JUBILEE

JUBILEE

a novel

JENNIFER GIVHAN

BLACK STONE
PUBLISHING

Copyright © 2020 by Jennifer Givhan
Published in 2020 by Blackstone Publishing
Cover and book design by Zena Kanes

Acknowledgments for permission to reproduce
song lyrics and poems start on page 303

The characters and events in this book are fictitious.
Any similarity to real persons, living or dead, is coincidental
and not intended by the author.

Printed in the United States of America

First edition: 2020
ISBN 978-1-5385-5677-1
Fiction / Literary

1 3 5 7 9 10 8 6 4 2

CIP data for this book is available
from the Library of Congress

Blackstone Publishing
31 Mistletoe Rd.
Ashland, OR 97520

www.BlackstonePublishing.com

for Lina

"I did not hold my head stiff enough when I met him and so I lost it just like the dolls."

Toni Morrison, *Sula*

PROLOGUE.
THE NIGHT WATER,
THE BRIDGE

Keep driving. Breathe deeply. Bianca prayed the words Mama taught her to pray.

Hail Mary, full of grace, the Lord is with thee.

Everything ached. But she had to make it to Matty.

She sucked in sharply at the thought of Matty. What would he say?

Off the road, tumbleweeds swept the dry arroyo beds. Stalks of alfalfa swayed in the Anza-Borrego night, their shadows dusting the earth. Mound after sage-smudged mound, like burial plots as far as the basin stretched in every direction, a pelvic bone, a sopa bowl scraped clean.

Monsoon season, the channels would swell, the quick rise and fall gathering mud and mosquitoes. Floodwaters would return. But this season of Lent, the embankment cradled rocks. Carrizo Creek and Alma Wash lay arid beside the mud caves, silent as salt-creek pupfish led astray, unable to find their way before sand swallowed water.

Blessed art thou among women.

Along the toxic Salton Sea, figs fell from palms and plopped to the brined beach. Black mission figs Bianca had peeled countless times with her teeth, sucking the pulp-pink flesh in the dirt lots behind her girlhood house. Summers, she had gathered the purple bulbs into the folds of her T-shirt then chucked their bulbous little heads off the mesa down toward the New River, watching the wine-colored skin splatter against the gorge.

And blessed is the fruit of thy womb.

Slip-faced dunes tilting their horns toward a brittle sky nodded solemnly as Bianca passed Seco del Diablo and Canyon Sin Nombre. Of the devil and without a name. The moon above had a name, La Luna Blanca. She'd sung to Bianca when Mama could not.

At the highway's edge, the Painted Rocks hunched restless as sleeping beasts at the mountain pass, signaling the way toward Palm Desert. Their tattooed bellies, their colorful graffiti, "Victoria & Angel 4-ever" and "Cynthia was here" and "Tres Locas," hushed by dark.

Holy Mary, Mother of God, payer for us sinners.

Bianca wiped her swollen face on her sleeve. She'd been crying again, her cheeks and the tender skin around her eyelids rawed with salt and rubbing. Her vision blurred with dehydration and exhaustion and the ceaseless fucking tears she couldn't stop. She should've asked Lily to drive her, despite the awful things her friend had said. Bianca was so exhausted she would have endured even the corrugated tin of Lily's snark to stay awake. Bianca turned the radio to a loud cumbia rock station and rubbed her eyes again, clearing the salt and haze, refocusing on the road. It was too late to turn back. Anyway, she didn't need her eyes. Not on this drive. She knew the landscape by heart. She didn't need to see it, filling the car with an ache. It was a rearview mirror she wished she could break. Years of floodplain evolution, the basin come to this: A woman driving home. A woman driving away from home.

Now and at the hour of our death. Amen.

She checked the back seat. Her boxer curled in a brown ball of fur, snoring in piglike grunts beside the rear-facing car seat. She couldn't see Jubilee. But she could imagine the steady swell and sink of chest, the pair of butterflied lungs, small wings flapping, steady compression of a fire bellow stoking the flame. Bianca let out the breath she'd been holding. "We're almost there, baby girl," she whispered as she thumbed the steering wheel like rosary beads, then recited the prayer again. And again.

Where Highway 86 met the 60, she left the Imperial Valley behind, its story stitched into her ribs, leaving her thighs and breasts and belly sore, a blood-soaked pad pressed against her crotch.

Left with the fork, past Beaumont, past mountain switchbacks and Chino's cow shit, toward Orange County, toward Matty. He'd know what to do.

The sky gathered a milky haze, La Luna Blanca playing hide-and-seek with the clouds. In girldom, hiding was Bianca's favorite game. She would slink into a laundry closet or the accordion-doored pantry where Mama kept her one bottle of brandy (for blessing the house, she'd said the time Bianca had caught her with it). And wherever she'd hidden, she'd wait. Girlchild tucked into a storage basket or flat-fished at the bottom of an empty bathtub in a dark bathroom, stifling the urge to giggle, the need to breathe. She wasn't even sure she'd told anyone they were playing. She would just climb in among the soft piles of linen or cans of stewed tomatoes and wait for salvation. She was so sure someone would find her.

She merged onto the 57S, toward Santa Ana, the radio threading static through the hills. By day, the cattle grazed like some postcard pastoral smack dab in the congested intestines where Orange and Los Angeles counties crossed. But tonight, shadows and darker shadows walled the asphalt beyond the metallic gleam of guardrail. It would only take one turn too sharp, too steep. One nudge of the foot, and off the edge she'd soar.

How had she ended up a twenty-year-old driving home to her family? She should've been a junior on a university scholarship. She should've been a writer working on her first collection of poems. Or, at the very least, in a coffeehouse somewhere beside some scraggly goateed undergrad or supportive Lily-alternative (insert college version of girlhood best friend here), snapping instead of clapping after each alliterated slam rendition of *Slay, Queen!* She should *not* have been bleeding. Not yet. Not this much.

In the city, light pollution made the stars impossible to see, but Bianca took comfort in the glowing haze above the chiaroscuro of buildings and houses: a nightlight in the sky whose dim bulb reminded her of the bedroom she'd shared with Matty at Bisabuela's house.

Matty didn't know she was coming.

Later Dr. Norris would ask what she'd imagined would happen when she got to Matty's. When Mama heard she was home, she would cross herself and praise the Lord her daughter was back for chocolate eggs and three-cheese broccoli casserole at Abuela's with the family. She'd be the prodigal daughter returned for Easter ham. Mama would insist she attend Mass. She could practically hear the aunts whispering, *Mija looks like caca. Pobrecita. What happened to her?*

Something *was* wrong. Deep down she knew it. But she couldn't think about that. Not if she wanted to keep driving, keep breathing. Even at two in the morning, the city kept an eye open. It yawned. It blinked bright red and yellow and orange. Gas stations and twenty-four-hour drive-throughs flickered as benign as white flies circling streetlamps in the Valley.

She exited at Main, where Santa Ana bordered the rest of Orange County. Matty and his partner, Handro, had bought a house and fixed it up, near the courthouse in the historical district, a few blocks from the public library where Bianca had gone the year before to hear Sandra Cisneros. She'd signed Bianca's copy of *Loose Woman*, a dog-eared, well-worn book of poems blessed by the living author herself: *¡Write on, chica!*

A few blocks later, Bianca turned right at the stoplight past the carnicería, the market with a squat merry-go-round outside the glass doors. At the edge of the parking lot, a cheery-looking Payday Loans with its green dollar symbols spray-painted onto the windows.

Downtown gave way to houses, colorful and cluttered. During the day, the paletas man would trudge through the neighborhood with his cart, ringing his bell, selling Popsicles and bags of churritos, crunchy pinwheels of pork fat with chile. Women with children would vend plastic cups of fresh melon slices, pepinos, pineapple. Some of their husbands and brothers would stand at the freeway's edge to sell flowers and bags of oranges.

Once, in the Valley, a man had stood in a parking lot selling a single orange. Gabe had been waiting for Bianca across the street in his truck, but she insisted on stopping to see what that man was about. He'd sliced the orange in half and to every person who passed he offered this one piece of fruit. Why this orange? Had he picked it from some nearby tree and chose to sell it rather than eat it himself? And who would want a halved orange, cut by a stranger in a parking lot? After she'd climbed into Gabe's truck, she'd realized she should've bought the orange from the man. He'd had a need. To fill that need, he'd offered his fruit. He'd sliced it open, so Bianca could see it was good, it was ripe and would taste delicious. She wished she could've been so open with her own need, so ready to slice her gift and offer it, with no pretense, no artifice. Simply a woman with an orange.

Santa Ana reminded Bianca of licking the lemon and chile from her fingers with Lily. The two girls would sneak the lead-filled Mexican candy Mama had warned Bianca not to eat or it would turn her blood black. Still she and Lily had pushed the sweet-spicy goo through the holes of the pop-top like worms, then squished it onto their tongues and spread it across the roof of their mouths until they went numb with heat. Bianca could handle it until she couldn't. Like her BFF's candor. For all her badass behavior, Lily could be chile-sharp. Bitter. Bile in the back of the throat. Driving away was milk, a salve to Bianca's memory. Leaving was bread in a burnt mouth.

Even leaving her Lily of the Valley.

The apodo fit her blond-haired, blue-eyed, porcelain-ivory-CoverGirl-foundationed best friend forever since junior high. Lily, no regular white girl. She ate chiles like pepinos, and not just the kind in the bag with onions and carrots, but the really hot kind they put into the blender for salsa. Lily could do the washing machine Selena-style like nobody's business and understood what a busticaca was. And in junior high, Lily had lined her lips with a darker brown than even Bianca had dared, when they were going through their chola phase. Lily still preferred the tangy granules of the candy called Lucas, like the boy's name, rather than a chocolate bar. And when they were kids, Lily poured lime crystals into her hand, sucking her palm then waving it all "Wáchale" at passing cars as they sauntered down Rio Vista shaking their hips (because that's how junior high girls walked anywhere) meaning both "Check me out" and "Watch it, man." She would bawl out anyone who tried to holler at them for real though, anyone who slowed the car too slow and rolled down the window. Lily would curse a storm and scare them off while Bee giggled and rolled her eyes, then her friend would link her arm through Bee's elbow and say something like, *Don't forget how that one girl ignored a guy's catcalls so he tracked her down and killed her. You can't mess with these scrubs.* To Lily's way of thinking, she was slaying dragons. She had protected them like that. Had understood she'd needed to protect Bianca. La Dreamer. La Empath. La Heart on Her Sleeve. Bianca had needed a practical Lily to pin her feet to the ground so she didn't go fluttering off into el cielo.

But Lily dealt in truths like lead around the neck and the ditchwater rising. Bianca couldn't stand her friend right now. She'd promised to text her when she was safe at Matty's. "Stay at my house, Bee," Lily had insisted. "Don't just take off in the middle of the night." But Bianca had to get away. She'd made up a story about not burdening her. A lie. No, she couldn't handle listening to Lily's shit opinions wrapped as tough love, callous dronings on what Bee should've done instead. What difference would it have made?

Or maybe she was afraid to show her Jubilee.

Matty's porch light shone against red bricks at the end of Woodland Street. The natives of Santa Ana pronounced it like the guitarist Santana with a Spanish accent, all one word. But the streets had English names like Baker, Treeline, or Moss. Names that conjured up forest images, though there were no state parks in Santa Ana. At Tía Lydia's in the ritzy beachfront section of Orange County called San Juan Capistrano, twenty miles away, all the street signs were in Spanish, and Tía's friends pronounced them funny, making Campanilla sound like "camp vanilla."

Bianca's legs ached, but not from driving her stick-shift all night. She pitched into the driveway behind Spacedog—Matty's nickname for the silver Nissan Sentra he shared with Handro. She yanked the parking brake and released the clutch, forgetting she was still in first gear. The car lurched, then died. *Shit.* She hadn't done that in years. Not since Dad had taken her out to the country beside the irrigation ditches and vegetable fields and taught her how to drive a stick because a girl should be able to do that kind of thing for herself. Exhaustion settled like powdered dirt onto her chest and shoulders; she fought to keep from resting her head on the steering wheel.

What would Matty think?

She pulled down the visor and checked her face in the mirror. Her forehead and cheeks glimmered fever-pink, slick and shiny with sweat. The bluish pool of bruises had yellowed to soggy pears across her cheeks and chest. Her dark hair matted in frizzy curls around her face. Her ass and inner thighs throbbed; the pad in her chonies clung hot and sticky against her skin. Her stomach hurt. But she was at Matty's. He would take care of them. He always had.

She glanced toward the house. She wasn't afraid, despite Santa Ana's reputation. The neighborhood was safe, though most people assumed otherwise. "You live in Santa Ana?" people asked, wide-eyed. "Isn't that dangerous? Especially for you guys?" Matty and Handro shook their heads. When they'd moved in, the handyman across the street had welcomed them, offering to fix up the place. Did they need help pulling weeds? With plumbing? Could he park his work van in the double driveway they shared with the neighbors since the house next door was vacant? Matty and Handro were fine with the firecrackers every holiday, the mariachi music weekends, and the avocado tree lobbing its fruit onto the grass in their backyard. And the neighborhood was fine with them, the mariposas in the redbrick house at the end of Woodland Street.

Bianca pressed chanclas to cement; a shockwave of cramping curled her over. Knees buckling, she hunched, hands to thighs. She could've been a leaf in an electrical storm, crinkled and burning.

Once the painful jolts released her to the dull, steady drum that had replaced her body, she pulled the handle, and the front seat swung forward. She reached back to unbuckle Jubilee, pink and fuzzy in a bunny-eared romper. Kanga cocked her unclipped ears and wagged her stump of a tail. Earlier that morning, back in the Valley, Bianca had balanced atop a lawn chair on the backyard porch of her empty girlhood house, then wrapped a cord around her neck and hung the slack around a patio post. She'd stared at her dog. She'd willed herself to kick the chair. To do something besides stand there, wobbly in bare feet, with the cord dangling down her chest. She'd closed her eyes and prepared herself to fall. But Kanga had barked and barked until Bianca climbed down and knelt on the slab of unfinished patio cement, still bleeding between her legs.

She hugged Kanga's brown neck and cried into her fur. Then she remembered Jubilee.

She'd broken herself into pieces, for Jubilee.

"Come on, girl," she said to Kanga. To Jubilee, "We're at uncles' house." Jubilee didn't blink or cry, but Bianca soothed her anyway. "Shhh, shhh, sana, sana," she whispered, patting the pink romper and resting the soft body against her shoulder. Bianca padded up Matty's porch steps and rang the bell.

Kanga barked. No one came.

She rang again.

This time, heavy footsteps across the wooden floor; Matty had woken up. Handro nearly floated when he walked, his petite frame almost hovering, a slender ghost gliding on the tip of his own long white beard in a Remedios Varo painting. But Matty was solid as sculpture.

The curtain rustled; Matty peeked out the door's glass window.

Bianca tried smiling, but her face wouldn't oblige.

Locks unchained, unclicked, and the doorway flooded with warm yellow light, revealing Matty, her massive older brother, his black hair sleep-rumpled, his dark eyes tired and confused. He was technically her half-brother through Mama, but Bianca would've punched anyone who said so, like she'd punched that bitch Vanessa at the Catholic school who'd called Mama a whore (she'd said "ho") for having kids with two different dads. Matty was her *full* brother.

"Bianca?" Barefooted and gym-shorted, Matty stared at her. "Are you okay?"

She nodded, tears landing on Jubilee's fuzzy hood.

His eyes narrowed into a frown. "Is that . . . a baby?"

Bianca nodded again, unsure whether he'd be loving or judgmental.

"Oh my God. Come in." He reached for her arm and led her into the house. "What happened?" He pulled her into his wide body for a hug. "Jesus, you're burning up."

She tried to speak. Couldn't.

"Here," he said, leading her to the couch, "let me hold your baby." He reached for Jubilee, but Bianca couldn't let go. She hadn't slept for days. She must've looked crazed. A La Llorona out of the waters, stealing dreams. "Bee, I'll hold your baby so you can rest."

She choked out a sob, letting him take Jubilee as she wobbled backward, landing on a couch that reminded her of the borrowed one she'd been bleeding on for two days, in the empty house-for-sale two hundred miles away. But soft and beige and beckoning, this one whispered *safe*. Whispered *let go*.

Her eyes fluttered. Matty said, "Wait, what the hell?" His voice reminded her of a flashing siren. It sounded an alarm. Something cold and blacktop and ugly. She squinted, willing herself not to fall asleep. Was something wrong with Jubilee? She tried opening her mouth to speak, but her tongue scraped sand. She'd become a noiseless womb. *Mami's here*, she thought of saying. But she couldn't recognize her own thoughts.

"Shit, Bianca. What's going on?" He seemed repulsed by Jubilee, holding her away from his body unnaturally. Was he angry Bianca had stayed in the Valley with Gabe, then come back with Gabe's baby? Matty had always hated Gabe. A childhood of abuse had given Matty a sixth sense that Bianca hadn't developed. Where she trusted everyone, he trusted no one. Yet surely Matty would forgive her mistakes, now that she was here, that she'd come home. Accept her for what she'd become. That's why she'd gone to him instead of Mama.

Hug her, she tried saying. The words wouldn't form. *Hold her tight. It's calming.*

"Bianca? What is this?"

She closed her eyes. Matty's living room swelled and shrank, a lung, breathing her in, breathing her out.

"Handro," Matty yelled. "Come help me. Something's wrong with my sister."

Jubilee was safe. The flashflood was gone. The arroyo was dry. Bianca was a lungfish. Drowning.

"Handro? Get my phone. I need help . . ."

Hail Mary, full of grace. Switch off the light and grant me peace.

And the light switched off.

Before Bianca's father had left for good the year she'd floundered at Holy Cross, he'd gotten sober. He'd changed. He wasn't the drunken asshole who called her brother a faggot and her mother a fat slob, but a man whose whole life could be summed up with one word: regret.

That night at Matty's house, Dad was there with her, she was sure of it, telling Mama he'd called the family and they were praying. Maybe he *was* there. When Bianca had nearly died, her dad, her red-bearded gringo, her mad scientist of a father, soft-spoken-with-the-alcohol-gone, had finally come to pray.

Mama was there. That was verifiable. As in, others would agree that she was in the room and not just a part of Bianca's imagination or . . . the other things they would say about her. Still, though she was flesh and blood, Mama's voice floated specter-like above Bianca's head. "Sana, baby girl. Sana." She meant *sana, sana colita de rana.* Heal, heal little frog's tail. The rhyme Mama had recited to her from girlhood, and she'd never outgrown. Translated literally it hadn't made sense. She'd asked Abuela why they prayed for a frog's tail to heal. Bianca hadn't understood the difference between dichos and prayers, or maybe there was no difference since Abuela hadn't corrected her. She'd only replied that the frog grows a new tail, a type of healing. Then she'd handed Bianca an empanada filled with mashed sweet potato.

Now Mama stroked Bianca's hair as if she were a child again, home sick from school. Bianca had sometimes stayed home even when she wasn't sick so Mama would take care of her, so she'd pay attention.

Mama lifted Bianca's arm, turned her palm over, held two fingers against her wrist. Did she have a heart? Was it beating?

Am I alive, Mama?

Mama's lips pressed against her forehead. But the dead couldn't feel, could they?

Mama smelled like rosewater. Could the dead smell rosewater?

"Has she said anything? Has she woken up at all?" Mama's voice was thorned with worry.

"No, she's been like that for an hour." Matty sounded thick and heavy. It reminded Bianca of the sourdough bread he loved to bake, yeasty and pungent in her memories. "I called you as soon as she got here. She was crying and rocking that . . . doll."

Jubilee. He meant Jubilee.

Mama was crying, and Bianca pictured rosewater. No, not rose. Holy. The kind she had sprinkled around their house. Tinged with alcohol. Waters breaking, no taking. Yes. Waters taking.

"Can you drink this, baby girl?" Mama put water to Bianca's mouth, and she drank.

Handro's polka-dotted socks poked at the couch's edge. He said, "I'll get a washcloth."

Mama peeled off Bianca's sweater, fingertips pressing the wet stains across her breasts, below each nipple. "Why didn't I drag you away from there, mijita? He hurt you, didn't he?" Mama gave guilt a voice. It hurt Bianca to hear.

She wanted to tell Mama to stop pressing into her stomach, stop prodding her; she tried moaning, but Mama only kept pressing her backbone, her abdomen, her thighs. Each kneading of Mama's hands into her skin throbbed, but not in the healing way of a sobradora giving a massage to get the blood flowing or cupping at the lungs to break up a phlegmy cough. No, Mama's hands were like knives now. Everything hurt. When Mama reached Bianca's buttocks, Mama called to God in Spanish. And Bianca knew. Mama had found the blood.

"Pick your sister up, mijo. We need to take her to the hospital."

"Mom, we shouldn't have left her there . . ." Matty's voice shook as he lifted Bianca off the couch. It scared her.

While her family carried her, wherever they carried her, she dreamt.

She hovered on a bridge, dirt-covered and crossing a concrete canal. Dippy Duck, the baseball-capped mascot to the irrigation district, stood at the other side calling: "Play it safe. Be cool, swim in a pool. Stay out, stay alive." She had swum in canals though, as a girlchild, used her blue-ribbon swim-team skills in the precarious ditches in the countryside.

Water rushed through the canal. Instead of carrying twigs and leaves, tiny corpses. Dozens of them. Tiny faces mired in scum, sealed in the ditchwater, swallowed by its rushing force. She lingered, transfixed by the mud caked in their hair, their toothless gums. Green, grimy liquid pruning their fingers.

From the bridge, she sat motionless in the truck. Gabe's pine-green truck on the bank between the ditch and stacks of sweet-smelling hay. They were a depression in the brown earth.

He reached across the center console and caressed her thighs, as she sat cross-legged in jersey-knit sweats. She recited John Donne.

> Sweetest love, I do not go,
> For weariness of thee,
> Nor in hopes the world can show
> A fitter love for me.

He buried his face in her hair and began sobbing. She called him a sissy la-la for all the times he'd told her to stop crying.

She was a stick. Lying in the mud. Beside tiny bodies. Drowned.

Mama had never told Bianca the story of La Llorona. She'd never sent her to bed frightened on purpose. Instead, they'd said their bedtime prayer together: *Now I lay me down to sleep. I pray the Lord my soul to keep. Guard me Jesus through the night, and wake me with the morning light.* Mama had omitted the most insidious parts of the prayer. She'd protected Bianca that way, deleting the dangers.

Bianca didn't learn until later: *If I should die before I wake, I pray the Lord my soul to take.* Gabe had taught her that, like La Llorona. Gabe and his mama, Esme.

Her stomach growled. She was waking, or coming back.

When Bianca was a girlchild, Mama had read her the gospels. A child comes back to life there too—through the miracle of belief. How crystal a thing, belief. How shimmering.

Bianca thought of Jubilee.

She opened her eyes. Hospital room. Clock on a wall. Wires and machines. A small salmon-colored pitcher on a tray.

"Mama?"

A monitor beeped.

"Mama? Matty?"

She pulled herself into a sitting position. She was dizzy and dehydrated still, that cotton on her tongue and lining her throat, but less fuzzy. Less prickly. She could keep her eyes open and focus on the objects around her. Balloons and a bouquet of white daisies. A card with a ballerina bear. She wore a hospital gown.

She tried her still-numb feet, pressing them against the linoleum floor. It was cold, but the jolts of pain were gone. It was like waking from a dream, unable to tell the difference between the dream and reality—how a young woman awakes believing for a moment she can fly. It isn't until the sleep crust wears away that the wings retract into the shoulder blades.

Mama told her later she'd been unconscious for two days, three hours, and twenty-seven minutes. Bianca had asked how many rosaries Mama had prayed. Mama hadn't kept track.

The urge to pee stung her bladder. The catheter pinched. Instead of pushing the red call button for a nurse, she called to Mama, but before Mama came into the room, Bianca remembered Jubilee. She needed her baby.

"Mijita? Baby girl?" Mama hassled through the doorway, a portrait of concern, and Bianca thought of the Bible verse Mama had taught her, how an angel had *troubled the water.* And how whoever stepped first into the troubled water was made whole.

In the room, Mama's gaze landed on Bianca sitting up in bed, and her face relaxed. She sighed and pressed her hand to the rosary around her neck, whispering, "Gracias a Dios." Mama had lost more weight since Bianca last saw her. She looked good, but tired. Her jet-black hair streaked golden around her face, covering any gray. But her face was Oil-of-Olay smooth. If she had wrinkles, they were well-concealed. So different was this thin, angular woman from the round giantess Bianca had grown up with.

"You're awake," Mama said, and she thanked God.

But her arms were empty.

"Where's Jubilee?" she asked. Bone tired. Bianca was still bone tired. And troubled. The water was still troubled.

"Who?" Mama's forehead creased. There they were. The wrinkles.

"Jubilee. My baby." Bianca felt cold. Wings retracted too soon. Or, cut off. She wanted to return to the place between wake and sleep.

Mama pursed her lips, tilted her head. The expression that flickered across her face was inexplicably sad. She looked at Bianca and said, carefully, "You didn't bring your baby."

Bianca scanned Mama's face, waiting for the punch. "Yes, I did. I was holding her when I got to Matty's. Where is she?" She stood now, stepped away from the bed and faltered, her legs buckling. A humming in her ears. Someone was singing. Or a memory of a song. "Matty?" *Come away to the water.*

Mama reached out, supporting Bianca's weight. "Let me help you." *Down by the water.*

"Help me find Jubilee. Matty had her."

The milk of Mama's eyes juddered sharply, muddying at the center. Like Bianca was a girlchild again and had done something terribly wrong. But Bianca couldn't focus on that.

"Matty?" Bianca called again, louder than was normal for a hospital. She didn't care. *Down by the banks of the hanky panky where a bullfrog jumped from bank to bank.* A nurse rushed in, ordering Bianca back to bed, checking her monitors, catheter, IV drip. Bianca wasn't pacified. "Matty!"

The nurse paged the doctor.

"Shhh, Bianca. Calm down," Mama whispered, stroking her daughter's tangled hair. "He's down the hall in the waiting room. I'll get him, pero cállate, the doctors will give you another shot."

Bianca felt like a child. Her pulse pounded in her ears. "Matty," she screamed again. "Where's Jubilee?"

And not a drop to drink.

When Mama came back into the room with Matty, he looked at Bianca with a mixture of relief and pity. "Bee?" His brows furrowed. "You didn't give me a baby."

"What?" *Like a bridge over troubled water, I will lay me down.* "Yes, I did. I drove her to your house." *And pray the Lord my soul to take.*

"No, Bee," he said quietly. "You drove this." He held her up as proof. She was still wearing her furry pink bunny pajamas. No one had changed her. "Not a baby. *A doll.*"

Sail on, silver girl. Sail on by.

The humming sounded like water. And water soothes. Water soothes the soul.

And what is a soul but a bubble in the void. But floating in the vacuum of nothing?

Dad had taught Bianca about quantum universes. He'd sat her down the way he had when he'd taught her about Mole day or Pi day (sometimes even brought her a slice of cherry pie that a student had given him). The way he'd taught her to drive, the way he'd taught her to ride a bike.

In the many-worlds hypothesis, he'd said, anything that could've possibly happened, but didn't, has happened in another universe.

Bubbles, bubbles everywhere.

In this one, Jubilee was alive.

Bianca stretched out her IV-wired arms. Mama nodded, and Matty handed over Jubilee.

Step into the water, child. Be made whole.

At some point, a therapist named Dr. Norris came in and evaluated her. In what sounded like something from an absurd Monty Python movie, he explained to Mama and Matty that Bianca was in shock. She'd need a low dose of Clozapine to start, antidepressants, and a weekly therapy session with him, but she wasn't a danger to herself or anyone else, humming Simon and Garfunkel and so on. She wasn't a danger, so she could go home. Bianca heard him. She heard them step into the hallway so they could ask their worried questions without her hearing. She heard anyway. She knew what they thought was happening. She knew what they thought.

But here's what she saw. *Once upon a time, there was a girlchild. A brand new girlchild, smiling. So innocent, so new. Her mama held her tightly, and she was safe. The end.*

After all, Jesus rose again, didn't he? And his mama must have held him. Mother Mary in a teal robe, clinging to her child—Pietà turned beautiful. Restored to babe in arms.

Bianca's daughter had returned. Her Jubilee. And she wouldn't let her go.

ONE
A WOUNDED DEER

WITH JUBILEE

Bianca bounded through the front door of the redbrick house, Jubilee tucked in her arms, and called out loudly for the guys to hear, "I met someone!" Then under her breath as she brought Jubilee to nest in the crook of her neck and shoulder, whispering into her curls, "A really *nice* someone."

Five months had passed. Bianca had reenrolled in college for the fall semester because she wouldn't go back to lying face down in the grass in the front yard the way she had after dropping out the first time and moving back to the Valley with Gabe, depressed as nobody's business but too stubborn to kill herself. Besides, she had Jubilee to consider. That's what she told herself. She said, *You absolutely cannot kill yourself because you have a daughter to consider.* Dr. Norris said her self-talk was an encouraging sign and Jubilee certainly would not want her to kill herself.

She could never be sure if she was joyful or manic, whether she was like her father dancing around the kitchen, him bare-chested in his weekend shorts and her stepping on his feet (*Dance me, Daddy!*) while he'd stomp her around the kitchen tile, how she'd thought he was so *joyful* when he wasn't shitfaced and shattering their belongings against a wall . . . Or whether she was getting better. Whether she was nothing like her father at all. Nothing like a body in a bathtub. Or his spitting image.

She was staying with Handro and Matty on Woodland Street,

attending Cal State Fullerton, a commuter school and easy to transfer into as a sophomore, unlike the prestigious schools she'd cared about before whose matriculation agreements had meant her credits from Holy Cross didn't convert.

At the redbrick house, going to college, raising Jubilee with the help of her brother and his boyfriend, none of it felt like pretending, at least not in the way it had with Gabe.

Matty watched Jubilee during the day while Bianca went to school and during her therapy sessions. Their relationship, now, in the redbrick house, reminded Bianca of the way it had been between them when Matty had helped raise her back in the Valley. Big brother, five years older, Matty had borne the brunt of Dad's drunken, bigoted rages, yet he'd still managed to be a loving stand-in—a brother turned caregiver when Mama was busy studying for nursing school or locked in her room crying and eating herself to sleep and Dad was mean-drunk. Matty had taught Bianca how to braid on Barbie's hair, how to cook arroz con pollo (without burning the red rice tar-black to the bottom of the pot the way Mama did), and how to sing along to all the musicals from deep in the diaphragm, where all her power came. Mama loved musicals as much as Matty, and she'd cry at nearly every one. They'd spend most weekend nights together watching all the classics before Matty got to high school and started going out with his drama-club friends instead. Their favorite was *Hello, Dolly*, and they'd belt out the tunes (*"Before the parade passes by!"*). Matty teased that Bianca sounded more like a country-western singer than a Broadway diva ("Not through your *nose*, Bee. From your *diaphragm!*"), but she didn't care. When they were singing along to *The Unsinkable Molly Brown* or *Westside Story*, just the three of them, there was no one ridiculing or hurting them. Mama protected them that way too. She thought she was protecting them with Bible verses, but really the musicals had made them the most resilient (*"I'm gonna feel my heart coming alive again!"*).

"Matty? Handro?" Bianca called when she didn't see them in the house. "Are you guys here?" She wanted to tell them about Joshua.

"We're out back, Bee," Matty called. "Grab a plate."

Still holding Jubilee, she tossed her bag onto the desk in the guestroom-turned-her-room. The guys had taken down Matty's framed comic book posters so Bianca could put up the wooden Frida reprints she'd bought four-for-twenty-dollars in Mexicali. The truth? Before today, Bianca had been mostly limping along. She missed her dog, Kanga, who, let's face it, had saved her back in the Valley when she couldn't save herself. Matty's cats had clawed the shit out of Kanga, so Bianca had sent her to live with Mama and Abuela in Buena Park, even though their plot of cement backyard didn't have any grass and Mama couldn't be trusted to take Kanga for walks or pet her belly. Mama acted like Bianca was made of china and would break apart any moment and it was all Mama's fault. Even Matty and Handro treated Bianca like a breakable thing. She wanted to believe she'd ever felt normal. That she'd feel normal again.

She turned Jubilee to face her, smoothing a creamy curl, pulling the hem of Jubilee's ruffled dress, and lifting the collar of a lace sock. Bianca rubbed the lace between her fingers, her gaze shifting toward the picture frame on her desk, which held a glowworm of a girlchild: Bee in third grade making her First Holy Communion at Sacred Heart. Mama had bought the white lace dress and flowered wreath from a swap meet in Calexico, the twin city bordering Mexicali, twenty minutes from her girlhood town, as close back into Mexico as Mama ever went. It wasn't safe, Mama had said. Still, Bianca had crossed the border often, with Gabe and his family, but Mama hadn't been back since she was a girl. In that communion picture, Bianca's lace sock scrunched an inch shorter than the other, rolled down to her ankle, so she looked as lopsided as her smile. Jubilee reminded Bianca of herself when she was a girl. She liked that about her.

"You hungry, baby girl? Let's go outside with uncles."

In the kitchen, she pulled a bento-box plate from the cupboard, fished the last Diet Coke from the bottom of the pack in the fridge, tucked it between her arm and Jubilee, then grabbed a baby bottle from the cupboard. She grabbed the pink high chair from the kitchen corner and, balancing her supplies, pushed open the screen door and stepped onto the cement patio where the guys were eating, each with a glass of red wine.

The August sun hovered low in the evening sky. The chickens the guys raised for fresh brown eggs rustled in their coop beside the stand-alone garage, which, along with the main house, had also refuged migrant families before the guys had bought it; all through the house and garage, in every room, bunk beds and makeshift cots had sprawled along each wall, and in the center of the garage behind a shower curtain, a single toilet the guys had since removed. The biddies squawking mildly as Bianca settled herself at the patio table were the second set of chickens, the first, victims of the neighbor's piles of debris beside the fence that formed a small mountain high enough for a vicious dog to climb over.

From the house behind them, beyond the jacarandas weeping their blue bells over the wooden fence, the hum of the neighbor's bolero music rose through a screen door, bridging the distance between the Valley and Bianca. Was there a soft guitar melody playing now on Rio Vista? How was Esme, Bianca's almost-mother-in-law?

"Hey, sister," Matty greeted her with his usual beat, with a warmth like a dry towel around her bare shoulders after a day of jumping off the high dive and practicing for swim team at the public pool. Matty wore khaki shorts, a plaid button-down, and Doc Martens, his regular writing uniform. She kissed him on the cheek, then Handro.

"You need help, hun?" Handro asked, standing and reaching out his slender arms.

"Sure," she answered, always grateful for Handro. He was the perfect boyfriend. For her brother, of course, but still. She smiled at his purple high-top Converse. She'd worn a pair in junior high, matching Lily's, with their short baby doll–cut dresses. "Can you set her in the high chair so I can fix a plate?"

Handro set Jubilee down in her chair then placed the bottle in front of her. This was their routine. In the beginning, she'd catch the guys side-eyeing each other, see the reluctance on their faces, but she couldn't focus on that. She needed this to be normal. And soon it was. They were a family. And family protected each other.

Handro asked, "Need me to feed her for you?"

"Thanks, but I'll do it after I eat."

"M'kay, hun." Handro smiled as he sat back down and reached for Matty's hand. If Matty still rolled his eyes at any of this, Bianca chose not to notice. At least in the way that one chooses one's eye color. The way we accept what we cannot control then call it choice.

Matty asked, "How was school . . . with Jubilee?" He'd had a meeting with his comic book editors, ironing out the details of the series he would launch in the coming year, at the springtime convention.

"My writing professor didn't mind." Bianca plopped a piece of fish and a vegetable skewer onto her plate. "It's technically against the rules, but Elena said as long as we stayed in the back and didn't disrupt class, it was fine." Matty hadn't wanted Bianca to take Jubilee, but she couldn't leave her alone. "There's something else I wanted to tell you guys." She set her plate down and perched at the edge of a patio chair. "I met someone today." She peeled a chunk of eggplant from her skewer and stuck it into her mouth, trying to act nonchalant though her heart was ricocheting as she awaited their reaction. Normal, she repeated to herself. Act normal.

"Someone famous?" Handro asked, sliding a bite of salmon into his mouth. "Is it James Franco? I've heard he goes to every writing program. That sleaze."

Bee laughed. "No, not someone famous. And I'm not in a writing program yet, tontito. I'm just taking one creative-writing class, for now."

Matty shook his head, and Bianca kept choosing to ignore any shade he might've been throwing. He always gave the air of being slightly above everyone else's conversation. Bee hardly noticed it anymore, though for the first few months, she'd had the distinct impression Matty was judging her. He cleared his throat, as if signaling them to rein in the nonsense. "OK, sis. Who'd you meet?"

"A guy in my class. A really nice guy."

"Girl, you waste no time," Handro said, winking. He leaned forward. "What's he like?"

"He's beautiful," she told Handro, pointedly ignoring Matty's grouchy expression. "His name is Joshua Walker. We have Mexican Art History together, and he hit on me today." She wouldn't call it hitting on her though. More like he was a gentleman. More like he seemed the complete opposite of Gabe, after Gabe became the complete opposite of the charming, puckish boy she'd met when she was fourteen. She brushed away thoughts of Gabe. Those couldn't lead anywhere but dark. She glanced at Jubilee. Took a deep breath. "He's sweet. Goofily charming." He'd invited her to coffee after class, and since it was just down the escalator in the student lounge, she'd agreed. Joshua had seemed nervous and called her *miss*. He'd pointed out that her last name, Vogelsang, was German. And when she'd said that her mother was Mexican and her father German, he'd said she was a Frida Kahlo, who shared similar ancestry. "He compared me with Frida," she said, the edges of her mouth crinkling.

"Did he meet Jubilee?" Matty asked.

Bianca glanced down, pushed the food around her plate with her fork. "She was asleep." Joshua had asked to see the baby. But Bianca had kept her covered with a blanket. Joshua hadn't pressed.

Matty made a noise in the back of his throat, then sighed and leaned back in his chair.

Bianca turned toward Handro. How fun it would have been if he'd been her college roommate when she'd tried moving out the first time. All that chisme, all that juicy gossip. Handro would've taken her to the gay bar where he worked and let her sing Liza Minnelli karaoke with the drag queens, whose long legs Bianca envied. She looked at Matty, his thick black eyebrows knitted. He moved his hand away from Handro's but said nothing. He looked a little like Walter Matthau in the *Odd Couple*, only he was the uptight one. Come to think of it, Handro reminded her of an easygoing Felix.

"Anyway, he has these intense, dark almond eyes, brown sugar skin, and a mass of shoestring curls piled on his head like copper wires. Like fireworks."

"Sounds gorgeous," Handro said conspiratorially. "Fireworks. Ay." He fanned himself dramatically.

"We bonded over art." She didn't add that they'd also bonded over the struggles of parenting as a college student. But she couldn't tell Matty that. She purposefully said nothing about Joshua's kid to Matty. She knew how he'd react. She did say, "He asked for my number."

"Honey, better wait and check him out first, m'kay?" Handro said. "Don't rush into anything." And her hopes for her ally in this battle faded.

Matty sighed louder. Bianca braced herself for a fatherly "talk," customary between them even when Dad was alive. "Hey, Bee, look, I don't want to spoil this for you. I love seeing you excited. But you've had a rough couple of years. Are you really ready to start dating?"

"Stop being so protective." She kept her voice haughty, but her stomach coiled.

"I don't want you hurt again. Too often you only think with your heart."

"Anytime we open our hearts, the world opens." She said this with as much poetic authority as she could muster and held tight to the thought of Joshua. They'd just met, but the idea of him was already blossoming inside some part of her she'd assumed ashen. His indefinable accent, somewhere between southern country and Los Angeles streetwise, the shyness permeating his politeness, his slightly dimpled smile. He was a package deal, he'd said. Him and his kid, Jayden. He'd worn a superhero watch and said it matched his kid's, just them two against the world, and he'd sounded so goddamn sincere, like Linus in his pumpkin patch, that she could've sworn her heart started flowering again right then and there in the campus quad. She wouldn't mention any of this to Matty. She'd had her fill of his lectures. What she needed right now was support. She was nervous enough. Kept fighting with herself over whether or not she deserved hope. And she needed Matty to reinforce Dr. Norris's encouragement to get back out there and make new connections with people. Joshua seemed like the best kind of people. And she was trying. Though it scared the shit out of her. She was really fucking trying.

"It can be dangerous," Matty said.

"So can driving, but we do that every day." Her cheeks were hot.

"Be careful, sister. You just got back on your feet. School's going well . . ."

"I'll be fine, Matty. Tell him, Handro."

"Hey, I haven't met the guy." Handro put his hands up in mock surrender.

"Well, *I* have a good feeling about him," Bianca said. "He's different than the other guys." He didn't stare at her breasts the whole time he was talking to her. Yet everything in his demeanor expressed his attraction to her. She looked Matty squarely in the face and said, "He's not Gabe."

Matty narrowed his eyes then quoted, in his oratorical voice, "A wounded deer leaps highest."

Bianca mocked a gasp, though truly, she was glad her brother had dished out his own poetic. They could put their drama skills to good use, communicating with each other at their most familiar level. And he knew she knew her Emily. "Yes, dear brother, but Ms. Dickinson has more to say on the subject, doesn't she? '. . . If I can stop one heart from breaking, / I shall not live in vain.'"

"Whose heart would you be helping, hun?" Handro asked, looking up from his wine glass, his slender hand resting on his slim-cut jeans.

"My own," she said, her voice clearer than it had been in months; she felt it.

And to this, even Matty raised his glass.

Joshua and his nephew, Jayden, did all right by each other, two strays in this fool world. But Bianca, she was a light. She'd stayed after class with him again, making their conversations in the coffee shop a regular ritual. She said something smart, which he would come to see was her norm. "Think about it. Remedios Varo, Leonora Carrington, Frida Kahlo. Mexico's three most prominent surrealist painters, all women. But they almost never come up when people refer to the surrealists. Why do you think that is?" She said the last part all sassy, like it wasn't a question.

He played devil's advocate. "You consider Frida a surrealist?"

She scrunched up her face, took a sip of her coffee. Man, she was cute. "It depends on what you mean by surrealism," she answered. "The images are almost always recognizable. They're taken from a reality we accept. But their *context* forces us to rethink their *purpose*. Think about it: If a teacup is covered in fur, I still see the teacup, though I don't know what to do with it or how it got that way. Did it get cold? Did it become mammalian? If a teacup can become like a mammal, can a mammal become like porcelain? And could this be the teacup's answer to all those metaphoric descriptions of women's porcelain skin? The images are recognizable. It's the placement. One or two steps to the side of their reality, that brings surrealism to life. All Kafka has to do is make Gregor Samsa a cockroach, and nothing else need change in the story. Same house, same family, same concerns."

"So, like, *The Two Fridas*. Or the Frida head on a deer. That's surrealism."

"Exactly. Frida said people thought she was a surrealist, painting nightmares. Yet she painted her own reality. So I'm saying reality *is* surreal. Know what I mean?"

He knew a little something about nightmare realities. He stared at her, the corners of his mouth flicking, like he wanted to laugh but he wasn't sure about what. Like he wanted to kiss this gorgeous, intelligent woman if she'd let him. He sensed hers was as old a soul as his. He must've been staring too long by the way she looked at him with eyebrows raised, her eyes slightly laughing back at him, like he'd missed a move in a chess match. He'd gladly be captured by this queen. He cleared his throat. "And you. You're a writer? You mentioned Kafka."

Her cheeks and ears reddened. "I write. I don't know if I'd call myself a writer."

"If you write, then you're a writer."

She smiled. "I have this dream that one day I'll write something important. Something true. Not true as it happened in reality, deeper than that. Something so true, it could never be real in this world. Not here. I don't know." She shrugged, and when she lifted her eyes to his, Joshua detected apprehension. She looked scared, almost. "I sound crazy, right?" she said, laughing. "Babbling about teacups and dreams."

"Hold fast to dreams / For if dreams die / Life is a broken-winged bird / That cannot fly," he recited, his cheeks flushed. "Langston Hughes wrote that. My favorite poet."

"I know that poem. 'Hold fast to dreams / For when dreams go / Life is a barren field . . .'"

"Frozen with snow," Joshua finished. She applauded.

He had to take the chance. If she'd stayed with him for coffee on campus, maybe she'd agree to a real date. "Would you go out with me, Bianca? We could go to the beach. I'll bring food." He talked fast so she couldn't reject him straight off. "We could make it family style. I'll bring my boy and you could bring your . . ."

"Daughter," she said. She looked at him intensely, and if anyone else had stared at him like that he would've been creeped out. But he liked it when she did it. Like he was a painting she was studying. He watched her golden eyes flicker as she deliberated.

When she didn't say anything, he nudged, "So you'll come?" *Please say yes, please say yes, please say yes.*

"Yes."

Huntington beach would be swarming with crowds on a Saturday in August, so Joshua had arrived early to claim a spot beside the pier on the amphitheater grass. He kept checking his phone to make sure Bianca hadn't texted him to cancel.

"Can I play in the sand, Dada?" Jayden had been calling Joshua "dada" since he could talk. After "cup," "ma milk," "ducko," and "nanana" (for banana), "dada" was up there with the firsts. Joshua had been there for them all.

"Stay close to the car," Joshua said, lugging a plastic ice chest from the trunk. On top of the chest, he stacked an oversized umbrella, a flannel blanket, and a duffel bag of beach toys. Over his shoulders, he hoisted two beach chairs. Around his neck he strung an army-green messenger bag packed with sunscreen, hats, extra clothes and underwear, windbreakers, Jayden's allergy medicine, and his inhaler.

Jayden reached through the rail, picked up a handful of sand, and threw it over his head. "Are we *moving* to the beach?"

"No, why?"

"You brought a lot of stuff."

Always be prepared. He'd learned that early. His older sister, Olivia, had birthed Jayden while coming down from God-knows-what, and she'd dropped him off at Joshua's dorm before splitting. She'd been in and out of jail, but Joshua hadn't heard from her in two years. After what they'd gone through in the system, he couldn't let that happen to the little guy. Child protective services had dragged him and Olivia out of their cokehead parents' house when he was thirteen months and Olivia was four years old, the same age Jayden was now. They'd stayed together in foster care the first couple years, but like everything else in his life, they'd been broken up. He couldn't remember their first place, but Olivia had told him a white lady took care of them, that she was nice, didn't yell. Gave them grape suckers. Joshua tried to picture the white lady who'd held him and changed his diapers, but he couldn't see her. So he pictured a streak of white light instead. A supercharged light that had infused him with special abilities. Second senses. He mentioned this to Olivia once, and she'd punched him in the arm, hard. "She was just a white lady, you weirdo. And you don't have any special powers. You're just a weird boy."

"Well why'd she send us back, then?"

"Had her own baby. A shiny pink-and-white one. Not all black and blue like you." She'd stuck out her tongue.

Joshua had said he wasn't black or blue but brown like a candy bar.

Olivia hadn't laughed. She'd hardly ever laughed.

"You'll be black and blue if they ever split us up and I'm not here to protect you, Joshy. Sissy boy. Bet you're gonna turn out gay." She punched him again, harder, but he didn't cry. "I'm just *Joshin'* you," she said, laughing finally. "You know I love you. I'm the only one who does." By Olivia's twelfth birthday, their foster mother Patti had sent Olivia back, but she'd kept Joshua until high school.

And when they'd grown up some more and Olivia had gone into the next system, the criminal justice system, he'd kept her kid for her. He'd kept her kid safe.

"Kinship caregiver," they'd called Joshua when Olivia became incarcerated. Quick fingerprints and a background scan had granted him temporary custody of Jayden, but he'd made sure to jump through every hoop to keep his nephew stable in his home, the two of them moving from the dorms to an apartment across campus. Soon he'd earn his bachelor's in human services and could become a youth counselor. He'd make it permanent then, make it official. For now, they relied on the foster care checks each month along with his scholarships and grants.

Like he said, they did all right by each other.

Crossing the boardwalk, they dodged bikers and joggers with dogs, heading toward the grassy steps where dreadlocked and tie-dyed musicians beat steel drums. The rhythm got Jayden pounding at the air with his palms and doing his imitation of beatboxing, spitting as he played. "Dada, I be jammin'," he said in his best Bob Marley.

"Ya, mon," Joshua said, arranging the picnic spread for Bianca. He asked Jayden if the girls would like it, but Jayden only said, "Can I have a juice?"

"Sure, grab one from the chest."

A few seconds later, Joshua felt ice chunks at the back of his neck. "Hey, you little turd, good shot, but quit wasting ice. I'm trying to make a good impression here."

"What's a 'preshun?" Jayden fiddled with the plastic straw in his juice box.

"*Im*-pression. It's like, we want Bianca and her daughter to like us. To think we have good manners and behave ourselves."

"But it's a lie! We're wild." He roared.

Joshua laughed. "We are wild. But let's pretend to be civilized—for the ladies."

Jayden sipped through his yellow straw. "Fine."

They'd gone to the stationery store the night before and picked a suede journal with gold-lined pages and embroidered flowers on the cover. On the inside flap, Joshua had written, *To Dreams. Write yours, Bianca.* Would she think he was a weirdo, or worse? Most girls assumed he was gay cause he was a "nice guy," as they put it. He didn't hit on them or make lewd comments or jokes. He hated sports. Instead, he watched cooking shows and reruns of old sitcoms. He and his foster mother Patti used to watch *I Love Lucy.* His favorite episode was when Lucy dressed up like Superman so her kid wouldn't be disappointed at his birthday party, but then the real guy showed up all buff and Lucy got stuck on the balcony in a bizarre getup and an old-school football helmet with pigeons landing all over her until Ricky found her and of course she had some 'splaining to do. Oh man, that was funny.

At the pier entrance, Bianca pushed that pink stroller down the ramp. The steel drums on the boardwalk beat in Joshua's ears. Her hair was tied in curls on top of her head and pinned with a bright fuchsia hibiscus. She had on this long, Aphrodite-type dress that reached down to the pavement with straps that circled her neck, shoulders and collarbone. Her cleavage showed, but barely, and when she stepped, the dress pressed into her thighs, and Joshua noticed the curve of her thick hips. She reminded him of a fetish from their Mexican Art class. She wore dangling bead earrings and bangles on her wrists, and her lips were shiny with gloss. *God*, he prayed, *you better not be messing with me sending this gorgeous woman sauntering toward me.*

He called her name, waving. She peered across the amphitheater, her face lighting up. A good sign. "Hey," she called back, heading toward him and Jayden. "Look at this spread," she said when she got to the picnic blanket.

He stood and hugged her. "You made it."

She hugged him back, warmly, like Patti used to. "This is fantastic. I'm lucky if I remember sunglasses and chanclas." She parked the stroller, locked the wheels, adjusted the sun visor, and sat. "She fell asleep in the car," she whispered, plopping her chanclas in the grass and tucking her bare feet beneath her.

Jayden watched Bianca intently, and when she'd finished arranging herself on the blanket, he jumped and shouted, "Ribbit, ribbit," leaping into her lap. "I'm a frog. Kiss me."

"Ay, hey there, mijo!"

"Kiss me." He puckered his lips.

She shot Joshua a bemused glance; he shrugged. "Well, since you're a frog, kissing you is the right thing to do." She planted her cheek to his lips and made a loud smooching sound.

"There, dada. I made a good *'preshun* like you told me."

"A good 'preshun?" Bianca said. "That *is* important." She grinned.

He wanted to reach across the blanket and press his face to her neck. He couldn't remember feeling this strongly about anyone, hadn't wanted to connect with anyone this badly. Not since a few shaky friendships at the group home after Patti's anyway. He averted his gaze from her cleavage, focused on the picnic. Busied his hands so he wouldn't turn into one of those frat-guy boors he loathed. But goddammit, she had beautiful breasts. He opened large plastic bowls of potato salad, macaroni and cheese, and fruit cocktail, and smaller containers of apple sauce, yogurt, pudding, and a bag of chocolate chip cookies he'd baked the night before. "Dig in," he said. "Oh, and I have something else for you." He pulled out the paper satchel from the stationary shop, handed her the gift.

She raised her eyebrows warily. Instead of reaching for the gift bag, she asked, "What's this?"

Jayden broke the tension, hopping and yelling, "It's for your birthday. Happy birthday!"

Bianca's eyes widened.

"Sorry, Jayden just loves birthdays," Joshua said.

Her confusion gave way to laughter, and she reached out and tickled Jayden's belly. "Tontito, you little silly boy." To Joshua, "I was afraid you'd take the present back if I told you it's not my birthday." She turned her attention to the bag, peeling back the tissue paper carefully, then pulled out the journal, running her fingers along the edges, opened the cover and made a strange little chipmunk noise, like she couldn't tell if she wanted to laugh or cry. "This is too much . . . thank you . . ." She looked at Joshua as if studying a painting again. "I love it."

He thought she would.

They ate ham-and-cheese sandwiches, pickles, potato salad, and cookies; Jayden mostly ate pudding and cookies, but Joshua let him be.

"I can't believe you did all this, really," she said between bites.

"It's just sandwiches."

She looked at him as if to say *it's not just the sandwiches and you know it.*

Jayden stood between them, his face close to Bianca's, and shrugged up his shoulders, cocked his elbows into wings, widened his eyes, and pulled his head low, turning it quickly side to side. Bianca watched, dumbfounded but amused, until he began screeching, "Who, who!"

"Oh, I know! You're an owl!"

He jumped up and clapped. "How'd you know?"

"You're a perfect owl, that's why. And I'll bet you're wise too."

He nodded solemnly.

Joshua said, "It's our spirit animal. Like Hedwig."

"I love Harry Potter," she said. "Will you read them to me sometime, mijo?"

Jayden hooted again, then turned sharply around, waved his hands in front of Joshua's face, and said loudly, "Can I go *play* now?"

Joshua prodded him from in between him and Bee. "Go on then, kid. But stay where we can see you."

Jayden stuffed more cookies in his mouth, then grabbed his bucket and ran down the hill to the sand.

"He's spectacular, Josh. Such a funny little boy."

"He keeps me on my toes."

"If you don't mind my asking . . ." She paused, bit her lip. "What's the story with his mom?"

Joshua had wondered when she'd ask. "It's not like you think," he said. "She's my sister, Olivia. And I don't know where she is."

"Your sister? Oh, you mean, Jayden's not your . . ."

"Son? Technically, no. He's my nephew. I'm his legal guardian, but it's more than that. We've been together since he was born."

Bianca leaned in closer. "He's lucky to have you."

"He's my only family, besides Olivia. It's us two guys against the world. My sidekick. We fight crime together." He did a ninja karate-chop. Bianca didn't roll her eyes. Instead, she laughed. And it didn't seem like the uncomfortable laugh other people did but a genuine I-actually-like-you laugh.

Down at the sandpit, Jayden dumped piles of sand on the boardwalk. "Hey, man! Cut that out," Joshua said. Jayden halted middump, throwing the bucket on the sand dune. "That kid," he said, shaking his head. "Well, I mean, you understand." He motioned toward the stroller.

She smiled, but it almost seemed forced. "I'd better check on Jubilee," she said, pulling back the sunshade.

"Jubilee. That's a beautiful name."

Now Bianca's face relaxed into an easy smile. "It means celebration. I grew up Catholic, and we memorized all the verses. In the Bible, Jubilee is the time of release and universal pardon. Slaves set free. Land returned. Debts forgotten. All kicked off with a trumpet blast."

"Trumpet blasts. An Emancipation Proclamation?"

"My dream, undeferred."

Joshua craned upright but couldn't see her. "I want to meet this little celebration."

"Of course. Just a sec, I need to grab her bottle." She reached into her purse and pulled out a small hard-plastic bottle with a pink plastic nipple. Joshua did a double take, unsure what he was seeing. It was a toy, a play bottle with pretend milk that disappeared when tipped over.

When Jayden was little, he used to suck on baby spoons for teething. "Does she play with that after she's done eating?"

Bianca turned around. "What do you mean?"

Then he saw Jubilee.

He knew it had to be Jubilee because Bianca held her like a baby, lifting the toy bottle to her mouth. Only her mouth didn't open. Man, what the hell? What was going on?

She wore a pink sundress made of terry cloth. Peeking from underneath were pink-and-white bloomers. Her short, tawny hair was parted to one side and fastened with a plastic butterfly barrette. Her eyes, wide open and clear, were gray, the color of a storm. Her lips and cheeks, puckered pink. A dimple indented one caramel cheek. On her wrist, a tiny charm bracelet with "Jubilee" inscribed. She was nonresponsive. Like a dead baby. He almost thought she *was* a dead baby. But no. A doll. The most lifelike doll he'd ever seen. A stone in Bianca's arms. A heavy rock in his gut. It clenched like the potato salad was turning bad inside him. He felt the urge to vomit. Not because Bianca wasn't gorgeous and mysterious. She was. But he was scared. Damn, this was scary. Was this a joke? Was he supposed to play along? He didn't get it. He shook his head.

"Bianca? What's going on?"

She stared at the doll as she pretended to feed it. His skin got all prickly like he was watching a horror movie. What would make this woman who seemed so smart and with it and pulled together act so . . . *insane?* There was no other way to say it, man. She was acting insane. His stomach dropped again.

She'd seemed so normal. She *was* normal. Right? I mean, everything else. But the doll? He looked at her carefully, quietly. Come on, she had to be joking. He waited for her to start laughing. She was pulling his leg. She had to be.

He sat up and peered into the stroller hoping the real Jubilee was there, waiting to be lifted up, that her mother the prankster was getting him good.

The stroller was empty. This was more than he'd bargained for. He put his hand to his head, rubbed his eyes. He felt so damn uncomfortable and could not for the life of him figure out what he was supposed to do.

"Um, Bianca?" He had to say something. This was too weird. He couldn't unpeel his eyes from her as she cradled that doll in her arms. She clucked and *tsk*'d as she moved, staring into Jubilee's eyes as she worked, then, in the softest, sweetest voice, began to sing:

"*Somewhere over the rainbow, skies are blue, and the dreams that you dare to dream really do come true.*"

Her song haunted him. It suspended them in this strange mise-en-scène, as if time had stopped, the spotlight directed on Bianca and her baby doll, and he had no idea if he was part of the play or a spectator in the audience. He exhaled. She wasn't playing. This was Jubilee.

"Oh shit, Bianca."

If she was listening, she didn't acknowledge him. He watched her. Watched as she swept baby-fine strands from Jubilee's forehead. She held the doll's body to her chest and sang. It broke his heart.

"*If happy little bluebirds fly, why, oh why, can't I?*"

She was messed up, bad. Bianca, who seemed so light, was heavy. It fell over Joshua like grief, had him there hunching. He scrolled the index of his memory, skimming his counseling books, flipping page after page. All the stories he'd read. What branch had broken inside her? What scar had healed thus? *Does it crust and sugar over—like a syrupy sweet? Maybe it just sags like a heavy load.* "Oh shit," he said again. And because he didn't know what else to do, because he couldn't stay there as sad as she was making him, he stood, mumbling something about needing to check on the kid, then walked toward Jayden, pouring bucketsful of sand onto the boardwalk.

He glanced back. Bianca held the plastic bottle to the doll's O-shaped mouth.

It was jacked up. Come on. It had to be a joke. She was testing him.

But she'd turned so bright when she pulled that doll from the stroller. Her face reminded him of Olivia's, the day she handed him Jayden. His chest hurt. He pulled his inhaler from his pocket and puffed it twice. Ocean waves roiled in the distance.

Joshua watched Bianca from the safe distance he'd created between them.

His stomach hurt. He thought of the home for troubled youth where he'd interned. Many of the patients were "prodromal," not yet fully psychotic but showing early signs of illness. Some of them scared the shit out of him. One boy had been killing small animals and drinking their blood, worried he might start drinking human blood. That was sick. But Bianca wasn't like *that*. Right?

Jayden was playing in the sand, oblivious to the potential danger. The boy hadn't been scared of her. If she were twisted, his boy would've sensed it. Kids know that stuff, right? He wouldn't have sat on her lap, wouldn't have treated her like a friend. Joshua was grasping at straws. What would Olivia have said about Bianca? She was gorgeous. And intelligent. She laughed at his dumb jokes. She liked the journal. She liked Jayden. She didn't seem sick. He couldn't imagine her killing anything. Couldn't imagine her having those dark thoughts. She didn't seem like a danger. *You should walk away, Joshy man. Call it. Time of death, call it.* It was crazy, and he was crazy for even considering walking back toward the grass, toward the woman on the blanket who'd already burrowed her way into his mind. Damn. Into his heart.

But he was curious. Maybe that's all it was at first. He wanted to find out more. He had to know—*why Jubilee?* Why did Bianca need that strange little doll, who almost looked like a living, breathing infant?

She called him back without calling him back.

She called him back, and he couldn't help himself, he needed to find out more. He needed more time with her.

What harm could it do to wait and see?

TWO
LA BEE

ONE YEAR EARLIER
BEFORE JUBILEE

In Gabe's kitchen, Bianca and Gabe's mother, Esme, chopped cucumbers, cilantro, and cubes of Monterey Jack cheese instead of the more expensive abalone. Bianca diced with quick, deliberate strokes, imagining the restaurant she and Gabe planned to open in the Imperial Valley. They would ask Gabe's dad, Hector, for help with the down payment—if they didn't chicken out. Hector was a huge, formidable man who scared Bianca. But Esme she loved. Esme she trusted. It was her house Bianca went back to instead of Mama's seven months ago when Dad died.

Esme threw the mixture into a deep plastic bowl, then peeled shrimp tails, deveined them, and tossed those in while sharing the latest chisme—which Valley women were cheating and in whose bed and why. But Bianca and Esme still never spoke of what had happened at the Clínicas de Salud Bianca's freshman year in high school.

A ceramic rooster cookie jar glinted against the faux marble counter. Esme's kitchen was decorated in red roosters that anywhere else would've been chintzy, but here they were comforting.

Outside, the lawn roasted in patches. Wilted yellow flowers spilt from cane cholla and barrel cactus. White flies, iridescent and smaller than grains of rice, orbited the streetlamps. The Rio Vista street sign was pocked with bullet holes where drunk teenagers had ricocheted through the alley with shotguns. Aluminum-foiled windows shimmered from the ranch-style stuccos squatting beneath palo verdes and mulberries, barricades against the 110-degree broil that relented only after midnight.

"If Gabe were my husband, I'd have left him," said Esme, "but since he's my son . . . Ay, hija. We've made a full-blooded Mexican of you. *La Bee.*"

Bianca pursed her lips, poured a chilled bottle of Clamato over the mixture while Esme squeezed lemon halves, shook Tapatío out in spurts. Once, while delivering tamales that Nana, Esme, and Bee had made, Esme told her comadre that Bianca was her nuera, daughter-in-law. But she never said it in front of Gabe. He was a mama's boy, which, in the Valley, wasn't necessarily bad. A man who treated his mama with respect would treat his own wife with respect, that's what Esme said.

Selena blasted from the stereo in the backyard. Gabe's rusted '66 Mustang hulked on a frayed patch of grass against the fence, covered with a tarp. Hector had promised to help his son restore it years before. But between them, most things remained unsaid or unfinished.

On the patio, carne asada sizzled on the grill with whole green onions— bulbs and all—habanero chiles, thick flour tortillas. Hector, a skewer in one hand, cerveza in the other, was a John Deere of a man, over six feet and three hundred pounds. When Hector found Gabe and Bianca in Gabe's bed when they were fifteen and seventeen, sheets pulled over her naked body up to her neck, he shouted in a growl deeper than her own dad's yelling, drunk and raging, *"Never let me see her in this fucking bed again!"* He slammed the door and drove away. Gabe had rubbed her thighs as she sobbed. "He's like that. He'll warm to you when we have our first baby." He said it like he didn't regret what they'd done. Regret: a metal scraping her mouth. She imagined what their baby would've looked like. Imagined herself growing beneath the tent of bedsheet into a carnival. Running away with her own damn self.

Two years later, when she was seventeen, beneath a star-pitted sky during winter break, she and Gabe lay in the back of his pea-green truck. Gabe was crying. Across the dirt road, red and green chaser lights blinked Merry Christmas from a farmhouse in the distance. "You don't understand," he'd said. And she didn't. It should have been simple: They loved each other. Wasn't that enough? She was a senior in high school, he a freshman in college.

He'd gone away to Cal State San Bernardino, three hours north toward the Inland Empire. The week after he'd left, Lily's mom had driven a drunk and babbling Bee home from a house party, and Bee's mama had rushed her to the ER where they'd pumped her stomach. Mama had grounded Bee for months; she would've allowed Gabe to come over, but he never did, not once did he come and see her like he'd promised, and Bee didn't know why until mid-November. Bee had gone to the Cattle Call parade on Main Street with Lily, and when she saw Gabe there, his arms around another girl, she'd fallen off the curb where she'd been buying watermelon with chile from a street vendor and sprained her ankle, but that pain didn't compare with the sight of Gabe's arm draped across another girl's shoulders, watching the floats of school children and rodeo queens passing by with another girl in Bee's place in the lawn chairs and blankets on the sidewalk beside his familia. Bee hadn't even planned on going; Gabe must have thought she wouldn't be there. She hadn't confronted him then. She'd been too ashamed. She'd left her fruit cup and limped back to her dad's car. They broke up over the phone, and she ignored his calls for the next month. She'd found out through the small-town chisme that the other girl's name was Katrina, and she went to San Bernardino with Gabe, though she was from the Valley, también.

Still, when Gabe had returned for winter break, he'd stopped by her house first to wish her a Merry Christmas, but they'd ended up driving out to the country between ditch banks and haystacks, where she gave in, gave herself to him, and afterward, he told her that he still loved her and never should've let her go. She hadn't gone anywhere, she'd said. They could still get back together. That other girl didn't matter. It was over. *What* didn't she understand?

"Katrina's pregnant."

The air had splintered, crackling like shards of ice. She'd sucked it in until her lungs ached.

She should've walked away then. She'd tried. She'd thrown herself into the novels and poetry books she loved, signed up for an online, dual-credit college literature class and read *Beloved* for the first time, filled every page of every journal she could get her hands on, transcribing the prickling songs of the cacti in her mama's garden, the troubled arrows of the penned horses' eyes down at the stables beyond the empty lots beside the river, the texture and taste of the pomegranate seeds growing wild in the orchards behind her house, the Saturday-morning before-sunrise chatter of the sleepy migrant workers gathering in the doughnut shop, their yawning Spanish, their gnarled, calloused hands, as she ordered her bear claw and sweet tea, last meal before she finally dragged herself to sleep. Her dreams; she wrote those too.

She'd earned scholarships to several California universities before she'd settled on Holy Cross. It was their music that had called to her. Their choir had put on a performance in the auditorium at school, and their haunted voices had spoken to the hole inside her. Of course, Mama had been thrilled.

But there's a hole in the belly of the earth. It swallows.

And it flapped open its meaty jaws. Made a meal of her father.

When Bianca had returned for the funeral, there was Gabe.

Now, Esme took the bowl of shrimp cocktail and a tray of saltines out to the patio. Bianca followed with a bowl of homemade salsa, made the way Gabe's nana had taught her. Blacken fat, green poblano chiles on the comal, "Pick them up fast or you'll burn the tips of your fingers," Nana had said, pinching her fingers together, snatching back her clasped hand and wincing, "¡Ay! How that stings."

"Bee," Hector called playfully from the barbecue. Grinning, he nodded toward the bowl in her hands. "You didn't make the salsa all soupy like the lasagna, did you? Remember, Esme? La sopa?" He meant the time she'd tried making lasagna for Gabe's whole family, and Hector had barked, "¿Qué es estó? ¿Sopa?" They'd all laughed at her runny casserole, her tomato-red face.

She forced a laugh. "Nah, Hector. I think I made it right this time. You'd better taste and make sure." She had to hide her feelings. She couldn't be too sentis. Unless she was drunk. And no one liked her when she was drunk.

Gabe pulled his green truck onto the treads of dead grass his tires had rutted into his mother's lawn, home from picking up two-year-old Lana from her mother, Katrina. She was a hurricane all right.

Through the open gate Lana flung herself into Bianca's arms. "Bee!"

"Hey, pretty girl. Qué chula." She picked Lana up, both smiling. But it also hurt, holding her. She wasn't *Bianca's* daughter. Though she could swear she saw a trace of her in there.

"Wanna play?" Lana's voice squeaked like a baby bird. Stuck them to the nesting place.

Bianca carried Lana toward the patio, where Esme scooped her away.

"Mi preciosa, mi princesa. Come to Nana." Esme snatched her so quickly, her voice and expression changed so suddenly, Bianca went cold. Lana was Esme's granddaughter. She was also a broken record in Bianca's memory. The Valley had a way of beckoning back its children. Children having children.

Clasping her arms across her chest, Bianca dug her nails into her skin as she watched Esme dance with her first and only granddaughter. Maybe Bianca shouldn't have returned to the Valley when Dad died. Her second semester of freshman year, she'd packed up before midterms and never returned. Maybe she should have stayed at Holy Cross on the coast, stuck it out there, stifling and dogmatic as it had been. Now she was stuck here in the desert—the way she imagined Dad, purgatorial.

Selena crooned the mariachi "Tú Solo Tú" in her husky voice.

"Come here, son. Man this grill," Hector called. With cerveza in hand, he marched over to Esme and grabbed her waist, pulling her to his gargantuan body and dancing her around the patio. "After twenty years with you, vieja, you're still the only one."

Lana squirmed out of their arms and toddled toward Bianca. Gabe pulled a bottle of beer from the cooler and popped the cap off with his teeth, letting it fall to the ground. He swigged half the beer in one gulp, watching his parents dance.

As the evening sun dipped behind the fence, the backyard barbecue had turned full swing. The rest of the familia, compadres, and comadres had arrived, parking their cars in the alley and funneling through the back gate carrying six-packs and paper bags of liquor. More food had been piled atop the plastic folding tables surrounding the wooden picnic bench, now mostly conchas and cakes, and people sitting or standing nearby occasionally waved the flies away.

Bianca had whisked away a pink concha before anyone else could and stuffed it in pieces between her cheeks as she helped Gabe put Lana to bed; the bright-pink pan dulce was her favorite, reminding her of girlhood holidays at her abuela's house. Reminded her of sweet things, this sweet bread. Reminded her of innocence. She was spilling the crumbs onto Lana's bedspread, but she didn't care. Gabe lay on one side of the queen-sized bed and she the other, with Lana in the middle as they watched *Strawberry Shortcake*. And as the little girl between them closed her eyes, Bianca whispered, "Sometimes I wish she were mine."

Gabe sprawled across his daughter's grand bed, a bed fit for a princess, his big feet hanging off the side, hands tucked behind his head. He closed his eyes briefly before answering. "I *am* sorry, Bee."

They'd spoken these words before.

When they were sure the baby was asleep, they crept out of her bedroom. On the patio Gabe grabbed three more beers. He handed Bianca one, chugged one himself, then opened the next as he sat in a lawn chair near the picnic table. Everyone prattling and laughing, Bianca perched at the edge of a bench, sipping a beer. Hector would be more generous in front of his friends. This was their chance to ask him for the loan. But how to break into the senseless banter?

Hector's compadre Frank complained his marriage had gone to shit when his wife went back to work. Hector laughed. "She stop making your tortillas, compadre?"

"You kidding? She never made tortillas. Even before that."

"Not like our mamis used to? Back in the good ol' days."

"Not with all this feminist independence mierda."

"Bee's a feminist. She's a college girl. Es verdad, Bee?" Hector was drunk.

Bianca nodded, though she was actually a dropout who'd soon be a college student again. After Dad's funeral, she'd found a job taking classifieds at the local newspaper, the *Desert Herald*, which was closer to writing than cashiering at Savers. She'd signed up to start community college in the spring (since she'd missed the fall deadline). She would retake the classes she'd dropped, sans biblical history, swapping it for contemporary poetry. That counted as a college girl, right?

"My daughter Adriana works at the bank," Frank said. "What about you?"

Bianca meant to say she worked at the Valley Press. But she'd been drinking and instead, she told him she was a writer.

Hector held his beer across his heart. Gabe rolled his eyes.

"A writer? So you don't want babies?" Frank joked.

Of course she wanted babies. That was her problem. She'd always wanted babies. Even when she'd let Esme and Gabe talk her into letting one go . . . for their future.

She nodded.

"I thought writers live alone, drink all day long, travel around Europe."

"I could take my kids with me to Europe. Or México." She used her Spanish accent, which she'd perfected when she'd taught herself to speak Spanish. Mama hadn't spoken Spanish to her or her gringo father. Another reason Bianca resented her.

"She wants to write about *our* people?" Frank winked at Hector. "Una gringa por la causa."

"My mama is Mexican," she said. If anyone heard her, they didn't respond.

"You're mixed up, Bee. You'd better pick: writer or wife. Right, Frank?" Hector laughed.

She chugged her beer, wiped her mouth, spoke up loudly. "All you do is sit around objectifying women as if we're set in stone. You relegate us to roles you've assigned and bark orders at us: Mujer! Grab me a beer. Make me a plate. Go get the ice. Why don't you get off your ass and get it yourself?" Her heart pounded. She couldn't believe she'd stood up to Hector. She didn't dare look at Gabe. They were supposed to be getting on Hector's good side, not accusing him of being a machismo pig.

But Hector laughed, then turned toward the grass behind him and spit. "Qué cabrona. Listen to this girl talk. What else, La Bee? Tell us more."

She knew he was making fun of her, but she didn't care. She was burning inside and the only way to keep from imploding was to let it out. "You think we like serving men?"

"Then why do you do it?" Hector demanded. "Why bring La Sopa over here?"

She looked toward Gabe, who stared at the cement. "Love."

For a second she thought Gabe would say something. Instead, he slumped farther in his chair, cradling his beer, its glass spout nestled against his chin.

"Ay, amor," Hector said, pulling Esme closer to him. "Mujer de mi corazón, mi vida," he sang. "Go get me a beer." He slapped her ass.

Everyone laughed. Bianca's cheeks reddened again.

"La Bee, you want your man to love you?"

Gabe shifted in his lawn chair, cleared his throat, said nothing.

"Keep that pot of beans hot. Right, son? That what you want?" Hector chuckled.

"I want her to keep her mouth shut in public," Gabe said.

"Muchacho, the woman's always right." Hector turned to his wife, "That right, mujer?"

"Mmm," Esme murmured, smiling as her husband kissed her. "But leave pobre Bee alone, Hector."

"Nah, she can handle it." He turned to Bianca. "So which is it then, Bee? Writer or wife? Your husband doesn't want you airing his dirty laundry. His caca."

She told him she would split in two, break the binary.

"There she goes with her fancy college words. Su poesía. Qué bonita, qué loca."

Bianca rose from the bench. She felt sick. Gabe followed her into the house. The patio door slammed behind him; he grabbed her shoulders and spun her around to face him. "Why do you always embarrass me in front of my family?" His face flushed from the beer.

"You don't mind when I talk like that with you," she said, mustering all the haughtiness she could. She was ready for a fight.

"That's different." He wiped his palms across the sides of his spiky hair and looked away. "They don't understand."

"They understand fine. You just never stick up for me. You used to love my poetry."

"I used to do a lot of things, Bee." His voice softened. She stared at him, the man she'd watched grow up. Tall and well-built with bronze skin that released a mixture of Cool Water cologne and sweat, he smelled like a beach in the desert. His broad shoulders were stretch-marked where his muscles had grown faster than his skin. His otherwise clear boyish face, slightly impish with his upturned ears, flashed a scar below his eye where he ran into the side mirror of his uncle's truck when he was little. Esme and Nana said he was a real travieso, would storm into the house in a fury, knocking plates of food off the table for no apparent reason. But then he would smile his charming dimpled smile and be forgiven. Not much had changed since then.

She sighed, the fight leaving her chest, her stomach. She was tired.

"Come here," he whispered. He pulled her to his body and wrapped his arms around her, pressing his lukewarm beer bottle to her shoulder. His kisses were rough, his sour breath hot against her face and mouth. This Gabe she knew well. She walked a fine line with him. He loved her or despised her when he was drunk. Tonight, he loved her.

She let him hoist her up, wrapped her legs around him. She was Coatlicue, Azteca mother of all creation, and destruction. She was Coatlicue, fumbling through the dark. She'd break through. She'd find a crossing—or create one herself.

Gabe carried her to the laundry room, locked the door, hoisted her atop the dryer. He reached under her sundress and pulled her thong to the side, pushing his fingers deep inside her, kissing her neck and breasts.

She was a snake. Careful. She could bite. She could. But didn't.

She combed her fingers through his short, black hair as she held the back of his head. They were drops of water on a hot comal. Their bodies scorched each other. They were not meant to make a meal, only to test the fire.

"You're sexy as hell," he groaned. "Mi poeta."

His breath against her neck. His voice in her ear. A voice that called butterflies from inside her. Made her think in clichés. Colored her dreams in red. *I've loved you too much too long too hard.* Red as the desert. Where oceans were dry as salt flats. Where red meant lost and lost meant dead.

"I love you," she said.

"Mmm . . . then let me fuck you."

He pulled her off the dryer and bent her over, face to machine. She pressed her ear against the cool, smooth metal and listened as he slid on a condom then thrust into her.

The echo of a seashell.

He leaned down and kissed her cheek when he finished. She straightened her dress and pulled up her chonies as he opened the door to the bathroom and took a piss.

"Hey, look. I'm sorry you felt uncomfortable out there. I don't want you making any scenes. We're trying to butter him up, right? So we might have a chance at a future, our restaurant." He zipped; she nodded. "Hey, come here," he said, his voice soft, playful. "You know I love you."

"Oh, yeah? Or you love my ass?"

He squeezed her ass. "Both. Now let's get your ass back outside. Don't get all dramatic again. Save that for your poems."

The first nights after he'd left for college, he'd promised to come home weekends but never did. She was imprisoned in her house. Mama wouldn't lessen Bianca's sentence even though she was losing it, caged in her room listening to Mama and Dad fight. Mama wouldn't risk Bianca getting drunk and ending up in the hospital again. Couldn't trust her not to hurt herself at a party.

Bianca had made a plan. She would be a writer. She would get out of town. She'd move to a big city like the postcard of New York her English teacher had given her when she'd admitted she wanted to be a poet but didn't know how since all poets were dead like Emily Dickinson and Sylvia Plath and her teacher hadn't laughed because he'd understood why she would've thought so. Instead he'd said she was already a poet, and there were others like her. Outside the Valley, there were such things as open mics and poetry slams and international competitions, and she could join them, she could win.

But then a birth and a death. Both like drowning. Dad had been drunk, and Bianca could never forgive Mama. She should have saved him. Compared to that, Gabe felt relatively easy to forgive. What were ninth-grade bloody thighs next to a father, drunk in a bathtub? The water must have felt so warm on his cheeks, his face, his eyes.

The stars. The beer. The mariachi music and night sky, blinking. She tried controlling herself in Gabe's backyard. For his family. For Esme. But the alcohol brought it all back. Sourness, bitterness rooted inside her, knotted and spindling her gut. A sick swishing. A turnip or sickly red beet. Pulled from her uterine strings to her feet. Splitting open. A cactus skull. Nopal on the patio. Prickly pear. A bright-pink cactus flower, sprouting then dying in sticky water.

The backyard swayed and dipped around her so she couldn't remember they'd been arguing. Faces blurred. She was drunk and screaming. How long had she been screaming?

Bile rose in her throat.

"You parade Katrina and Lana around like you're a family, taking them to birthday parties like *I'm* the other woman. While I wait for you like an idiot. Soy estúpida. I'm so fucking stupid. Putting up with it. Are you ashamed of me?"

"Bee, you're drunk, shut up." Gabe yanked on her arm.

"No, they should know. They should know what you put me through."

"I never asked you to come back. Sit your drunk ass down, show some respect."

"Ooh, Gabe, you'd better control your woman," Frank teased. "Looks like someone can't handle their alcohol."

"Looks like someone can't handle their business," Hector said. He glared at Gabe.

"Shut up, old vatos," Esme countered. She turned to Bianca. "Mija, don't you think you've had enough?"

The backyard spun; Bianca steadied herself on a stucco pillar beneath the patio, then staggered onto the grass toward the swing set where she and Lana had played. She jumped onto the swing, standing straight, knees locked, rocking back and forth. "I *have* had enough."

"What the hell is she doing?" Frank asked, chugging the last of his beer. "She really loca?"

The neighbor's dog barked.

"Get down, Bee. You're gonna wake up the neighbors. You want them to call the cops?"

She kicked him. "You fuck me nights then go play daddy to Katrina's baby."

Gabe threw his bottle at the slide, glass smashing against aluminum, beer trickling down like tears. He'd almost hit her with the glass.

"Shut up, Bee. Shut the fuck up!"

"Hey, son, you'd better take her home," Hector called. "This isn't funny anymore."

"Tell them, Gabe." Bianca wouldn't stop. "Tell them how we had a baby too. Tell them how I lost her. How you *wanted* me to get rid of her. How Esme took me to the Clínicas."

"That's enough," Gabe yelled, covering her mouth and heaving her off the swing over his shoulder. "You're going home."

Gabe hoisted her across the lawn, clutching her tightly. She was going to be sick. She knew he'd throw her in his truck, drop her at home. The house would be dark. And cold. And silent. She wanted to stay at Esme's house. To wake up to a family. Not broken by a father's death.

She bit Gabe's hand.

"Fucking bitch." He dropped her onto the grass. "You bit me."

"I'm sorry," she sobbed. "I don't want to go back there tonight."

She wilted, a heap on the grass, her dress wadded, revealing her chonies.

"Esme," Hector muttered. "Take her to bed."

She could stay. Hector said it. She could stay . . .

Esme helped her up, wiped the grass from her dress and smoothed it over her ass and legs.

"It's okay, mija. You had too much to drink. We understand."

"I lost the baby, Esme. I lost her. She bled down my legs. You saw her.

My little cactus flower. You saw her." At the end of her freshman year in high school, when she was fifteen years old, she'd had the abortion Gabe and his mama had encouraged her to have. The beginning of her senior year, Gabe had made a baby with someone else. Bee imagined her little cactus flower blooming in Lana's bed, instead of the gray-eyed baby sleeping in her place. She choked as she sobbed, "I want her back."

"Shhh, Bee. Cállate. I know you're upset, but Hector doesn't know about that. You'll break his heart. Please stop, mija. Please."

"For Christ's sake, Esme, what's she talking about? Get her inside," Hector called.

"Ay, mujeres," Frank clucked. "What can you do with them? That one's sure got spirit though, don't she?"

Esme took Bianca inside, while Gabe sank into a patio chair and grabbed another beer.

Before the glass door shut, Hector asked, "Son, what the hell have you done?"

THREE
REBORNS

WITH JUBILEE

Bianca asked Dr. Norris if he believed in love. His office was in Anaheim, the next city over from Matty's, off the 57 freeway near the giant
red *A* at Angel Stadium, but she'd never been there because Dad had
been a Dodgers fan. Outside in the courtyard was a wishing fountain;
copper pennies and silvery-shining quarters and nickels and dimes,
each representing someone's desire, covered the aquamarine tile. Before
every visit to Dr. Norris, she dropped in change from the wallet she
kept in Jubilee's diaper bag or, if Jubilee had stayed home with Matty,
in her canvas book bag with a scene of the tattooed tree outstretching
her branches to hand the boy an apple from *The Giving Tree*. Bianca's
wishes were always the same but they came out as prayers. It took her a
long time to discern what she was telling herself since her thoughts had
sometimes become muddled in her mind, like speaking another language in a dream and she knew what it meant in the dream but when
she awoke she realized she couldn't speak that language so she must
have been making up the words.

They seemed so real in the dream.

On Dr. Norris's wall hung a picture by an artist named Tanguy whom
Bianca didn't know anything about, but she could tell he was surreal and
she liked that about him. The painting was called *The Lovers*, and it

would have taken a real creative mind to comprehend what he'd meant because the whole painting was underwater and the so-called lovers were comprised of salt bones, taupe mineral deposits, curvy-lined wishbone figures like various parabolas on a piece of ocean-colored graph paper that nearly puzzled together but not quite.

The painting was like splitting the wishbone with Matty. And it made her think of Gabe. But at her therapy session after the picnic on the beach, it made her think of Joshua too. Above the lovers, smaller pieces of the same bone material floated haphazardly, unconnected to any larger bodies. One figure looked like a woman's torso, another the head and horns of a white-skulled buffalo, and another a dancer's lithe leg bending in a jazz-style arabesque, or a fishhook.

The Lovers hung beside Dr. Norris, and Bianca often studied it while avoiding discussing the disarray of her life or her unresolved anger at Mama and Matty since Dad had died or why she would rather stay home and care for Jubilee than go out and make friends. She didn't know the answers to any of those things. But she began to find the most remarkable possibilities in the painting. The day after the picnic, she also decided the wavy-boned figure she'd thought represented the lovers lying together not quite fitting was only *one person*. The other person stood at a distance in the sand, her long black hair coiled around her salt-pillar body, the long clean bone of her spine growing up from the ocean floor.

All of this had prompted her to ask Dr. Norris what felt like a ridiculous question. She knew the purpose of their visits was to "unshock" her—as Mama would say when she called or showed up at Matty's with a box of the pan dulce from the Mexican bakery down the street, always with several pink conchas: "Baby girl, you have to keep seeing Dr. Norris, so he can unshock you." Bianca pictured him jumping from behind his desk and yelling or growling in his scariest voice. She would scream and throw her hands in the air the way they do in cartoons except her eyes wouldn't pop from her face; she would be cured and could stop taking the antidepressants and antipsych meds and could go back to Abuela's without everyone looking at her as if she were about to unzip herself and reveal a hideous monster beneath her skin.

They all acted glad enough Jubilee and Bianca were home, but their kindness felt like a facade. She told Mama while wiping the sugar dust from her mouth and sprinkling it back into the pan dulce box, "I'm not shocked," but then refused to talk about Jubilee except to say she needed her and would everyone please leave her alone because if she didn't have a home here, she'd go find one somewhere else. Matty would tell her to stop being dramatic, and Mama would get that look like either the beans had made her gassy or she was about to cry. Of course they wanted her home. Of course they didn't wish she'd stayed in the Valley. Of course Jubilee was perfect. After a few cycles of that scene, they left their questions about Jubilee to Dr. Norris, who'd mostly left Jubilee out of it and instead asked about Bianca's childhood and what had happened before she moved to Santa Ana.

A few times, they'd ventured into Dad's history of mental illness, and once she'd admitted how she used to float through the hallways upside-down when she was a girlchild. *Was she really floating, or had it just felt like floating?* he'd asked. She'd shrugged. When he mentioned dissociation, she began humming. And never brought it up again. Sometimes, when she was supposed to be talking about herself, instead she told him the plots of the novels she loved and watched to see if he caught on and knew she was shitting him. He never let on, though she suspected he knew.

Dr. Norris spoke with a Scottish accent like the priest at St. Bruno's, where Mama would sometimes drag Jubilee and her to Saturday-evening Mass and try to get her into the confessional box. But Bianca had drawn the line and said they'd wait in the pew beside the statue of Mary and the ever-glowing prayer candles, which appeased Mama. Bianca only liked going to church to listen to the priest's accent, which reminded her of Mel Gibson in *Braveheart*, though neither Dr. Norris nor the priest looked anything like the long-haired, stallion-riding William Wallace.

"Something's happened, Bianca. You seem more relaxed today." Dr. Norris's short brown hair balded at the edges, his facial expression welcoming, the smile lines at the corners of his eyes and mouth like little rivers. Bianca might have told him about Joshua, so inviting were his mannerisms and that accent, but something told her he might react more cautiously than Matty, so she held back. Instead she asked if he believed in love.

He answered with a clarifying question of his own: "Love at first sight? Or love over time? Or both?"

Since she didn't know what she meant and was tempted to launch into a Shakespeare sonnet ("Love is not love / Which alters when it alteration finds, / Or bends with the remover to remove"), she shrugged and curled her legs beneath her on his therapist's couch (typical beige pleather).

He asked if they were still talking about Gabe, or if she had someone else in mind, but she assured him it was purely rhetorical, that she'd discovered those lovers on his wall weren't conjoined after all but separated by ocean and sand and whatever material they were made of.

He said he'd always thought of the lovers as the other swirling figures at the top, searching for matching pieces.

"But that's just it," she said. "What if you find a matching piece? What if you find another salt bone and it matches your own strange shape and you fit together and everything seems perfect?"

"Well isn't that the goal of love?"

"I don't want to lose my own shape again."

"Then don't," he said, as if it were the simplest thing in the world, holding on to one's self.

After the beach, Joshua had searched online and found dolls called Reborns. He'd typed in "baby doll delusions" and found a documentary about women in the UK who collected Reborns, lifelike dolls painted to look like newborns, with the same purple veins, skin folds, iridescent eyelids, mohair dyed by hand and stitched into the scalp to match the downy hair of a real baby. Women custom-ordered dolls from artists called Reborners. Advertisements on eBay promised:

Send me a photo, and I can make a replica of your baby.

Facial features, hair color, eye color and weight will be done to your preferences.

I can make up a birth certificate also with names and dates that you choose.

Custom babies start at $500.00.

Prefabricated Reborns went for a hundred bucks, and even cheaper on Amazon.

Therapists endorsed the Reborns for dementia patients, particularly women; hugging the dolls released oxytocin, the same as nursing mothers release when they breastfeed. Holding and tending to the dolls helped elderly patients in nursing homes feel more relaxed and calm. One old woman kept her doll with her at mealtimes, while the nurses wheeled her through the hallways, at bedtime. All the nurses went along with it, like it was her real baby.

Some people thought the dolls were creepy. They posted so in the comments. Reborns fell into the uncanny valley, the way robots that were too lifelike inspired disgust instead of awe. The closer to humanlike a thing got, the less we humans could accept it. Strange creatures, we were.

But Jubilee wasn't like that. She didn't repel Joshua. He'd always been attracted to the strange, and the sad.

He'd collected action figures since childhood. He knew everything there was to know about comic books. The X-Men series had been his bible since boyhood. It had saved him as he shuffled from foster home to foster home, protected him and given him strength all through his teen years, when Patti sent him to the group home. None of the jerks there could touch him. He was Beast. Didn't a part of him believe the worlds of Marvel and DC actually existed? Didn't a part of him rebel if a storyline infringed on the canon he so revered? How were dolls any different?

After their first visit, Jayden said, during bath time, "Jubilee's not like the babies at daycare. She doesn't cry. She's kind of a lump." He stuck soap bubbles to his face to make a beard, then added, "I still like her though."

Joshua explained that Jubilee was a really quiet baby. Babies cry to ask for something. Maybe Jubilee's mama already knew what she needed, so Jubilee didn't need to ask.

Kids are so blunt that if Joshua had said anything else, Jayden was liable to hurt Bianca's feelings. It wasn't really lying. For Jayden, his stuffed animal Walter was real. A furry dog he made at Build-a-Bear, with a little heart he put in the dog's chest himself. Walter went to recess with Jayden every day. Once, Walter was lost at the park, and Jayden was crying like a real person had vanished. He made himself sick crying. Joshua took him back to the park with flashlights, and they found Walter in a tunnel slide. It wasn't just a stuffed animal to him, it was a best friend. What was the difference between belief, the imaginary, and therapeutic representation? Was Bianca's reality any less valid?

Joshua would allow Jayden to come to his own conclusions. For now, Jayden accepted that Jubilee was real. Perhaps in some ways Joshua *was* lying to him. But Joshua already lived in his own world anyway, through his superheroes. Even though the "rational" adult part of him knew that he was just a weird boy grown into a weird man, part of him still believed he had special powers, a second sense. Maybe Jubilee was Bianca's second sense.

The wounded boy in Joshua remembered how powerful belief could be.

He called Bianca later that week, then again, and again. They'd hung out at the park on weekends with Jayden, and talked into the witching hours most nights. They met at the bowling alley on campus in the basement of the student center a couple of times before Jayden's pickup time. Since Bianca never took Jubilee to school, it all seemed so normal. He wouldn't know, since he'd never dated anyone before her, but he'd have bet they looked like any happy new couple.

The first day she invited him to her house, he was that weird mixture of nervous and excited. It felt like fieldwork, like an exploration. He'd get to watch how Bee lived in her own environment. Not in a clinical way. Only, that's how he'd reconciled any misgivings. She was his case study.

He pulled up to her brother's house in Santa Ana. On the front door hung an autumn wreath decorated with leaves. A pumpkin sat on their porch mat. It seemed normal enough. He walked up to the porch and knocked on the door.

Bianca answered, dressed in cotton shorts, a long-sleeved flannel, and fuzzy slippers, all bright pink. She looked sexy even in pajamas. She kissed his cheek and invited him in. He followed her with the tingle of her lips still on his skin.

She'd already sketched a portrait of her brother during their many late-night phone conversations. Matty was a freelance tech writer and editor, but he wrote and illustrated comics, well-known amongst enthusiasts, which Joshua was. Joshua didn't know Matty's work, but he was eager to learn. Joshua *did* know that Matty watched Jubilee for Bianca every day she went to school or tutored at the writing center. He gathered that Matty also watched Jubilee whenever Bianca went to what she referred to as "appeasing her mother" appointments, which Joshua had gleaned were therapy sessions, though she wasn't forthcoming about anything related to her past or Jubilee and he was still afraid to ask her point-blank.

"Josh, this is Matty," she said. "Well, Matthew if you want to be fancy about it, but I call him Matty and so can you. Handro, well, Alejandro, is at work." She'd told Joshua that Handro worked at a gay bar downtown. They entered a nook past the foyer set up like an office. Lining the walls were black-framed pictures of comic book characters Joshua didn't recognize. The room was decorated in red and black, koi fish paintings, Chinese letters. A black-and-white photo of a little girl who looked like Bianca on a tree swing foregrounding a wooden fence leading to the beach. Matty sat at a desk chair and stood when they came in. He was taller and broader than Joshua, but he sensed something similar about them, something in the way Matty looked at him, as though he could've been a stand-in Matty. He shook Joshua's hand.

"It's nice to meet you, Josh. I've heard amazing things. Bee hasn't been this happy in a long time."

Bianca nudged Matty in the ribs. "You're not supposed to *tell* him . . ." She twisted her shoulders and lowered her chin, and in a deep exaggerated voice, she drawled, "Keep them guessing, always, darrrling . . . Keep them guessing." Was it all a game she'd lost the rulebook for? Was she playing from some alternate set of instructions the rest of them only needed to find?

"You're too much," Matty said to her, his voice not resentful but more complicated than Joshua could decipher in that moment, so he recorded it in his list of mental notes, cross-tagged under *brotherly protection* and *how are families supposed to love each other?* When Matty squeezed her shoulder, she recoiled slightly. A lesser observer might not have noticed, but Joshua did. She put her arm around Matty and hugged back, the cognitive dissonance so palpable in the room it was a wonder none of them were morphing into creatures beneath their disguises.

"Hey, Matty, Josh is a comic book aficionado. You should take him to Comic-Con next May." Joshua had told her he'd wanted to go to the annual comic book convention in San Diego. He'd never done any of the things he'd wanted to. Before college, he'd won a round-trip flight to London. Only he couldn't scrounge up the money for backpacking, not even for bunking in hostels. Mostly he'd been afraid to go alone. He wished he could say it was Jayden that kept him from traveling, but that'd be a lie.

Matty said he'd be glad to take Joshua, that it would be fun. Joshua made another mental note at the way he said *sure* and *fun*. He *seemed* genuine, but Joshua knew how even genuine sometimes masked condescension, how he could've been teasing and Joshua wouldn't have realized it until later.

Bianca said, "Matty's always trying to recruit new comic book fans, right, brother?" Then she added, smiling, "And pad his booth with supporters."

Matty asked Joshua's favorite comic character. "Beast, easily."

"An X-Men fan." Matty winked at Bianca, and again Joshua couldn't tell if he approved or was laughing at him in code.

"Hey," Bee said, clapping her hands. "What if we all went on this trip? I could take the kids out to the beach while you guys are in the convention. We could go to Sea World."

"The kids?" Joshua asked, laughing. He looked toward Matty, who raised his eyebrows.

Bianca's smile vanished.

"What kids?" Matty asked, frowning at his sister.

She'd meant Jubilee and Jayden, but Joshua couldn't account for the tension at his mistake. Bianca crossed her arms in front of her chest. "Josh knows who I mean," she said, her voice flat. She stared at her slippers against the linoleum floor of Matty's makeshift office.

Joshua felt the rope of his stomach hockling into a knob, but not for the reason he probably should have felt sick. She'd invited him on a family trip, and he'd insulted her. "Of course we can bring them," he said, trying to lighten the mood of the room. "That would be fun."

Matty looked at Joshua as if trying to figure something out. "More than Jubilee?"

"My nephew, Jayden. I'm his guardian."

"Oh." Matty's voice was cold.

Bianca looked like she was about to cry. Joshua felt compelled to apologize for something though he didn't know what. Matty filled the silence. "So, Beast? Good old Dr. Hank McCoy. Before or after he grew blue fur?"

Bianca walked back toward the foyer and disappeared behind a corner. Joshua watched her leave before turning to Matty, who'd sunk back down into his swivel chair. Joshua had so many questions. Instead, he answered Matty's question. "I can relate to him in either misshapen form."

Matty sighed. He opened his mouth then closed it. Sighed again.

"Do you think I should say something to her?" Joshua asked.

"About Jubilee? No. Listen, Josh—she's in a bad place right now. I haven't seen her as excited and, well, normal, as she's been since she met you. I honestly think you could be amazing for her. But I can't expect you to hang around. Hell, I'm her brother and sometimes I can't figure out what I'm doing playing house for her, um, well, you know . . ." He couldn't say *doll*, could he?

"It's not role-playing then." Joshua tried to keep his voice lighthearted, like he was in on the joke. Matty shook his head and stared at his hands; his fingers were red and raw in patches.

After a few seconds, Matty said, "They've met—your nephew and Bee?"

"He adores her."

Matty picked at his fingers with his nails. What wasn't he saying? He grabbed a comic from the pile on his desk and handed it to Joshua. "Let me know what you think."

Joshua thanked him and turned to leave, but Matty reached for his arm. "Hey, Josh, if you want to take off—it'd be the *sanest* thing to do." He narrowed his eyes.

Bianca was rattling pans in the kitchen. She was singing.

"She cooks when she's upset," Matty said.

"I'll go help her," Joshua said, and Matty half smiled, his eyes warm again. Like Joshua had passed a test.

In the kitchen, Bianca was chopping vegetables and singing a Spanish lullaby, but what struck Joshua more than the sweetly doleful tune combined with the sharp knife in her hand was the steady clicking of a rocking baby swing, a sound he remembered from Jayden's babyhood. In the living room, Jubilee, placid and unmoving, was propped beneath a set of colorful stuffed animals dancing above her on their spinning mobile.

Bianca saw him and stopped singing. Then she looked down at her cutting board and, still chopping, said, "We're trying Thai food tomorrow. Pad Thai noodles, vegetable spring rolls, yellow curry, and sweet-spicy pineapple fried rice. And the pièce de résistance? Fried plantain à la mode. You and Jayden should come." She looked up at him so hopeful and so hurt. He looked again toward Jubilee in the living room; beside the swing was a little statue of a Buddha burning incense on the mantle above bamboo stalks and a fish tank.

"Of course we'll come," he said, turning back to Bianca. "What are you making now?"

"Chile rellenos," she said, holding up a poblano from the cutting board and scraping out the seeds. "Nana taught me to make them for love."

"Like a potion?" he asked, moving toward the steel-gray kitchen island, pulling a bar stool out and sitting down. She smiled, her face shining, steeling his nerve to continue flirting. "May I taste?"

She frowned a little, squinting one eye like a sailor. She was the cutest damn woman he'd ever met. "These chiles don't taste good until they're blackened, but there's sweet tea in the fridge, and pan dulce in that pink box." She nodded to a pastry box on the bar.

Joshua picked a sugary brown pastry that looked like a little pig and bit into its leg. Gingerbread. It was pretty tasty.

"Oh, you picked the marranito," she exclaimed, watching him.

"Is that bad?" Should he spit it out?

She laughed. "No! The marranitos are my second favorite. Little piggies. Little puerquitos." She smiled vaguely, wistfully, like she was just remembering something. "I used to raise pigs, down in the Valley."

She hadn't talked much about where she grew up, and he wanted to hear more. But she'd resumed her chopping and humming and didn't seem inclined to continue the livestock conversation, so he let it go, found glasses in the cupboard and served them each a glass of tea from a pitcher. After a few moments of silence, he said, "I knew who you meant, Bee. Before, in Matty's office."

She nodded, taking a sip of her tea and choking back a sob. Soon her tears were falling onto the chiles, and she made a joke about *Como agua para chocolate*, how she would accidentally poison them with her sadness like Tita did the wedding guests by crying into the cake. Joshua wanted to take Bianca into his arms. Whatever had broken inside her, he wanted to fix. There were clues, of course. Bits and pieces in what she'd told him about her past that fit together with whatever she was doing with Jubilee. She'd had a boyfriend, who'd had a baby with someone else. She'd been cryptic. It stung that she hadn't told Matty about Jayden, but Joshua hadn't admitted everything about his own complicated situation with Olivia and the courts.

"Too late," he said about the poison cake. "I'm already sad."

While Bianca cooked, cracking eggs and coating the chiles before throwing them onto a hot skillet, he thought of Patti's house. He hadn't been around a woman cooking in a long time.

He leaned in to taste a piece Bianca offered him, after wiping the grease on a paper towel. "Cuidado, Joshy. It's hot."

"No one's called me Joshy in a long time." He bit into the chile.

"You don't like it?"

"No, it's fine. I like it. It reminds me of Olivia, that's all."

"Do you ever hear from her?"

"Not in over a year. We've been looking. It's weird. She loves Jayden. She just can't . . . you know . . . get her act together, I guess. She's a mess. She's family, I want her to change, but I don't know. She's . . . Olivia. Growing up, she was like a mom but then she'd bully me worse than anyone."

Bianca leaned over the table, setting down the food; she looked at Joshua with her hazelnut eyes shining sad and focused. He said, "I ran away to find her the first night they separated us. I didn't find her that night either. Didn't know where to look. Patti came searching for me in her car, calling out, 'Joshua,' but she pronounced it with a *y* like Yoshua. 'Yoshua, where are you?' I felt bad for running. I hated her for sending Olivia away, but I understood. Olivia was mean. So I stepped into the streetlight holding my backpack with all my comics and ramen noodles, and waited for her to see me. She pulled over and said, 'Yoshua, I was so escared' in her thick accent, then she crossed herself and hugged me."

"*Yoshua*," Bianca whispered. "I like that." She was hugging him; he was crying. What was it about this woman that cut through him? Loving her would be like slicing onions. Loving her? Damn. Loving her. "You can blow your nose on my shirt if you want," she said. "It's nice and soft."

He pulled away, sniffling. "Thanks, but I've been snotted by Jayden. It's not pretty. I'll use a napkin."

"Suit yourself. But I would've snotted you," she said, winking. She poured him another glass of tea; he gulped it down, ice and all. She laughed. "I guess you like it." She hadn't said anything about Jubilee, hadn't checked on her in the swing or made any gestures that she was worried about her. He took that as a hopeful sign.

Bianca leaned against his chest, her face nestled into his neck. "Your hair smells good, like baby oil," she said, breathing him in.

"You like baby smells," he whispered.

"True." She pulled a curl toward her nose. "Still, it's good." When she let go and the curl bounced back in place, she laughed. "Springy curls."

"Will you write a poem about my hair?" he teased.

"Sure. Here it goes: *Oil, oil everywhere and not a bite to eat.*"

"That's awful."

"You didn't give me time to think."

"Fine. I'll expect a *serious* poem next week."

"Be careful what you ask for, Joshy," she said, using a mock mysterious voice again. Then she lifted two chile rellenos with a spatula and set them on his plate, beside the pile of rice. She called Matty into the room, and they had the most hopeful meal Joshua ever remembered having.

FOUR
BAR CRASHING

BEFORE JUBILEE

Bianca hated waiting as much as she hated the Valley. It was Friday night, almost a week since she'd had made a fool of herself in front of Gabe's entire family, and he still hadn't shown up. He'd promised to come over to the empty house-for-sale around the block from him where she was now crashing alone with her family ghosts since Dad had died and Mama had moved back up to Whittier with Abuela.

Her girlhood house: a long, squat, beige-stucco ranch-style similar to Gabe's only hers was so beige it was almost mustard-yellow and shuttered and the garage had been converted to a family room by the previous tenants, an elderly couple who'd wallpapered the whole thing in hideous paisley patterns that made her dizzy, and there were incongruous, black-steel bars curling across the windows, sharply pointed at the ends. The garden had gone to seed, the veining trellises spidering up the walls and encroaching upon the windows and roof. She'd agreed to help tend it, to keep it tidy enough to sell. But Mama's green thumb had turned black on her daughter. Bee couldn't keep a potted plant alive, and the best she could do for Mama's garden was remember to spray it with a hose every week or so.

Inside the house: a strange mash-up of borrowed furniture, pieces she'd dragged over from Lily's garage around the corner, pieces that didn't fit or match or fill even a quarter of the empty space; a love seat in the middle of the room, a mosaic lamp on the floor, a checkerboard for a table, a mini-fridge. Mama had sold the appliances for funeral money, so Bee did laundry either in the sink, with strawberry-scented Suave shampoo, or at Lily's—but there were so many people living there, including Lily's chronically ill mother and elderly and ornery grandmother they called Little Gran, it was always a hassle—or at Gabe's. His mama still did his laundry, but Bee slipped some of his dirty items in with her own. It made her feel like they were a real couple who washed their chonies together.

Gabe had said he would bring giant Jaliscience burritos from across the tracks on the Eastside, and they could watch movies in bed. He forgave her for causing un desmadre, that ruckus at his parents' house the other night. Forgave her drinking too much and saying fucked-up things in front of his whole family. And he was sorry for the way he'd responded. He should've been more sensitive, after all they'd been through. This weekend would be just the two of them, like old times, he pinky swore.

Real quick though, he needed to stop at a happy-hour meeting with his coworkers, to get on his boss's good side (since his boss was Katrina's big brother). When Katrina got pregnant, Gabe had still intended to finish college. He'd worked a forklift in a warehouse every night in Rancho Cu-camonga and hoped to go back to school after the baby came and Katrina was settled with her mom in the Valley. But driving the three hours back and forth got old fast, so Katrina's brother got Gabe a forklifting job at a feedlot he managed in Westmorland, where Gabe could spend his lunch breaks at Katrina's mom's trailer, hanging out with Lana.

Bianca tried his cell phone. It had been hours since he got out of work and surely he'd done his diligence at the bar, but he didn't answer and she didn't leave a message. She would wait exactly seven minutes longer before calling Lily.

Moonlight filtered through her parents' old curtains. Mama hadn't taken them down when she'd moved out. (She'd said, "I can't stand it here, mija. If you want to waste away with that no-good boy, fine. But you'll have to do it alone.") Dressed-up in her rhinestone jeans and paisley halter top, Bianca sprawled out on the full-size mattress she'd bought at a yard sale when she'd moved back, the only item she'd actually bought for the house. She flipped her journal to the gothic story she was working on. It wasn't any good, but it helped her feel less like a college dropout. In her story, a woman was watching antiquated sconces cast shadows, which flickered on the parlor wall in her husband's empty manor, until Bianca believed the shadows were inching toward her. It was all very Daphne du Maurier. But not quite Hitchcock. She figured if she were living in a haunted house, the least she could do was use the Mary Shelley atmosphere and write a ghost story.

But inspiration wasn't coming. Her thoughts sludged, muddying the water. She couldn't dredge anything useful. She set down her pen and reached toward the flame of the Cristo candle she'd bought at the dollar store, set on a teacup saucer she'd taken from Lily's house then placed on the floor beside the mattress. In a plastic holder, it was white with a picture of Christ holding a lamb around his neck, flowers around the frame. She picked it up from the carpet and poured the wax into her palm, creating a candle-wax replica of her handprint, like Lana's handprints. *Gabe's girl. Not mine.* In Gabe's hallway, Esme had hung a small round clay molding tied at the top with a pink polka-dot bow; in it, two tiny hands and the words, "Baby's First Handprints." Not their baby's, not the-baby-who-never-existed.

Like the protagonist in her story, all the lights in her house were on because she too was terrified. Of family ghosts. Of familiar spirits. Of blood. She missed her dad. But she willed herself not to think of him right then. Not while she was alone. Instead, she focused on balancing the candle as she lay on her back, stabilizing it on her navel. It flicked as she breathed in and out. If she were a curandera, a healing woman, she would pass an egg over her chest and stomach. She would crack it into a glass, and the yolk would reveal the cause of her trouble. Her susto. Gabe's Nana taught her this. She didn't know if she believed it any more than she believed in the Cristo candle, but she liked the idea. Anyway, she'd rather be a healing woman than a sick one. Rather a blazing woman than the kind who waited around. She was done waiting. Done putting up with Gabe's bullshit. His seven minutes were up.

The red-hot flush scuttling up her cheeks and neck squelched her usual fear. She was ¡*La Bee!* looking for a fight.

Her cell buzzed. Lily—a mind reader.

"You feel like going boyfriend hunting?" Bianca asked.

"I already have a boyfriend. Sam. Remember? Did you kick Gabe to the curb?"

"Tonight might be the night."

"He's with Katrina?"

"I think so."

"What an asshole. Do you have a plan?"

"Bar crashing."

"I'll be ready in ten minutes. Should I bring my brother's baseball bat?"

Bianca didn't doubt Lily was serious. "I don't feel like getting arrested tonight."

"Fine," Lily said. "But if that bitch tries anything, I can't make any guarantees."

Bianca laughed then hung up, slid on her high-heeled wedges (because she didn't own a pair of cowboy boots, which she regretted since they'd befit such an occasion), and checked her reflection (crimson cheeks and tousled curly hair—Gabe could eat his heart out), before rushing to her white five-speed Cavalier and reversing fast down the driveway. She felt like a race-car driver, shifting gears quick and rough. This car was the one thing from Dad that Bianca had managed to keep her mother from selling or pawning or throwing away. This car he'd taught her to drive and let her borrow whenever she needed. She'd begged her mother. *Dad would've wanted me to have it.* And finally, Mama had relented. Sometimes Bee felt like she was driving a hearse. But mostly, she felt powerful.

Halfway down the block around the corner, she swerved into Lily's driveway and honked twice. Her yellow-haired best-friend-forever appeared at the door wearing her usual band-logo T-shirt (Bianca never knew the bands), jeans, and a pair of pea-green Vans. Lily stuck out her tongue.

"¡Vámonos, muchacha!" Bianca called. "Get your brave ass in the car. I'm on a mission."

"What's with you tonight, crazy lady?"

"I'm on fire!"

Lily pulled a cigarette out of her purse and rolled her window up long enough to light it. "Yes. I gathered as much," she answered, puffing easily.

"I meant why. All last week you were a moping, crybaby mess. Why the sudden change?" Lily offered Bianca a drag, and she pulled the sweet stinking thing to her lips. Gabe hated when she smoked, refused to kiss her when she had sour-singed smoker's breath. But tonight, who the hell cared?

"I'm tired of being second-class, Lil. That's what. So I don't have Gabe's kid. That doesn't mean I'm not worth something. She was a fluke, no? A condom break."

"Who? Lana?"

"No, not her. I meant Katrina. I *do* love her little girl. That's the problem. It's all twisted. It's all so goddamn twisted."

"Turn that frown around, chica. Or turn it into a sneer. Come on, show me some teeth. How about some rabid dog eyes?" Lily snarled like a deranged animal.

Bianca laughed so hard she choked on the smoke.

Outside town, they sped through the countryside, past fields of broccoli and onions and the overwhelming pungency of the beef plant, the smell of death. Bianca plugged her nose. She hated driving to Westmorland. Since Katrina, she associated it with gut-dropping loss. Forget the Honey Festival. It was a tiny town more stifling than Brawley. And populated by boyfriend-stealers.

In the parking lot of the first bar she tried, they spotted Gabe's pine-green truck and pulled in.

"Are you sure you want to go in?" Lily asked.

"Hell yeah," Bianca said, but she wasn't sure. The veins in her neck were itchy, like a too-tight necklace. The blood in her ears pounded.

It was a dive bar called Hops & Rods, with corrugated aluminum siding walls plastered with neon beer signs, electric guitars, and posters for local bands. Like the inside of a warehouse it had iron rafters, along with a small stage and a long, orange bar designed from two hot rod Chevy Bel Airs. No wonder Gabe liked this place. In high school, Bianca had pretended to care about the classic car magazines he'd shown her, teaching her to distinguish a Shelby from a Camaro. She'd cared as much about his car obsession as he'd cared about her poetry. Did Katrina like hot rods and muscle cars? Or only having sex in them with other girls' boyfriends.

Bianca searched through the crowd and spotted them: Katrina, at a high shop-style table in the middle of the bar with Gabe. Undeniable evidence. Gabe ran his hands through his spiky hair the way he did when he was irritated. Katrina shook her head. Katrina, with her bobbed, mousy brown hair, pug nose, and thick stumped eyebrows, as if she shaved them in the middle instead of plucking or having them waxed so the space was too big between her small brown eyes. Like a Muppet character. Short, petite, and plain. Her face had a pinched look, like she was squinting in the sun. She wore a pair of khaki shorts and a navy-blue tank top, and although she was thinner than Bianca, she was nowhere near as pretty. What had she been majoring in at Cal State San Bernardino before she dropped out, and what had Gabe seen in her?

"What do you want to do?" Lily asked.

"Order a drink," Bianca said, shaking, her voice gone flat as old seltzer. Gabe's aunt had told her she drank a beer after work to *take the edge off.* Of course, that was before the three or four beers that came later, so it was a big joke in his family that only one beer was necessary to take the edge off. But Bianca needed that—the edge off.

Her stomach churned but she chugged her beer anyway. They didn't see her.

A random rock and roll song played on the jukebox. The place was packed. Her chest felt explosive, her palms slick. The beer roiled inside her stomach, curdling her throat. She felt like crossing herself and praying to Sandra Cisneros. *Come on, La Bee! Hold your head up high!* Sandra might have told Bianca in her high-pitched voice, her hoop skirt flowing around her red-studded cowboy boots, turquoise looped around her neck.

Silently, Bianca mouthed Sandra's words as she crossed the bar, a prayer: "I'm 'sharp-tongued, / sharp-thinking, / fast-speaking, / foot-loose, / loose-tongued, / let-loose, / woman-on-the-loose / loose woman. / Beware, honey . . .'" She'd admit it: "I'm Bitch. Beast. Macha. / ¡Wachale! / Ping! Ping! Ping! / I break things."

She looked back at Lily, planted at the bar, gesturing her onward and motioning in a way that meant *Rabid dog eyes! Go!* Bianca nodded then inhaled, wallpapering her face with a broad, plastic smile, a pink flamingo across her mouth like *I'm fine. You can't hurt me. All those mornings I made you breakfast, blaring your favorite CD while I cooked*—Hotel California *and scrambled eggs, the warm smell of flour tortillas rising through the air—not real.*

Instead, the mask on the outside said, "Hey guys. Why wasn't I invited to this party?"

Gabe jerked his head up, his shoulders rigid. "Shit, Bee." His voice was halting and shaky. "You scared me." Bianca almost laughed at how pathetic it was, watching him stand and reach for her. He tried pulling her into a hug, but she swatted his arms away.

Katrina knotted her hands in front of her on the table, staring at her fingers and refusing to look up. Coward.

Gabe asked what Bianca was doing there. She asked him the same.

"Why, what time is it?" He grabbed his cell phone from his pocket. "Shit. I'm sorry. We got caught up talking about the baby."

"Mmm." She scrunched her face and pressed her lips together, mocking belief.

"Hey, can we go talk about this somewhere else?" he asked, reaching out for her again.

"No. We can't." She scooted from his arms and sat in his empty chair across from Katrina.

"What are you doing?" Gabe stammered. "Come on. Don't get her involved in this. I screwed up. I should've called you." He looked boyish in his work uniform, a short-sleeved button-down and brown shorts. His company-logo'd baseball cap laid on the table. He was a pubescent boy caught in the closet. Almost laughable. But she could tell he wasn't drunk.

She took a swig of his beer, slammed the bottle down on the table. "Don't get *her* involved? You're kidding, right?" A caustic laugh spurt out from within Bianca, the bitter taste of bile rising in her throat. *Ping!* "Katrina? We need to talk outside. Woman to woman." She hoped she sounded more confident than she felt. She felt like a sham. Like a hole at the bottom of the ocean.

Katrina flashed her an icy glare, then rolled her eyes and said, "Sure."

As Bianca stood, she offered Gabe a cloying twisted smile. "Lily's at the bar. Would you be a doll and go keep her company?" Bianca was ridiculous, but she couldn't care.

He grabbed her arm, jerking her tightly to him. His beer breath in her face, hot against her neck. "What are you doing, Bee? Seriously. This isn't funny. Please don't screw anything up for me and the baby. I've been working this out with Katrina. Please don't fuck with her."

"I'm the one you shouldn't fuck with." She broke herself from his grasp, pulled away and stared into his face. His deep-brown eyes muddied with worry, his eyebrows furrowed. He was telling the truth. "I want to talk to her," she said over her shoulder as she walked away.

Lily signed a knife-slice across her neck then winked. What would she say to Gabe? Nothing pleasant.

Out in the muggy desert air, past a thatched-roofed palapa bar replete with surfboards and fishing nets strung from the wooden fence, Bianca followed Katrina onto the hard-packed dirt of the parking lot. Nearby, canal water whirred as it rushed over the embankment.

Bianca spoke first. "What's going on with you two? I have a right to know. Are you sleeping with him?"

Katrina hesitated.

"What did I ever do to you, Katrina? I've helped take care of your little girl for months, and—"

Katrina cut her off. "Yeah, and I don't appreciate her coming home talking about you, either. You think that feels good? To have your own daughter come home and talk about how much she likes her father's whore."

"The fuck? Whore? Are you kidding me? You're unbelievable. I've loved that man since I was a little girl, you manipulative cunt." There, she'd said it. She was trapped in a trashy daytime talk show. "He was my first *everything*. Before I even knew what everything was." She was red-faced and short of breath.

"You knew enough though, didn't you?" Katrina said.

"What's that supposed to mean?"

Katrina pursed her lips and crossed her arms.

"Please?" Bianca urged. "Imagine you were me. How would you feel? Tell me. *Please*."

"Please nothing," Katrina snapped, rolling her eyes and thrusting her chest out. "You have no idea what I've been through with him. Having his baby. Raising her alone. Everything I've gone through because of him."

Bianca's gut pitted, her teeth clenched. A rush of heat surged up her neck and face. "No, I don't know. My baby died before it was ever a baby. I never took vitamins or ate saltines by the boxful. Gabe never rubbed my belly." Her head spun. Her baby floated, pendent above their heads or bramble swishing through a ditch. "No, you heartless bitch. I don't know what you went through." She was screaming. She wanted to kick Katrina. To yank her by her dull, brown hair. "But you know what I went through? I went through losing all that for nothing. For goddamn nothing! Because you swooped in and screwed everything up anyway. And I hate you for that. We were supposed to get out of here. My baby was supposed to have meant something."

"You're a murderer, that's what you are." Katrina spit the words at Bianca, who keeled in, her legs giving out beneath her. Something cracked inside her. She felt it cracking. Wire casings like wings of dead moths. She couldn't talk. The air had been knocked out of her like the time she was Superwoman on the swings and Dad had pushed her into the air but she'd flown too high and crashed hard on her chest and the words wouldn't come and there was Dad, holding her. She couldn't breathe.

She dropped to one knee and clutched her stomach. "Why would you say that?" Sobs rocked her body. She didn't have a heart. It wasn't beating. "Why the fuck would you say that?"

"Gabe told me what you did."

"What *we* did. What *we* did. *Together.*"

Katrina looked down at her, eyes narrowed, forehead creased. "He wouldn't let *me* do that to Lana. Said he couldn't take losing another baby."

Bianca choked a sob, heaving. "Ay, God. Please stop it. Katrina, please fucking stop talking." She wanted to call for her dad, the bar crashing down on her.

Gabe came outside and saw Bianca on the ground. "What the hell? What'd you do to her, Katrina? Goddammit!" He pushed Katrina out of the way and knelt down beside Bianca. "What happened, Bee? Did she hit you?"

Bianca shook her head. She couldn't look at him. She'd scraped her uterus for him. She'd given everything for him when she was still a girl and not old enough to take care of herself, let alone anyone else. She'd come back to him empty. And here was Katrina, doing what she couldn't. Standing on her own. Raising a kid on her own. A single mama. Small and strange looking, but proud. And powerful. She had a baby, didn't she? And that made her so goddamn powerful. She called the shots. She pulled the strings. Tears puddled onto Bianca's halter top, streaking her cheeks black with mascara. She wiped her mocos away with her hand. She must've looked pathetic, crying in front of a woman who despised her.

She took a deep breath. "You told her about what happened at Clínicas?"

"Oh fuck," he said. "Stupid Katrina." He stood back up and faced his baby's mom. "I told you not to bring that shit up. I knew I couldn't trust your big mouth. What the fuck did you say to her?"

"The truth, you asshole. That she is what she is. A baby killer."

He raised his hand to slap her then pulled back, clenching his fist. "Get the hell out of here, Katrina. You goddamn bitch. I don't care if you threaten me again with Lana. Go ahead and try taking me to court. I'll get a lawyer and take her away from *you*. But don't you ever call my girlfriend that again. Do you understand? She was a fucking kid when I knocked her up. A fucking kid! And I told you that when *you* were threatening abortion, you two-faced bitch. When *you* were threatening to kill yourself. God, I can't fucking stand you."

Bianca sucked in air. Her head throbbed. She didn't know what to think.

"Whatever, Gabe. You're the two-faced one here," Katrina said.

"No, don't play like that. You tell her the truth, Katrina. I'm not joking. You've hurt her enough tonight. Tell her why I was here with you."

Katrina heaved a sigh. She stared at the ground. "Fine. Whatever. I don't care anymore." Her voice sounded hollow, like the tin of empty beer cans. "He was defending you tonight, Bianca. Telling me I need to stop fighting him when it comes to you taking care of the baby. That you're his girlfriend and I need to accept that." Her voice was neither kind nor spiteful. It was matter-of-fact, resigned. "And I'm not sleeping with him." She tucked her hair behind her ear then said, "Gabe, you can pick up the baby tomorrow if you want."

Gabe nodded. "Fine. Now leave us alone." He scooped Bianca from the ground, holding her to his chest. She was stiff and lifeless in his arms as he carried her to his truck, setting her on the hood. "You know I'm so sorry," he whispered, burying his head in her chest. "Not about tonight. About everything." His face against her cold skin felt warm and damp. "Don't listen to her. She's crazy. Jealous. You know that."

Bianca wanted to believe him. *Sandra Cisneros come give me strength.* But she was too tired to fight.

FIVE
LETTER TO JUBILEE

Who understands why I needed you?

Why I need you still?

I'll tell you a story my mother told me:

One summer, Mama's eight-year-old brother disappeared. A baseball-capped man on a bike snatched him up and threw him in the back of a pickup before dumping him in an alley in Buena Park, warning him to wait cause he'd be back. Mama's brother knew to run. He ran to a gas station and called home to his mother who'd locked the other children inside while police helicopters circled the neighborhood.

Mama's mother beat her after that summer. She used to grab her dark hair, pinch her chin, and slap and slap anywhere on the body her flat hand landed as if mom were a dusty rug, a roach on the bathroom wall.

Because she was the eldest daughter, Mama bore the brunt of Abuela Celia's fear.

Mama used to cry sometimes walking me down the street to my best friend's house, tears finally breaching her long silence. She'd never let me get lost. She'd never let go. A mother doesn't let go, she'd say.

It wasn't a lie.

SIX
CURSED LIGHT

WITH JUBILEE

Cursed objects. Contenido maldito. Joshua had been researching dolls, okay, obsessing over dolls, these past almost-two months he'd been hanging out with Bianca.

He'd become a fixture at Matty and Handro's house since that first dinner together, hanging out with Bianca after class whenever Jayden was in daycare. Sometimes he'd bring Jayden over, though he suspected Matty didn't appreciate having a chattering kid in the house. Bianca swore her big brother adored them. But Joshua felt the undercurrent troubling whichever room or open space Bianca carried Jubilee into, and he marveled, silently, at how she flitted about in the light she created, this bright, lightning creature who ignited everything around her till it all buzzed and hummed with chaos, crackling wires, all the while she clung tightly to her calm: that doll in her arms.

Lately, he'd wondered if Jubilee was a blessing or a curse. He'd framed it in that binary (Bianca loved the word *binary*; she dropped it into at least half their discussions, always stressing that they should break the binaries, and she'd gotten him hooked on using it too) after happening across an island of dolls near Mexico City in his research, La Isla de las Muñecas, an island on Teshuilo Lake in the Xochimilco canals where some claim that over fifty years ago the island's guardian had found a child, drowned and clutching her doll, washed up on his shore, and with them, a curse. When mysterious happenings began, troubling things, he strung the girl's doll in a tree to ward off the ill spirits, but over the years he collected and hung doll upon doll, since the spirits were unsatisfied and craved more. The island became infested with ruddy, decaying dolls dangling from branches, wired to fences, some decapitated, all mud-splattered, hundreds of them—tangled limbs and naked bodies and bulbous heads, grinning and grimacing alike, many reaching out among the palms and ferns and tall grasses as warning.

Some say he was honoring the girl's spirit, at first. It had begun as tribute, an altar, before taking the bizarre twist and veering into horror.

Joshua had tried not to picture Jubilee among those terrifying, hanging dolls.

Not to picture Bianca as the caretaker of such a place.

A decade ago, the article had said, the island's keeper, the doll fanatic, had been found drowned on the same shore where he'd supposedly found the little girl when the curse began.

Bianca had called in sick to her writing-center gig, she'd said, because they had a rough night, Jubilee and her, they hadn't slept well. He'd offered not to come over as planned, to let her get some rest, but she'd insisted he come anyway.

Matty answered the door with the half-smirking, half-exasperated expression that Joshua had come to believe was the only mask he wore, his costume of protective-but-good-natured-nevertheless brother. He held a Dark Horse Comics mug and wore cutoff shorts, a short-sleeved button down, and sandals.

"Hey, it's Beast," Matty said, his tone friendly. Joshua smiled, appreciating this gesture of familiarity, nicknaming him, recognizing that he was becoming a staple in their lives, like they relied on him, like he and Matty now shared a common purpose: watching over Bianca.

Joshua nodded back. "How's it going?" He stepped inside the redbrick house, taking in the electric energy he felt radiating from Bianca's space down the hallway, the manic pixie vibe she often exuded that left him high and craving more.

"It's been a night, I'll tell you what."

"She okay?"

Matty chuckled slightly, took a sip of his coffee, shook his head. Never let slip his good-natured-brother mask. "Nothing more than usual."

Joshua didn't let himself wonder why none of this scared him. Why he was so eager to wrap himself in the tangled limbs and breast and belly of a woman whose island caretaker stood here in the hallway, passing the torch to him: shift change, changing of the guards.

He stopped at the little table outside her door, on which perched a fishbowl and a five-dollar goldfish. "He's mine," she'd declared. "I call him Blue. *How blue it'd be, swimming back into oblivion.*"

"Where's that from?"

"It's a piece of a poem I've had swimming in my head. It has something to do with Eve's children rescued from the waters of Lethe . . . I haven't worked it all out yet, haven't committed it to paper."

He shivered, recalling her words and their ominous echo of the island of dolls. He hadn't stumbled across that part of his research yet, when she'd quoted her poem, so he'd just told her a lame story of how, before Jayden, when he'd lived in the dorms his freshman year, he'd heard that it was possible to swallow a live goldfish in one piece then regurgitate it still alive. So on a bet, he tried it. The fish came back out, tail flapping. But a few minutes later, it'd died. "I felt bad," he told her, "but I won the bet. He came out alive, even if only for a little while."

She'd answered that he was horrible for killing it, then admitted a part of her wanted him to try it again, to test if it was still true. Or if a fish could ever beat the odds. Undrown.

Now, he wondered if he could have used her poem as a segue into the island of dolls. Gauge her reaction. With her knowledge of Mexican history and haunted things, maybe she already knew of it.

He knocked on her bedroom door, expecting her to mumble "Come in" from her bed, and he stiffened at the hope of climbing in beside her, breathing in her vanilla-and-orange-peel scent, pressing his face into the crook of her neck, her dark hair streaming around them both, pulling her soft belly and the cup of her hips against him. They hadn't slept together yet, not officially. Honestly? He was probably less ready for all that than she was, even with her baggage, and that was saying something. But damn, it felt good to lie beside her.

She didn't answer.

He knocked louder.

Still nothing.

He looked back down the hall toward Matty's alcove but Matty had already put his earphones back on and was clacking away at his keyboard.

Josh turned back toward Bee's door, listening for her, but heard nothing.

Should he text her first, before barging in? Had they been together long enough that he had a right to open the door? It felt like an invasion of privacy.

He put his hand on the knob and flicked, slightly, to check if it was locked. When it gave, he turned it completely, his pulse quickening, and opened the door, calling. "Bee? You here?"

The half-light through her purple curtains cast an ethereal flush across the many faces of Frida hung across her walls, alongside the other Mexican surrealist painters she loved, all women of course. Reprints she'd found cheap on the border where she'd grown up, she'd told him, striated color across cheap cardboard but still beautiful mirrors of the original works. A thin figure with a magical contraption feeding stardust and dark matter to a caged crescent moon with a long, thin spoon through the bars. A blue ghost-shelled woman peering into a small, wooden box from a shelf and seeing inside her own blue, flickering face.

Stuff like that.

He glanced around the dim room.

Bianca wasn't in bed like he'd expected but hunched on the floor beside Jubilee's bassinet, her back toward him. Was she sleeping? Crying?

He couldn't help for a moment seeing her as the drowned island woman of the dolls.

Maldito. Cursed.

Then he saw she was moving, scribbling. He inched closer, afraid to disturb her.

He watched her writing the way he and Jayden had watched

archaeologists at the natural history museum through the glass with their headlamps and paintbrushes, dusting the bones so lightly. She was filling the journal he'd given her at the beach.

If she noticed him, she gave no sign. She only perched on her knees, hunched forward, journal on the floor, pen to the page, filling line after line. She could have been praying at an altar.

Jubilee lay in her bassinet, a baby blanket tucked to her chin, her hazel eyes closed. Like the Reborns he'd seen online, Jubilee looked so lifelike, she could have been sleeping. It was as if her eyelids would flutter and her little mouth would make sucking motions in her sleep. Even the veins bluish beneath her infant-thin skin appeared in the detailing of her face and neck, the dimpled infant rolls at her knees and thighs, the wrinkles in her tiny feet and hands. Every time Joshua looked at Jubilee in her crib, he felt the urge to press his hand against her torso to check for breathing. They stayed in that strange tableau a few moments, Joshua standing silent, watching, trying to understand what he was seeing.

Bianca must have known he'd come in, for a minute later she stretched her arm toward him, gesturing for him to join her on the floor.

"Hey," he whispered, kneeling beside her. "What are we doing?"

"Writing," she said, and kept scrawling. He watched the loops and curves of her handwriting, observing the ragged edges of line ends emerging in patterns as she wrote. She didn't stop where the journal's page prescribed but where she decided.

"A poem?" he asked.

A few moments of silence. He thought she hadn't heard him.

Then she answered. "A letter."

A few weeks later, Joshua was alone with Jubilee. Bianca had gone into the next room to talk to Matty, she'd said, and left Joshua in her bedroom. He stood above the bassinet, watching for the telltale rise and sink of her chest the way he'd spent the first few nights with Jayden after Olivia had left him without a single instruction and he had no idea what he was doing, but he knew breathing was important. Joshua stroked her hair with his fingertips. Today she wore a yellow onesie, baby ducks stitched across the chest, fuzzy bloomers, yellow socks. All premie clothes. He'd gone with Bianca to Target a couple of times for baby essentials, premie diapers, premie onesies. She'd bought an actual baby bottle, stopped using that plastic doll one he'd seen at the beach. They'd said nothing about it, but he guessed she'd thrown it away.

He still hadn't asked Bianca straight out, *Why the doll?* Couldn't work up the nerve. Didn't want to risk upsetting the island. Every once in a while she would say strangely poetic things, and he kept mental notes. She'd say things like she was "sewing her life together from corpse-like memories and joy so unexpected it deserved every chance at breath it got, every side stitch, every gluttonous inhalation." He'd hold her and tell her how beautiful her poetry was. How he was glad to be a part of the joy.

He stared at Jubilee, her eyes closed. He tried talking to her in the voice he'd used when Jayden was an infant but he couldn't manage it and soon found himself confiding in her as if she were some kind of hoodoo doll instead, a juju baby that could absorb his fear and confusion, releasing him. "Hey, Jubilee. What's she recovering from, little girl? You know, don't you? I think you know."

He hadn't meant to, but he picked her up. Her body was heavier than he'd expected. He placed her head against his shoulder and swayed back and forth, patting her and whispering, "Shhh . . . shhh . . ." the way Bianca had. It felt like an experiment. Only, it also felt real. He made another mental note: she smelled like Bianca and baby powder.

"I'm gonna stick around, you watch. She's going to be okay. I know she's going to be okay." He rocked and patted. A warning flickered. *You're losing it. She's sucking you into her world.* He squelched it down, kept holding Bianca's baby.

Bianca returned to the bedroom, saying she needed to change Jubilee. Joshua watched. Beside the bassinet was a dresser with a terrycloth changing pad. From a wicker basket next to the pad, Bianca pulled out a tiny diaper, wipes, and powder. She changed Jubilee, pulling off first the bloomers, then removing the diaper and throwing it in the wastebasket. Of course

Jubilee had no genitalia, but Bianca wiped her as if she did. While she worked, she cooed and sang. "*This little light of mine, I'm gonna let it shine.*"

Joshua was becoming part of the study. He stepped into the painting. He was all in. He quieted the voice nagging at him since he'd met her, since he'd rowed up to her island, since she'd lured him to the shore and he'd stepped onto the beach, willingly, and he joined in her song, throwing his whole self into whatever strange game they were playing.

"*Hide it under a bushel? No! I'm gonna let it shine.*"

She smiled over at him each time he sang "*No!*" with such emphasis they were both laughing through the words.

When she finished, she held Jubilee close and sat on the bed. From the nightstand, she lifted Jubilee's bottle and fed her. Joshua was so high on endorphins from all the laughing it almost seemed natural. Almost.

"Hey, can I ask you something?" Joshua asked. He pulled out his therapist's mental notepad of questions. He'd dole them out one at a time, gauge her responses, change tactics accordingly.

Her face still glowed, ruddy from laughing, but her smile faded slightly. "What's up?"

"When I first met Matty, he seemed upset when I mentioned Jayden." He cleared his throat. "And you say he adores us, but every time I bring Jayden over, Matty seems, I don't know . . . sullen or frustrated. Do kids just bother him?"

She set Jubilee back in the bassinet, walked over to the window where the purple curtains draped open; he followed her gaze past the stucco wall to an avocado tree in the neighbor's backyard. She wrapped her arms around her chest.

He was tempted to fill in the silence with an apology. He often felt like he was walking on eggshells around her, but he had to admit that was part of her allure. Her current always buzzing, and he could never tell when she'd spark. She'd stormed out of the office that first day after Matty got all weird about Joshua and Bee both having "kids." And each week since then, she'd crackle a little more. Like he was getting through to her. Like he was helping her uncover whatever was burning her up inside. Like they were making progress. Part of him felt like a little boy, hiding under the bed whenever the social worker would come, every time Bianca got angry. But the stronger part, the older part, felt like the social worker coaxing her out from under the bed. He sat on her office chair and leaned back, his hands locked behind his head, as if letting her know he would wait for her reply.

She turned toward him, her expression guarded. Sad. She took a deep breath. "When I was with Gabe, he got another girl pregnant. Katrina. I was in high school still, he'd gone off to college. He was supposed to wait for me. A year. I'd follow him then, we agreed. But he couldn't wait, I guess. We'd been together since I was fourteen, he was a year older. He didn't love her. He said it was a mistake. I tried staying with him. But it was hard, seeing her in the passenger seat of his truck. I'd be walking home from school my senior year, walking alone past the carnicería and donut shop and laundromat toward my house—just a block away from his—and they'd pass by. On their way back from her doctor's appointments. He'd call me to apologize. Tell me the baby was making her really sick. She had that pregnancy sickness that makes you throw up nonstop. He was really good to her. I got it all twisted in my mind for a while, believing it meant he'd be really good to me too. When I got pregnant." She looked away from Joshua, toward the floor, her cheeks flushed bright red, her neck rashed with embarrassment or shame, Joshua couldn't tell which, but he sensed her discomfort. He probably should've been confused (*why would she have still* wanted *a baby with him?*) but Joshua knew firsthand from falling for Bee the heart knows no reason.

"It's all right, Bee. I know you had a life before me. I'm not upset. You can keep going."

"My mom found out about it, small town, rumors. She said I couldn't go to prom with him; he had responsibilities to someone else now, and I screamed I'd never forgive her. Matty came down to the Valley and told me I had to break up with Gabe. That coming between them, keeping a father from his child, was wrong. *I wasn't.* I didn't mean to. Matty said he'd never forgiven our father for not being his *real* father. It wasn't Dad's fault that Matty's father abandoned him and my mother. But Matty made me feel small and stupid. He called me pathetic. Called Gabe a consolation prize, a white elephant gift. I shouldn't want him anyway, but what I was doing, he said, was degrading myself by playing the other woman and standing in the way of a family . . ." She was crying. She wiped the tears from her cheeks with her wrists, wiped those on her shirt. "I gave up my UCLA scholarship and went to Holy Cross University instead. Their choir came to the Valley and something in their song sounded like redemption. I wanted God's forgiveness, maybe. Or Matty's. I broke up with Gabe and left early, right after graduation, spent the summer at my Tía Lydia's in San Clemente. Matty had given me the Destiny's Child album *Survivor* because, he said, I was. Katrina had the baby, and I thought I'd get over Gabe. But when our dad died, I got back with Gabe. Matty found out and said he wouldn't speak to me as long as I was seeing that lowlife, he called him. And he stayed good to his word. He didn't speak to me the whole time I was living down there. He iced me out completely until I moved back into his house."

Joshua stood up and moved to hug her, but she bristled. "I'm glad you told me," he said. "I hadn't realized Matty was so stubborn."

Bianca chuckled mirthlessly. "Oh, he's stubborn all right. Downright pigheaded. Thinks he's always right. Always knows what's best."

Joshua murmured understanding. "Older sibling syndrome. My sister has it too." He kissed the top of Bianca's head, and he felt her relax in his arms.

She looked up, her grimace given way to softness. "I'm lucky to know you, Joshua Walker," she said, and pressed her body to his, her breasts against his chest, her thighs between his legs. She traced her lips against his neck, kissing upward toward his mouth. "Lucky," she whispered again, her breath warm and tingling in his ear.

"I'm the lucky one, Bee," he said, his voice husky. He wanted her. He wanted her so badly he forgot he was supposed to be studying her. He kissed her until he forgot he'd been troubled at all.

SEVEN
BLOODY MARY

BEFORE JUBILEE

She was fifteen again; she was always fifteen. She wasn't supposed to take a bath for several days after the D&C, but she didn't care. She needed the water. She filled the tub lukewarm and clear—no suds, for those stung—and dipped herself gingerly past the water's edge, then deeper. When she submerged completely, she allowed the water to rinse the words again and again over her. Dilation and curettage. She imagined a cactus flower opening wide, and bleeding. She opened her eyes. Whatever gift she had given, she prayed Mother Mary would return to her tenfold. When the time came. She would birth a nation. She would birth the stars. She would birth a newness that would emerge on the other side of the water.

She held her curettage flowers, red swirling in the lukewarm tub.

Petals in her palms—& floating away.

That was then.

Fifteen and nineteen were worlds apart.

She was a college woman now, or would be again, soon. She still had time.

She wouldn't go into the bathroom she'd used as a girlchild, growing up in the now-empty house. That bathtub was fucking cursed.

She used her parents' master bath, really a bathroom as tiny as her girl-hood one, not really "master" in the way she thought of fancy homes on the rich, white side of town. The only differences were that it was attached to her parents' old bedroom—now hers, with her mattress on the floor and her small television-VCR combo propped on a plastic bin—and that their bath-room had no tub, only a shower.

Showers were safer.

Steam fogged the bathroom mirror so she ghosted, invisible.

She turned on the faucet, cupped the water in her hands, let it drip down the mirror, a rivulet, an artist pouring turpentine down her acrylic failure, a girlchild again invoking Bloody Mary.

There she was.

Bianca in the flesh.

Her family had left her.

Her boyfriend had a baby with another girl, who called her a murderer.

The desert had swallowed her back into its belly, and she was trying so hard to stay afloat.

She applied her makeup, tucked her dark hair into a messy bun, put on her *Desert Herald* polo shirt and jeans, fed the boxer the last of the puppy food, and went to work, where she'd take calls all day from folks across the Valley looking to yard-sale their junk, find homes for their ani-mals, locate their lost/love/jobs. She'd make poems out of classifieds. Hide haiku in the ads.

All the while strumming, *I'm alive, I'm alive, I'm alive.*

EIGHT
SORRY AFTERWARD

WITH JUBILEE

It wasn't supposed to be part of his investigation. He'd taken Bianca to Disneyland for some carefree, case-study-free fun. It was supposed to be the happiest place on earth for Christ's sake.

Disneyland was decorated for Halloween, with a giant, orange Mickey Mouse jack-o'-lanterning the entrance and *The Nightmare Before Christmas* enshrouding the usual Haunted Mansion. On Main Street Plaza, an automaton fortuneteller glowed outside the entrance to the old-fashioned ice cream parlor. "Let's find out our fortune," Joshua told Bee, pulling a dollar out of his pocket. "What does Madame Fortune-teller think of us, *together*?"

"What if she tells you the girl you're with is totally bonkers? Leave her at once?"

"I could either unplug the witch, exposing her for the fraud she is. Or I could run. *Are* you totally bonkers?"

"Yes."

"Thank God. Me too." He inserted the dollar into the machine. A coin tumbled down and dropped into his hand. "Insert coin for your fortune." He handed it to Bianca. "You do it."

She kissed the coin then released it into the slot. The white bulbs lining Madame Esmeralda's booth lit up. The fortuneteller opened her eyes, gazed into her crystal ball, which turned from dull gray to hazy blue, clouds of smoke swirling inside. She bobbed her scarfed head. Seconds later, a card shot into a slot in the booth. Joshua pulled it out, cleared his throat, and read in an official tone: "Hear ye, hear ye. Madame Esmeralda's Prophecy proclaims: *You sometimes have a desire to destroy things, especially in your younger days, for which you are sorry afterward.*" He paused, reflective, then made a sour face. "The witch got it wrong. That's not a romantic reading."

"That reading's meant for me," Bianca said, somber. He'd meant this as a joke but she seemed to be taking all of it too seriously.

"Nah, that was crap. Esme's a fraud." He shoved the card into his pocket, slung one arm around Bianca's shoulder, and held Jayden's hand with the other.

"Strange you say that," she said. "Esme's my ex's mother's name." Her voice was flat.

"Bee, I'm sorry. I didn't mean anything." Her intensity attracted him to her, but sometimes a small part of him wished she'd lighten up. He wondered what would happen if he ever said this aloud.

"No, I know. It's fine." She squeezed his hand resting on her shoulder.

"Let me buy you an ice cream, as apology. Me and Jayden like the fudge-dipped cones best, right, kiddo?" Jayden nodded, licking his lips.

"You read my mind," Bianca said.

The shop smelled of fresh-baked waffles. They ordered three cones then sat at a booth in the fifties-decorated diner, with checkered tabletops and red-vinyl chairs with metal frames. As a person of color maybe Joshua should've critiqued or at least mistrusted nostalgic Americana, yet he found it comforting. Patti had liked fifties kitsch. She'd wanted to be Lucille Ball. "Man, I miss it at her house."

"Why'd you leave?"

Joshua looked over at Jayden, who was engrossed in his cone and watching kids shop for candy in the next shop, so Joshua lowered his voice and explained to Bee how Patti couldn't keep him. No room once her son and his family had moved in. The son had lost his job. At first, Joshua had slept on the couch and let her son and his wife have his room. Her grandchildren had the other spare room, Olivia's before she went to the group home. Patti had said she'd put up bunk beds so Joshua could share with her grandkids, but he'd told her he'd rather sleep on the couch in the living room, near the warm kitchen, where he could smell whatever she was cooking. That had made her laugh. But he'd overheard her son arguing with her. Patti shouldn't keep Joshua. He wasn't like them. Not family. The house was too crowded. His social worker, Ms. McCall, came then, and Patti cried when she hugged him goodbye. *Be a good boy, hijo. Remember how much your Patti loves you, Yoshua.*

"What a jerk. That jealous pendejo." She glanced over at Jayden, a guilty look on her face for cursing in Spanish. She mouthed *sorry* to Joshua.

"It was a long time ago."

Melted ice cream dripped down her hand. "You'd better finish that," Joshua said. He pulled a folded piece of paper from his wallet. "I saved this from a fortune cookie. *When you have only two pennies left, buy a loaf of bread with one and a lily with the other.* Survival and beauty. They sustain me. Survival, I've got. Beauty, I've been searching for."

"Where did you come from?" she asked, sweeping her hand across his face.

He shrugged, smiling in a way he hoped was charming. "You ready to go build Jubilee a bear?"

Jayden heard that part and, chocolate all over his face, yelled, "Yes!"

They skipped through the plaza, arms linked, Jayden scrambling to keep up, Joshua pushing the stroller too fast. People stared, but they didn't care. Bianca laughed, breathing hard. "You remind me of who I used to be," she said.

But a few steps ahead, she froze, transfixed by the window display of a store. Huge photos featured newborns, sleeping atop bright flower petals. On the display-case shelf, dolls posed the same as in the photos, some wearing flower costumes with petals on their heads.

The shop was called Anne Geddes. Joshua had never noticed it before.

In the doorway, a saleswoman in a black dress cradled a doll in her arms.

It looked like Jubilee.

Bianca stared as if in shock. Her hand went rigid in Joshua's, her eyes opened too wide. She steered the stroller away from the store.

Joshua followed her, holding Jayden's hand. "They look so real, don't they?" He hadn't meant to confront her with her demons, hadn't meant to turn this into a therapy session, but sometimes it seemed like all she needed was a gentle nudge, like she was so close. He couldn't help himself. "Like Jubilee?"

"Jubilee's not a doll."

"I didn't say that."

She stopped and turned to face him. "Is that what you think?" Her voice was cold. "You think I'm crazy? I know what people think of me. At the park with Jubilee, the other moms stare. I know Jubilee is different." She said *different* like it was a shard of glass on her tongue, slicing her. She glared at him, then turned abruptly and pushed the stroller into the crowded walkway, away from Joshua and Jayden.

"Hey, Bee. I didn't mean that," Joshua called after her. "I was only pointing out the resemblance."

Jayden looked upset. "*Is* Jubilee a doll?"

Joshua had too many fires to put out, didn't know what to say, so he just grabbed Jayden's hand and pulled him into the crowd after Bianca.

"I'm not crazy," she said again when he and Jayden caught up with Jubilee and her outside the House of Blues, with its smell of smokehouse barbecue and the soulful music of a saxophone.

"I know, love. I know."

"Jubilee's not like that."

"No, she's different, isn't she?" He grabbed her hand and squeezed, and she let him. "Can't we forget it? I was stupid."

She rolled her eyes, turned again, but Jayden grabbed her hand before Joshua could say anything else and said, "Come on, Bee. It's okay. Let's go make a bear for Jubilee."

She smiled weakly at him, and Joshua's stomach coiled. He watched helplessly as Jayden led her into the Build-A-Bear shop, and sighed. He'd already messed everything up. What could he do but follow?

In the shop, Bianca remained guarded and said almost nothing to Joshua, though she was sweet and motherly as usual to Jayden, who seemed appeased, stuffing and dressing and giving a heart to matching giraffes for him and Jubilee.

"It's like magic," Jayden said, laughing, as the stuffed heart started beating.

NINE
THE RESTAURANT

BEFORE JUBILEE

A few nights after her disastrous bar-crashing, Bianca peeked through the slits in Gabe's fingers as he covered her eyes and whispered, "Almost there." He was taking her out to dinner to make up for the burritos he still owed her, and as he parallel parked, she looked around, speculating where they were supposed to eat. He'd wanted it to be a surprise, but she didn't know any restaurants in this neighborhood that were still open. So many things had closed since she was a girl.

The summer before her freshman year in high school, Lily and Bee had spent every night together, staying up until morning, prank calling boys, playing truth or dare, stirring up batches of rice crispy treats or muddy buddies, watching movies. They'd traipse off to the Donut Shop on Main Street at the westernmost side of town, three blocks south of their houses, traveling one of two ways:

1.) *Shaking their hips down the busy Rio Vista* if they wanted to check people out and pause on their trek to talk smack with whomever drove by or happened to be out on their front lawn, or late at night when they needed the protection of the streetlights and the neighborhood watch signs and the porch lights. Rio Vista kept them safe.

2.) *Sprinting through the potholed back alley* if they wanted to get there fast, like if they needed a sugar rush from chocolate old-fashioned doughnuts and sweet tea with crushed ice ASAP, or if they felt like getting spooked by the unlit empty lot that stretched to the end of the town limit where old, shopping-cart-pushing vagrants camped out and lit bonfires in barrels and, probably, there were ghosts kicking it too. That was the summer before she'd heard of La Llorona roaming the New River, which flowed in the ridge below the cliff and, folks said, green and soap-scummed, carried industrial, urban, and agricultural waste from across the Mexicali border, killing all the fish and reeking worse than the beef plant during the hottest part of summer. Swimming in the river could give a body rashes, sores, or make them violently ill. Mama had told her all that stuff, but she hadn't told her about La Llorona.

Sure, they'd played Bloody Mary in bathroom mirrors, sprinkling water on the glass and chanting *Bloody Mary, Bloody Mary, Bloody Mary*, and they'd played light as a feather stiff as a board. But never La Llorona. If Bianca had known about La Llorona then, poor sad woman who drowned her babies in a fit of rage and heartbreak then prowled that frothy, stinking river where old men and boys fished but never ate what they caught, perhaps mistaking all the other dead and glowing things entangled there for her lost ones, she would've been scared for sure and never would've gone through the alley by herself, day or night. She never would've met Gabe washing his pea-soup-green pickup truck in the driveway of his corner-house where the alley met that empty lot. He never would've seen her racing by, her chanclas slapping at the gravel, her dark ponytail flapping at her back, her thick thighs and round hips already pouring from her cuffed jean shorts, her breasts already filling her paisley tank top. He never would've called to her, asking where she was going so fast (she should have kept running). Then she never would've left her yellow-haired best friend behind and scrambled into Gabe's raised pickup to jump the dirt hills behind his house like a dune-covered stunt-track, not scared that anyone could fly off the cliff and into the river. Not thinking that trucks or loving or the country could be dangerous. Before that summer, she never knew what lay behind the palm trees and branches and rolling mounds of dirt and scraps of junk and trash and, probably, homeless people's huts.

But she did run through the alley. She did meet Gabe, just two years older, sixteen to her fourteen, but those two years he filled with all the things Mama never had. Caldo de rez and sticky red rice, filling her belly like embryonic fluid. After Gabe, the world was all nanas and cerveza and brujas and chile con carne and chupacabras. After Gabe, she'd turned into a La Llorona herself.

On Main Street, she let Gabe lead her blindfolded by his hands out of the car and onto the rutted sidewalk; she pressed her chanclas to the concrete, trying to feel for the cracks. She was torn between annoyance and excitement at the theatrics, not like the Gabe she'd gotten used to since he'd gotten Katrina pregnant. In high school, pre-Katrina, Gabe had loved surprises. He'd thrown Bianca a surprise party for her fifteenth birthday because Mama couldn't afford a quinceañera. Gabe had promised Mama there wouldn't be any alcohol, so when she showed up in the backyard, everyone hid the beer and tequila, and Bianca pushed her mama away, telling her they were hanging out with friends, that it wasn't a party for grown-ups. She still felt bad they'd lied to her. Bianca would've loved a real quinceañera. She would've loved that father-daughter dance.

The toe of her chancla caught on a snag in the concrete and she staggered forward.

"I've got you," Gabe said, laughing, holding her firmly.

She laughed too, but her body stiffened. "Where are we going?"

"Hang on, Bee. You'll see in a second." She could hear it in his voice that he was smiling, an impish thing who could barely contain his excitement. She also heard keys jangling and the opening of a glass door. A *ding-ding* sounded as they walked through. What she didn't hear was any other sound, no voices, no plates and dishes clanging, no music or television playing in the background.

She pulled off the blindfold and looked around. Wait, what? The restaurant was abandoned, empty. It seemed clean enough, booths and chairs stacked neatly at the edge of the room, no roaches scuttling across the floor, no dirty dishes stacked in piles at the bar. There were water glasses at the bar, clear and sparkling crystal. But this wasn't a restaurant anymore.

A For Sale sign hung in the window.

"What are we doing here? There's no food," she teased.

He pulled her toward him. "We're gonna buy this place," he said, hugging her tightly. "We're gonna fix it up. We're gonna start our restaurant, Bee."

She jerked her head back, searching his face. Was he joking? It wasn't like him to play tricks. His dark eyes danced and the corners of his mouth were upturned in a sly smile. He was being honest. She could tell. "But how?"

"I talked to my dad. It wasn't easy, but he's willing to help us get started. We'll have to pay him back, but hey, it's something."

"Oh wow . . ." She breathed out slowly. She'd thought Hector hated her after the barbecue. She'd thought Hector would never forgive her, now that he knew her secret; she was sure he would never look at her the same. She never would've expected that he'd be willing to help them. She felt a pang of longing for her own dad.

She looked around the almost-restaurant, allowing the shock to wear off, the swollen feeling of gratitude to sink in. "It's ours?"

"Well, not yet. It belonged to my dad's compadre and comadre a while back, but the wife got sick and they had to shut down. He let me borrow the keys so we could check it out." He squeezed her hand.

She almost couldn't believe this was Gabe saying these things. Gabe. The guy who wouldn't move in with her. The guy who wouldn't marry her. Who had to check everything with his baby's mom so he didn't make a wrong move and risk having his daughter taken away from him. Was this that guy? Or . . . was he sorry for what'd happened at the bar in Westmorland, keeping true to his promise to change? To go back to the Gabe Bianca had known before Katrina and Lana? Before he'd turned into some alternate version of himself—that angrier, more critical version she'd grown to despise. She pressed her face into his chest, laughing. This was real. She and Gabe would start a life together. All the darkness of the past two years was melting away.

Standing in the middle of the restaurant, *their* restaurant, he lifted her chin and kissed her softly on the mouth. "I know I've screwed up, Bee. But we'll fix it. Like this place."

She nodded, beginning to imagine what they could turn it into. "We can paint the walls red and yellow and orange like shades of desert sunset. We can play mariachi music and have dances on Saturday nights.

Cumbias. Fiestas. Jarabe Tapatío. Oh, and I'll ask Nana to help us with the menu. Of course we'll have your favorite, fried fish tacos with pico de gallo, authentic Puerto Vallarta style, made special for Fridays during Lent . . . menudo on the weekends." There'd be color and cultura. Chips and salsa. And it would be theirs.

"I was thinking of a sports bar," Gabe said, snapping her out of her reverie.

She frowned.

"Yeah, like a Lakers theme. We could have flat-screen TVs everywhere, showing ESPN and MTV. It'd be a restaurant too, but mostly, you know, beer and snacks, like quesadillas and hot wings."

"I hate sports. You know that. I hate *going* to sports bars. Why would I want to *own* one?" He let her hand go, and she watched the light fading from his eyes as he knitted his eyebrows and sighed, ran his hand through his spiky black hair.

"What are you doing, Bee? Why are you ruining this? I'm trying to do something good for us here, and you're picking a fight. I thought we were just sharing ideas."

It was stupid to fight; he was right. They could hash out the details another time. This was a celebration of possibility. She wanted to go back to holding hands and dreaming with him. But the memory of wringing herself dry, for him, wouldn't leave her alone. She looked at him, this man she loved, and saw loss. She couldn't help picking at the scab that would never leave the wound. Under her breath, "I was thinking of a more traditional place, that's all. More romantic."

"But come on, Bee. Let's be realistic. You think that would make good business sense? Think about it. Most of the bars stayed open even when the restaurants closed. We've got to think about demand and profits, or we'll sink ourselves into a hole."

"You're sure proud of that one year as a business major, aren't you?" As his face crumpled, she regretted saying that. "We can have a bar, I guess. But I want mariachis and dancing, not TV."

"You've gotta think about cost, Bee. All that costs money."

"Dancing is free."

"Fine. You dance." His voice had gone cold.

She drew away from him and walked toward the bar. She imagined women in folklórico skirts twirling like butterflies around the tables, tapping their black high-heels to the rhythm, their colorful ribbon-woven braids gleaming in tandem with their spinning. She imagined standing at the front of the room singing a ranchera while couples danced around her, cowboy boots and wide-brimmed hats touching. *Ay ay ay ay, canta no llores.* Her bisabuela used to sing to her in the bedroom she'd shared with Matty: *Cielito Lindo, los corazones.* "I don't want a bunch of drunken borrachos watching football or soccer or whatever in my restaurant."

"Katrina understands," he mumbled.

Bianca's insides turned to ice. "What did you say?"

"Nothing. Forget it."

"Like hell I'll forget it. Did you tell *her* about this place? Before you told *me*?" Doubt and suspicion surged through her anew. Maybe Katrina had been telling the truth. Maybe Gabe was a two-faced liar.

"Look, it's nothing. Shit, Bee. She's my friend."

"Your friend? Your . . . friend?" She spit the words as if they were bitter chiles. "So for all your big talk, nothing's changed."

"Calm down. Jesus Christ. I just mentioned I was thinking of buying a restaurant."

"Okay, Gabe. *You* buy a restaurant. *You* do whatever you want with it. *You* share it with whomever you choose. You always do what *you* want anyway."

Gabe stomped toward her across the room, and for a second, she was afraid he would hit her. His face was dark and frustrated. His fists were clenched. But she didn't recoil as he grabbed a clear glass sparkling from the counter and hurled it across the room. She stood still and silent as it crashed, shattering against the white plaster.

"Why do you make everything so damn difficult?" he asked, his voice a hollow drum. Bianca didn't know. She didn't know why she made everything so difficult. She stared at him, but he wouldn't look into her eyes. He sighed deeply, his shoulders and chest heaving as he exhaled. "I'll be in the car. Lock the door." He dropped the keys on the bar where the glass had been and walked out, the door sounding a hopeful *ding-ding* after him.

Bianca reached for another glass from the bar and held it up to her left eye, gazing toward the wall where a matching glass had shattered. As if through a crystal kaleidoscope, she searched the broken pieces for color. She saw none.

TEN
LETTER TO JUBILEE

I write poems for us, mijita. The world brightens in the dark forests of meta-phor. I'm grateful for the strength you give me. I'm learning to love girls like us, gritonas and lloronas but chingonas too, like Sandra, fighters, baby girl, with the strength to kill gods, with the strength to realize they were never gods to begin with. Mira—

> *Girls like us*

> *Light La Virgen candles for protection*
> *sometimes from ourselves*

> > *Morgue numb, rib-cracking,*
> > *petal backward, unblossoming*

> *Girls like us learn to save ourselves*
> *memory slipping like snakes down the throat*

> > *Bind our heart-hands, burn*
> > *& never cry out*

Girls like us have been crying for a thousand years,
never stop crying

    We know
    something is breathing, is alive

        Girls like us swallow fish & glow & fin
        nightwise through rivers, ditchwater girls

We fight drowning by learning to breathe
underwater, gills full

           All backwater summer, white flies seethe
around girls like us

Backhand, back-sass, break-bone girls—
when our survival depends on how far we backbend

    in haystacks, stain our skin
    red, hex your father's gods, dip them in batter

fry for tacos & serve them back
with cilantro & limón

        lick the chile from our fingers.

ELEVEN
SUCH SWEETNESS
WITH JUBILEE

Something was different in Bianca after the Anne Geddes dolls; Joshua sensed it. Bianca had already invited him and Jayden to Thanksgiving dinner at her abuela's and didn't renege. But most of his calls went to voicemail. He should've been relieved. Jayden hadn't brought up what happened outside Anne Geddes, but it had shaken Joshua. What was he supposed to tell the kid? He was in love with a delusional woman? Wouldn't that screw him up worse than having Joshua for a dad/uncle? What Joshua had learned about Bee so far: she needed a lot more help than he could give.

But he was scared to lose her.

He and Jayden dressed up for the occasion; they even wore matching ties.

What would her family think of them? Would her abuela be like Patti?

"I'm nervous," he whispered to Bianca, holding her hand as they walked the front path toward her abuelos' gated community. She looked beautiful, wearing a deep-blue dress and matching heels. She'd dressed Jubilee in a lighter blue dress. Joshua had picked them up at Matty's so she could give directions to her abuelos' house. They lived thirty minutes down the 5, toward Knott's Berry Farm in Buena Park.

"They'll love you. Believe me. You're perfect." She sounded genuine, like maybe she'd forgiven him for the *doll* slip.

"I don't know about that."

She smiled and squeezed his hand. "You're a knight in shining armor." After she'd given him the cold shoulder all week, this behavior was a major surprise. Why the change? If only they'd had more time to talk privately before he met her family. He wanted to bask in her warmth, but he still felt like he was missing something, and it unnerved him. Maybe he'd have to learn to feel a bit wobbly, a bit disoriented around this woman.

"Me too?" Jayden asked from his arms. "They'll like me too?"

"You, mijito? You, they'll adore." She tickled under his chin. "But prepare yourselves, guys. My family is huge. No. Huge is an understatement."

The house was impressive. Two stories with a manicured lawn and sculptured bushes. This was nothing like Patti's in Pomona. Joshua felt out of his league. Bianca opened the door without knocking; Joshua took a deep breath and held Jayden tighter.

She wasn't kidding. From the doorway, he stared in shock at the crowd: dozens of people spread across the long linen-covered folding tables beside the formal table in the dining room; they stretched into the living room and entryway. A colorful chandelier hung above the main table, beside an oak china cabinet. The spacious room, filled to capacity, hummed with noise: loud laughing, conversation, children crying, dishes clanging, aunts setting out the food.

"It's like a restaurant," Jayden whispered.

"Hey, everyone," Bianca yelled above the din. The room quieted and "everyone" turned toward them. Joshua tried to smile, hoping he didn't look too nervous.

"Mija!" A small, round-faced woman with short, dark hair and glasses approached, arms extended. "You brought your novio."

"Hi, Abuela." Bianca kissed her cheek. "This is Joshua Walker and his son, Jayden." She nodded toward her abuela, who was wiping her hands on her apron. "This is Abuela."

Joshua smiled, genuinely this time. Although Abuela's amber complexion was flecked with brown liver spots and skintags, her taut skin and the glow of her aura made her appear much younger than Joshua suspected she was. Bianca so resembled her, Joshua could've taken Abuela for Bianca's mom. He extended his hand to shake hers and said, "Great to meet you, and thank you for inviting us to your home."

Celia embraced him and Jayden both in a warm hug. "Ay, mijos! We've heard so much about you from our hija. Pásale, come in. We're starting the blessing."

Bianca led them through the crowd to a table near the back, squeezing between dozens of cousins, boyfriends, girlfriends, spouses, and children, all dressed up. Joshua was glad he'd thought to dress them up too. He and Jayden were the darkest faces in the mostly Latinx room, though he did see one Hawaiian-looking woman and a couple of much fairer-skinned people, even one or two blonds. Some family members nodded and smiled warmly, shaking his hand and hugging or kissing Bianca, who clutched Jubilee to her chest. Some of the family looked at Jubilee strangely, a few shook their heads. Bianca held her head high as she passed. The majority of faces were welcoming. But Joshua couldn't help being self-conscious. Bianca acted oblivious to the stares and whispers. Did she know how they looked at her? Did it bother her?

Behind Bianca's chair, against the living room wall, a high chair was set up for Jubilee, one of the four around the table. Who'd left it there for the doll? Matty and Handro?

"How do you know all these people?" Jayden whispered as they took their seats.

Bianca laughed. "They're family."

"They're *family*? Whoa. That's a lot of family."

Bianca's lips quirked and she winked at Joshua, who'd been thinking the same as Jayden.

Trays and bowls were brimming over in the middle of every table all around the room: sliced turkey and ham, candied yams in melted marsh-mallows, green bean casserole, mashed potatoes, stuffing, rolls, and a pretzel-crusted Jell-O salad covered in what looked like whipped cream but Bianca said was sour cream. Her Tía Lydia made it, and it was *sooo* good. Joshua *had* to try it. Aside from the food, on gold-trimmed china plates in front of them were thin, white candles. A tradition in Bee's family that had started the year her bisabuela had died; in honor of Bisabuela's memory, they each took turns passing the fire to light their candle and say what they were thankful for. Everyone participated, and Abuela usually cried.

When Joshua's turn came, he said, "I'm thankful for you all welcoming me into your home. And for my boy, Jayden, who brings laughter to my life. And now, for Bianca . . ." Glancing at the highchair, he added, "and Jubilee." Bianca kissed his cheek when he lit her candle. She looked toward the head of the table. A woman nearly identical to Bianca watched them. She was thinner and graying at her temples, one elbow on her place mat, her arm supporting her forehead as if she had a headache, and the other hand on a necklace around her neck. Joshua watched her thumbing the beads; it was a rosary. Rosana. He'd recognize Bianca's mother anywhere. Someone, an aunt maybe, put an arm around her when Bianca said she was thankful for *fathers*.

Mama was nearly last to give thanks, before Abuela, who did cry as Bianca predicted she would. Mama was thankful her daughter had come home. But Bianca didn't even look up at her.

After dinner, Matty called Joshua to join him and Handro. Most of the male cousins were watching TV in the family room. Bianca had taken Jayden with her female cousins and their children to play upstairs, and for a brief moment, Joshua wondered if Jubilee somehow helped Bee feel like she "fit in" with a family where all the women (even the college-age, younger women) seemed to have children in tow. Again, this was a case-study note he'd have to file away in his memory, since he definitely couldn't ask her outright.

Bianca's brother and his partner looked cute together. Bianca called them her favorite guys. Matty was taller and wider. Something about his demeanor made Joshua want to impress him, gain his approval. "Josh is an X-Men fan," Matty told Handro. "He's the Beast."

Joshua nodded.

"You should come with us to Comic-Con in San Diego next year then," Handro said. "Matty's debuting his new comic—it'll trend so hard, watch, it'll transcend X-Men." His voice was enthusiastic and melodic, as if singing instead of talking. Bee had said he was a host at a swanky gay bar in Orange County, which seemed perfect, he was so friendly.

Matty said that was a good idea but gave Joshua a look that meant *Are you gonna be around in a year?* In defense, Joshua blurted out something about how much he liked Matty's sister, adding, "She's smart and classy. Already, she acts like a mom to Jayden."

"Isn't that problematic for you and your kid?" Was he trying to be an asshole? Or was he genuinely concerned? "What do you tell him about Bee's doll?"

"It's a coping mechanism, right? She's not *insane* or anything."

"My mom says we need to unshock her." Matty crossed his arms in front of his chest, frowning. "I'm not so sure."

"What shocked her in the first place?"

"Has she told you about her therapist?"

"She's mentioned her 'appeasing-her-mother appointments,' but she hasn't actually given any details."

"Don't you think you should ask her?"

Was Matty trying to make Joshua feel like an idiot? "I wanted to let her work through it in her own time, not push her. Besides, I thought therapy was supposed to be confidential."

Matty sighed. "After our dad died, she was a wreck. She couldn't be consoled. Not by me, not Mom, not anyone. She stayed in the Valley with that douchebag she called a boyfriend. She told you about Gabe?"

"The rough sketch anyway. He sounds like a player."

Matty picked at his cuticles. Handro put his hand on Matty's leg. "She showed up at our house in the middle of the night right before Easter. She collapsed on our couch and when she woke up, she acted as if the doll was alive and she was its mom."

"*Her* mom," Handro corrected. "Not *its.*"

"Sorry. *Her* mom." He sounded irritated, a scratch to his voice Joshua hadn't heard before. He seemed calm around Bee and handled Jubilee with care. "I should know better by now. We never call Jubilee a doll. She's Bianca's *baby.*" He said this last part as if he were reciting a script; it wasn't mocking, exactly, but Joshua understood what Bee meant when she'd said her brother was a talented actor in high school; she was surprised he hadn't pursued a theatrical career. His current role: patient brother who loves his sister. He'd masked his true feelings well. Joshua hadn't realized he was so frustrated about having to pretend for Bee.

"Why do you do it?" he asked. "I know why *I* go along with Bianca. Why do you all?"

"Because we love her," Handro said.

"Look," Matty said. "We were afraid she'd gone crazy, that we'd have to send her to a mental health facility against her will. And I'm sure you know by now what it's like to go up against Bee when she doesn't want to do something or disagrees with you." He chuckled, and there it was, the brotherly love that Joshua had sensed before. "Luckily, her therapist said she could be treated at home, with meds and therapy, and a lot of patience from us." He looked toward their mom, and Joshua followed his gaze. Bianca still hadn't introduced them. "Bee's angry with her," Matty said, as if reading Joshua's mind.

Before he could respond, Bianca's mom stood in front of them. "Am I allowed to meet this handsome young man?" Her dark hair curled around her face the same as Bianca's, only Mama's was streaked with gray. Joshua noticed again the string of beads dangling from beneath her cream-colored sweater. He thought of Patti and her rosary and stood to shake Bianca's mom's hand.

"Good to meet you, ma'am. I'm not sure about handsome, but I'm Joshua Walker."

"Bianca's been keeping you a secret." She kept his hand in hers. It felt rude to pull away.

"I'm not sure about that, ma'am." His palms were sweaty.

"Oh, Mom, leave him alone." Matty's voice was playful and casual again. "Bee's upstairs with Jayden."

Bianca's mother let go and sat in an empty folding chair beside her son, smoothing her slacks.

"Mom, Josh wants to know why Bee hasn't introduced you two yet."

"You mean a more compelling reason than I'm a nag?" She laughed. "She assumes I would say you could be the unshocking cure my baby girl needs to get her life back on track. Watching you interacting tonight, I'd say I'm correct."

Damn, he could see where Bee got her intensity. Did this woman actually expect *him* to *cure* her daughter? He didn't even know what was *wrong* with her daughter. He was just playing along because he liked her so much. But *unshocking* her? He didn't know about that. He assumed she meant Bianca suffered from PTSD, but he'd never heard anyone phrase it the way Mrs. Vogelsang did. *Keep it cool. She's teasing you.* His mouth sandpapered. He couldn't form a response.

Matty came to his rescue. "That's putting a lot of pressure on him, Mom."

"Well, it's true. When my girl came home from the Valley, she was a mess. Before that, she'd been lost. We couldn't reach her. *I* couldn't reach her. When she showed up with Jubilee, she was stronger. We saw our Bianca again."

"So we go along with it," Matty added. "Hell, I babysit for her."

"Is she delusional though?" Joshua asked, regaining his composure. "It's not a choice she's making?" He recounted what he'd found online about dementia patients and role-playing.

"She has a tough, stubborn streak I both admire and don't understand," Rosana said. "If she were playing, she wouldn't let us in. I'll tell you though, mijo, she's never referred to Jubilee as anything but *her baby.*"

Joshua told them how upset she'd gotten at Anne Geddes.

"She's not ready yet," Matty said.

"But you can help her," Rosana said.

The pit of Joshua's stomach felt empty although he'd just eaten a huge Thanksgiving meal. Why did they think a weirdo like him could help Bianca? He wasn't a counselor yet. And Bee was a feminist. She wouldn't want a *man* to fix her problems anyway. He understood that much about her.

Matty cleared his throat and sat forward in his chair, leaning closer. Joshua wanted to scoot away but couldn't without appearing rude, so, uncomfortable as he felt, he forced himself to stay conspiratorially close to Matty. "Josh, I have to ask you. What if she doesn't recover? What will you do? Spend your life with my sister and her doll?"

"Ay, leave the poor guy alone, Matty," Handro said, hugging his partner's shoulders. "They're dating, not getting married. Right, guy?"

"I mean, I could imagine myself marrying her . . ."

The words were out of his mouth before he could stop them. What was it about this family that made him open up? Any family really. He wasn't used to family. He wanted to hang his head in embarrassment, but he looked up to see the damage. Bianca's mother's eyes had lit up while Matty's darkened. Joshua wished he could take back the insanity he'd just put out there. His heart thudded. *What are you saying? Marrying her? Before dinner you weren't even sure she still wanted to be your girlfriend. You idiot.* His dress shirt and collar felt too warm, his tie too tight around his neck. He loosened it. Bianca's mother rubbed her rosary beads between her fingers. She said nothing.

Matty asked, "What does Jayden think of her?"

"Who? Jubilee? He loves her." Joshua was glad for the change of subject. "I can't tell if he believes in Jubilee the way Bianca does or not. It's a game he loves playing with Bee."

"We're all playing the game, aren't we?" Matty said, his voice bitter.

"Ay, mijo, it's not forever." Rosana patted her son's hand.

"It's been months, Mom, and nothing's changing."

"Everything's changing," she said, looking at Joshua. "This young man is changing everything."

Joshua stood up, too quickly not to seem rude, but he didn't care anymore. He needed air. This conversation was a crazy train. He'd meant to get some answers about a woman he cared for, not become some kind of savior.

As though she sensed they'd pushed too far, Rosana took his hand in hers, said, "Give my daughter time, mijo. She'll come around."

These words would cycle through his mind for months to come. *Give her time.* He didn't know why he'd told her family he'd consider marrying her, but he did know he wanted to spend as much time with her as possible.

Whether he needed to throw away his case notes or throw in the towel, he wasn't sure.

Jayden fell asleep on the ride home, worn out from the new people and full of pie. Joshua carried him upstairs to their apartment, Bianca following. He had offered to take her home, but she wanted to stay.

She still hadn't mentioned what had happened the other day at the Anne Geddes store, but she did ask what Joshua thought about her family and whether or not her mother seemed genuine. "What do you mean?" he asked, lugging the sleeping boy through the apartment. When she didn't answer, he turned to look at her.

She shrugged. "I don't know what to think of that woman."

He waited to see if she would explain, and when she said nothing else, he turned back toward Jayden's room to deliver his sleepy parcel to his bed. He didn't mention the intense conversation after dinner, or how strong Rosana came on. Instead, he plopped Jayden gently down.

"I'll change him," Bianca said, handing Jubilee to Joshua.

This was new. A good sign. He watched with his usual interest as she helped the stiff little zombie boy into his night pull-ups and pajamas, his arms and legs hanging limp. From the doorway, Joshua held Jubilee like he would a stuffed animal, in one palm against his thigh, then caught himself and propped her against his shoulder, hoping Bianca hadn't seen.

"Night-night, mijo," Bianca whispered, kissing Jayden's forehead. Something like a fishhook caught inside Joshua. He couldn't tell if it hurt or not.

Before she could slip away, the zombie awoke. "Bee, you forgot a story."

"Tontito. Were you pretending to sleep?" Jayden's eyebrows shot up. She'd caught him! Bianca laughed. Joshua couldn't pin down what he felt at their camaraderie.

She picked a book from the shelf and read: "There was once a velveteen rabbit, and in the beginning he was splendid. He was fat and bunchy, as a rabbit should be; his coat was spotted brown and white, he had real thread whiskers, and his ears were lined with pink sateen."

Jayden listened, spellbound. When Bee got to the part where the fairy turns the velveteen rabbit *real*, hopping on his haunches with the other forest rabbits, Jayden sprang from the bed then crouched on his rump and twitched his nose. Joshua laughed. How long would it stay like this? Jayden playing along. Joshua—playing along.

He liked the justice of the velveteen rabbit proving himself in the end.

"If he'd been my bunny," Jayden said, "I'd have known it was him right away."

"Hmm. Then you're a smart boy. Time for bed, mijito."

"Can I say good night to Jubilee?"

Since the Anne Geddes store, Jayden had asked a few times if Jubilee was a doll or real. So what if the kid believed? What harm could it do?

Joshua brought the doll from the doorway to the bed, and Jayden kissed her nose. "Night-night, Jubilee Bunny."

He switched on the constellation nightlight, which glowed blue against the wall (Jayden's favorite was Ursa Major, the Great Bear), then he and Bianca left the room, keeping Jayden's door cracked so the hallway light could shine in. He was afraid of the dark.

At a safe distance from the boy's room, Joshua whispered into Bianca's neck, "Spend the night?" He wrapped his hands around her waist and kissed her shoulders from behind as he nudged her toward his bedroom. He'd wanted to pick her up and bury himself inside her all evening. He'd been so worried she would leave him. Yet here she was.

"Yes," she whispered, taking Jubilee from Joshua. "Let me put her to bed first."

He pulled his body away from hers and moved toward the bed while she set the doll in the bassinet and covered her with a blanket. She did *not* go through the whole bedtime routine he'd witnessed many other nights. Another good sign.

Now she turned to him and began undressing.

She'd slept over before, but this felt different. The nights Bianca had spent with Joshua, he'd held her close to his body but nothing more. His dick throbbed at the nearness of her thighs and ass, cradled against him, but he hadn't wanted to pressure her. The truth was, he'd been scared. What would she think of the way he made love? She'd had a life before him. Her ex was her first. Did she shape to the curve of his body? What would she think of Joshua's body, his style? Let's face it, he didn't have a style. He had nothing to compare her to. He'd been a weirdo kid, a loner young man. The farthest he'd ever gotten was an awkward kiss with a sort-of friend at senior prom. But now, he ached for Bianca. Hoped that would be enough to carry him through.

She pulled her dark-blue chiffon dress over her head, revealing a matching bra and lace thong. He'd anticipated this for three months, if he was honest with himself. He moved off the bed and came toward her, pulling her body against his.

She was crying.

"Did I do something wrong?" he asked, her tears on his skin. "Am I hurting you?"

She held her hand to her face; he cradled her cheek in his palm.

"No," she said. "The opposite."

He traced the lines of her stomach and breasts.

They were both made of scars, like her stretch marks, white and jagged and beautiful.

He kissed each one.

In the story of La Llorona, a woman comes unhinged from unrequited love. She drowns herself by drowning her babies. She is lost. She is gone forever to the riverbank. And her song sounds of death.

This is no kind of ending.

This is no kind of love.

Rivers take, yes. But rivers bring back.

Joshua came inside Bianca with such sweetness (*I know of a river that empties into a gulf in the belly of Mexico. I know of an ocean that belly spills into, of salt I must drink, brindled fish I've become. Salt on my skin, my lover is drinking too. I know of a cycle that carries away what is clean, what is made clear. I know rain. I am rain. Love, let me rain into you. I know groundwater, freshwater. Oh love, the river is coming. Listen. She's singing again*).

TWELVE
NIGHTBLOOM

BEFORE JUBILEE

The Brawley public library didn't have many books, but it was a life source to Bee. She wouldn't start at the community college for another couple of months, and she didn't have enough money to buy books. Her job at the *Desert Herald* paid a little above minimum wage, but she was helping Mama pay the mortgage on the house-for-sale and when it sold, she'd have to find somewhere else to squat. She also had gas and groceries and puppy food and health insurance. Books weren't a luxury but a necessity, and if she could've eaten the pages rather than the ground beef tacos she sustained herself with, she would have. But the library made it possible for her to eat both books and tacos, and she was currently living on Gloria Anzaldúa and Ana Castillo, one for sustenance and the other for sweetness, both of which she needed. Anzaldúa wrote, "Awareness of our situation must come before inner changes, which in turn come before changes in society. Nothing happens in the 'real' world unless it first happens in the images in our heads." Bianca tried imagining a world in which fathers don't violate their households, in which mamas teach their daughters to be strong rather than cower in a corner, or a world where cowering in a corner, too, is a kind of strength. Perhaps Mama had been teaching Bianca a survival tactic.

Mama was the living one, after all.

Yet here, now, Bianca felt defeated. She could've been so much more.

But when she looked in the mirror, she saw a shadow. The aftereffect of something bright and glorious. Its absence.

She hadn't always been obsessed with babies. There was a time she believed she would change the world, lead a movement, follow Dolores Huerta and Sylvia Mendez, Ellen Ochoa, and Sonia Sotomayor. Where her bisabuela had picked pecans and oranges in the orchards, climbing the tallest trees with her small girlbody, dropping the fruit to the baskets below where her tías and tíos and primos stooped to pick those that had fallen on the ground; where her abuela had sewn in the garment district in downtown Los Angeles with her bisabuela, both women taking the bus each morning and evening, making the beautiful dresses to be sold in Beverly Hills and maybe worn by a movie star; and where her mother had cared for the ill, had gone to their crumbling homes, those diabetic elderly dying in the heat in the Valley—Bianca would grow and tend to the broken world, would find where it ached and heal it, would locate its source of ugliness and make it beautiful.

Only, since she'd met Gabe and become La Llorona, she'd been growing the ugliness inside her. She could sense it warping the roots from within. The cactus flower had dropped from her when she should have been having a quinceañera, blooming across the dance floor in a bright, sequined dress, not spending the night at her boyfriend's nana's across town so that her mama wouldn't know what she'd done, not taking a Tylenol for the cramping and eating the caldo de rez they'd made for her. They'd taken such good care of her.

Had they done it for her? Or for their son's chance at a football scholarship?

She'd never know.

What she did know: She was blessed with a safe procedure. She was blessed with women to check her for bleeding. She was blessed with choice.

Only, she hadn't chosen for herself.

She hadn't.

Awareness must come. And it did. Too late.

If she'd chosen for herself, she would have chosen the cactus spines. She would've chosen the one night a year the night-blooming cereus uncoils its moon-white skirt, opens its opalescent throat, and allows the bats who've flown hundreds of miles with their young clutching to their fur as they swim through the air, half starved from waiting, to drink their fill and feed their next generation of creatures who can see through the dark. She'd have been a Queen of the Night and taught her daughter to give her body to no Gabe.

She knew that, deep inside.

Where Anzaldúa and Castillo dwelled, where she fed on the nectar of their toughest blossoms.

These truths would moonstone in her palm and she would grasp her hand shut, hold it tight to her heart, and try to carry it with her toward the front door, out onto the walkway, into the world.

Until Gabe would bend her over. And call her gordita or cochina. Chubby girl. Dirty girl.

She'd open her palm, and the stone had turned to dust.

She swept it away on her jeans.

A daughter doesn't solve anything; she needed her mama to tell her this.

But she makes the world a lot less lonely. A lot less ugly.

THIRTEEN
THE SIGN
WITH JUBILEE

After Thanksgiving, Bee stayed with Joshua most nights. She only returned to Matty's for clothes and essentials. It all felt so natural, though a wriggling worm in the pit of his stomach kept reminding him that he was acting as irrationally as his almost-live-in-girlfriend. He pushed that nagging whisper down. When he was with Bee, it almost *felt* like Jubilee was a real baby. Bee was that convincing. Or he just needed her warmth, needed her glowing.

One morning, a few weeks after Thanksgiving, Bianca told Josh the news she'd been keeping secret because she hadn't wanted to jinx it. Jayden was still in bed, but she and Josh were sitting together with coffee and a plate of cinnamon rolls, their textbooks open. Finals loomed. She curled her legs beneath her on the couch in what Jayden called crisscross applesauce.

"I'm going to New York," she blurted, her words ballooning toward the ceiling.

Joshua looked up from his psychology textbook, a lopsided grin spreading across his face, though his throat felt sandpaper rough. The first thought that rushed through his mind: he hadn't realized she was well enough for long trips across the country. Then a sting of shame: had he thought his almost-live-in-girlfriend, the woman he was trusting around his almost-son, was too unstable to travel across the country? He cleared his throat and spoke carefully. "That's amazing, Bee. When? For how long?"

She told him about Elena, her writing instructor, and how, several weeks before, she had told Bianca about an NYU workshop for undergrads during winter break. She had recommended Bianca for a minority scholarship and given her the application materials. Bianca submitted a sample of her poetry along with the application, and they'd accepted her. Between the NYU financial aid and a Cal State travel grant, the trip was paid for.

She just had to get on a plane and go.

She'd never been on a plane before, she told him. A few years ago, she'd had no idea there were such a thing as writers' workshops. She'd had no idea there were other living poets. They taught her the dead cis white guys in school. She'd soaked all the rhymes in and could say them by heart. But they hadn't spoken to her directly, hadn't climbed into her window and whispered, *You're safe*. She knew Emily Dickinson and Sylvia Plath because she wrote to them in her journals, pages and pages of responses to their poems, pages and pages of their responses to her, or at least, as she imagined their voices in her head.

At Holy Cross she'd found out that Sandra Cisneros was giving a reading at the Santa Ana public library. She'd found her books online and devoured them like Nana's enchiladas. Like posole on New Year's Eve. She'd filled her belly with her red-hot words—

> You my saltwater pearl,
> my mother, my father,
> my bastard child,
> heaven and hurt,
> you my slavery of sadness,
> my wrinkled heart.

Bianca wanted badly to be a Loose Woman like her. To shake loose. Shake free.

She told him all of this, and yet, she said, "I can't tell if I'm excited or scared."

Joshua shut his textbook and listened between the lines. This kind of passion he'd only seen her pour into Jubilee, now she was talking about something *real*. Had this been the sign he'd been waiting for? A sign that she was truly on the road to recovery? "This is incredible, Bee. *Excited*. I think that's what you should be." He turned and faced her again, hiding his relief and hope, trying only to show his enthusiasm and support. "You should definitely go."

"But what about Jubilee? Matty has meetings. He's getting ready for Comic-Con. I can't expect him to watch her the whole time."

"I'll watch Jubilee for you," Joshua told her. "You're a writer. You need to write."

Bianca stood and leaned her whole body toward him. "You're right. I *am* a writer. I'll go."

Rosana didn't want Bianca to go to New York. She was afraid it would shock her worse. She reminded her to take her meds, take them every day and not forget because she didn't want her having a crazy episode like an addicted starlet she'd heard about in the big city (as if they were not living right outside Los Angeles, but Mama lived like anywhere she went was a small town). Anyway, Bianca wasn't an addict, she told Mama. She didn't want to take those meds in the first place. They made her fuzzy.

Mama asked if Dr. Norris approved, but Bianca only shrugged and promised her she wouldn't go all Zelda Fitzgerald on her. When Mama looked at Bianca with a blank face, she told her how Zelda wrote her only novel in six weeks in a psychiatric hospital. She was a ballerina. A mother. A gifted writer whose gift had been squelched and stolen by her husband.

Mama said, "Just take your meds."

But Bianca would've liked to go all Zelda. Imagine? Just letting go . . .

She'd read that critics considered Zelda's prose "unpolished" for its excessive use of "flowery" metaphor.

Bianca liked Zelda's prose.

She needed flowers against the concrete, dandelion weeds growing out of the cracks and turning into pinwheels for wishing.

She thought about the restaurant with Gabe. How it had all evaporated, a dream she'd only half wanted anyway, but colorful nevertheless. And this was New York. This was the girlhood dream. The big one. The postcard from her high school English teacher that said *Follow your dreams*.

Bianca was falling in love with a man who loved her back. No, Josh hadn't said those exact words in that exact shape, but before, in the Valley, Gabe's *I love yous* had been empty. When Josh told her to go to New York, 'it was as if he were saying, *Your dreams are beautiful*. When he believed with her, it was easier to believe in herself.

The weeks leading up to finals, Bianca was spending most of her time at Josh's. Her brother looked hurt each time she left, but he didn't say anything. He had Handro. He should have understood.

Between finals and New York, she only had a week's break for Christmas. The wires coiled in her gut kept raveling and unraveling whenever she thought about leaving. Jubilee slept in the bassinet beside the couch. Bianca had helped Jayden to bed in his dinosaur footie pajamas, and she could hear him snoring from his room. He reminded her of Lana and that scared her. Why was she playing house with another family? She'd gone right from Gabe's to Josh's.

They sat on the floor in Josh's living room, studying. The words on the page of her novel blurred. She stood and stretched. "I need a break from madwomen in attics."

"You still writing about that Hitchcock movie you showed me, the one with the obsessive, controlling housekeeper who burns the house down like Bertha?"

"I'd prefer to call her Antoinette."

"Yeah, from that other novel you like. What's it called?"

"*Wide Sargasso Sea*." She loved that even if Josh couldn't remember the names of all her novels, he remembered what she'd told him about them. The Brontë sisters had enchanted her when she'd discovered them in high school. At Holy Cross she'd encountered Jean Rhys's novel and fallen in love, the way her narrative was nonlinear and broken, like life, like memory. And although Rhys had written it as a biting response to its Romantic predecessor, Bianca couldn't help believing it had always come first, her white Creole sister Antoinette with her colorful bird and patois, her magical nanny Christophine, from whom she would've learned the ways of *obeah*. She'd told Josh this, how she was living in a stream-of-consciousness novel, only writing it herself.

Romantic literature set off a hankering for chamomile tea. She offered to make Josh a mug too; he nodded but didn't follow her into the kitchen. She set Jubilee in the high chair Josh had bought from the Goodwill along with other baby items. She hadn't asked for all those things, and it felt like luck or fate she'd found a man like him. She was dizzy, as if dehydrated. She wanted to tell Josh about Dr. Norris, tell him everything. But he'd think she was crazy. Like Gabe had.

She wasn't legally required to see Dr. Norris. No one threatened to check her into a hospital, and no one knew what destruction she was capable of.

The knot in her stomach snaked. She was Coatlicue, the serpent woman. Snakes-her-skirts. Snakes-her-love.

She leaned over a trash can beside Josh's kitchen sink and threw up.

"Bee?" Josh came into the kitchen as she wiped her mouth with a napkin, still gripping the trash. "You have a bug?"

She nodded.

He felt her forehead. "You're cool and clammy. Here, sit down. I'll take this out." He took the garbage and led her to the dining table.

"Probably nerves."

"About finals?"

"I was thinking about New York, about flying."

"You'll knock them dead with your poems. They'll ask you to stay, offer you a residency."

"I couldn't stay."

He kissed her forehead, gently. "I wouldn't want you to stay."

He left to take out the trash.

Her head throbbed. She decided to tell him what she was afraid of.

"I started a short story a while back but never finished it," she said when he came back into the kitchen and began pulling two mugs from the cabinet.

"You *should* finish it."

"It brings up so many memories I'd rather forget."

"Could be cathartic."

It was time to talk about therapy. She knew it was. She'd alluded to it many times but hadn't straight out told Josh she was seeing a shrink. "Dr. Norris says the same thing," she ventured. She felt nauseated again, and pulled away. She watched the tea kettle; soon it would start whistling.

Josh closed the gap between their bodies. "Dr. Norris is wise."

She turned around, Josh's arms still clasping her waist like they were dancing. He didn't seem jarred by her admission.

"He's kooky and has this Scottish accent I adore." Josh's smile crinkled his slick brown skin, dimples like small eyelets in his cheeks. "He tells me I'm a 'different lamp than I think I am.' That I only wear the shade I think I'm supposed to, and that going to New York is a step toward a new lamp shade. He says I should write a book about my life. Well, my lamp. He says I'll shine brighter if I take the shade off." She motioned her hands above her head like taking off a hat, lifting her arms high in the air, twirling around in Josh's arms like a ballerina. "Do I shine?"

"Always."

She stopped twirling, steeled her nerves. "He says I'm not crazy."

His eyebrows furrowed for a moment. He looked at her as if seeing her for the first time. As if she was a surprise. She liked the way she felt about herself when he looked at her.

"I never thought you were."

FOURTEEN
USELESS MOON

BEFORE JUBILEE

Fantasies. Maybe that's all Bianca and Gabe had. They'd shifted their dream to the restaurant, as if what they fixed in the kitchen could heal them too. But they couldn't work together much less live together if all their conversations ended in arguments. They hadn't talked about the fight since he'd shown her the abandoned restaurant. Now they were going to a club in Mexicali with his cousin from Los Angeles, forgetting their troubles the way they always did: chasing tequila with beer.

Bianca had mixed feelings about Mexicali. It was only a forty-minute drive from Gabe's house, and they'd often crossed the border to party since the drinking age in Mexico was eighteen. But the children selling chicle on the side of the street made her sad. The women holding out the empty baskets of their hands. Her mama had told her stories of the pregnant mothers crossing the Colorado Desert through the Mexicali Valley. Same as her bisabuela's pregnant mother: by foot and, sometimes, hands and knees. She'd crossed the Chihuahuan Desert at the Jornada del Muerto, which could be called the Journey of the Dead. Before she'd died in childbirth, Bisabuela's mother had heard her girlchild's vibrant cry. That girlchild's cry delivered life to the rest of Bianca's family.

Mama had delivered the babies of the crossing mothers en el otro lado. Mama had nursed them at the hospitals, dehydrated from weeks through the hundred-degree heat, bursting at the seams with the new life they'd given their hijos. She'd nursed their wounds too. From climbing the fence. Jumping. Or falling. One woman had fractured both legs. When Mama had recounted her experiences in the hospital, Bianca had thought of the date trees she'd climbed in the back lots and how painful it had been to fall from just a few branches high. Her own bisabuela had picked pecans and oranges up and down the orchards of California from the time she was a small girl, climbing into the trees and dropping fruits and nuts to her family—the aunts and uncles who'd taken her in, all migrant field workers who'd picked their way across New Mexico, Arizona, and into California—until she ran off to marry a blue-eyed Spanish man and began sewing in the garment district in downtown Los Angeles on Alameda Street. Since then, none of Bianca's family had accrued any wealth, but their lives were far less precarious than those here, on the Mexicali streets.

Bianca pressed her face to the glass, watching the children weaving through traffic with their boxes of hard, bright gum. Gabe said he felt like a spoiled jerk, driving his fancy truck while mothers and their kids sat on the curb with nothing. When he said things like that, Bianca believed they still had something in common.

In the club, cumbia rock blared on the speakers. Bianca leaned her body into Gabe's as he propped against a stool at the bar chugging another beer while she gulped down a second tequila shot, scrunching her face and clenching her eyes tight from the warmth stinging her throat. His breath hot and acrid against her neck, she loved him best when he was a little buzzed. He treated her nicest that way. How quickly it could turn. How quickly she'd be upside-down, stomach aching, calling out for Mama. Mama whose bedroom in the empty house-for-sale she'd return to, drunk, like Dad of her girlhood. Was Mama praying her rosary now? *Hail Mary, full of grace, keep my daughter safe. Keep my daughter sound and safe.* If so, Bianca couldn't hear her.

"It sucks you couldn't find a friend to keep my cousin company," Gabe said close to her ear, his hands on the slight lonjas at her hips, a mini muffin at the top of her jeans. She tried not to care that she was gaining weight, getting rounder.

"Yeah, sorry. Can't he meet someone here?"

"Nah, he's not like that. Look at him, he's miserable." He nodded toward his cousin, alone at a table at the edge of the dance floor.

She let the buzz enhance her confidence, put on a pouty face she knew he found sexy and told him she wanted to dance.

He kissed her mouth and squeezed her ass. "Let me go check on him real quick."

Bianca swayed with the music, allowing it to fill her with the cumbias she'd learned at quinceañeras and high school dances. Her own mama didn't dance anymore, hadn't since she'd married Dad, except for the exercise videos she'd done to lose weight so he'd stop calling her lard ass.

Suavamente, bésame. No one had taught her the steps, but she'd caught on from the girls dancing around her. The washing machine meant shake her hips as if polishing wood. Some moves were like the pony Mama had taught her from Richard Simmons videos: balance on the pads of her feet, heels up high, even in high heels. One two three, one two three. Like the waltzes she'd performed in recitals, only more shaking. Her favorite was when she and Gabe would crisscross bodies together, forming scissors with their hips and legs, hips locked together, one arm each extended, elbow bent, hands clasped together, opposite arm hung around each other's waist, feet apart, his knee between her crotch, and they'd swing, back and forth, round and round, fast and bouncing. ¡La quebradita!

In his arms, she felt sexy, felt he was sexy. With Gabe it was all show. With a muscular frame bulked up by his intermittent lifting and a flippant, borderline cocky (in that friendly playful way) attitude toward others, he radiated macho masculinity. Still, in bed, Bianca could tell he felt he had something to prove. He'd told her once after making love how much his dad's expectations hurt him. How he couldn't get anything right. The summer in high school he'd hurt his back and couldn't play football anymore, he went to live with Nana, deflated by his dad's reaction. *All those years of training down the drain.* Isn't that how Bianca and he felt with each other? Why they clung?

He sauntered back across the bar, pulled her tight toward his body, dancing her in time, his pelvis tipped toward her hips, his head close to hers. For a moment, they were an elderly couple dancing at the Chili Cook-Off fiesta, outside the rodeo arena. They were his parents dancing in the backyard or at a wedding. For a moment, his hair grayed, covered by a wide-brimmed Stetson, his DC skater shoes replaced by shuffling cowboy boots. Her strappy platforms transformed into closed-toed pumps, nylons thickened into stockings.

"Sorry, Bee. My cousin wants to leave," he said, still holding her close. "We're going to Miau-Miau instead." The strip club. Bianca's pulse quickened, gut lurched. She told him no.

"We came out here for him. He came all the way from LA, and I promised him a fun time. Besides, it won't be bad."

"Gabe, I hate those places. You know that. Can't we hang out here? Please?"

He pulled away from her. "You should've brought a friend for him, then we could've danced like you wanted. We're leaving. Let's go." He signaled his cousin to head toward the exit doors then tugged her arm, steering her away from the cramped dance floor beside the bar.

At the door of the strip club, a fat baseball-capped bouncer checked her driver's license and nodded. This club was dark and smelled dankly of vinegar and even stronger of cigarettes. Gabe draped his arm around Bianca's shoulders. "It's fine, Bee. We'll order some drinks and stay here a few minutes so my primo can get his kicks, then we'll leave. I promise."

Thick frays of yarn pulled inside her stomach. In high school, a bunch of them had gotten together to watch *American Beauty* at Eloisa's. Despite its critical acclaim, she'd hated it. It felt perverse to her, that dad. She guessed that was the point. Everyone had a twisted side. Everyone had alligators in the swamp. In a book about being a writer, she'd read Stephen King's essay. All you need in this world is love, he'd quoted Lennon. Then added, *as long as you kept the gators fed.* In this world, some men fantasize about teenage girls. For all Bianca knew, most men did. Dads jacked off in the shower. For all she knew. What did she know about dads? Some dads killed themselves in the bathtub. But she wouldn't want to watch a movie about that. It was enough to know it existed.

She'd stopped reading Arundhati Roy's *The God of Small Things* for a month when she'd frozen on the scene in which the Orangedrink Lemondrink Man in the theater lobby puts his warm, hard flesh into the little boy's hand. Estha, the little boy who'd been kicked out of the talkies theater for singing Maria's parts in *The Sound of Music*, the way Mama and Matty and she sang to all the musicals (*"Before the parade passes by . . ."*), who couldn't stop singing even in the lobby, who went back to his Ammu and had to be rushed out of the theater to the bathroom and held over the dirty toilet to vomit. She froze because she was there with him, in the lobby. She wanted to scream out *Don't go behind the drink man's cart. Don't take the sweets he's offering you. Go back to your mama. Turn around, little Estha.* Or at Ammu, *Look what he's done to your boy. Slice his neck, Ammu. Call the police. Take it back. Take it back into you. Take Estha back to where he'll be safe.* She'd wondered for a long time what art was for. To show us what we needed to see, dim and dirty in this world, or to imagine something other, some *Pan's Labyrinth* where little boys aren't sexually abused and little girls aren't killed by stepfathers, and women don't dance nude for drunken men out of economic necessity.

Which version of reality? Frida impaled with a bus rail. Frida sprawled on a blood-soaked Detroit hospital bed, her little Diguelito pink and perfectly formed but dead. Snail and machine and wilting purple orchid strung in the sky like balloons, held in her hand on the bed by veins deeply red. Frida, a broken column—

Or Remedios Varos's long, strange figures sailing the Orinoco River in giant goldfish teacups, women gliding along passageways on their hair, hovering above the checkered tile on tiny pointed toes. Labyrinths in smoke. Séances and floating objects.

Neither, Gabe would tell her. Both, she wanted to shout.

He ordered them each a beer, and she sat, mouthwashing hers, watching. She didn't even like beer. He leaned over and clutched her waist, whispering, "They've got nothing on you, babe." He'd misread her as usual.

"It's not that. It seems sad."

"Most of them are ugly anyway." He pointed out a woman with jet-black hair sweeping the small of her back, her red lingerie already splayed on the platform, one black stiletto high in the air, one wrapped around a pole. She didn't have any other body hair. Did she shave every day or wax? Bianca could never wax her pubic hair. She'd tried once. It tugged at the soft, stretchy skin where thigh met pelvis, ripping off a strip of skin, leaving her chafed and limping for days. When she'd shaved, she'd itched like crazy, her chonies become a torture device. As a girlchild, each time she'd showered with Mama, she'd seen the fuzzy dark patch and assumed that's what women have. Dark splotches on their privates and wide, dark-brown stains on their chichis called nipples.

"She's not ugly," Bianca said. "She was probably a beautiful dancer at one time, the way she can arabesque like that." The dancer was stunning, like the women in Gabe's *Maxim* magazine or on his Budweiser posters, with pouty red lips and thick jet-black hair tumbling down her shoulders, the obsidian of her eyes glowing in the spotlight.

"She's haggish, if you ask me. Her skin pudgy in the middle, you can tell she's had kids. I'll bet if you look closely she's all stretch-marked."

"What the hell?" The rope in Bianca's stomach knotted. "I have stretch marks and a pudgy stomach, and I haven't had kids. And anyway, so what? So what if she has stretch marks? Most women do. Cabrón. You're such a chauvinist. What am I even *doing* here with you?"

"Oooh, someone's drunk. Getting feisty there with the cuss words. Getting all tough in Spanish."

She sipped her beer until it became tasteless in her mouth. "I was only pointing out they're not all perfect. Sexy, yeah, but not perfect. Most of them have children at home."

My body never stretched with new life, though it bears the marks. My breasts never flowed with milk, though they hang like heads. Poem fragments swirled around her alcohol-fuzzed head. Aloud, she told him at least they were bringing home money for food. At least their children had clothes and shoes. At least they weren't selling their children.

He called her a spitfire drunk, ready to sting, ready to attack. He was laughing at her. She hated him like this. Hated his patronizing.

Onstage, the woman with jet-black hair squatted at the edge of the platform to collect folded-up bills from the men crowding around cheering and whistling. English or Spanish, catcalls sounded the same. Bianca looked away.

"I thought that wasn't allowed," she said, referring to what some of the men were paying to do one after the other to the woman with jet-black hair. "Like that rap song you explained, no sex in the champagne room?"

"It's not illegal to touch and tongue pussy here." He wasn't looking at Bianca.

"It's disgusting. They're like deer at a salt lick." Her head reeled again. "I don't feel good. Can we leave now?"

"Stop it, Bianca. My cousin's barely having a good time. Close your eyes then and go to sleep if you're sick. Stop being such a baby."

"I don't want to be here." She said it loud enough that the bartender looked up, motioned to the bouncer, who came over to the table.

"¿Hay problema?" he asked.

"No, lo siento. Mi novia está loca, es todo." He was sorry she was crazy. Yeah, him and her both.

The bouncer nodded approval but said in Spanish that he'd better keep her quiet or he'd kick them both out.

Gabe apologized again in his broken kitchen Spanish, and when the bouncer walked away, he pinched Bianca's thigh. She yelped, and Gabe said, "Shut the hell up, stupid. You want to get us in trouble? Look, if you don't like it here, go wait in the car."

She told him to give her the fucking keys then.

"Are you serious?" he asked, his eyebrows raised. His eyes were laughing at her, but she stared at him straight through her blurring vision.

"Yes. Give them to me."

"Whatever. Suit yourself. You'd better not try going anywhere. You're too drunk to drive. Just stay there and sleep it off." She wanted to say she wished she could sleep *him* off, but instead she scooted out of the circular booth from underneath the table, almost tripping on the step, then stumbled out the door. He didn't follow. Behind her, cheering and whistles.

In the truck, she locked the doors, double-checking they'd all locked, then pulled off her strappy black platforms, letting them drop to the floor mat. She propped her nyloned feet beneath her and wrapped her silver sweater over her dress and lycra knees, curling them into her chest. She'd gotten all dressed up for fucking nothing. She was a useless Christmas tree the day after. She turned the key halfway in the ignition for the radio. All that came in were Spanish stations, and she was tired of loud music, but she found a Spanish love song station, leaned back against the headrest, crossed her arms as if hugging her own damn self, and blinked back the tears stinging her eyes. Outside on the curb, a man puked into the gutter, wiped his face with his sleeve, and staggered off with his brown paper-bagged bottle. Behind the truck, half a block down, a metal cart squatted beneath a tent strung with white Christmas lights and red-and-green plastic flags, selling little foil-wrapped tacos on doubled corn tortillas, trays of carnitas, carne asada, lengua, carne adovada, diced onions, cilantro, radish slices, pico de gallo, lime wedges, and salsa. No, she wasn't a Christmas tree. She was a fucking taco cart.

Her stomach lurched, head reeled. She was too scared for sleep. She wanted to call Mama like she'd done the night of the barbecue, raging drunk, dry heaving into Esme's bathroom sink, still screaming to Esme, *I lost the baby, Esme. Remember? I lost her*, while Gabe hollered at her to shut the hell up, of course Esme knew and why open old wounds. She wanted to call Mama and scream at her, *You lost Dad, remember? You lost him!*, like it was her fault. But she didn't get cell reception in Mexico. And she didn't want to hurt Mama. Not again. Mama had driven down to bring Bianca home once. Bianca had said she couldn't leave Gabe, but could Mama buy her a dog so she wouldn't be so lonely at night? At the *Desert Herald*, she'd taken a classified's call for boxer puppies, and could Mama get one for her? So Mama went back to Abuela's and left her there in her empty house with a brown, floppy-eared boxer who sprawled on the carpet with Bianca, howling as she cried.

Useless moon, too beautiful to waste—Sandra Cisneros was no help to Bianca tonight. *Sometimes a woman needs a man who loves her ass*. No. Sometimes a woman needs a man who won't let her wait in the car alone, in the cold, in the dark, with the taco man and the puking drunk on the sidewalk. Sometimes a woman needs a man who won't promise to take her dancing then drag her instead to a strip club because his cousin wasn't having fun. Sometimes—a woman doesn't know what she needs. Especially when she's nineteen, drunk, and sad as a useless moon.

FIFTEEN
NEW YORK, BLACK BLOSSOM

WITH JUBILEE

New York City revealed a secret. In ice-breath and snowflakes, the smell of urine and garbage on the streets, mazes of high-rises and billboards and twinkle lights making pandemonium of Bianca, alone, without her family, time rewound itself.

She'd never been on a plane. She ordered ginger ale and ate hard, brown gingerbread cookies. When the captain announced rough air, Bianca gripped the armrest and imagined herself on the Ferris wheel at the Midwinter County Fair. The plane wobbled as it turned over the dark Atlantic Ocean where white birds dotted the black water like a stippled painting. She forced herself to keep her eyes open and take everything in, despite the turbulence. When she deboarded, the wind was furious and cold as needles, colder than even at the beach in winter.

Her first taste of NYC: a slice of pizza on a flimsy paper plate, slopped cheese and basil and grease she savored while following the signs toward the AirTrain. A mother and a little girl waited at the sliding doors. Bianca reached for Jubilee. She'd forgotten for a moment that Jubilee wasn't with her.

Her bones stung with cold. In the elevator, she pulled out the heaviest jacket she'd brought, a fuchsia peacoat with large black buttons down the front and a matching beret. Her reflection in the elevator glass appeared *city chic*, even if her teeth were chattering; the cold made her feverish as a

girlchild again, refusing to take those pink chewable Tylenols she'd squir-
reled into her cheeks until Mama had left the room, then spit into the
toilet bowl, watching them disappear in a swirl of rose-colored water.

Adult Bianca hadn't brought her meds to New York. She hadn't taken
them since Thanksgiving, despite Mama's warning. Dr. Norris had advised her not to skip doses or risk brain shivers. Was that what she felt
now? Her teeth chattering? An electrical pulse running down her brain?
It was nauseating.

When the doors opened, the crowd corralled toward the AirTrain,
where the doors were closing again. She watched the city whir past. Leafless trees praising the overcast sky; brownstone buildings and bundled
children playing on the sidewalks; brick apartments so tall she wondered
how people carried up their groceries.

She managed to get herself onto the train at Jamaica Station, with Penn
Station as her stop, although she'd nearly screwed up. All those trains and
the confusing ticket kiosk; a throng of agitated people in line behind her, she
panicked and put sixty dollars on her card though she only needed five for the
tram since the train was a separate ticket. So when she left, two weeks later,
she gave her Metro card to a woman bundled in newspaper in a stairwell.

Bianca trudged up the stairs from Penn Station toward the street
above, the sky shimmering silverfish, an ad for *Kinky Boots* flashing sap-
phire. She thought of her mama and Matty. She wanted to tell them, *We
made it.* Her mama had always wanted to see a Broadway show.

When Mama was a girl, she and her older brother had been dropped
off at the movie theater with enough money to watch whatever marathon
was playing, including the old-school musicals she probably wouldn't have
seen otherwise, glamorous and hopeful. The theaters had been a babysitter
when Mama's parents worked several jobs each to pay the bills, but those
musicals had been a life raft. Anything was possible. Anyone could sing
along. Some nights, when Dad was drunk-raging and breaking Mama's
things (her abuela's dishes, her record player, her collection of model
horses she'd scavenged from thrift stores and yard sales and displayed on
shelves), Bianca would see Mama mouthing the words to the songs, and
sometimes, softly, so softly, humming the tunes—*"Don't tell me not to fly,*

I've simply got to / If someone takes a spill, it's me and not you / Who told you you're allowed to rain on my parade."

For a moment, Bianca forgot to be resentful or annoyed with her mama, and only wished she were there, holding her hand.

Up the subway-station stairs, amidst the crowds and garbage and glam (and snow! NYC was snowing!), she wanted to pause in awe in the stairwell, unmoving, unbreathing, but the crowd shoved her toward the wall and her luggage slipped from her hand. She pushed back against the other bodies and made her way toward the sidewalk.

She had no idea how to get to the writers' house though she'd printed out a map. The streets compressed like a miniature of a city. She couldn't make out which way was south.

Behind a roasted chestnut cart, a woman with a Caribbean accent and ruby-red braids stopped scooping the blackened nuts into a paper cone and smiled when Bianca asked her was south this way or that, and the woman pointed her arms perpendicular to Bianca's to show she'd been pointing east and west. The woman's warm smile widening at Bianca's confusion, she handed her a crackling bag as she explained how to get to Greenwich Village. Her mixture of patois and standard English reminded Bianca of the Spanglish that Esme used, and she listened more to the lull of her voice than her actual words. As she thanked her and made her way down the street with her paper cone, all she could remember of the instructions were which direction to start and the taste of chestnut on her tongue.

The Lillian Vernon Creative Writers House stood three stories; leafless and flowerless branches of plants, no doubt green and lush in the spring, vined the bricks and porch rails, now covered in thin trails of ice. Bianca's nose pinkened in the cold.

At the buzzer, she introduced herself to the voice in the box, resisting the urge to tell the gatekeeper inside that she was Coatlicue, goddess who bore destruction, who bore death, that she was undone, she was girl-becoming-something-other.

Instead she said, "I'm Bianca Vogelsang, here for the writers' work-shop." And just like that, they let her in.

Lining the brownstone's walls were pictures of famous writers; some she recognized, like Gwendolyn Brooks, the first black woman poet to win a Pulitzer. (Bianca had looked up whether any Latinas ever won in poetry, but none had.)

A youngish man in khakis and a billowy pastel scarf knotted around his neck and shoulders descended the narrow staircase and welcomed Bianca as she was leafing through a volume of thesis work from the previous year's MFA graduates, struck by one poem about a homeless transgender poet on the street turning tricks for food money before being accepted into NYU's writing program. A line described a teacher who'd given them (the transgender poet preferred this pronoun, a footnote said) money for groceries, but they went out and bought poetry books instead. She could relate and was grateful again for the public library that had kept her fed.

The youngish man introduced himself as Chad, a recent graduate of the MFA program, in charge of the undergrad residency. He handed Bianca a canvas book bag emblemed *NYU Creative Writing*; nestled inside was a glossy pocket folder with the two-week workshop and lecture sched-ule, along with her room assignment and a brass key. She felt professional and empowered. She held the key in her palm as she made her way to her room, lugging her pink roller suitcase each step up.

While Bee was away, Joshua did some detective work. He'd sat in the car, Jayden and Jubilee each in a car seat, while Bee dragged her suitcase into the airport terminal. Then he'd parked at the observation deck so Jayden could watch the planes take off. And for all the times it should have hit him before, it finally sank in. Without Bee in the car, all that was left was him and his boy watching her fly away. And a doll, buckled like an infant in the back seat. He had to know what was going on.

He drove to Matty's house, where Jayden pointed out the guys' cat curled in the windowsill and once inside, he followed the cat toward a back room. Joshua tossed Jubilee onto the sofa like any regular doll and watched for how Matty would react.

Matty saw but only said, "What's up, Josh? Is Bee okay?"

The back door opened, and Handro's voice came through the kitchen, "We have company?" He appeared in the dining room doorway, holding a bottle of wine, a grocery bag, and a bouquet of flowers. "Oh, hey, Josh." He kissed Matty on the lips. Joshua noticed Matty didn't exactly kiss his partner back. "Look what I found at the farmer's market on the way home." Handro held the flowers up to Matty's nose. "Delicious?"

"They're beautiful. I'll get a vase."

While Matty was in the kitchen, Handro whispered, "You think our little bumblebee will be *safe* in New York?"

Joshua began to ask what he meant, but Matty returned with the flowers in a vase.

"Did something happen at the airport?" Matty asked.

Joshua shook his head.

"Come sit down." Matty and Handro exchanged a glance. Matty said, "I've been worried about her all year, Josh. I've gotta tell you, I don't know how good any of this is for her. Staying with you most nights, going so far away . . ." His tone blamed Joshua for his sister's newfound independence.

"She *seems* happy," Joshua said, without the conviction he'd felt earlier. But it was true. Bee *was* happier with him. She was getting better. New York proved that. She'd left Jubilee with him and ventured out on her own.

"She's mentally unstable, Josh."

Joshua's gut clenched. Handro cleared his throat and narrowed his eyes, as if he wanted to tell Joshua something but not in front of Matty.

"Well, you go along with it," Josh retorted. "We all do."

Matty picked at his raw cuticles. "I don't want to push her away again."

Joshua clenched his jaw. "What actually happened to her? I mean, what *is* Jubilee?" He felt like a jerk asking, like he was betraying Bee. He thought of her on her little island, tending the shrubbery.

Matty shrugged. "She's a doll, Josh." He looked hard at Joshua. "How long before you give up and break her heart, and she's back here again, in my house?"

Joshua pulled his inhaler from his pocket, puffed it twice. What was Matty's problem? He wanted to help his sister. He loved her. "I won't break her heart."

"It's more complicated than that." He sounded irritated, his cheeks and nose flushed, his forehead creased. "When I found out you had a son, you know what I mean . . ." He nodded toward the bedroom where Jayden had gone to play with the cat. "I couldn't help worrying about you guys. Bee, yes. But, well . . ." He sighed. "I've been worried about you and Jayden."

"She's not crazy." It had become Joshua's mantra. "I trust her. *Don't you?*"

"What, with Jayden? Yeah, of course. She wants to be a mom."

Handro said, "She *is* a mom."

Matty rolled his eyes. "It's dangerous, okay? When someone's been hurt as much as Bee. I don't want anything bad to happen."

"I wouldn't let anything happen." He wasn't getting anywhere with Matty, not when he mistrusted his intentions. What had happened to the guy who liked Joshua for Beast, who said he hadn't seen his sister this excited in a long time? He thought back to Thanksgiving. He hadn't seemed so angry then. What had Rosana said? *Joshua is changing everything.* Did Matty think Joshua was changing things between him and his sister, taking Bee away? This hadn't gone well. He got up to leave, calling out to Jayden and grabbing Jubilee like a rag doll, tucking her between his arms. "I'll see you later, guys."

Before he stepped out the door, Handro pulled him in for a hug. "My bar. Tonight."

Joshua nodded, and Matty closed the front door.

At the car, Joshua debated strapping Jubilee into the car seat. For the first time he could remember, he felt angry at Jubilee. His hand hovered above the seatbelt as he debated pulling the strap, clicking it. *You're just gonna feel like shit if you don't do it.* He strapped her in.

Later that evening, he dropped off Jayden at the Cal State Fullerton daycare and took Jubilee as far as the parking lot of the bar, but he couldn't bring himself to take her inside. He walked back to the car, cursing himself and imagining her suffocating without the windows rolled down. *Snap out of it, Joshy. She's a doll.*

The bar was Orange County ritzy. He'd never gone to bars, much less gay bars. On the stage, a drag queen sang something he didn't recognize. Handro stood beside a tall table of young men, slick-haired, thin, with tight-fitting clothes. He looked up from where he was leaning toward one of the men, chatting conspiratorially, and waved Joshua over. Walking toward the group of well-dressed men, Joshua felt clumsy and awkward in his baggy jeans, zipper sweater, and tennis shoes. He hadn't combed his hair. It'd probably frizzed into an Afro.

"Hola, Joshy." Joshua liked Handro, the way he said *hola* with an affected *h*, a mixture of the Spanish and slang for *holler*. Handro kissed his cheek. "Meet my friends." He pointed each man out. "Ernesto, Brian, Lolly, and Stefan." Lolly wore makeup. "Well, my lovelies, I have some business to attend to with Joshy here." He winked at Joshua, and Brian made a catcalling sound. "Not *that* kind of business, naughty man. You know I'm taken. Joshy's Matty's sister's boyfriend." The men exchanged a glance. "I'll check with you all later. Enjoy the show."

They sat at a table in the corner, and Joshua asked if Handro would get in trouble for sitting with him while at work. "Hell no! They love me here. M'kay—look, Joshy. Let's get serious. I know Matty can be hard to read. I've lived with him for years and still can't tell what he's thinking. But you need to know, he doesn't hate you."

"Then why does he act like he doesn't want me dating his sister?"

"Honestly? Feels guilty."

"For what?"

Handro uncrossed his legs and sat forward. "He feels like it's *his* fault Bee's the way she is. When he went to the Valley, he said cruel things about her dad. So insensitive. He thinks he pushed Bee toward Gabe. That she would've come home sooner, before she went all . . . well, you know."

"But what does that have to do with me?"

He reached for Joshua's hand. It was strangely comforting, holding another man's hand. Joshua had never done that before. "He worries you'll leave her worse than Gabe did."

He filled in the gaps Matty hadn't told Joshua. Last Easter, when she showed up at their doorstep, Bianca had been bleeding and feverish, at times incoherent, at times nearly catatonic.

"Bleeding where?"

"A botched abortion, most likely."

Joshua thought back to the first time he'd met Jubilee on the beach. He'd thought she was a joke. With Bee gone, it was like the magic had faded away, and Jubilee returned to the lifeless object he'd first seen. She was a doll he'd left in the car. A doll who never cried, never got hurt.

Handro squeezed Joshua's hand. "Just promise us you won't hurt her, and we'll believe you."

Bianca wrote another poem in New York. It had nothing to do with New York.

> I Believed All Poets Were Dead
> & that I'd be the only poet in the world.
> I had no idea there were others
> besides the Frosts & Dickinsons, never
>
> heard of coffeehouses or spoken
> word. Where I grew up, we barreled
> bonfires & burst kegs. Ended in ERs
>
> for drunk-driving quads in the sand or trying
> to keep up with the boys, drink for drink—
> but I loved poetry, even if I didn't know
>
> where it lived. Poetry tasted like the chile
> con limón on the rim of the plastic beer cup,
> smelled like alfalfa in the menudo pot.

I ate it with a knife. Though I met Frida—
she was a painter & she was dead.
I want to be the first Latina poet

to win the Pulitzer. I looked it up online.
None ever has. Do they dare
look us in the mouths? At my

scholarshipped writers' conference
the one Latina editor lifts her pointed Jimmy
Choos from beneath the speakers' panel

& says, I'm tired of reading about barefoot Latinas.
All the Latinas I know wear shoes—
& they're fabulous shoes.

Maybe it had everything to do with New York.

Another poet at the Lillian Vernon House, Makayla, said she'd planned
on attending since she was a sophomore in high school. She asked Bianca
how long *she'd* been a writer, and Bianca said she'd been writing all her
life but had taken only the one class with Elena. Makayla said her mother
helped plan her future writing education as soon as she saw it was her
daughter's passion. She'd attended a prep school that taught her classical
Latin. She'd studied with poets Bianca had to look up, though she nodded
along while Makayla talked, faking the funk.

Makayla had long hair the color of oatmeal and angular features.
Her mother was Catholic and her father was Jewish, and they'd both
strayed from their religions and married each other to stick it to their
parents. She had athletic legs and a flat stomach she showed off in the
bathroom by walking around in bikini underwear and bra. She said
the heater made the house stuffy. Her mom had gone to Princeton; her

mom's parents had wanted her to go to the Catholic college that her sister went to, but she secretly applied to Princeton since it was 1969, the year the university first started allowing women to enroll. When accepted, she took the letter to her parents and told them, "Look, I got in. I have to go." What a badass, her mom. How different Bianca's life might have been if Mama had ever tried sticking it to *her* parents, applying to college when they'd told her she couldn't go. Instead she'd married Matty's dad. Then married Bianca's dad.

Over breakfast at a bagel shop the second morning, Makayla told Bianca that she attended Stanford, earning a degree in comparative literature. She was studying Spanish for Yaul (pronounced Shaw-ool like Saul in the bible), her Argentinean boyfriend. Makayla said she wanted to understand what his mother muttered under her breath. Bianca wanted to tell her about Esme but didn't. Makayla's experiences all seemed so sophisticated compared to Bianca's.

Makayla's friends at school wanted her to go out for girls' nights but she preferred staying home with Yaul. He was her first boyfriend. She told Bianca all the "gritty details" about their sexual escapades. It all sounded so carefree, so fun. Not gritty at all. Bianca said nothing.

"What about you?" Makayla took a bite of her bagel and strawberry schmear. "Do you have a boyfriend or do you go out for girls' nights?"

It was such a strange question, posed like that, in its rigid binary.

"I have a daughter." The words stuck on Bianca's tongue, like she'd been eating raspberries and the prickles had implanted themselves in her mouth.

"Oh," she said, her bagel hanging limply beside her. "Did you, like, *want* her?"

Bianca nodded, tears stinging her eyes. She didn't tell Makayla she'd wanted babies since she was a teenager, how when Makayla was in prep school, Bianca was planning life as a mother . . . because that's what women in the Valley did, the brown women like her.

She excused herself and beelined toward the restroom. Those goddamn brain shivers and nausea. She splashed water on her face and looked into the mirror, seeing Jubilee in the reflection. She tried calling Joshua to check on her, but he didn't answer. She breathed in deeply for five, out for five, like Dr. Norris had coached her, and recited Emily: "Hope is the thing with feathers / That perches in the soul, / And sings the tune without the words, / And never stops at all." After she'd repeated the first stanza five times, she looked in the mirror. Bianca in the flesh. No ghost.

At the table, Makayla apologized. "It's just that you're young," she said. "I couldn't freaking *imagine* having a kid right now. It's hard enough with only myself to take care of." Bianca sipped her tea. Makayla dropped the conversation and talked instead about how last year she'd met the US poet laureate, who'd complimented her poem.

A few days later, before New Year's Eve, she and Makayla took a cab to Times Square, which was chaotic and claustrophobic, then to Central Park, which was lovely—dusk, full moon over the trees. It reminded Bianca of girlhood, but with skyscrapers in the distance instead of bales of yellow hay. They went to the Met, open until nine p.m., later than any museum Bianca had ever been to. She paid the student price for admission (not just "any amount over a dollar," though Makayla only gave a five) because Bianca believed in the arts, in their power to save people like her. Twelve dollars well spent, even if she couldn't get a bag of chestnuts on the way home. She'd grown a taste for them, yellow-soft and meaty inside.

Her favorite painting in the gallery was by a French artist Bianca had never heard of, Marie Denise Villers, called *Young Woman Dreaming*, the plaque claimed had mistakenly been attributed to a man named Jacques-Louis David. Bianca was grateful the art historians had gotten it right. The work might have been a self-portrait—the way the woman leaned protectively over her canvas as she sketched, the way the light emanated from the canvas itself, first illuminating the artist's belly and chest, working toward her pale face and daffodil-colored hair. How could historians ever have believed it was painted by a man? All the companion paintings by men, of women drawing or sewing or playing the piano as high-society women did in the nineteenth century, the activities came across as hobbies, duties, ways to pass time. But in Villers's work, Bianca sensed urgency and secrecy. She leaned in closer to listen.

The young poets ran into a concert off Fifth Avenue as they left the

Met. Bianca felt dizzy at the loud classic rock that reminded her of Dad and she searched for his reddish beard in the crowd, for his sparkling blue eyes and Grateful Dead T-shirt, with a bottle of beer in each hand: one for himself and one for her. *Dad, come back. I need you.*

She couldn't make out any faces except Makayla's, pink from cold and laughing while pulling her hand and tugging her through the crowd yelling, *We're having an adventure,* as they were corralled in tight lines down the sidewalk until they broke free. Bianca's feet cramped from all the walking, and her skin was clammy, but they kept walking toward Times Square through the noise and ghosts. She had to cover her ears. Finally Makayla steered them into a corner café. Bianca's face was numb; her stomach ached with hunger.

She'd spent all her cash on the museum ticket, but Makayla offered to buy her a sandwich. They sat at a window bench, watching people hurry past, Makayla chatting about her boyfriend not knowing what he wanted to do when he graduated; they were all still kids figuring out their lives, Makayla said. Though it was freezing, a naked woman sauntered through Times Square with her body painted like an American flag, advertising God knows what. Bianca's stomach turned. Inexplicably, the smell of citrus mixed with paint.

When she came back from the restroom, Makayla said, "God, Bee, you keep going to the bathroom. Are you, like, *pregnant* or something?"

Dad's many-worlds hypothesis came to her again. In every moment, every decision we make, every possible outcome is happening somewhere—in dimensions we can't reach with our limited senses but that must exist according to quantum data. How a particle can't possibly be a wave and a particle at once, how it can't be blurry and shapeless because we are clear, our world, it has a shape. Yet they *are* both at once. They are both fuzzy and concrete. They are both waves and particles.

Bianca was pregnant.

She hadn't wanted to see it, so it hadn't existed.

Makayla spoke it into existence. Bianca could no longer ignore the proof of her body. Sore, sticky nipples, swollen all over, bloated, foggy brain, overwhelming smells everywhere.

The next day was New Year's Eve, which meant it had been over a month since Thanksgiving, since she and Joshua had first slept together. And her period had gone missing over Christmas. She hadn't seen it because she'd been so focused on Jubilee.

The next day in workshop, poet Rigoberto González read from his poems about Latina women in *Black Blossoms*, dangerous and fierce women, his mother, murderesses and the murdered, Frida and Lizzie Borden, the unsung invisible women.

When he read "when the sun sets next it will // blossom with the blackest mushrooms and the moths / will lay their eggs on your leathery smiles," Bianca thought of what blackness or beauty could be blossoming inside of her. When he read her poetry and told her it was a beautiful, aching work with a strong voice of authority, when he gave her recommendations of awards she should submit to along with his business card so she could email him revisions because he was eager to nurture a new Latina poet . . . she was still seeing the pink cross that bloomed so bright on the test in the writers' house bathroom.

In this world, in this hypothesis, Bianca was pregnant again.

SIXTEEN
LETTER TO JUBILEE

I'm another riddle, my daughter. I've done it again. Three times in six years. I'm an even equation; two by two we're blue, two by two I lose you, only I refuse another bitter transformation. Tell Sylvia Plath the first time it happened it was an accident. I'd thought I could become Coatlicue, my daughter. What does that make you? I thought I was so tough. But for what?

I was wrong.

I was wrong to hold on.

But I can't let go.

When the boys take you out to the country, though the moon may be full and the hay may smell sweet as painted earth and sweetened sky silhouette back seats . . . and the boys tell you that you don't have a choice, and you think you don't because all you want is respect, all you want is love, but not the kind that ends in a stale truck bed, not the kind that ends with your mouth screwed open in its little o—

O please know that you don't have to stay and sacrifice, you don't have to yellow the mound of hay.

I wanted to be revered. I wanted to be sacred.

Cherished.

A spiderwoman. A fat cow.

And sometimes a girl shoves her ass onto a boy like a baboon if she thinks it'll mean recognition, in the end.

No. I'm hanging on to myself now, baby girl. I'm selfish as gold, and I can't afford the past.

Anyone else might see artifice or illness. But I see atonement. I see redemption.

I need a way to keep on breathing. Tell Sylvia Plath to let me go—

O let me keep on breathing.

SEVENTEEN
THE GRAVEYARD

BEFORE JUBILEE

Not all ditches are deep enough for swimming. Especially in the desert. When the floodwaters come, they make rich, porous homes for the pupfish and minnows, make rapids that'll carry them safely to more stable bodies. But when the waters recede, that small life must bore into the mudholes to wait, dredging pockets of wetness beneath the hard dirt until the sky opens its mouth again. Unless the ditches are cement and meant for enduring drought, meant for perennial irrigation. Then the fullness of their bellies or emptiness, their rushing into rivers or dribbling to spittle on the chin, belongs to the whims of farmers, of nature, of need. The opening of a gate. The running of the bull-waters.

No, the ditches are not always full. Sometimes they are barely scum ponds. Foam at the maw of a dog.

Even so. A body can drown in as shallow as an inch or two. All it takes is the stubborn lungs to keep gathering in what would dam them, ignorant lungs. All that evolution. All that breaking down at the gas-exchange chambers. All that flooding of the blood-gas barriers.

A body can drown in such a dribble of water. The damage held in those traitor lungs, anxiously trying to diffuse all the wrong round molecules, puzzling together all those ill-fitting shapes in a child's shape-sorter box. H_2O in the O_2 slot. The way a star will never squeeze through the triangle hole. Though a body may gasp.

Dad had taught Bianca the periodic table. They'd memorized the elements set to *Orpheus in the Underworld* (*With oxygen so you can breathe / And fluorine for your pretty teeth*).

The H in the topmost left, atomic number 1, the lightest element, most abundant chemical substance in the universe. The O in the top third column from the right, atomic number 8, highly reactive, like Bianca, readily bonds with most compounds.

Readily bonds in ditches. In children's wading pools. In bathtubs.

The saddest part was, Bianca was a strong swimmer. Always had been.

If only her father had asked for her help.

"Hair of the dog, loca," Gabe said, handing her a mug, his voice morning-husky, playful. He'd been too tired and drunk to drive the extra block back to Bee's empty house after the strip club in Mexicali, so he'd let her crash with him.

She still wore her party dress, though she'd left her nylons wadded up with her platform wedges on Gabe's floor, beside the weight bench he still used but never with the same motivation as when she'd first met him in high school, when he still had hopes of a football scholarship. Why they'd convinced Bee to let her cactus flower go . . . Then he'd taken a hit to his back that he never recovered from. Not after surgery, not after physical therapy. He'd thrown away his football gear, and they'd never mentioned it again. Now he only used the bench in fits and starts. Bianca imagined it a saguaro cactus, tall and proud, with its goalpost arms reaching toward the sky. Spindled with long, needled thorns. And along the top, a crown of saguaro flowers, bright white and smelling of overripe melons.

She reached out from under the bed sheet, took the mug from Gabe. She could smell the pungent tomato juice and spices before she brought the Bloody Mary to her mouth, but when she looked into the mug, a shock of thick red wafted a faint iron smell through her, so she had to close her eyes and chug to keep from gagging.

She got it halfway down before she had to stop for air.

Gabe was smiling wryly at her. "Feel better?"

"Never," she said, heart-on-sleeve.

He came closer, wiped the tomato juice from her upper lip. "Sorry about the mugs. My parents had a party last night, and all the glasses are still in the sink."

She smiled now too, thinking but not saying aloud, *Tontito, why not wash one then?* Instead she said, "I can pretend I'm a wino this way, hiding my liquor in plain sight."

He kissed her. Tenderly, the way he had when he was still a boy and she was still a girl. Before they'd grown and fucked everything up.

She pulled back, groaning but not with passion. "My head hurts."

"You drank half of Mexico last night." He chuckled.

"Did I?" She remembered dancing, she remembered the strippers and being angry, so hurt. But had she drunk more after that, after she'd gone to sleep it off in the truck? When alcohol was involved, Bee couldn't often remember everything she'd said or done. It scared her, mostly because it reminded her of Dad. "Do you know why they call it hair of the dog?" she asked him.

He squinched his eyes in a mock thoughtful expression. "Mmmm, no. Lay it on me, Profesora." He squeezed her ass, pressed his face against her neck, kissed her collarbone.

Her red-bearded father had taught her this. He'd also read to her from his two favorite Roberts—Burns and Louis Stevenson—in his best burr, his birthright and hers, although her dark skin and hair in this Valley had cut her off from her Anglo side. "It's from a Scottish folk remedy for rabies; plucking hair from the vicious dog and applying it to the wound will cure the infection." She pressed her fingers together and tweezed a piece of Gabe's baby-fine black hair, pulled it out.

"What the hell?" He groaned then playfully bit her shoulder. "I'm a dog now, huh?"

"A vicious one."

She dropped the strand of hair into her mug, feeling like a bruja, a powerful witch. And gulped the rest down.

Shakira sang, *My hips don't lie*. Gabe's ringtone. He was low-key obsessed with Shakira. They'd seen her on Univision, before she'd crossed over to Gringo pop lovers, when she was still a so-called political rockera with black hair, singing angsty Spanish calls-to-arms. But Gabe loved the blond, belly-dancing version better. Of course he did.

He reached across the bed to the floor, fished his phone out of the jeans he'd worn to the club, tapped the screen.

"Who was that?" she asked.

"Alarm."

Did his eyes shift upward to the left, a sign of lying? Bee couldn't tell.

"Why'd you set an alarm for a Sunday morning?"

"To remind me to call Lana."

She wanted to say, *how sad*. He needed an alarm to remember to call his daughter. But then she thought, she wished her Dad could set an alarm to call her. She said, "Oh, that's sweet."

He took the phone into the next room, and Bee, alone with her empty mug, got up, smoothed out her wrinkled dress, and went to see if Esme was awake yet, maybe needed help with breakfast.

Turned out Lana had a fever, pobrecita. Gabe and Katrina fought over why she hadn't called him. Lana was two years old. Did Katrina still need to call Gabe every time their baby was sick? Yes, she did. Dammit. Of course she did. He wanted to be there. He had a right to be there. Why was she always trying to keep his kid from him?

Bee heard this version when Gabe relayed it to Esme, as Bee browned the tortillas in the skillet and scrambled the eggs for the migas.

When it was finished, he guzzled down the breakfast, pecked Esme on the cheek, and said, "Come on, Bee, I'll give you a ride home on my way to Katrina's."

Hadn't he meant Lana's?

Bee didn't even care this morning, honestly. She was so fucking tired. Of course he hadn't invited her. Did she even want to spend her Sunday in his baby mama's trailer in Westmorland, listening to them fight over their feverish toddler?

God no.

Her head throbbed.

"I'll call you later, okay, punk?" A sobriquet he'd called her since high school, but right now she felt like his kid sister, his fuck buddy. As she stepped out of the truck via the side rail, he said, "I love you."

She knew he did. She also knew it wasn't enough.

If she explained why she was digging in the backyard with the rusted shovel Dad had left in the shed on the side of the house, who would have understood?

Not Gabe, that's for sure.

She would've called Lily, but Lily was dealing with a houseful of demons of her own. Not quite as literal as Bee's. But nearly everyone in Lily's house had one ailment or another, and Lily's forever-boyfriend Sam meant well but never quite got the hint that sometimes girlwomen need *alone time*. As in, girls only. Things between Lily and Bee hadn't been the same since they'd gotten a Gabe and a Sam. No, she couldn't call Lily. She had her own frustrating life and didn't need Bee's added drama. *Therefore do not worry about Bee, for Bee will worry about herself. Each Lily has enough trouble of her own.*

Her oft-neglected boxer scampered around Bee as she gripped the shovel and struck the hard dirt beneath the dead, yellowed grass where a girlhood swing set once stood, before its metal hinges sagged and warped, the slide rutting inward, a sharp, jagged tuna-can lid, and they'd had to tear it down before it collapsed. It was a good thing Gabe had dropped Bee off; she'd almost forgotten about Kanga, and the pobrecita had needed her breakfast too. It was a wonder she could keep this puppy alive.

What had she been thinking, getting a dog in her precarious existence? Always hovering on an edge. She couldn't scrape together enough money for dog food a few weeks back and had cooked up the ground beef she'd bought for her own tacos, fed the dog a whole bowlful. Lord, the vomit. She hadn't known any creature could vomit such copious amounts. Bee felt horrible. She had no right to be a dog mother. Much less any human creature's mother. And that thought had gripped her with a sadness she still hadn't been able to shake.

Rust flaked off the shovel handle onto her hands. She could already feel blisters forming. She gripped tighter. The weeping shade tree in the center of the yard kept her from the sun, but the humidity in this desert, even in November, clung her sweat-heavy dress to her in minutes. She still hadn't taken off her dancing clothes. Her dad had planted the lebbek tree, an Indian deciduous he'd read about in the *Desert Herald* (in a section called the Horticulturalist, which gave plant advice for their plot of desert) and had gone out and bought a fledging, planting it dead smack in the center, so when it grew, and it grew rapidly, requiring little moisture in the soil, it would cool almost the entire yard. He'd read the article aloud to Bee, and she'd loved the poetry of the journalist: "Another strong point in their favor is the ease with which they may be transplanted at all ages, with little danger of loss." She loved the shade tree's other names too. Its apodos: *flea tree, koko, woman's tongue tree.* With its tufts of downy dandelion, its long, iridescent, string-bean seed pods. She could see the fleas and the tongues, slipping in and out of the leaves.

Sometimes she'd pluck as many tongue pods as she could, peel each one back, give each round seed a name before planting it in the dirt, praying she would sprout into a girl who could talk back, sassy, a girl who could speak for herself.

The problem came when she started seeing real tongues, not seed pods but slick, pink, slimy things, wriggling from the branches.

Severed tongues. They floated her to the ceiling at night. Kept her pinned where she shouldn't have been.

Had Bianca floated through the hallways at night, upside down, before the tongues?

She must have.

Had it begun the night Dad first attempted suicide? At Bisabuela's house in Los Angeles? His slurring, seizured exit through the hallway and into the night when Bee was four years old.

Bee had two fathers growing up: 1.) the fun-loving Dad who danced her around the kitchen on his feet; made her the jelly to his peanut butter sandwiches; rode her on the back of his bicycle, always with a helmet; pushed her on the swing set beneath the shade tree he'd planted for her, reciting, *Oh, how I love to go up in a swing, up in the sky so blue*; taught her as many numbers of pi as she could keep track of, insistent they could follow the irrational number into infinity. That father had carried her into infinity.

2.) the other Dad. The mean drunk. The terrifying drunk.

And only one of them had died.

The mean drunk had stayed with her. He haunted her.

> One need not be a Chamber—to be Haunted—
> One need not be a House—
> The Brain has Corridors—surpassing
> Material Place—

quoth the Emily. "So that now, to still the beating of my heart, I stood repeating," sayeth the Poe. Her hands ached in the familiar way of the shovel. How far down had she hollowed last time?

As she thrust into the plot of backyard, scabbed over from her latest dig, she recounted as many words as she could for *house*, starting with Frida's Casa Azul, Blue House. Split house. Hothouse. Icehouse. Fish house. Dollhouse. Broken doll. *Scratch that.* Broken house. Greenhouse. Black house. House of cards, crumbling. Slaughterhouse. Housewarming. Welcome home, baby. Hell house. Or was that hellhound? Sugarhouse. Housefly, buzzing on the dog vomit house. Houseplant, wilting. Madhouse. Ay, there's the rub. Angry fucking haunted house. Root house. Belly house. Father house. Dead house. Severing her from *before* and *after* house. Too many *befores* and *afters*. Severing her like the seed pods of her women's tongues. House tongue.

She'd never told anyone about the abortion. Not even her parents. Especially not her parents.

Thud. The shovel knocked against wood, a familiar sound. She dropped to the ground, and on hands and knees began digging with her hands, dry, rocky soil caking under her fingernails. Kanga sniffed at the edges of the hole, pawing curiously at the clods of dirt that Bee was scooping to the edges; she didn't shoo away her dog. She'd never had company out here before, not like this. It felt nice not to be alone. And not to have to explain what she was doing.

Sweat beaded her neck and forehead, as she cupped her hands into the earth and dredged up the wooden box, the size of an old-fashioned milk crate that could hold half a dozen glass, quart bottles of milk, lidded; she'd found the crate in her dad's chemistry lab at the high school, where she used to visit sometimes when she was a little girl, mildly sick, and Mama was working because there was no other family in the Valley. So she would curl up in Dad's lab, making a bed for herself beneath his desk, his lab coat for a pillow. Other times, when school had let out early but her brother had commitments, Dad would pick her up and bring her back to his lab, and she'd wander around reading all the labels on the bottles of chemicals, playing with the eye-washing station, swiping her finger along the countertops searching for traces of magic in the science.

In one storage closet, she'd found a crate of beakers and wanted so badly to conduct experiments of her own that she pulled it out and headed toward the swivel stools and counter when she tripped on the linoleum floor and lurched forward, dropping the crate and all its glass contents. Dad had found her gingerly picking up the largest chunks.

She'd expected him to scream, like at home. Her body instinctively waited for the flinch. But instead he asked if she was all right. She nodded, and he got the broom and dustpan. After they'd finished cleaning, he'd taken out another set of equipment, filled one beaker with water, added phenolphthalein, then poured the mixture into a second beaker he'd filled with a base. In this way, he changed water into wine. The glass of clear water turned spectacularly bloodred. Bianca had gasped in wonder and delight, clapped her hands. "Another, Daddy. Another!"

Whether he'd performed another or not, she couldn't remember, but he'd sent her home with the crate, filled with a few supplies (sans chemicals beyond basic kitchen-pantry ingredients) so she could recreate her own experiments whenever she wanted.

As the years, too, changed from water to wine and her father's alcoholism worsened, Bianca buried the box. Not empty. Its contents:

1.) The Nutcracker pin that broke her mama's heart. When Bee was a tin soldier in the ballet, a professional show put on by the Yuma Ballet Company, who'd come all the way from Arizona and recruited young dancers in the Valley, Mama had been so proud. After the final curtain call, when all the other girls' moms brought them flowers, Bianca's mama had given her a gold-plated Nutcracker pin. Bianca had been so angry, she'd shoved it back in Mama's hands, tears streaming down her face. She'd never gotten flowers before, had wanted to be just like all the other girls in town. In the car ride home, Mama had said, her voice low and plaintive, *Flowers wilt, mija. I wanted to give you something that wouldn't die.*

2.) Bee's first communion rosary. From the day of her mismatched lacy white socks and the pristine dress, the white-flowered wreath and satin slippers that Mama had bought for her at the swap meet in Calexico. Bianca had lost the dress and socks, the wreath and ballet slippers, or maybe Mama had put them away in her cedar chest at the end of her bed. But the rosary Bee had kept in her bedroom. And she'd put it in the coffin box when she wasn't a girl anymore.

3.) The baby outfit she'd shoplifted the day she'd found out she was pregnant. A simple, yellow onesie. Though in her heart, she knew it must've been a girlchild. Come to save her. She'd kept the pregnancy test too, its cross still marking someone was there.

4.) One jagged face piece of the porcelain doll her father had smashed in a drunken rage. Bee couldn't fit all the bruises into the box. But this doll named Penelope she'd loved all through girlhood. What was left of her. She fit. Mama had thrown away the rest, but this piece had hidden under Bee's bed. And she'd salvaged it. Buried it here.

In the graveyard of broken things, stolen things. Her father had stolen her girlhood. Gabe had stolen her girl. Or at least, the girl she'd been.

You're not supposed to exhume bodies in a graveyard but Bianca couldn't help it. She had to hold the skeletal remains under the lebbek tree, its tongues warbling in the desert heat. She had to lie on the matted grass and clutch the dirt while the dog ran off to sniff out a neighbor's cat. She had to hold them until she buried them again. She couldn't let them go.

EIGHTEEN
HEART. BEATING

WITH JUBILEE

Joshua watched Bianca hanging her Frida Kahlo reprints on his bedroom walls, which had been bare before she began refurnishing, and he liked the new colors. *The Broken Column. Still life with Pitahayas.* Monkeys, monkeys everywhere. Portraits in beads and parrots. But *The Two Fridas* was Bee's favorite; she'd said: "One woman, a part of another woman, cauterizing her own heart. Two women in one. One hanging on. The other letting go." All while balancing atop their bed, hammer in one hand, wooden painting in the other, nail between her lips.

Instead of backing off as Matty had advised, Joshua had asked Bee to live with him for real, and she'd agreed. They'd gotten her a background check and fingerprint scan since she'd be an adult living in the house with Jayden, same as Joshua had when he'd first become a kin caregiver, but she'd passed that with flying colors—though he had to admit, a part of him had been scared she wouldn't. He felt a little ashamed he was so relieved to see in official documentation that she had no history of arrests or convictions. He'd ticked that off his mental list. Whatever had happened to her in the Valley, it hadn't been criminal.

The past few weeks though, since she'd officially moved in, she'd been moody and sullen. He wouldn't go to Matty again. It wasn't so bad; nothing he couldn't handle. He'd heard that women could act bizarre—you know, hormones. Besides, compared to Olivia, Bee was a cakewalk. He hadn't lived with a woman since Patti and that was back when he was a kid, so he hadn't paid attention to whether she'd left tampons in the trashcan or whatnot. He just figured Bee must've had a painful period because she went to the bathroom a lot and wasn't interested in sex. He didn't ask more than if she needed anything. He didn't want to be insensitive so he gave her space. She let him cuddle her in bed and she still kissed him. He could've kissed that woman for hours, asthma flaring or not, though he could swear since he'd been with Bee, everything was better, even his asthma. He needed his inhaler less and less.

He helped her move into his place the week she got back from New York. They wanted it settled before the spring semester. After he'd finished loading the last of her things into his car and gone back to get her goldfish, Matty had taken him aside through a sliding glass door to the side yard and warned him that though she seemed fine, to watch her closely. He repeated *mentally unstable*, and Joshua shifted the fishbowl in his hands, uncomfortable. "She could still relapse, you know," Matty had said. "She's not *cured* or anything." He said *cured* in a way that made Joshua think he wanted her to relapse. But that was crazy. He'd probably misread his tone.

Now Bee was all moved in, and they'd set the goldfish on a table in the living room to make it official. She and her Jubilee were living with Joshua and his boy. Nothing left but to hang artwork in their bedroom, she'd said.

"I have big news." She stepped down from the bed where she'd finished nailing in *The Two Fridas*. She sat cross-legged on the comforter, staring at Joshua.

He took a deep breath, trying to gauge whether it was good news or bad, her moods had been so quirky lately. But she looked cute sitting there all serious for an important meeting in her pajamas, hammer in her hands, and that watermelon glow that hadn't left her cheeks and face since she'd moved in with him. In fact, she looked more beautiful than ever.

"Okay," he said, freezing in a stiff, robotic pose, mock bracing himself, playing along. "I'm ready. What's the good word?"

She set the hammer in her lap and said, her eyes straight at his, "I'm pregnant."

He stared at her, waiting for her to crack a smile or jump up and start laughing and say she was teasing him and he was so gullible. But she stayed composed, returning his gaze without flinching. He cleared his throat, the muscles in his neck and jaw tensing.

"You are?"

She nodded.

He pulled out his inhaler and puffed. Seriously, there was no air in his lungs. There went his theory she'd cured his asthma. "When did you . . . you're preg . . . really?" *Why are you questioning her? You think she's lying? Like one of those fake pregnancies? You want to ask her for the damn pee stick?*

Bianca nodded again, and her face looked like it might crack, this strange half-smiling, half-on-the-brink-of-tears. "I can bring you the sticks I peed on as proof."

"Nah, I'm good. I mean, I'm sorry."

"You're sorry?"

"No, I'm sorry for asking you like that. I'm . . . I'm . . . You're pregnant?"

She threw a pillow at him. She was crying but in this weird hiccough way like she was also laughing only she was crying. "I am. With child. In calf. Half-caff. Knocked up."

He wanted to hold her. But he couldn't move. He stared, transfixed by her, cross-legged on the bed, tank top hugging her breasts, the thin material showing the outlines of her nipples, rounded belly, and hips he couldn't get enough holding.

Could she handle this? Were they ready? What about Jayden?

She frowned. "Josh, are you upset?" She looked at him like he'd run over Kanga and threatened to run over her too. "Why aren't you saying anything?"

"I'm . . ." He grabbed his inhaler, puffed it twice more.

"Great, I've sent you into an asthma attack." She rolled her eyes melodramatically.

He strode across the room and lifted her from the bed, wrapping her legs around him. "*You're pregnant?*" he asked again, as if those were the only words he knew.

She laughed in that same hiccough way. "Yes. I'm pregnant."

He held her in the air, clasping her feet around his torso. He kissed her forehead, her cheeks, her lips. "We're having a baby," he said.

"*Another* one."

His stomach dropped.

He glanced past her at the bassinet in the corner of the room. She'd replaced the playpen he'd set up there for her with the one from her old bedroom at Matty's, the one that rocked and vibrated and played weird "womb" sounds. Bee was pregnant. With a real child.

And mostly Joshua was happy. But also, it was hard to breathe, like his heart had grown too large for his chest. There was no room for his lungs.

Bianca stopped seeing Dr. Norris. His receptionist called to reschedule the appointment she'd missed, and when Bianca told her she wasn't returning, Dr. Norris called, in his Scottish accent that slayed her. He was concerned, and why had she made such a hasty decision when they were beginning to make progress? She stood on the balcony of Josh's apartment watching traffic cross the 57; she pictured Dr. Norris as William Wallace or Mama's priest, riding a horse into battle for her. She'd never needed him, she said. It was Mama's idea to unshock her in the first place. She was fine.

While he talked, Bianca stared at the arboretum, catty-corner to the freeway. The sugar pines were her favorite. They never lost their leaves, when all the others yellowed or bared their branches toward winter. The cactus were resilient too. But shorter, so she couldn't see them over the garden walls, not like the tall pines and oaks and firs.

Dr. Norris asked about Jubilee.

She reminded him their sessions were voluntary. It was her right to end them. He was calm in a patronizing way that soothed her, which she hated, because she fessed up about Joshua. She didn't owe Dr. Norris anything. She would never have to see the psychiatrist again, and it wasn't his business what she did in her noncrazy life. But something about his soothing accent and the fact that she could also picture him inside a confessional booth, the phone offering the anonymity of a veil, made her want to swear to this neutral territory that she'd moved past the Valley and that Joshua took good care of her (not that she needed taking care of . . . with those fucking conventional and misogynist undertones . . . but also, it was true).

Dr. Norris asked about her meds, and she told him she'd had to stop taking those a long time ago because she was pregnant. She steeled herself for a speech, but instead Dr. Norris said, "It sounds like you've found a way to reshape yourself from that wishbone you loved. You've found a way to reconcile the floating pieces of *The Lovers*."

She had to put her phone down for a second to wipe tears from her face and the screen of the phone with her sleeve before she could say anything. The arboretum's trees were nodding her on in the breeze. Dr. Norris had remembered what she'd said about his painting. He'd understood what she'd meant when she began splitting—self from self.

"Thank you, Dr. Norris. I think I'll miss you after all."

Joshua marveled at how the semester had commenced and somehow they were making it work, their situation: college students, Bee pregnant, raising Jayden. They'd picked classes to coincide with each other's schedules, and he still had foster care money for Jayden and his grants and scholarships for growing up in the foster care system himself. Bianca had scholarships and loans, and her part-time job at the writing center, so it didn't feel like a stretch in the beginning, their new state of affairs. He drove them all to Matty's to drop off Jubilee in the mornings, then to campus where Jayden went to daycare and they went to class, and in the afternoons they picked up Jubilee then all went home together. Like a family. Yeah, it was weird they had to drop off and pick up Jubilee, but he didn't want to tip the scales. They were fine. They were normal. It was such a small detail.

He went with Bee to her ob-gyn, but that first appointment, she asked him to wait in the lobby. "I'm embarrassed about the pap smear," she said.

He said he understood, but he didn't. *You sure she's not lying to you about this pregnancy?* This wasn't the fifties anymore. He hadn't expected to wait like the husbands in old sitcoms. But he respected Bee, so he waited outside.

At the next doctor appointment a month later, she asked him to come in because the ultrasound tech was there. "I want you to hold my hand when the tech looks for a heartbeat," Bee said. She was all jittery and cold, which made him nervous too. But he was relieved. Bee was letting him in. She was telling the truth. He felt ashamed for doubting her. "I'm ten weeks," she said. "The heart should've been beating for a while. It's not always detectable this early. I hope they find it."

"Don't worry, it'll be there." He said it, but he was scared. Things he loved got taken away. His sister, Olivia, for instance. He had no idea where she was. Jayden never asked for her anymore, not since Bee had come along.

Bee clutched his hand as the tech squeezed cold jelly onto her skin and began sliding the monitor around. Joshua held his breath and imagined for a split second what would happen if the tech couldn't find anything. If from her white coat she looked at them sadly, shaking her head. For a split second, he imagined everything falling apart.

Thump-thump. Thump-thump. A baby. The tech found it. A baby he'd helped make.

Tears smeared Bee's cheeks. He put his face to hers and whispered, "Marry me." *Stay with me. Sign the papers that show me I'm yours. That I'm real. That we are.*

At first she looked at him as if he'd told a wildly inappropriate joke. Like he was a clown and needed to stop messing with her. His heart beat so loud he swore she could hear it. She didn't say anything for so long, he was choking on his own heartbeat against her silence. He was tempted to start laughing and pretend to *be* a damn clown.

Then she grinned and wrapped her arms around his neck. "Yes."

He kissed Bee and the tech was clapping, saying, "Congratulations."

The baby was real. Bee was marrying him.

Then why was he still scared?

Sundays, if they'd finished all their papers and studied for their exams, they visited the Getty Museum, a white castle atop a hill overlooking UCLA, the school Bianca said she should've gone to, pointing it out on the tram that carried them upward from the street-level entrance where the park-and-ride bus dropped them off to the marbled museum stairs.

"But then you wouldn't have met me," he answered.

"Ever the optimist, Joshy."

Los Angeles glimmered through the glass, so pristine from the tram. The Getty was a favorite spot in the city; every time he visited, he turned from pauper to prince, and riding up toward Olympus, he felt, just briefly, the separation rich folks must've felt in their sparkling, white architecture high above folks like him and his little family.

Bianca, who was beginning to show, held Jayden's hand as they stared out the window. Joshua tugged off the straps of his heavy backpack, chock-full of everything he needed, and dug through the front pocket for the camera. He sifted through a miniature first-aid kit, flashlight, batteries, cell phone charger cords, and Swiss army knife. It had taken a few years, but he finally stopped carrying a change of clothes for himself the way he'd done growing up, since he'd never known when he'd need to run. He still carried a change of clothes for Jayden, because accidents happen.

He snapped the picture, and Jayden asked, "Bee, what do we get at the *getting museum?*"

She smiled and winked over at Joshua, aware he'd been photographing them. "You mean, the *Getty* Museum?"

"That's what I said, the getting museum. What do we *get* there?"

"An appreciation for works of art."

"Huh?"

"You get to fall in love with art."

"I already love him."

"Who?"

"Art!"

Bee smiled wide, tickling him. "Tontito, you got me."

They stepped off the shuttle and climbed the white steps, everything shining and clear as a fantasy. A photograph of a family. Joshua's own version of the American dream.

"What's the sign say?" Jayden asked.

"The J. Paul Getty Museum," Bee answered.

"I thought this was Art's museum."

As they walked around the galleries, Bee's phone rang several times though she never answered, and in the East Pavilion, staring intently at the late-Renaissance art, she silenced it.

He'd never pried before, but something about this family outing as an engaged couple with a baby on the way piqued his interest and gave him the courage to speak up. "Hey," he whispered, "who's been calling you all day?" She didn't answer immediately but kept her gaze fixed on the painting of *Lot and His Daughters* by Orazio Gentileschi, and for an uncomfortable moment, he wondered if it was her ex, the notorious Gabe he'd heard about with such disdain from Matty.

"The bible *twists* . . ." she said, nodding toward the painting of two women in a cave, shielding their father, who appeared to be grieving, from the destruction beyond. Bianca said nothing else, but the melancholy in her voice told him her mood had shifted from playful to somber in the time it had taken him to ask her who'd called. He was accustomed to her mood swings, but even he had to admit that her sidetracks, her evasions, sometimes grew tiresome. He knew loving her required patience. And he had that in droves. A kid waiting for parents who never came learns all the waiting games.

He didn't press. He could wait.

It wasn't until later that evening as they sat together, legs tangled on the couch reading for their separate classes, once Jayden had gone to bed and Jubilee was laid down in her bassinet for the night, that he asked again.

She didn't even put down her book. "That was no one, I told you." (No, she hadn't told him. But he wouldn't start a fight.)

And one last time when they brushed their teeth for bed, after she'd eaten a few saltines to sop up the sleep nausea.

"Seriously, Bee. Who was on the phone?"

"Joshy. What's going on? Why are you acting so inquisitive? It was just a solicitor. I blocked their number."

"Why are *you* being so dodgy? If it were a solicitor, why didn't you tell me the first time I asked? And come to think of it, that's a diligent solicitor, calling you all damn day."

She stopped brushing and turned toward him, paste foaming at her mouth, but said nothing. Any other day he would've thought she looked cute. He shoved his toothbrush into the holder. He couldn't remember being this mad at her, and he couldn't even pinpoint why. He just couldn't understand why she was keeping more secrets from him. The past, fine. But whoever was calling was calling *now*. Why didn't she want him to know? He sighed. "Just forget it. You have toothpaste on your face," he said and walked out of the bathroom.

After she'd fallen asleep hugging her pregnancy pillow, he got up and took her phone into the bathroom. Tried a few different birthdays for the code. His. Hers. Nothing worked. He couldn't get in without her knowing.

Then a text message flashed across the screen. "Mija, I hope you're safe." It was from someone named Esme.

He typed Jubilee into the password box. The screen unlocked.

Esme had texted Bee a dozen messages over the past several months, all of which were unanswered. The predominant theme was *I miss you and worry about you and hope all is well.*

His stomach clenched as he clicked over to another string of unanswered messages in her log. "Bee answer me. I'm sorry okay? I was an insensitive shit! But this has gone on long enough!" and "Chica! I've tried calling you 100x! Answer me!" and "I don't have your fam's # & this isn't funny. I just want to know you're okay" and "If I have to drag my ass to LA I will" and "Sigh. I hope you're safe. Love you forever."

They were all from someone named Lily.

He said nothing that night, to keep the peace. He was biding his time. He told himself, *She will open up to me. I know she will.* At least it wasn't her ex. Just a fight between friends. Esme and Lily. Esme sounded familiar, but he couldn't quite put his finger on where Bee had mentioned her. Bee's childhood bestie. He'd never had one, so he didn't know what friendship was like beyond the movies. And from those he inferred girl fights could be catty and vicious. He didn't need to get in the middle. He was sure Bee would tell him all about it, in her own time. Like she always did.

The weeks leading up to the wedding were hectic. He hadn't meant to upset her, not at the apartment laundromat. He'd had every intention of allowing Bee to bring Lily up on her own. But as they went through their routine (her loading the dirty clothes into the washers and him folding the clean clothes) they discussed who would come to witness and sign the marriage certificate, and he couldn't help himself.

"Are you going to invite your friend Lily? I'd love to meet her." He almost slipped and asked about Esme too, but couldn't remember what Bee had said about her, and she would've known he'd been spying.

Instead of answering him, she dropped the bag of quarters into the washing machine and cursed. He stopped folding, sighed, shook his head. This woman. He crossed the aisle to her and started fishing out the coins. "You trying to launder our money now?"

She smiled but said nothing.

Once all the quarters were back in the bag, he lifted her onto a machine, and she wrapped her legs around him. He put his forehead against hers, sighed again.

"You got wedding jitters or what?" he asked. "You want to call the whole thing off? Or run to Vegas?"

She smiled again, but her eyes were wet with tears. She shook her head no.

He sighed. "Is there something you're not telling me?" He wanted to add, *You are cutting people off who are trying to contact you. I feel like you're cutting me off too.* But he held his tongue. How could he say that without admitting he'd invaded her privacy?

"Josh, it's complicated, okay? Lily's in the Valley. And that's all in the past. I just want to be here, now. Nowhere else."

He pressed his head to her chest. "Fair enough."

"Hey, Josh."

"Hmm?"

"Let's get married," she whispered.

"It's a date."

She said she was here, now. But dammit, he wasn't so sure. Not two nights later and she was screaming from the bathroom where she was giving Jayden a bath. "He's DROWNING!"

Joshua ran from the kitchen, heart pounding.

She kept yelling as he stood in the doorway confused about what was happening.

"Fucking help him, Josh! He's drowning. I can't. I can't!"

She hunched on the tile beside the toilet.

Jayden, covered in bubbles and holding a plastic pirate ship, sat upright, staring at Bee.

"Are you hurt, little guy?"

He shook his head.

"He's fine, look, he's fine."

She looked up from the toilet bowl, toward Jayden in the tub.

"Bee? What happened?"

"He was drowning," she said, softly.

"Were you playing underwater, Jay? Did you stick your head under the water?"

"No, Dada. Can I get out?"

Joshua grabbed him from the sudsy water and wrapped him in a blue monster-hooded towel. As he covered the boy's dripping curls with the hood, Joshua told Bee, "I'll dry him off and get him in bed. Are you all right?"

She said nothing, but kneeled to stand. With his free hand, Joshua helped her the rest of the way up. But she didn't follow him into Jayden's bedroom.

Joshua helped Jayden into his pajamas. Jayden asked, "Why was Bee yelling like that? Was she mad at me? Did I do something bad?"

Joshua's head hurt. What the hell had happened?

"No, sunshine. You didn't do anything wrong. Bee gets scared sometimes. I think it's the new baby." He tried explaining to him about pregnant women, but Joshua wasn't sure he understood any better than Jayden did.

That night, Bee lay in their bed, comforter pulled to her neck. Joshua sat beside her.

"What happened, Bee?"

She shook her head.

"Did you remember something?"

He could have sworn she looked at him with a flicker of recognition, some emotion he couldn't pinpoint. Like she wanted to tell him something. Like guilt.

She turned away, toward the window, the lights from the arboretum and university glowing against the dark glass. "No."

"Jayden thought you were mad at him."

She was crying now. She wiped her face. "I'm sorry."

In the weeks following, he asked her what had happened in a few different ways. Played the waiting game some more. Gave her more time. Shifted tactics. Asked again.

She never answered.

He'd read in a book called *Suspicious Minds* something that hit him with the gravity of their situation. The authors said that although delusions appear to be irrational thoughts, they are *normal* thoughts about abnormal *experiences* caused, most likely, by brain disorders. When someone has a strange experience, they try to make sense of it. They say a delusion is a rational mind coming to grips with bizarre psychological events.

He didn't believe Bee had a brain disorder. And he didn't think her therapist had suspected that either, otherwise he wouldn't have let her stop attending her sessions (she wouldn't tell him so, but Joshua gleaned the meaning behind her words and didn't press when she told him she was free of the unshocking Dr. Norris). But that *bizarre experience* part sank in. Whatever had broken in Bee had congealed in Jubilee. Joshua told himself they were fixing it together.

It never happened again. He didn't let her give Jayden a bath by herself again either, but still. He told himself it was normal for a pregnant woman to freak out. Hormones. Jayden was fine. The date was set. Nothing had really happened. It was a silly scare. She didn't need a therapist. He was practically a therapist himself. He'd figure this out for them. She'd open up. He'd help her open up. They were fine.

NINETEEN
GHOST ALREADY

BEFORE JUBILEE

Bianca used to like the rodeo. It came to Brawley each November, Cattle Call Park filling with kettle-corn-eating swarms of townsfolk for the event that claimed them statewide fame. The two hotels in town booked up. Main Street held a parade. The rodeo itself transpired in the river's northeast basin, the rich white farmer's side of town, where the only houses that could pass for mansions spackled the few blocks saddling the cliffs above the park. People from all over the Southwest came to watch cowboys and cowgirls barrel race and rope calf. Cars flattened the sallow grass. People trudged dusty fields toward the arena. Sparkly-booted girls in pink-fringe cowboy hats and suede-vested boys in Wranglers flashed through the crowd. The smell of barbacoa mixed with musty alfalfa, and the metallic chain-linked fence engulfed them as they approached the booths of concessions below the bleachers. Sweet, salty kettle corn stirred in black, cast-iron cauldrons sold for five dollars a bag, Mama's favorite part of the rodeo. Bianca had brought her a bag every time she'd gone without her. Now, she considered mailing one to Abuela's. But deep down, she didn't want to send her mama anything sweet.

As they wandered the concessions before the show, Gabe held Bianca's hand on one side, Lana's on the other. His little girl had recovered quickly from whatever'd fevered her the weekend before. They'd already attended the Chili Cook-Off and the Cattle Call Parade, but Lana's energy hadn't seemed to wane. She'd been chattering all morning about the horses and floats and could she buy this trinket or that sugared snack.

Gabe steered them toward the Budweiser stand. Its line stretched farther than any other, longer than the kettle corn line. He bought two cups, and no one asked questions though Bianca didn't show ID and couldn't have if they'd asked.

Esme had gone ahead with her comadres and was already in the stands when Gabe, Bianca, and Lana took their seats on the benches near the bullpens, facing the afternoon sun. Bianca didn't say anything when Gabe handed her a beer; as she sipped it, a girl she knew from high school sang the National Anthem all *American Idol* style, kicking off the rodeo. People cheered and yelled as the first event unfolded: wild bronco saddling. Only men ran into the arena, though women joined in most of the other events. The bullhorn blasted. Bianca peeled paint chips from the bench as she watched, the sticky mess clotting under her fingernails.

A few minutes later, Lana complained the sun hurt her eyes. Bianca shaded her with an oversized umbrella Esme had brought, but Lana wasn't appeased. She demanded a hot dog, so Bianca offered to carry her down to the stands to buy one.

"Come on, chulita," she'd said, taking the girl by the hand and leading her down the bleachers. Though she didn't earn much at the *Desert Herald*, she made enough to buy her boyfriend's daughter and her a snack. She sat beside Lana at a Sequoia-shaded picnic table, crunching churritos with lemon and chile between her teeth and licking the spicy sauce from her fingers while Lana stuffed a hot dog into her mouth in too-big bites and got mustard all over her face. Longing washed over Bianca. *Lana. Won't you pretend you're mine?* Girl with sticky yellow mouth. Woman with sticky yellow ache. They were a landscape. That needed smudging. *Lana. I want to be a mama.* She wiped Lana's mouth with a napkin. Lana chatted about the food, the booths, the grass, the cowboys.

They finished eating then headed back toward the bleachers, stopping under the metal stairway to admire the horses in their holding pens. She swooped Lana up and leaned her against the fence for a better view. Girl giggling at horses. Brown, with flies in their eyes.

Outside the fence encircling the arena an asphalt road curved a mile round. It's where she and Gabe used to run in high school. When she was still a cheerleader, and he was still the boy who'd knocked her up.

Beyond the road, a playground and picnic spot with built-in barbecues. How often she'd zipped past birthday parties, screaming children, piñatas strung from trees. Holding Lana, it wasn't so ridiculous. *I thought that would be us.* This had been their favorite place. Before she'd realized what she'd let go in the Valley, that depression in her belly. *I was too young.* The way they ran, they were preparing for their sprint out of town. Gabe would call out between breaths, "Come on, punk, just a little farther." She'd bite her lip, lift her head, and keep running. It stung her chest. Her legs throbbed. But she ran. After they'd gone a few times around the arena, he'd yell, "Let's go up the hill." He, bounding up the asphalt, climbing out of the dell and she, plodding along after him, huffing and puffing. If she lagged behind, he'd look over his shoulder and mouth, "A few more steps. You can make it."

Lana fell asleep on Bianca's shoulder, and for a moment Bianca considered herself quite motherly before she decided all small children who haven't napped will tire after eating and wandering around in the afternoon sunshine. She sighed and held the girl tightly anyway as she crept back into the stands and plopped beside Gabe, feeling too nostalgic. And bitter. He didn't notice, only offered her a plastic cup of beer. Esme took Lana from Bianca's arms when she saw Bianca holding both the girl and the cup. Bianca said nothing, but the lingering warmth where the girl's breath and sleep-dampened skin had been now felt prickly and strange. The clamminess of a fever breaking, without the relief. She chugged the beer. It was bull-riding time: each rider had eight seconds. Eight measly seconds. "Look at that poor jerk," Gabe said, laughing at a thrown cowboy being chased by a bull while the rodeo hands waved and zigzagged so the cowboy could flee the ring.

She stared at Gabe. Boy she'd watched grow into man. Man she wasn't sure she liked. Lana curled on the bench, her feet propped on Bianca's lap, her head on Esme. Bianca lifted Lana's legs off her and set them on the bench. "I'll be right back," she whispered to Gabe, but he didn't look at her.

"All that beer," he said, moving his big feet out of her way. As she scooted over him, he slapped her ass, but she didn't let him see her react. She lurched toward the aisle, heading toward the bathroom stall, but when she got there, retching, she only hovered above the toilet, waiting for something that wouldn't come.

Outside the bathroom, while she rinsed her hands with drinking fountain water, she realized some guy stood nearby watching her and chuckling. She wanted to tell him to fuck off but decided not to start a fight with a stranger, especially not one wearing cowboy boots.

"The sink's not working in the lady's room either?" He flashed a smile that meant *I don't know what destruction we're capable of.* His hair was the color of summer squash beneath his cowboy hat. His green eyes playful. He wore tight Wranglers and cowboy boots.

"No, it won't turn on. I know this isn't exactly hygienic, but I had to do something."

"Let me get you a paper towel," he said. "Hang on." And for some reason, she did. He strode (there's no other way to describe his cowboy walk) to the other side of the building where he asked someone behind the booth, "Excuse me, ma'am, may I please have a paper towel?"

When he came back, his smile inviting and startling as ever, he held out a stack of napkins. "This is the best they could do," he said, handing them to her.

"Thank you." The veins in her neck fluttered as she wiped her hands in the compulsive way she might have were she Lady Macbeth instead of La Llorona. When she finished drying, he took the crumpled napkins, threw them into the trash barrel, then kept his hand out to shake hers.

"I'm Luke, by the way."

"Luke, I'm Bianca." Her stomach roiled again, but in the way that meant hunger not illness. "Do you work here or do you just enjoy standing outside the restroom handing women napkins?"

"I rode in the show today," Luke said. "And hey, don't knock the napkins. This is a great way to pick up the ladies." He winked, and Bianca tried hard to remember the scar on Gabe's cheek. Or his smell of Cool Water cologne. "Did it work on you?"

She shook her head, wondering what he smelled like. She wasn't quite close enough.

"Aw, darn it. I was sure I had you at paper towels."

She laughed, aware of the heat prickling her neck and cheeks, and the fact that she sounded like a silly eighth-grade girl, opening herself to loss. "Well, thanks again, but I should get back up to my seat. Someone's waiting for me."

"Oh, of course," he said, and she pretended to ignore the disappointment in his voice. Given enough time, hope faded. Hope, that thing with feathers, fell ceremonious as tombs. She misquoted Emily, but it still felt true. "You're so pretty," Luke said, "of course you have someone up there. Is it serious?"

"Dead serious."

"That bad? Well, I know a cowboy who'd be glad to revive you."

"You're too kind, cowboy." She couldn't believe she'd said that aloud. "You are the cowboy, right?"

"Yes, ma'am." He took his hat off and gestured a bow.

Her chest matched the stomping from the arena. How easy it might have been to give in. To walk away. How easy it might have been to let go. But the sticky yellow girl up in the stands caught the rutted burial ground inside of her, and she knew she couldn't. "Even so, cowboy, my someone has been around awhile, and I think I need to finish the rodeo with him."

"May I at least buy you a beer?"

"That, you can do." Her face felt hot, and she eyed the stands again, making sure Gabe wasn't watching.

"Well, let's go then, pretty lady," he motioned her to pass, touching her elbow. She focused on the Budweiser sign instead of his tight jeans.

After buying two drinks and handing one to her, Luke raised his cup to hers and said, "Cheers. To what might have been great, were there not someone *up there.*" Then he motioned his cup to the bleachers. "And to that lucky guy up there."

Luckiness tasted sour in Bianca's mouth. "It was nice to meet you, cowboy," she said. "Thanks for the drink." He tipped his hat, and she walked away. But when she climbed back up the stairs and sat beside Gabe, he asked how she'd gotten the beer. She handed it to him, considering lying. Instead, she settled on the truth. "A nice guy at the concessions bought it."

"Wow. That was *nice* of him." He took a sip. "And what did you do to deserve it?"

"Nothing. He saw me standing there and asked if I wanted a beer."

He made a sarcastic grunting sound and looked at her like she was one of those rag dolls people buy to scream obscenities at, frustration dolls. "Yeah, right," he said. "That guy was trying to get in your jeans."

"Gabe, just drink the beer. Free beer is free beer."

"Yeah. Right."

"Here, let me have some then." She grabbed the cup back from him and chugged it.

"You looking to get drunk?"

"Maybe."

"You know what I do to you when you're drunk?" He smirked in a way that made her feel muddy, and she checked whether Esme or Lana noticed, but one was watching the rodeo and the other was sleeping. Gabe pulled her close to his body, but she felt herself becoming ghost already, some unfortunate legend. The kind you already know the ending to but read anyway because there's something powerful pulling you through. Like it would hurt you not to finish.

In his pine-green truck after the rodeo, after he'd dropped off his daughter with Esme and took Bianca out to the country, past Brandt road, past the fields of alfalfa, between the haystacks, beside a canal flowing with irrigation water, Gabe groaned, "So you like to pick up nice guys at rodeos? You're a little slut who lets guys buy you beer?"

He unbuckled her seatbelt then pulled her across the bucket seat to his lap, her ass on the steering wheel. She didn't think to open the passenger door, to press chancla to packed dirt, to jump into ditchwater. "Are you a slut, Bee?" He slapped her face, his palm flat against her cheek. He tore open her blouse, squeezed her breasts together.

"No," she whispered, kissing him back, not sure if they were playing a game.

He laughed, clenching her shoulders. Then he pushed her away from his body, held her in front of him, looked hard into her face, and she got her answer. "You're not?" he asked, his voice cold and flat. "Then why did you let some jerk hit on you?"

"It was just beer, Gabe." She didn't want to apologize. Why should she apologize? She hadn't done anything wrong. "Can't we let it go?"

"You want me to let it go that my girlfriend is a puta whore? Fine. I'll let it go." He pushed her hard from his lap, slammed her to the passenger seat, yanked her jeans from her hips to below her ass, unbuttoned his own jeans, climbed on top of her and thrust in. She didn't cry out, but she could taste the blood-salt in her mouth where she'd bitten her own skin. "Is this what you wanted, puta?"

"No," she whispered.

He thrust harder, tearing at her skin. She winced.

"No," she said again, louder.

But he wouldn't stop.

Girl with sticky yellow mouth. I was much further out than you thought. Mama's favorite kettle corn stirred in a wide, black cauldron. Drowning in sweetness. She's yours, not mine. I'm yours, not mine. This world is yours, not mine. It is too cold always.

"Say it, say you're a slut."

I used to love you. We snuck up to your Nana's rooftop across the tracks, wine coolers in your back pocket as we climbed. Lay on the sleeping bag you'd heaved up there, mapping ourselves in the stars. Reading each other's palms.

"Puta whore. You wanted that drink. You took that drink. Now tell me what you are."

Chaser lights blinking, across the street. And somewhere in the distance, a girlchild swimming. Under a bridge. Through ditchwater. Immobilized, arrested by stones, a fish without fins, her scaly body slick with desire. No, not desire. The girl is swimming for her life.

"Tell me, goddamn you."

On her hands and knees, her face pressed against the bucket seat, tears rolled down the upholstery, stains at her cheeks. *Out, out damn spot. Life's but a walking candle. And I haven't gone for weariness. I've just gone.*

"What? I can't hear you."

"I'm a slut."

"That's right." His fists through her hair, pressing her down, down.

She had to leave Gabe. She finally knew that.

TWENTY
A SLICE OF
WEDDING CAKE

WITH JUBILEE

Joshua married Bee on a brisk early-March afternoon, the ceremony held at the historic Norwalk courthouse where Bee's parents had been married twenty-one years earlier with Bee in her mama's belly. Only Rosana, Matty, and Handro came to witness. Joshua wished he could've invited Olivia and Patti but had no idea how to contact them. And either outcome, whether they'd shown up or ignored his invitation, would've hurt.

Joshua married Bee despite or perhaps in spite of any misgivings.

Matty had taken Joshua aside before the wedding and given him another of his take-care-of-my-sister speeches. Joshua had become inured to Matty's big-brotherly ways and, smiling wide, thanked him.

During the ceremony, Rosana held Jubilee, but Jayden stood beside Joshua, his best little man in matching sky-blue vest and bow tie, both with hair greased into corkscrew curls, cocoa butter brightening their faces. The justice of the peace was a woman with thick burnt-sienna braids in cornrows and a broad smile. She didn't blink an eye when Joshua's bride stepped through the artificial flower-wreathed arches cradling a motionless, fabric-and-vinyl painted baby whose skin folded and dimpled in at her tiny hands, whose downy hair curled in patches on her indented skull. As if it were everyday a beautiful woman walked down the aisle holding a doll she then handed to her mama. Or maybe the justice had believed

Jubilee was a living, breathing infant—as many people had, from a distance. As he had, when he first met Bianca.

Bianca wore a vintage-style lace dress, sleeves to her elbows, scalloped edges around her collarbones; she'd bought it from a thrift store, she'd told Joshua, recalling a girlhood horror story she'd read about a woman who wore a secondhand wedding dress, only to die on her honeymoon from embalming-fluid poisoning, for the dress had come from a corpse bride. She'd laughed wryly when she told him this, and he'd marveled at her darkness, her light. *It's my poison dress,* she said. He'd laughed and answered, *Let's get it dry cleaned, just to be safe.*

Once she reached him at the altar, she whispered, "Do I make a lovely corpse?" Her long curls were swept to the side and clipped with an orchid, and she wore dangling pearl earrings. She looked like a sea queen. Something regal risen from the depths.

"A perfect corpse bride," he whispered back, winking. "I'm the luckiest man alive."

When the justice said, *till death parts you,* Joshua pictured Bianca and him on the silt-thick marsh of the island of dolls, hand in hand, frozen. He shook his head to rid himself of the macabre image, and she cocked hers slightly, watching him. He took her hand, ceremony be damned, pressed it to his lips. Mouthed, *I love you, Bee.* She smiled, whispered, "Don't make me cry."

When Joshua married Bee, he and Jayden were swept into a family.

They'd planned to go out for dinner afterward, but Rosana insisted they stop by Abuela's so she and Abuelo could congratulate them. The family understood they didn't have money to spend on a wedding since they were saving for the baby, but newlyweds, Rosana said, still deserved a blessing.

"Does everyone know you're pregnant?" Joshua whispered behind Rosana's back, but Bianca only rolled her eyes and shrugged.

From the courthouse steps, Jayden asked Bee to hold him, and Joshua laughed because that boy was big enough he didn't need holding. Of course, Bee scooped him up, and Jayden wrapped his legs around her waist and clasped his feet together at her back. "You're ours now," he chirped, squishing her cheeks between both his hands so her face looked chubby.

"Yes, I am," she said, laughing and puckering her lips as he brought his lips to hers.

They all piled into his Ford Focus; Joshua buckled Jubilee's car seat and Jayden's booster seat. He leaned into Bee as he opened the car door for her, kissing his wife, his beautiful island bride. She whispered in his ear, "The wonders of this world."

"Congratulations!" Bianca's entire family was crowded into Abuela's living room, dressed in Sunday clothes and holding presents, spilling into the dining room and up the staircase. Cousins, aunts, uncles, abuelos, padrinos, madrinos, compadres, all filled the sprawling house, which was decorated with streamers, balloons, and a handmade sign reading "Blessings to the Newlyweds, Bianca & Joshua." A wedding cake with turquoise piping and flowers towered in the middle of the dining room table. Abuela came from the kitchen, apron-waisted, wooden spoon in hand. Her short brown hair coiffed elegantly, her brown eyes, soft.

"Mija. Mijo, come in," she said. "We made a party for you. And Jayden, mijito, come to your abuelita." She stooped to kiss him, but he grabbed the spoon and wiggled out of her arms. Joshua raised his eyebrows and shot him a stern look that meant *be polite.*

"Can I help you cook, Abuelita?" Jayden asked, sugar-voiced. That kid.

"Of course, mijo. Wash your hands first and no running in my kitchen."

Jayden ran to the bathroom, dropping the wooden spoon on the floor. Joshua bent to pick it up. "He's a handful, I know."

"Don't worry about it, mijo. He's fine. You go be with your wife. We'll take care of Jayden. Go sit down. I'll fix you a plate."

Bee's cousin, noticeably more pregnant than Bee, her popped-out belly button showing through a maternity dress, introduced herself as Bella (pronounced with a *y* instead of an *l,* which he knew meant beautiful in Spanish). Bella took Jubilee's infant car seat from Bee, unfastened and held Jubilee close to her body, above her own protruding belly. A crazy impulse came over Joshua, and he was tempted to touch his wife's cousin's pregnant stomach. Bella smiled at them, and Joshua felt a twinge of guilt. *She knew what you were thinking, weirdo.* People did it all the time, touched pregnant women. But the thought made him feel dirty. He scooted closer to Bee, grabbed her hand and entwined his fingers between hers.

"Does she need a bottle or anything, Bee?" Bella asked, in a way that creeped Joshua out. Even though Rosana, Matty, Handro, and he all played along, it was surreal seeing it from an extended family member. It was like she'd intruded upon their game. And the affectedness of her tone irritated him. He watched to see how Bianca would react.

Did she seem skeptical too, or was he projecting?

"Thanks, prima," she said at last. "There's a bottle in my bag."

The discomfort was broken by Tía Lydia, who came up briskly and kissed each of them on the cheek. He knew that Tía Lydia was a preacher's wife, and he noted her pearl-pink suit and bright-fuchsia lipstick, which Bee had mentioned before. A kiss mark on someone's cheek in the Flores household meant Tía Lydia had been there. He wiped his face with the back of his hand.

"Did you see the cake I made for you?" she asked.

"You made that, Tía?" Bee said, pulling away to hug her aunt with both arms. "It's gorgeous. Thank you."

"Thank you," Joshua echoed, a strange mixture of claustrophobia and gratitude. For a second, he imagined Olivia's dark face in the crowd. Again, he wished for Patti. She would've been proud. She would've liked Bee (sans doll, but still).

Bee squeezed his hand. "I'll check on Jubilee. Hang out with the guys in the family room."

He watched from the kitchen as Bianca buzzed into her abuela's dining room with that halo of self-assured belief encircling her and reclaimed Jubilee from Bella. Beside her, another cousin, Dora, nursed a baby under a blanket. All of Bee's female cousins were either pregnant or had young children. Joshua reluctantly headed into the family room where the "men" watched football (except for Matty and Handro, who were outside with Bee's mom at a patio table, and Jayden, who stood on a step stool in the kitchen, helping stir a pot). Abuelo and the rest of Bee's male cousins and uncles spread out across the couches and folding chairs, drinking beers (Abuelo drank Pepsi instead of beer) and eating chips, intermittently shouting at the television, joking and laughing. An uncle called out, "Hey, Josh. Come in, man. Take a seat." Joshua took a shallow breath, stopped himself from pulling out his inhaler. He dropped into an empty folding chair, feeling robotic. He should've stayed with Bee or gone outside with Matty when he had the chance. Now he was trapped.

"Hey, man." Another uncle, this one much younger, came and sat beside Joshua, shaking his hand. In his other hand was a beer. His breath reeked of it. "I'm Oscar. Bee's tío." He was light-haired and green-eyed, and the cuffs of his black button-down shirt showcased the tattoos on his forearms.

Joshua shook his hand. "Hey."

"So you married Bianca? You sure you know what you're getting into there, homeboy? She's pretty loony." Joshua's jaw clenched, muscles stiffened. He thought back to Thanksgiving, how not all the faces they had passed in the crowded family smiled as Bee walked past with Jubilee.

"Don't talk about my wife that way," he managed through clamped teeth. His heart rate sped; he reached for the inhaler in his suit pocket.

"Look, sorry, man, but somebody should tell you. My niece is sick. Batshit. Mental."

Abuelo stood and smacked his son on the head. "¡Ay qué la fregada, Oscar! Have some respect for your niece. That's his wife." He turned to Josh, the age lines on his forehead and around his eyes furrowed deeper. "Don't listen to him, hijo. He's had too much to drink."

Oscar ducked away from his father but didn't let up. "Everyone protects her, but this pedo stinks, man. I'm sick of this loony bin. I've been holding my peace a long time. But it's not right, you feel me? You have that little boy to think about." He motioned toward Jayden in the kitchen, who'd been busy with Abuela.

"You leave him out of this," Joshua said, his face burning. But Jayden had already turned to watch the commotion.

"Come on, mijo, let me go show you my roses outside in the front yard," Abuela said as she ushered Jayden out of the kitchen. He looked toward Joshua, worried. Joshua nodded.

Matty, Handro, and Rosana rushed in through the screen door.

"What's going on in here?" Matty asked.

"Oh great, here comes the silence patrol," Oscar mocked, rolling his eyes. "The keep-everything-a-big-secret police."

"Hey, what the hell is wrong with you?" Matty said, his deep voice rising. The back of Joshua's neck felt prickly. He hadn't meant to start a fight.

"Cool it, man," Oscar said, laughing. "I'm only warning this poor sap what he's getting into with your crazy sister. Since I'm the only one who cares this shit is insane."

"Oscar," Bee's mom snapped. "You're drunk. Leave it alone."

"Look, thanks for the advice, Oscar," Joshua said, forcing a chuckle. "I know what I'm getting into, okay? I love her."

"Fine, play house with the loca. What do I care?"

"What'd you call her?" Matty demanded. Handro put his hand on his partner's shoulder, bracing him, or holding him back. Matty's demeanor reminded Joshua of a bull.

"You heard me. Your sister's loca, and everybody knows it. Watcha gonna do, mariposa?" Oscar laughed.

Matty shrank back against Handro then balled his right fist and moved toward Oscar, but before he could reach him, Abuelo stood in front of him and yelled, "¡Basta ya! Muchachos, that's enough," slamming the remote control against the coffee table so the battery case fell open. "This is my home. And I won't put up with this disrespect." He turned to Oscar. "You'd better shut your mouth, son, or get out of here with your vulgar language."

"Yeah, Oscar, let it go, man," another uncle said, reaching for Oscar's colorful-sleeved arm, but Oscar shrugged him away, puffing out his chest defensively. A bird with his plumage.

"Hey, why's everyone so quick to defend Rosana's misfits, eh? You're all so politically correct now you can't even speak the truth? The loca, the mariposa, the negro," Oscar mumbled. "I just call it like I see it."

Joshua sucked in sharply, his stomach aching.

"That's it. Get out," Abuelo yelled, the veins in his neck bulging. "I don't know where you learned that kind of behavior, muchacho, but not in my house."

Bianca stood in the doorway, clutching Jubilee. How long had she been there? What had she heard?

"Thank you, Abuelo," she said, moving into the room and kissing him on the cheek. "We'll leave instead."

Joshua felt sick. *It's your fault, Joshy.* His chest tightened as Bianca turned to Oscar and slapped him hard across the face. Her uncle's eyes darkened, but he didn't flinch or shift to strike her back.

"I'm not deaf, or crazy. You homophobic, racist pendejo."

She took Joshua's hand, steered him out the front door. They had to leave their own wedding party. His throat thickened.

Outside on the porch, Abuela was letting Jayden pick her roses. "These are for you," he said, handing Bee a bunch of white and yellow. "They have prickles."

Bee kissed him, wiping the tears from her own face.

"I'm so sorry about that, mija," Abuela said. "My son's pigheaded. Some people just don't get it. But we love you."

"I know you do, Abuela. Thank you for the party."

With her flowers in one hand and Jubilee in the other, Bee led them away.

They didn't have time to settle into a married-couple routine before the outside world found them. It had started with Oscar at the wedding. But a few days after that, Bee reclined on the apartment balcony reading, Jubilee beside her in a portable baby swing, and Joshua watched them from the living room where he'd just gotten off the phone. They hadn't discussed the wedding party, even after Bee's mom had brought them a Tupperware with a slice of cake and a Ziploc baggie with the plastic bride and groom toppers.

Bee wasn't reading her book. Joshua followed her gaze to a beam adjoining their porch with the neighbors' where a glass jar of raspberry-jelly water hung from a string wrapped around a rafter. Inside, dozens of yellow jackets stacked on top of each other to keep from drowning. What a sick joke. Maybe he'd ask the neighbor to take it down.

Bee's hair webbed around her face. Someone with a need less intense than Joshua's might have been turned off by the pulsing ache she came with. The sadness she carried like a candle, illuminating the gold of her eyes, gathering around her the way incense fills a room only after burning the stick. She was the curled edges of paper after the fire but before the ashes. He'd married her. Sadness and all. He'd married her and she was having their baby and there was no turning back.

Through the screen, her eyes flickered toward him. "It's cruel, luring them to their death."

He stood to join her, pulled out his inhaler, puffed it twice. "At least they die happy."

"Drowning would be the worst way to die," she said. "Drowning in sticky red water." Her face was pale and beads of sweat appeared above her lip. She seemed nervous, agitated. "Sometimes, I feel like a beekeeper, setting the trap. Other times, I'm struggling to get out but mired in muck." Joshua nodded though he didn't understand what she'd said. He was accustomed to her poetry, her strange moods. He thought of Jayden in the bathtub. She'd screamed that *he* was drowning. They remained silent as she stared at the yellow jackets, until she broke the silence with the question Joshua had hoped to elude a few seconds longer. "Who was on the phone?"

A pit formed in his stomach. "Jayden's caseworker."

"What's up?" Bee sat up straighter, leaned toward him.

The sick ache had been welling inside him since Oscar said that stupid shit at the wedding. "Random visit. She's coming over next month. It happens sometimes in the foster care system." He said it to placate Bee. Or himself. But he didn't believe it. His gut felt too tight. No one had visited him and Jayden in almost two years. He couldn't imagine anyone in her family would've called. But it didn't seem like coincidence.

Although Bee smiled, her eyes didn't crease, so her smile wasn't genuine but pasted to her face. "That's normal, right? Nothing to worry about? You're a great guardian."

"Not just me, Bee. *We*." He said it aloud, the reality of the situation sinking in. He'd thought they'd have more time. Next month was too soon. He leaned against the patio rail, resting his head against the metal. "*We*," he repeated, sighing.

"Do you think they'll approve of me?"

He could've punched himself for not thinking this through earlier. Of course a social worker would have to come. He'd been stupid to think otherwise. He said nothing.

Bee bit the cuticles around her nails. "What if the she calls me unfit too? Like Oscar? I know what people think of me. Gabe thought I was unfit."

"Gabe?" A pang of unexpected rage shot through Joshua. He felt like smashing his hand through the jelly water jar, throwing it against the balcony. "That bastard who caused you all this pain in the first place? How the hell would he know? How the hell would anyone know, but you and me?" He looked up and saw she was staring at him, an unreadable expression on her face. He couldn't read her. That was the problem. He sighed again. "Look, the only thing anyone can say about you is that your love is tough. Stands at the edge of the cliff. Insists on flying."

"This was a mistake. Marrying me. That's what you're thinking."

"Dammit, Bee. That's not what I'm saying."

"I love Jayden. You know that, right?"

Joshua kneeled beside her, put his head in her lap. He'd find a way to show the caseworker they were fine. He looked at Jubilee in that swing. When had Bee's treatment ended and his own delusion begun? He had to be honest with himself.

"You're not unfit," he said, his head against her belly.

Two nights later, she knelt on all fours in child's pose on the living room floor. Prenatal yoga. She leaned over and stretched her body into a bridge, modified downward facing dog, knees bent. Her belly wobbled beneath her tank top. Joshua watched her. Ragdoll. Sun salute. Back to the mat. He watched as she wobbled, fell, onto her belly.

He knelt beside her. "Are you hurt? Does anything hurt?"

The Bianca he'd fallen in love with would have been laughing. Would've made a self-deprecating remark about her clumsiness. This Bianca whispered, "She's dead. I know she's dead." Then louder, "Fucking help me, Josh!"

"Calm down," he said, freaked out by her hysteria. "You didn't fall hard. She's fine." They didn't know the gender. But Bee had said *she*.

"Jubilee," Bee cried. "She's dead. I know she's dead."

What the hell? "Hey, hey." He lifted her face up to his. "Shhh . . . Jubilee's fine. She's in her crib. And our baby is fine too. Want me to call the doctor, see what she thinks?"

Bee nodded, still crying.

He helped her up and walked her to the couch. "You sit here and rest. I'll call right now."

"Can you bring me Jubilee?"

What had she meant, she killed Jubilee? The fetus inside her? Or the doll in the bassinet? Could she tell the difference?

Joshua went to the bedroom, picked up Jubilee, handed her to Bee.

"Hey there, little girl. Mama's here. You're safe. Mama's got you."

"Bee . . ."

"Yeah?"

I'm scared. I'm scared you're gonna fall apart. I'm scared I'm gonna lose you. I'm scared for Jayden, and I don't know what to do. I'm not your therapist. I'm your husband. Your brand-new husband. I'm in over my head. "Nothing. I'll call the doctor. You relax."

In the kitchen, he dialed the doctor. From the living room, Bee hummed "Somewhere over the Rainbow." She sang it every time she was upset.

Now it upset him.

TWENTY-ONE
LETTER TO JUBILEE

There are windmills and there are dragons.
(You can be anything you want to be.)
I'm a fisher queen. Forever floating in your blood-murk sea.
Forgive me.

TWENTY-TWO
A FLOODY PLACE

BETWEEN JUBILEE

Lily had been Bianca's best-friend-forever but she hadn't invited her to the wedding. She hadn't told her she was getting married—

Time was a construction. Time was fluid. In the many-worlds hypothesis, time was no arrow. It was everything happening at once. It was still happening, somewhere.

In the valley, Bee had tried not to bother Lily with her soap opera shit. Not that Lily would have minded. But even Bee was tired of herself and Gabe. This time though, Bee needed her BFF.

Lily was there in three minutes flat. She used her key to let herself into the empty house-still-for-sale, her footsteps echoing through the bare hallways.

"Where are you, Bee?"

Bianca slumped over on the bathroom floor, half dressed, her boxer's flat snout-of-a-muzzle resting on her naked thighs. She held a pregnancy stick.

Time was cyclical. Time was broken.

Lily appeared in the doorway, her blond hair swept away from her face in a ponytail. She never went out without curling her hair and bangs because she hated her forehead and how greasy her hair looked slicked back. "What's it say?" Lily nodded toward the pregnancy test.

"Positive." What else would it have been?

"Oh." She squatted on the rug beside Bianca. Lily knew how conflicted Bianca had felt when she was fifteen. How much she'd wanted a baby to glue together the broken glass inside of her. She also knew how Bianca's mama and dad had fought. What had happened to her dad. What family meant to Bianca. How she felt when Gabe had one with Katrina.

They were both quiet a while, Lily staring at the pee stick like it was a poisonous insect. "Do you know how far along?"

Bee shook her head, hiccoughing a sob and wiping snot from her face with the back of her hand. It could have been any of the times Gabe forgot a condom or used the pull-out method like she was a dirty sock. She hadn't been keeping track of her period, didn't even know how late she was. Only that she felt like shit and couldn't stop vomiting. She shuddered to think she'd been pregnant long though. She'd been drinking like a fish.

"So what's the verdict?"

Kanga perked up, wagging her stump of a tail, waiting for someone to pet her. When no one did, she settled her face back on Bianca's lap. "I meant to leave him, Lil. I've claimed it so many times. But this time I meant it . . ."

She couldn't tell Lily about Cattle Call. Couldn't admit what happened in Gabe's puke-green truck. What humiliation. What degradation.

Time was a joke. How even in those awful minutes, cells joined. Cells clung. Signaling a second chance. Forgiveness, maybe. Redemption. But at what cost?

Lily raised her eyebrows. "But, you changed your mind . . . because you're pregnant?"

Kanga snored from her place on Bianca's lap.

Bianca lay flat, rubbing the bath mat's shaggy rungs between her fingers. Her reasoning sounded so wired with faults in Lily's cynical voice. Where was her feminist mierda now, she wondered, thinking back to Hector and his compadre making fun of her. She felt like a joke. She felt heavy. Even her blood felt heavy. Yet somewhere in that mess, in that swollen, heavy sea, a pink, iridescent jellyfish clung. And if she didn't touch it, maybe it wouldn't sting her. If she didn't move from this bathroom floor. If she didn't move a goddamn muscle.

"You don't have to stay, you know." Lily said it with such startling frankness, lying on her stomach beside Bianca, stroking her hair. "You have a choice."

This time. This time she had a choice. "Remember what Gabe used to be like? Before Katrina. Before Lana. Before he hurt his back and lost his scholarship."

"What was so different?"

"This one summer morning, I remember, the desert air smelled like a sweet mixture of cow manure and hay . . ."

"You're gross, Bee. Cut it out with that poetry shit and tell me what happened." Lily chuckled, realizing what she'd said. "Poetry shit, like, your poem was about cow shit."

Bianca wadded up the toilet paper in her hand, threw it at Lily. "Fine, you poetry-hating philistine. Shit or not, Gabe came to my house early to take me to this fruit stand on the Eastside over by his Nana's house at the edge of town because I said I'd never tasted a mango. He pronounced it like a Spanish word, like *mongo*. So we went and chose fresh fruit, then went out to the fields where he set this picnic. He said we'd follow each other out of the Valley and take the world by storm. It was cliché, I know, but I believed it."

"Yeah, except he couldn't keep his dirty dick in his pants long enough for that to happen. How long did he last away at college before he knocked Katrina up? A month? I don't buy it. What? You tell him you've got his kid growing inside you all fat and cute, a little Gabey baby, then all of a sudden he's supposed to morph back into a good guy?"

"When you say it like that, of course it's stupid. But I don't know, Lil. It's possible."

"Yeah, it's also possible I could drink soap and blow a bubble out of my ass."

Bianca rolled her eyes. "You're so crass."

Lily gave a wry grin. "That's why you love me."

Bianca pinched Lily's thigh.

Time was a dick.

Bianca scratched Kanga behind the ears. She'd made up a song to the tune of Credence Clearwater Revival's "Suzie Q"—*Oh Kanga Roo, Oh Kanga Roo, Oh Kanga Roo, baby I love you, Kanga Roo.* The puppy followed her everywhere through the empty house, waiting for her outside the shower, licking the water that leaked through the cracks in the linoleum. Would a baby be so different from a puppy?

Bianca was ridiculous. She had other plans. Bigger plans. She had to leave Gabe.

"So come on, chica-dee. Tell me. Should you stay or should you go? *If you stay there will be trouble. If you go there will be double.*"

Bianca rolled her eyes again.

"Seriously, Bee. I can help you pack. I'll drive you up to La La land myself. Back to your mama. I'll hate to see you go. But I hate to see you hurting even more."

"I've loved him since I was fourteen, Lil. I can learn to love sports bars."

"Ugh. I knew that's what you'd say." She made a gagging face. "Hey, I don't want to be the one to let you down, but I've got to tell you. I've been holding it in, but I can't let you go on like this. If Gabe treats you this badly now, he'll only treat you worse if you stay. Face it, he does not want this baby. *You* want this baby. He doesn't. Wake up and smell the dirty diapers, chica. He's an arrogant jerk. What kind of drunken role model will he be for your kid? He doesn't freaking deserve you. If you keep the baby I will support you one hundred percent, but if you stay with this son-of-a-bitch asshole, I'm outta here. You always said you wouldn't turn into one of those women waiting around for a man who's out with other women. Well, with this jerk you're one of those women. What happened to that fighter spirit? What happened to La Bee? Where'd she go? Why'd you let him take her out of you? He's a loser. He didn't change when he had what's her name. He won't change for your baby. Take your little fish of a kid and get out of this Valley. Go home to your mama and Matty, to people who care about you. I'm washing my hands of the whole damn thing if you insist on staying with him."

Bianca narrowed her eyes, her pulse fluttering in the veins of her neck, her cheeks hot. "So what? You're giving up on me? You're my best friend, but you have no fucking idea what I've been through. You make it seem easy, like I could walk away. To what? To being a single mom? To a family who will make me feel guilty the rest of my life for having a child out of wedlock? You know my mom. The Saint. Santa Rosana. I can already hear her saying extra rosaries for me, her sinful daughter." She sighed, leaned down and squeezed Kanga's thick neck. Naked on the bathroom floor, scratching a dog with one hand and holding a goddamn pregnancy stick in the other, she felt like a still life. A painting she would have loved, if it didn't hurt so much. *What the Water Did*, maybe. Who could she blame but herself though? *What the Bee Did*. Stung and stung and stung. She sighed again. "Frida always went back to Diego."

"Your painter hero?"

Bianca nodded. "It's all over her journals, her undying love for him no matter how awful he fucked up. No matter how badly he hurt her. Hell, Lil—he even fucked her sister!"

Lily snickered, then shook her head. "Look, I won't trashtalk your saints. But that sounds like no kind of life. Talk about suffering for your art."

"She divorced him at one point. But remarried him a year later."

Lily scoffed, shook her head again. "Damn. Well, there you go. Looks like there's no talking sense into you, if you're determined to follow Saint Frida. But remember, even saints fall."

"Don't let my mom hear you say that." They were silent a moment, then Bee grasped Lily's hand. "Just don't abandon me like my family, promise me. Whatever I decide. Don't make me choose between him and you."

"Jesus, Bee. You're in bad." She pulled her hand away and smoothed a piece of yellow hair that had fallen out of her ponytail. Then she reached out with both arms and hugged Bee's shoulders, squeezed her in a tight mama-bear embrace. "You know I'll stay and help you. I always do. But I predict this'll only end with your heart broken again. And that baby? God only knows."

Time wound itself like lights around a Christmas tree, choking. Flashing sirens.

Bee dragged her ass off the floor, got dressed, and followed Lily back to her house, where they dug through the Christmas decorations. "No one can feel like shit when they're Christmas decorating," Lily said, cradling an absurdly large plastic reindeer.

"Watch me," Bianca said, but she strung tinsel and lights anyway.

Next, Lily lugged in a plastic storage container of wrapping paper, tissue, boxes, and bows.

"I don't even have any presents to wrap this year," Bianca said. "I'm broke."

"We're gonna wrap empty boxes and put them under the tree so it *looks* like you do."

When they finished wrapping and tying and curling ribbon, Bianca stood back. "It looks like people live here again."

"Don't leave the Christmas lights on all night, Bee." Lily clicked off the switch. "You could start a fire."

Bianca tried to laugh. But it hurt when she laughed.

Time was a body. Her body was a floody place.

The holidays disappeared. She spent the day with Esme while Gabe went riding his quad in the desert. He asked her to go, but she felt sick. He didn't even notice she wasn't drinking. Instead of meandering through the desert with Gabe and his friends, Bee spent the day in Esme's kitchen, woozy, cooking spicy pork, steaming the tamales, and preparing the champurrado, a thick chocolate atole they made with toasted masa harina and water, piloncillo (brown cones of unrefined cane sugar), cinnamon, and Mexican chocolate. It smelled delicious, and Bee had loved it since childhood (when she used to eat the dark, hard discs of Mexican chocolate straight out of the box, so bittersweet and granular, even though they were supposed to boil it into a drink, Mama used to scold her). But now, every smell in Esme's kitchen made her nauseous.

Esme said, "You look sick, mija. Go lie in Gabe's bed and take a nap," and brought her some of the champurrado and pan dulce, mothering her the way she had before. Except there was no blood. No pad. No absence. Just heaviness.

Whether left on a bathroom floor or thrown away, even time faded like the lines on a pregnancy stick. Sometimes they grew so faint a body could barely make them out.

Maybe Gabe did not love her. Not enough. But she was Esme's nuera, her daughter-in-law, even if Esme's son wouldn't admit it. Bianca held Esme's grandbaby inside her. Hector would warm to her. Gabe would love her again. She could make up for what she'd done. What she'd failed to do. All would be right in the Valley because she was pregnant again.

But she couldn't tell Mama until Gabe married her.

And he would. She knew he would.

TWENTY-THREE
THE FIGURE

WITH JUBILEE

As Joshua and his little family pulled up to the apartment after another Sunday afternoon at the Getty, a figure perching on the steps to their building came into view. She wore baggy jeans and a loose T-shirt, and her hair formed a dark pom-pom atop her head. She was tiny, but her hunched posture made her look even smaller. She held her knees to her chest. She reminded Joshua of a ghost. She was his sister, Olivia.

"Is that her?" Bee asked, as if she'd been expecting her.

"Yes." Joshua cleared his throat. He reached for the inhaler in his pocket. What was she doing here? It had been nothing but Murphy's law since the wedding. Everything that could fall apart did . . . including himself.

"Do you think the social worker called her? Because of what Oscar said?"

His stomach clenched. "God, I hope not. You and the kids stay in the car. Let me go talk to her and find out what's going on." He pulled the parking brake.

The last time Olivia had gotten out of jail and visited Jayden when he was a baby, she'd left him in a motel while she went on a drug run. She was a no-show the first two court cases. Joshua didn't know she was out. *She's gonna try to take Jayden. Be careful. Don't let her get the upper hand. She can't have him. Not for a weekend. Not ever.*

Joshua moved closer to where she slouched on his stairway and noticed she looked sallow, ashen even. The usual cocoa of her skin was more like waxy butter. The bloodshot Red Vines of her eyes were gone, replaced with a strange yellow glow. She reminded him of an alley cat, scraggly and defensive. He thought of Jayden's spirit animal. The owl hovered above, wary.

"Hey, Suga." Olivia's mouth cranked upward mechanically, as if trying to lift off into a full-blown smile but stuck on the uptake. "You look fancy." Joshua had worn dark-wash jeans, a button-down shirt with the sleeves rolled up, and black boots to the Getty. He and Bianca liked dressing up for family outings. Bianca had worn a long maxi dress to hide her baby bump (though Joshua liked it, she insisted she looked "fat") and strappy sandals. They'd dressed Jayden to match Joshua, except the kid wore black-and-white Converse lace-up low tops. They were teaching him to tie his own shoes.

His palms felt clammy and his stomach hurt. It was eerie, like he'd reverted to a little-boy version of himself. Olivia had a way of making him feel small and scared. He couldn't tell if he was upset or relieved. He hadn't heard from her in so long, part of him wondered if she could've died. He managed, "Hi." She started to stand up, but he motioned for her to stay. "I'll join you." He sat beside her, wrapping his arm around her bony shoulder and squeezing her softly. Was she as brittle as she looked? Would she crumble if he squeezed her too tight?

"I'm back," Olivia said, like those words didn't carry the weight of their lives.

The first time she'd left, they were kids. The first time she'd broken her promise. Maybe she'd resolved to follow their parents' footsteps. Maybe she'd been waging war inside herself, screaming out not to become them, but scared as hell that no matter what she did, she would end up becoming them anyway. They had an aunt from Tennessee who'd visited Patti's once, Aunt Arlene. She'd told them how their father had run off with their mother, left his wife and three daughters in the lurch. The ex-wife and daughters still lived back East, Arlene had said. She'd come out to California to find John's other kids after their father died. A drug-induced seizure. Joshua and Olivia hadn't known anything about their father, much less that he'd died. Joshua didn't feel anything when she'd said his name, John. He was only a story. Arlene had said she didn't know where their mother was. Arlene hadn't gone to the funeral, if there'd been one.

Patti had stood in the kitchen, listening from a distance, giving them time with "family," though Arlene didn't feel like family to Joshua. He wanted Patti to come in and hug them, but she didn't. She couldn't have known what that "family time" would do to Olivia.

Arlene had said she couldn't take them home with her. She'd had no idea his kids were growing up orphans, but she was no good with kids. Never had any of her own. She was a traveler. She had friends all over the country, flitted here and there throughout the year, staying with each one a while, not long enough to wear out her welcome. That's no life for young'ns.

After that, Olivia started hiking her skirts, rolling up the cuffs on her daisy dukes. She tore the sleeves off her tees and cut lines in the back, like she'd been attacked by a chupacabra. When the calls about her smoking at school came, Patti was appalled. No, she was *not* raising a hoodlum, she'd said. No, she was *not* her mother. She didn't *have* a mother. Olivia was her *ward*.

When Olivia began screaming at her teachers, refusing to do her work, wearing a smug smirk across her face, like "kiss my ass," Patti threw up her arms. Was Olivia testing her? Was she testing how far she could push before Patti would snap or testing whether Patti was good for her word? Would she have moved her kids to a neighborhood where Olivia couldn't have been friends with the cholas and gangbangers? Would she have sent her to camp? To see a counselor?

One night, Joshua had gone upstairs to Olivia's room where she lay on her bed, smoking and listening to her headphones, and begged her to cut it out. Patti would send her away if she didn't. But Olivia had only hugged him then shut her bedroom door in his face. She was breaking her promise. Maybe she couldn't help it. Not then, not ever.

The day she cussed Patti out for taking her cigarettes away, Patti called the social worker. She couldn't handle her anymore, she'd said. Take her away.

Now Joshua let go of Olivia's shoulders and turned to face her. "You just get out?"

She shook her head. "I've been out a while."

"Where've you been staying?" He pulled away slightly, trying to suppress his anger. He hadn't wanted her to come. But knowing she'd been out of prison and hadn't come over? That hurt.

"A friend of mine and her boyfriend been letting me crash there. I been there a couple months. Before that, here and there, you know." She wiped her nose with her hands. Then she began peeling the cuticles on her fingers. They were yellow, like the glowing ink of a highlighter had seeped into her fingernail beds. "My friend's pregnant though, so she's all grouchy, and I'm gonna have to get outta there soon, when the baby comes. But seeing her get all big, her belly button poppin' and shit, her boyfriend fussin' all over her . . . reminded me of my kid. Reminded me how it was with him, before. I know he was only inside me a few months before we were in jail. But there was a minute I thought it could be different for me and him. My friend got clean when she found out. All fast and shit. I guess that's the difference between me and her. That's my problem."

"We've all got problems, Olivia."

"Not you. Look at you, Joshy. All spiffy and successful. College boy."

"I'm graduating this semester."

They seemed like themselves. Big sister, little brother. "No way," she said, grabbing his chin and shaking him playfully. "Way to go, kid. Look at you. How'd you get all the brains and all the heart too? You musta' stole my share."

"You've got a lot more heart and brains than you think. It's never too late to change."

"Nah, Joshy boy. I made my bed."

"You talk like you're an old lady. You're not even thirty. You can't throw in the towel."

"Aw, kid," she shook her head. "Life's given up on me."

"What does that mean?"

"I'm sick."

Joshua looked at her skeptically. She didn't look well, true. But that didn't mean life had given up on her. What had she come for? Money? He took the bait. "Have you been to the doctor? You have insurance? I can help you. You don't have to worry about that." He still got his monthly stipend for foster care, on top of the leftovers from scholarships and financial aid.

"I been already." Her voice was scratchy, but he could hear the sadness beneath the smoke. She looked him straight in the face; he saw, for the first time, hopelessness in her eyes. That rage she'd carried all her life, that mean streak he'd known, that Olivia who burned coming and going all the while she was near you, that sister he'd loved from a distance because hearts can only take so much, was replaced by someone quieter. Beaten and done fighting. "At the clinic they told me it's my liver, from Hep C. It's too late though, 'cause my liver's already gone to hell. Cancer, Joshy. It's cancer."

Something squeezed his lungs. "Aw jeez, Liv." He breathed out shallow puffs. Couldn't catch his breath. "Aw jeez . . . Liv. Jeez. Can't we fight it? Can't we do something? I can find you a doctor. UC Irvine hospital is right nearby. We can take you there. Or UCLA or wherever."

She shook her head. "It's no use."

Tiny and brittle, she held him, much bigger than her, as he wept like a little boy again. "I'm so sorry, Liv." He pulled away, wiping his face on his arm. The honey of her skin was the yellow of jaundice. Not drugs. Cancer. She was weak, not because she was coming down, but because she was dying. She wasn't here to take Jayden away. *Dying.*

He looked toward the car where Bianca had turned around in the passenger seat to face the kids. She sang and clapped with Jayden, who, through the tinted back window, laughed and clapped too.

Olivia followed Joshua's gaze to the car. "That your girlfriend?"

"My wife, Bianca. She's a writer. We met at school. She's great with Jayden."

"I knew you'd find someone perfect, Joshy. She's beautiful. Latina?"

He nodded. "Her dad was white, but her mom's Mexican."

"Hmm. She's pretty. But can she do Jayden's hair?" Her voice was playful, and she nudged him in the ribs. He couldn't remember the last time they'd joked around.

"She's meticulous with his curls."

Olivia took his hand. "Can I see him? I've got no claim. I just want to hold him a minute. My kid."

"Liv, I want you to. You can, of course, but . . ." His mouth felt sticky. How could he tell her she couldn't take him?

She must've sensed it. "I'm not gonna take him, I promise. He's your guys' boy."

He exhaled slowly. She wasn't there to fight him. They wouldn't have a custody battle. He nodded *yes*.

"I won't make a fuss, I promise. I just want to talk to him. I need to hear his voice. I won't tell him I'm sorry, 'cause he won't know for what, and how could I explain? But I'll know how sorry I am. And God will. That's enough for me. I want to tell him goodbye."

"You don't have to say goodbye, Liv. You can come again."

"Nah, Suga. It's better this way. It took all I had to get here today."

He squeezed her shoulders again. "Okay. Let me go talk to them real quick, then we'll all go upstairs." He wanted to feel grateful she'd come back just because she'd missed them. But she was dying. What the hell was he supposed to do with that knowledge?

At the car, Joshua knocked on the passenger window. "Can I talk to you for a minute, Bee? Out here?" She bit her lip as he helped her out. He called back to Jayden, still dancing around. "Hey, bud, how ya holding up there?"

"Hey, Dada. Who's that on the stairs? Who are you talking to?"

"That's your Auntie Olivia," he said, trying to sound cheerful. "You'll go say hi to her in a minute, but I need to talk to Bee real quick. Can you stay put a few more minutes, big guy?"

"Yes, but I'm thirsty," Jayden whined.

"I know, kid. We'll get you some apple juice in a minute."

"But I want juice now."

He closed the door and turned to Bee, who was chewing on her bottom lip. "Did the social worker tell her what Oscar said? Is she here to fight?"

"Nah, it's not like that."

Bianca closed her eyes and exhaled. "I was so scared."

He sighed. "She's sick though. Liver cancer." The words fell heavy.

"That's awful. I'm sorry, Joshy." She touched his arms, which he'd folded across his chest. "Does she need anything?"

"Nothing. That's not why she's here."

"So she doesn't want Jayden back?"

"She wants to meet you. Wants to know everything is fine before she leaves."

She glanced toward his sister, forehead creasing. "Does she know we're married?"

He nodded.

Her smile cracked, but he could tell she was relieved. "I don't know what to say to her." She gripped his arms tighter. They turned back toward the car, and Bianca unbuckled Jubilee from behind the passenger seat then held her to her chest.

Joshua let Jayden out, who yelled, "I have to pee. Clear the way. It's coming out."

"Hang on, bud. Hold it in." He swept him over his shoulder like an injured soldier and ran, calling out, "We'll meet you inside." He ran past Olivia, laughing. "He's gonna burst." Joshua saw from his peripheral vision that she'd stopped, waiting for Bianca. His stomach coiled. He opened the front door for Jayden then quickly returned to the stairway landing where they were already chatting without him.

"Joshy," Olivia said, "Your wife's even more beautiful up close."

He smiled, taking her elbow, Bee following with Jubilee pressed to her chest. *Calm down. She'll think it's a toy. Be cool.*

As they entered the apartment, Bee asked, "Does anyone want iced tea?"

"Sure, hun. I'll have some," Olivia said.

Still squeezing Jubilee, Bee nodded then disappeared into the kitchen.

Normal, normal. Everything seemed normal. So far, so good.

Then Olivia poked Joshua in the ribs. "Hey, Joshy boy, I know you're a good dad and all, but you let Jayden play with dolls?"

"Jayden's four years old, Liv. He's not too old for dolls."

"You gonna make him a sissy boy like you?"

"That's mean, Liv. You know I hated it when you called me that."

"Sorry. Can I talk to Jayden?" He led her back to Jayden's room where he was playing with trains.

"Hey, kiddo. You remember Auntie Liv, right?"

"Hi, Auntie."

"I told myself I wasn't gonna cry when I saw him," Olivia whispered, then, aloud, "Hey there, Jaybird. I brought you something." Joshua hadn't heard that in years. She'd called him that when she'd first come to visit. He'd grown up, and she'd missed it. Olivia reached into her purse and pulled out a picture. A bent-edged snapshot.

"Who's that baby with you, Auntie?"

"That's me and you, kid."

"Wow, you've known me a long time."

"I have." She wiped her eyes and scooted closer to Jayden. "Can I play trains?"

He nodded, and she reached down, pulling his body close to hers. He let himself be hugged.

Joshua leaned against the door, watching her kneel beside him. She ran her fingers through his spiral curls, brushing her hand across his cheek as he pushed his trains along the railroad table.

"He's perfect, Joshy. You been taking good care of him."

He marveled at how well-worn that picture had become. She must've carried it with her through some rough places. Joshua had held the disposable camera. She'd just gotten out of jail the first time. He'd steeled himself for when she'd take Jayden back. But she never did. She had no claim to him. She'd said so. The court said so. Then why did he feel guilty?

"I'll let you two play."

"Dada, you forgot my juice."

"Oh yeah. I'll be right back."

Olivia looked up and winked. She wasn't always mean.

Bob Marley's "No Woman No Cry" drifted into the hallway from the kitchen. *Little sister, don't shed no tears.* The three of them had listened to his greatest hits while making breakfast earlier that morning. "Dada, Bee be jammin'." They'd all laughed. "Yeah, mon." *In this bright future you can't forget your past.* Three glasses of iced tea remained untouched on the kitchen counter. But Bee was nowhere.

He poured Jayden apple juice then walked toward his and Bee's bedroom and opened the door. She drooped at the window overlooking the arboretum, clutching Jubilee, rocking her. She sighed when she saw him. "I'm an intruder."

"She's my sister, Bee. Not an ex."

"I know, it's . . ." She held Jubilee to her chest, making soothing noises. It bugged him. The way she averted every crisis by holding that—

A knock on their door. He turned around. Olivia stood in the open doorway. "Sorry. Didn't mean to interrupt. Jayden sent me to find juice."

"Oh yeah," he said absently, handing her the juice. "I forgot."

She hesitated. "Sorry to bother," she stammered, looking over at Bee. "Hey, Joshy, can I talk to you?"

"Sure," he said, stomach dropping as he walked toward the door. Before closing, he glanced back at Bee. She just kept rocking Jubilee.

After taking Jayden his juice, Olivia joined him in the hallway. "Jayden told me he had a new baby sister named Jubilee."

He cleared his throat. "Well yeah, Bianca's pregnant. We're having a baby."

"No, that's not what he told me. He said he already has a baby sister. His *Bee* lets him hold her and help change her. He says she's like a doll but not really cause she's real, like the Velveteen Rabbit." She looked at him hard. "What's he talking about, Joshy? That doll your wife was rocking and singing to? What kind of game are you playing with my kid?"

She had a point. But he had it under control. He stood taller. "He's not your kid anymore, Liv. He's my son."

"What's going on? Your wife crazy? I saw her with that doll. Rocking her. Wasn't it in a car seat?"

He balled his fists, clenched his jaw. "Okay, look. Bianca's gone through a trauma. The baby's a coping mechanism."

She scrunched her face, grimacing. "Are you kidding me?"

"It's fine. I've got this. I'm a counselor, remember?"

"Not yet you're not. What about Jayden? You think this is good for him? He's in there telling me he's got a doll for a sister. What kind of sick shit is that?" Her lips curled into a sneer and her face twisted.

"Calm down, Liv. Let's go outside. Don't upset Jayden." How many hysterical women could he handle? He wished Olivia would leave. Why'd she have to come back? Why'd she have to be dying? Why'd she have to be Olivia?

"Fine. But you best explain to me what's going on around here."

He opened the front door and led the way downstairs to the patio. Olivia pulled out a cigarette and lit it.

"Should you be smoking? Isn't that dangerous with your illness?" He coughed. She knew smoke triggered his asthma. It always had.

"Don't turn this around on me, kid. What's going on with your bride? She wacko or what? You find her in a mental ward? She one of your patients?"

"Olivia," he snapped. "Do not talk about my wife that way. Jesus! You barge in here after all this time without any word, and now you start disrespecting my home and my family? Look, I'm sorry you're sick. I'm sorry your life has been shit. But none of that's my fault. I'm with Jayden because you never showed up, Liv. You never showed up." He hadn't meant to yell. He'd never yelled at Olivia before. But what right did she have to talk about Bee that way? She didn't even know her.

Olivia's expression gnarled as she sucked her cigarette. "Josh. Tell me the truth. What's going on with your wife?"

"I don't know."

"What?"

"That's the truth. She went through something. I don't know what. She already had Jubilee when I met her."

"Where?"

"I told you. At school. She's not crazy, Liv. She's not. She's . . . in denial. It's shock. Everything else in our life is normal. Everything. She's a good mom. You've got to trust me. I know what I'm doing. I can handle this. Jayden just thinks it's a game."

"I don't think so. He seemed pretty convinced."

"It's like the books we read to him. It's magic. Make-believe. Fairy tales."

"And later? When he's grown? What then?"

"She's getting better. We're fine."

"I thought you were smart, Joshy. I thought you were the smart one. I gave you my kid 'cause I thought I could trust your judgment. What are you doing? Use your head. You think a social worker's gonna give her Jayden? You think you're gonna get to keep him? She's delusional. And it looks like you are too."

"That's not fair. You don't understand. It's not a delusion. It's . . . it's . . ." He couldn't breathe. "Can you put that thing out?"

"Sorry." She stomped out the butt on the sidewalk. "Don't have a panic attack."

He wasn't a little boy anymore. She wasn't his big sister. She'd left. She'd never shown up. He'd done the best he could. Bee was a good woman. She was everything Olivia wasn't. "It's asthma, Olivia. Not anxiety." He dug around his pocket for his inhaler. *Shit.* He'd left it upstairs.

Her voice softened. "I didn't come here to fight."

"I know."

"I'm scared for you. This situation you're in, it's messed up. You know that, right?"

"Hey, Liv. You don't understand. She lost a baby, and her doctor says carrying a doll is an unusual but *normal* way to cope with it, and I'm helping her through it. It's like PTSD."

"No social worker's gonna let you guys get away with this. You've got to realize that. Then what, Joshy? You gonna let him go into the system? You gonna let them take him away like they did us?"

It hurt to breathe.

"If it comes to it, who you gonna choose? Your wife? Or my son?"

"I've got it under control, Liv."

"Like hell you do. You don't get this straightened out with her, and I mean quick, I'm gonna call the court, Joshy. I don't want to. God knows I don't want to. But come *on*. You think I'm just gonna let you leave my boy with a crazy? I wanted that for him I'd a kept him myself. You take care of this shit now or I'm taking him."

The real world had found them.

From where he stood, he had to protect his wife from the outside. He'd taken that role willingly. He'd known how she appeared to others. He hadn't cared. But Jayden? How would he keep the system from grabbing him away?

TWENTY-FOUR
PLEASE DON'T LEAVE

BEFORE JUBILEE

Saturday night dinners at Nana's were Bianca's favorite. They'd barbecue outside on the grill, and Nana would make potato salad and homemade tortillas. Other times she'd make a huge pot of posole or albondigas, Gabe's favorite.

That night, two nights before New Year's, Bianca served herself a heaping plate of rice, beans, cheesy potatoes, and chile con carne. Esme's comadre Belen, who was in town from Orange County, had come for the dinner. Belen and her ex-husband Frank were Gabe's padrinos. They had a daughter named Adriana, whom Bianca had heard about for years but never met. That night at Nana's, Belen bragged about Adriana as usual, telling everyone how she'd gotten a job working as a teller at the bank in Newport Beach, and she'd bought herself a silver Mazda Miata.

Every time she mentioned Adriana, Bianca wanted to gag. She could blame it on the morning sickness, but Adriana was the cause. From what Bianca could tell, Adriana was nothing special, but Belen gushed on and on about her to Esme, who *ooh*ed and *aah*ed. It bothered Bianca, how possessive she'd become of Esme's attention.

She'd wanted to confirm the pregnancy at the Clínicas before telling Gabe. She hadn't wanted a false positive. Earlier that afternoon, the nurse had confirmed it; the doctor had calculated ten weeks based on Bianca's last period, which she'd dug through journals and calendars and the haze of the past few months to remember. It was safe to tell Gabe.

She went for a second helping of everything, more rice, more beans, more cheesy potatoes, more chile con carne. Gabe saw her piling the food on her plate and asked snidely, "Don't you think you've eaten enough?" A knot in her stomach. She might have been overdoing it, but he didn't have to point it out in front of everyone. Besides, she was hungry.

"No." She sucked the word in the way she might breathe shallow after eating a chile, to keep it from stinging. "And there's a reason I'm so hungry." She motioned for him to follow her through the back door into the yard that his Nana shared with the neighbors. "I need to talk to you."

He followed, fidgeting with his cargo pockets like he wasn't interested in whatever she had to say. "What's up?" he asked, impatient. They stood beside the outdoor washer and dryer, on the side of the house, beside Nana's rose garden. Bianca leaned against the washing machine while he shuffled back and forth in front of her. Her stomach uncoiled in the way that meant she'd need the restroom soon.

"Do you love me?" It had popped into her head and felt ridiculous spilling out of her mouth, jagged as rock candy. Too sweet. Too hard.

"Ay, Bee. Don't start again. Come on, not now. Does everything have to be a dramatic scene?" He began to walk away.

She pulled him back. "Gabe, wait. This is important, and I won't make a scene. Stay and talk to me, please."

When she'd gone to visit Nana after moving home from Holy Cross to tell her that Gabe and she were back together, Nana made the sign of the cross and thanked God. By the time Gabe and Bianca were standing in her yard on New Year's, Nana probably questioned whether it was God that brought her back. None of Gabe's family acted outwardly angry with Bianca for the scenes she caused, because, really, they weren't *that* bad compared with Katrina's and the scenes her family caused. Katrina's brother had knocked over Esme's backyard fence at Lana's first birthday party (Esme had told Bianca this, since she hadn't been invited to the party).

"I won't make a scene," she said again. His face softened, his body relaxed. He lifted her atop the washing machine, face-to-face with him, though he usually towered over her, a foot taller and still as broad as when he'd played football.

"Of course I love you," he said, resting his head against her chest. "I'm sorry I've been such an ass lately. I know this whole situation is hard on you. I know it hurts you. That's why I never asked you to come back to the Valley, why I was so proud of you when you went away to school. You deserve more."

With his body pressed to hers, she put her arms inside his hoodie sweatshirt's front pocket, keeping her hands warm the way she'd done when they were in high school. "Remember that night at the fair? You locked your keys in your car in the parking lot, so we waited by the FFA pig barns for your friend to bring you a spare set. It was so cold and windy. I asked you to my sophomore Baby Ball. You said yes."

His eyes were bright, and Bianca could see again why she'd ever loved him. "I'd never been to a dance with anyone before." He sounded almost shy, the way he'd been when they met.

"You danced pretty good for a first timer."

"I danced good with you."

"I'm on a bench again, Gabe. Hoping you'll come sit with me . . . wait with me . . ."

"What do you mean?"

"I'm pregnant."

He lifted his head from her chest, pulled back, looked hard into her face. "You sure?"

"I took a test at the Clínicas. I'm ten weeks."

"Bee . . ." His forehead wrinkled, he shook his head as he stared at her knees, still pressed against his stomach. "What are we gonna do?"

"We could be happy . . ." She put her hand on his cheek, pulled his face toward hers, took his hands and wrapped them around her waist. "We could dance." She swayed against his arms. When he half laughed, she whispered, "Let's keep it, Gabe."

He started crying. Softly at first but then in heavy rib-shaking sobs, his tears soaking through Bianca's sweater. "I can't." She tried pulling him away to look at him, but he clung to her. "I can't . . ."

"Why can't you?"

"We'd never get out of here, babe. You're asking me to stay here. To keep forklifting, all my life forklifting. You're asking me to keep working in a feedlot, delivering seed. I already can't afford to take care of Lana and Katrina and get myself a life."

"What about the restaurant?"

"It's a stupid dream, Bee. Come on. You must know that. We don't stand a chance down here. I already feel trapped. This was not supposed to happen now . . . Not again. Not like this. I'm not ready." He wiped his eyes on the back of his hand, his voice firm. "Sorry, but I'm not."

She pried his head from her chest, looked at him straight in the eyes. "Ready or not, Gabe. What do you want me to do?"

"Can't you get it taken care of?"

"How many babies am I supposed to lose for you, Gabe? How many will be enough for you? And why only mine? Why not Katrina's?" She shoved him away, hopping down from the washer onto the grass, feet sinking into the soil.

"Fuck, Bianca. Why are you throwing that in my face? I told you she was lying about that. Lower your voice."

"You act like you don't care. You don't care that our baby bled down my legs."

"Please don't start making a scene. Please. Let's go. Come on, we can talk in the car. Don't say that shit out loud. My nana will hear . . ." He grabbed her arm, but she pulled away.

"Why should I care?" She was yelling.

"Be angry with me, fine. I understand you're angry with me. But don't say things that will hurt Nana. She didn't do anything . . ."

"Is everything all right, mijo?" Nana opened the back door, peeked through the screen.

"Yes, Nana, sorry. We're fine," he called, controlling his voice, his dark eyes pleading with Bianca to stay quiet. "We need to leave though, but thank you for the food."

"Ay, ¿por qué?"

"Bianca feels a little sick, that's all. Talk to you later, Nana, love you."

"Okay pues, be careful driving, you two." She blew a kiss through the screen. "I'll tell your mom and everyone you left. Are you sure you won't take a plate with you?"

"No thanks, Nan," he said.

"Bye, Bee, feel better, mijita," she called.

Bianca looked at Gabe then turned back to Nana and smiled, "I will, Nana. Love you."

They drove the two miles across town to the other side of the tracks without talking. She felt drunk and vomity, though for once when they were fighting, she hadn't been drinking. Her stomach churned. When he pulled into her driveway, he left the car on. She asked, "Aren't you coming in?"

"No, I think we need to cool off and think about things tonight. I don't want to argue." His voice was quiet, the bitterness seeping out of him and lying between them in the cup holders, murky.

"Please stay, Gabe. Please." Her voice was shaking. "Please don't leave."

"I'm sorry, Bianca. I'm not trying to be an asshole. I need to think about things. Clear my head. Give me some time. I need some time to process this."

She didn't move to open the door.

"Come on, Bee. Please get out of the truck so I can go home. I'm tired. We'll talk in the morning. I'll come over, and we'll talk. I promise. Get out of the truck."

She sat still. *The Nerves sit ceremonious, like Tombs.* Emily understood why Bianca couldn't move.

"Bee." He reached across her lap and opened the latch, shoved the door open. "Please. Let's not get into this tonight. I need some time. Go inside and get some rest."

She hated him. She hated his truck. Hated his face. He was mean. He said he loved her, but he didn't. If she didn't move, he might push her out. He'd done it before. Why did she want to stay and fight? Why would she rather hear him scream than go into an empty house, alone? Though it was insane, she wanted her father. He'd been just as mean to Mama. Is that what was happening with Gabe? She was having daddy issues? How much more of a cliché could she get?

The bile rose up, burning her throat. She gagged.

"Shit. Bee, turn over."

She threw up in her hands and lap, vomit splashing across the seat, onto the floor.

He yanked his seatbelt off, jumped out of the truck, ran around to her side. He unbuckled her, turned her toward the driveway, pulled her hair back. It was too late to salvage anything; she'd soaked her clothes, shoes, the seat, the floor mats. Once she stopped heaving, he helped her out of the car. "Come on," he said softly. "I'm here. I'll help you." He held her close to him, despite her stench, leading her up the dark walkway, her slick clothes sticking to him. She'd forgotten to turn on the porch light again. "Do you have your keys?" he asked.

She nodded, dug into her jeans pocket for the keys, apologizing as she handed them over.

"You couldn't help it. We'll get you cleaned up." He helped her inside, led her down the hallway and turned north at the fork, toward her parents' old master bedroom. "You gonna throw up more?"

"I don't think so." The ghosts couldn't hurt her when Gabe was around. She let him help her into the bathroom the way he'd done so many nights when she was drunk and staying with him at Nana's, the times he'd propped her onto the toilet to pee without falling over and hitting her head on the sink. He helped her shower and get into her pajamas, then he changed himself into basketball shorts and an undershirt before putting their clothes into the stoppered, soap-filled sink, since Mama had sold the washing machine at a yard sale before she'd moved to LA. It was too big and old to haul, she'd said. From where Bianca sat cross-legged on the mattress on the floor, bolstered by pillows, she heard him outside washing his truck beyond the sound of ocean; he'd turned on *Finding Nemo* on her thirteen-inch television. She fell asleep to cartoons most nights.

When he came back in, he said, "I'm sorry I yelled at you."

She didn't answer. In the background, Dory was forgetting Nemo's dad, Marlin, again.

"I can stay tonight if you need me to."

She nodded, and he kicked off his shoes, checked his cell phone, then plopped onto the mattress. "Good night," he said, turning over, away from Nemo. "Let me know if you need me."

She sat still and watched the water. Even on a small screen, it was so blue.

In the middle of the night, she awoke to Gabe's loud snoring. Her stomach still wobbled, queasy, but she didn't feel like vomiting. She stared at the ceiling where a brown water stain was forming. When she relaxed her eyes, the way she had as a girlchild, lying on the grass in her front yard to watch cloud formations, it looked like a sad old woman hunched and carrying firewood on her back, her head hung in either exhaustion or despair. It morphed into a rhinoceros, depending on how much Bianca squinted. Then the woman was back, not carrying firewood but a baby in her rebozo. Her baby was crying, but the woman didn't know how to make it stop. So she cried along with it. They unsettled Bianca's stomach like too many beers or another ill-timed pregnancy, that crying woman and her crying baby.

She couldn't watch anymore. She felt voyeuristic. What could *she* do to help them? She was a blob on the mattress of the floor, a water stain on the bed.

Bianca wanted to get up and pace the halls, crawl into Mama's bed between her and Dad as if she were a girlchild again. But she was already in Mama's old room. Mama's bed was gone, and Bianca wasn't a girlchild anymore. She could never crawl between Mama and Dad ever again.

She felt four years old, lying in the dark cradling her own damn self. She remembered those uneven bangs she'd chopped herself and the ballet slippers cemented to her feet all summer. Mama couldn't pry them off her. Bianca used to hunch under the round oak table at Bisabuela's house where she'd shared a room with Matty, swallowing whole packets of Sweet'N Low. She'd rip apart pink paper after paper, pouring the bittersweet granules straight onto her tongue and letting them melt there like Eucharist, until Mama caught her and spanked her with her chancla.

Bisabuela's house meant escape. The night that Dad had stuck his head into the lion's mouth, that great fool, and lived. Bianca most clearly remembered scrubbing out with a sponge the Crayola shapes she'd scribbled on the walls, and Bisabuela's avocado tree pitching its fruit at Bianca's head while she swung on the set below, Dad or Matty pushing her. *Oh how I love to go up in a swing, up in the sky so blue.*

In that house, she'd lain foot to head with Matty in his bed, which he'd let her crawl into when she was night-frightened, which was often, while he sang to her.

The night Dad washed down his Prozac with a few beers, he seizured through the halls like a wild sword-swallowing performer, his shadow staining shapes too dark to scrub away. The way Bianca remembered it, Dad called for her from the boiling pot of his body, a doorway seething. Girlhood was white and shaking until she couldn't remember where he went or why but only that he needed help. Memory interpreted through the wash of color and sound—a big brother's baritone singing *go to sleep* and Bisabuela's yellow hands folding eggs into the pancake batter in the morning when one's father was gone.

Fifteen years later, she was walking the red dust of Chaco Canyon in her imagination, following Bisabuela's people, who only entered the sacred ruins to pray for their ancestors. *Did you mean to end it, Dad?*— the broken pottery Bisabuela warned her not to touch—shards meant for the spirits. A piece of an article she'd read in *Smithsonian Magazine* pinned itself to her: *The very act of remembering can change our memories.* She wanted to remember Dad there, in Chaco Canyon, against the clay, against the constellation of stars where Bisabuela's ancestors tracked the sun, the moon, their entire lives.

She wanted to touch Gabe, to find something concrete to hold her to him. She closed her eyes, imagining she wasn't something already broken.

When she opened her eyes to the faint-yellow morning, Gabe stood in the doorway putting on his shoes. She blinked, sleep crusted in her eyes.

She looked again. No, he was taking his shoes off. He was returning from somewhere, carrying a white paper bag. She pulled herself up onto the pillow, rubbed her hands across her puffy face, trying to smooth back her tangled hair. She felt swollen from crying and vomiting. But she was starving.

"Hey there." He wasn't smiling, but she could tell he wasn't angry. "A peace offering. With extra salsa."

He handed over the bag, which held two giant Jaliscience breakfast burritos. She tore open the paper, poured salsa onto the warm, soft tortilla, then stuffed a corner of the burrito deep into her mouth and bit down, scooping bacon, potato, and egg between her teeth. She couldn't remember ever eating before that morning. Couldn't remember ever being so ravenous—as if she could open wide and swallow the entire room into herself, Gabe and all, and still not have been filled. She was a snake, guarding her nest. (Here was Gabe, offering her peace, and she was imagining herself a venomous creature, eating him like prey.)

"Thank you," she said after huffing several bites.

"Pregnant women are always hungry. I realized that's why you were eating so much at Nana's." He laughed, and Bianca felt a stitch in her side she knew was jealousy. Had Katrina been so hungry? Had he brought the same food to her? The burrito felt tainted.

He lowered himself to the edge of the mattress, and Bianca scooted her legs away so he could sit. "I'm sorry about last night. I was shocked is all."

"Shocked? You should know babies happen when you don't use a condom."

He shrugged his shoulders. "Well, it doesn't matter now, I guess. What's done is done. But you were right last night. This is my responsibility. I do love you. I shouldn't have been so mean to you. You didn't do anything wrong." He ran his hands through his spiky hair. "What I'm trying to say is, yes. Let's dance. Let's have this baby. Let's be a family."

She dropped the burrito onto her lap. She couldn't believe what she was hearing. Family. He'd said family. The classification of living things. Kingdom, phylum, class, order. No, *family*.

She sprang up and lunged toward him, and he hugged her, really hugged her, laughing. She buried her face in his neck, and he didn't ask her to move. He just held her.

"And hey," he said, "we can raise him or her by the beach. We should go up there and check it out. Maybe it's still possible for us all to get out of here."

She nodded, her forehead and chin bobbing against the fold of his collarbone. His skin was slick with her tears—forgiving him. Forgiving herself.

TWENTY-FIVE
OUT OF THE BUBBLE

WITH JUBILEE

The April air gusted through the Bank of America parking lot. Joshua tugged open the heavy glass doors of the Social Services office tucked on the side of the bank's brick building in downtown Pomona. He hadn't expected to return as a grownup. The place was hidden. A person might never know it existed if he'd never had reason to visit. Joshua wished he never had reasons. Not as a kid. Not now. He'd made an appointment a few days earlier and stayed nervous all week. Bee didn't know he was there.

His body clenched as he strode past the security guard and toward the check-in desk. "May I speak with Ms. McCall? She's expecting me. Joshua Walker."

The receptionist glanced up at him, another black face in the crowd, then pointed toward a pad of paper. "Sign in and have a seat. I'll let her know you're here."

Joshua nodded and signed his name, glancing into the playrooms beside the waiting area, colorful and vibrant. He'd played with that bead maze as a kid, pushing the green circles up the spiral rungs then letting them fall to the other side like wooden people on a roller coaster. He'd watched other children visiting their parents in those rooms, hoping his parents would come. They never did.

He turned away from the upbeat mural on the wall and sat across from a young pregnant woman. He felt irritated, his body buzzing with anxious energy.

He hadn't seen Ms. McCall since a week after high school graduation when she'd given him a pen with the inscription "Oh, The Places You'll Go" and hugged him, the off-to-college-boy, goodbye. Ms. McCall had been his childhood social worker. The only constant in his life. She took him away when no one wanted him. Placed him somewhere new. Fresh start, she'd always say. New beginning. Keep your chin up. You're a bright boy with a good heart. You'll go far. Joshua needed her guidance.

The pregnant woman stood and walked toward the bathroom. She looked six months along. Bee wasn't quite as big. Though at five months, her belly was expanding steadily. Every night, he watched his wife as she lifted her nightgown and stood in front of the mirror, tracing circles across her middle. Sometimes she listened with the stethoscope Rosana gave her. Bee liked the whirring sound of the ocean inside her. She told Jayden that a fish was swimming inside her. Joshua's own stomach flopped. What would Ms. McCall say? Was Olivia right? Had Joshua blown it? Could Olivia take Jayden away?

"Mr. Walker? Ms. McCall will see you now. Do you know where her office is?"

Like the back of his hand.

Shuffling down the fluorescent hallway, he felt like a boy again, holding Olivia's hand, loving and hating her for always getting them into trouble. Social workers were like gods. Deciding fates. Coordinating lives. Matching families. Picking up pieces. Sometimes smashing those pieces to bits.

He still hadn't decided what story he'd tell her. Would he change names to protect the innocent? If he told her the truth, he'd be giving up control of the situation.

Ms. McCall sat at her large desk, a petite woman but round, with skin darker than Joshua's and amber braids pulled into a bun atop her head, decorated with a large red flower that matched the silky blouse beneath her blazer. Just as he'd remembered her. "Hey, Joshy. It's been a long time," she said, grinning. "How are you?"

"Doing well, thanks. I'm graduating with my BS in Human Services this semester, going into a marriage and family counseling master's program in the fall."

"I knew you'd make it. You've always been a shining one. I never had to worry about you. So what can I help you with? You mentioned a family situation on the phone."

This was it. He had to break the bubble.

He steeled himself to tell her about Bee, but the words wouldn't form. He couldn't admit his predicament. It was too dangerous. What if she had connections with the Orange County social services agency? What if she knew whomever they assigned them? What if Olivia had already called? He couldn't risk telling the whole truth and facing the repercussions. Better to keep the cards in his hand. Better not to become vulnerable. He'd had to trust her growing up, but social workers, like gods, could be fickle, and he couldn't afford to lose. Instead he said, "Well, it's not about *me*. I have a concern about a *client* situation I need some advice about."

She raised her eyebrows slightly. Doubt flashed across her face before she smiled again. "Ask me anything, honey."

"A client of mine is hoping to adopt from foster care. This client's husband is already a legal guardian, and they're about to put in the paperwork for adoption. Everything looks good as far as a stable home and income, all that."

"Sounds promising," she said, nodding and smiling. "So what's the issue?"

He exhaled. "She, my uh, my client, has an, um . . ." *What? Has a what? Say it. Tell her what she has.* "A delusion."

"A delusion?" Her smile vanished.

"Yeah. She went through a trauma and is coping by maintaining a complete denial." He felt like he was betraying Bee by sitting there, talking about her like she was a patient.

"What type of delusion is it? Erotomanic? Persecutory? Has schizophrenia been ruled out? Is she undergoing treatment?"

"She's definitely not schizophrenic. I'm not sure there is a classification for her specific manifestation. She believes a baby doll is her daughter."

"A baby doll? As in, a toy? She believes a toy is real?"

"Yes."

"Wow. That's a major issue, Joshy. If I were aware an adoptive parent had such a serious delusion, I certainly would not relinquish control of the child to that person. If I were assigned to the case, I would refer her to counseling, most likely once a week for whatever length of time necessary to work through the grief and trauma fueling that delusion."

"But what if the doll was her type of treatment? Have you ever heard of Reborns? They're a type of lifelike infant doll, and sometimes they're used for therapy. They've had success treating female dementia patients with them because they remind the women of motherhood, a time when they were useful and needed. A time they could nurture."

"Hmm . . ." She knitted her eyebrows. "But this client of yours believes the baby is alive? That crosses the line of treatment, doesn't it? That's a loss of grip on reality. I mean, if she could truly believe a doll was a living, breathing child, what would stop her from suddenly believing the foster child in question was a zebra or an alien? What would keep her from believing he was demon-possessed in need of drowning? Do you see what I'm getting at? A delusional person cannot be trusted with a child. I'd need to see a clear indication of recovery, of working through the trauma, of having a clear handle on what's real and what's not, in order to even consider placing a child with that person. I'm not saying it's not possible to recover from something like that, but it would be difficult."

She made Bee sound ugly.

"So your recommendation would be to halt the adoption process pending treatment and further evaluation?" He hated the official words coming out of his mouth. Hated them clinking on his tongue. He longed for softer words. Words filled with hope and promise. The kind not found in textbooks or courtrooms.

"That's right, hun. I'd give it time. Maybe look into alternate placement for the time being." *Alternate placement? What have you done, Joshy? You fool. You're messing this up.*

"But the husband is the legal guardian." His voice came out high-pitched. His neck prickled. "Why would alternate placement be needed? He doesn't have any issues to work through."

"As long as they're married, they're considered one unit, honey. One family. Unless he's applying for individual adoption of the child without the other party, he would most likely not be granted the placement until the home situation is deemed conducive to the child's well-being. Living in a home with a mentally ill parent, even if the other parent is stable, could be detrimental to the child. Social Services needs to protect the child. Isn't that the number one concern here? The child?"

He nodded. Under. Control. He reached for his inhaler, puffed it twice.

"Joshy, honey? Are you all right?" She pushed the Kleenex box closer. *Pull yourself together, Josh.* "I'm sorry. I'm sad for the family."

"This job can be so stressful. So overwhelming. You've got a good heart, Joshy. You always have. I'm sure you'll do the right thing for your . . . client."

"Thank you for your time, Ms. McCall."

"Anytime. Let me know how it goes."

"I will."

He could tell her how it would go. The family would stay together. He wouldn't let anyone smash the pieces. Wouldn't let anyone play god with his life. Not anymore. He had promises to keep. Secrets to stifle. He had a baby to hide. A wife to protect. A boy to hold onto. A life. He had a life. He couldn't let go.

He sat in the parking lot, shaking. He yelled into the rearview mirror, *What the hell do I do now?* He punched the steering wheel.

Grasping at straws, he pulled the scrap of paper from his wallet with Olivia's phone number on it. She'd given him the number at her friend's house and said call her as soon as he'd figured out what he was gonna do. She'd be waiting, she'd said.

He dialed the number slowly, hands trembling. His fingers felt numb, corpse-like.

"Liv?" he asked, voice distant, like it didn't belong to him.

"Yeah, Suga?" He could hear her coughing, muffled through the receiver, like she'd put her hand over the mouthpiece.

Tears blurred his eyes. He choked back a sob. "Please don't call the court. Please don't take Jayden away from me. Please. I've had him since he was a baby. I'll make it better. I promise. Bianca will get better. But please give us a chance. I couldn't live without him."

She sighed, ending in a deep cough. "I know, Joshy. I know you do. But I had to think of Jayden." She coughed again. "I already called the social worker, I'm sorry. That doll was just too weird. I had to call and tell them something."

He leaned back against the headrest and closed his eyes, tears streaming down his cheeks. He willed himself not to hear what she'd just said. He hung up the phone.

A social worker called Joshua a few days later, citing a concerned relative. She never mentioned Olivia or a baby doll. Maybe his sister hadn't told the whole truth, just suggested the social workers pay a visit. Part of him wanted to call Olivia and thank her at least for that much, but he was still too angry. He could've handled it, but Olivia hadn't trusted him. That was her problem. She gave him her son, but she still didn't trust him, after all these years.

Even though the social worker hadn't yet made any specific allegations, the situation still wasn't ideal. He needed a plan. On the phone, he did some damage control, telling the social worker how they planned to adopt Jayden and other respectable things about their lives he thought she'd like to hear. Bianca was an English major, he was becoming a counselor. They were going to San Diego a few days after her visit on a family vacation. That sort of thing. She seemed pleased, and when they got off the phone, he felt hopeful.

They still had a chance. He could fix this. He *would* fix this.

TWENTY-SIX
LETTER TO JUBILEE

Children are buried on the moors.

One mother I read about returned daily to search for her child.

She died searching.

One of her child's murderers wrote to her from prison and claimed she could take her to the body.

What a cruel joke.

The body.

Buried.

One murderer was a woman. The devil's wife.

The papers said that was worse than being the devil himself.

A woman should have known. A woman's maternal instinct should have kept her from doing harm. What a potbelly of lies.

In prison, she wrote that her lover could've told her the earth was flat, the moon was made of green cheese and the sun rose in the west, and she would've believed him.

Darling, this is not a letter I should be writing to my daughter.

But someone has to tell you the truth.

Someone has to make you understand.

Here's where a mother goes wrong. Here's where a mother turns herself into a hole and swallows. Here's where she turns herself into a whole prison and waits.

I didn't listen to my mother.

Why should you listen to me?

I'm the aswang—the bruja who flies in the night and swigs the belly of pregnant women. I'm the fear of corpus, the fragment of night terrors. I'm alive, but you're . . .

. . . in my arms.

The truth swills us both like brujas.

(I remember the devil's wife.

I remember.)

Inside I'm crawling, baby girl. Crawl back to me. I'll reclaim you the light.

(If you're determined to make your way back to the earth, come back through me.)

I can't ask you to forgive me. I can't ask you that.

TWENTY-SEVEN
FREE BIRD

BEFORE JUBILEE

Gabe took Bianca to the Newport Channel Inn, a small blue-and-white motel three minutes from the beach. They'd stayed there once before when she was still at Holy Cross; they'd liked it because it was cheap and close to the ocean. They were in Newport to look at apartments, get leads on jobs, begin staking out a new life.

But first, they watched the water. They sat on the beach on a motel towel. Gabe steadied Bianca as she sank into the sand. Her loaded belly ballooned in front of her when she sat, squishing out, pressing against her sundress. She kicked off her chanclas and buried her toes.

They'd once run naked away from beach patrol along that strip of shore in the middle of night, carrying their clothes in a bundle, laughing hysterically. She couldn't imagine running anywhere now. She was heavy. Carrying high. Abuela would've plucked a hair from her head and tied her wedding ring to it—if she could've gone home, if she'd had a wedding ring—and let it swing in front of her belly. If it swung side to side, it was a boy. If it swung around in circles, a girl. "Remember when we made up?" She nodded toward the pier. "Lana just born."

"I remember. She was perfect. Small and wrinkly." He paused. "When Katrina was in labor, she asked me to marry her."

Bianca turned to him. He'd never mentioned that before. "What'd you tell her?"

"I couldn't say anything. I couldn't stop thinking of you."

Something inside Bianca ticked like a broken clock. "What am I supposed to say to that?"

"I don't know." His voice was scratchy.

"Fuck." She buried her feet deeper into the sand.

"Fuck off?"

"No. Just fuck." She stared at the water, letting his hand rest on her shoulders. "I spent too much time watching this ocean, trying to get over you. Trying to settle the family picture of you with Katrina and your baby in my mind. Torturing myself. Figuring out the reasons you chose her over me. Trying to understand why God let her baby live but let mine go."

"That wasn't God, Bee. That was us."

She pulled away from him. "That was a mean thing to say, Gabe."

"I'm sorry. I didn't mean to ruin your life," he muttered under his breath.

They sat quietly for a few minutes before she spoke again. "At that stupid Christian college, I almost died too. Like my coward father. I almost died there. Then you called me. How cliché is that? You said you were coming to pick me up, so I hung up the phone and scrambled across the hallway to the Fontana girls' dorm room." She was laughing wryly, so sorry for herself she nearly couldn't stand herself. "The girls across the hall reminded me of how I was in high school, remember? Latina cheerleaders. Clichés. But at least they didn't know it. They were always awake, so I pounded on their door and screamed, 'I have a date! Can you straighten my hair?' My hair, Gabe. Not Nietzsche. My hair. You know Nietzsche said metaphor is a desire to be somewhere else? He meant it as a jeer, but he's right. God, how right he is."

She looked over at Gabe. He was smiling in a way she couldn't tell if he was genuine or making fun. He was staring out into the ocean but still listening.

She kept talking. "After twenty minutes in their room with a round bristle brush and blow dryer, I raced back to my room, pulled on some tight jeans and a tighter sweater. I had a date. With you. My father wasn't dead yet, and you were coming to get me. I rushed down the five flights of stairs to the sidewalk below and waited on the curb for your stupid green truck to pull up. Like old times. Like the years in high school when you'd flown around the corner to pick me up, and we'd ride together, music blaring. Lynyrd Skynyrd. You remember?"

He nodded. "Yeah, it reminds you of your dad." He started singing, softly. "*If I leave here tomorrow, would you still remember me?*"

She was crying. "When we were free, Gabe. When we'd roll down the windows and cruise Main Street, taking the long way to school."

"We've always taken the long way, Bee."

"On that pier, you held me. You told me you'd missed me."

"I miss you like hell every time I'm away from you."

"Then why do you push me away?"

He shook his head.

"Those fishermen reeling up eels beside us? Your breath against my neck? The fog and the sunrise . . . were those nothing but dreams? Cinematic? Unrealistic?"

"We wouldn't be here if I thought that."

"How long will you love me?"

"*Lord knows I can't change,*" he whispered, his voice cracking.

She tried not to roll her eyes. She was so tired of being cliché. Tired of being a cardboard version of the woman she was meant to be. She knew *he* couldn't change. But the problem was, why couldn't *she*?

They looked at apartments all afternoon, but the cheapest one they found was eighteen hundred bucks a month, plus utilities. Why did Gabe want to move to Newport? Why couldn't they move inland? Anaheim or Santa Ana would've been cheaper. They could've lived near Matty. Okay, neither man would've wanted that. She sighed. The farther inland they went, the more like the Valley it got. She could see it on Gabe's face when they arrived at the beach. He wanted water after all that drought.

She felt as out of place in Newport as she had at Holy Cross. Everyone blond or sun streaked. Everyone with a perfect body. She felt like a brown blob staining the ceiling. Conspicuous. Untidy. The boys had treated her like a fly on the wall. Her "brothers" from the adjacent fifth floor on the other side of the freshman dorms had laughed at her hair net when she worked in the kitchen to help offset the cost of meals because Mama couldn't afford the full mean-plan otherwise. They'd ignored her in her bright hula dress and lei at the Hawaiian mixer. Not light not dark. Not thin not elephantine. She'd made no impression on them. She was not their sister, not girlfriend material. She was nothing. To Gabe she was something. Sexy as hell. His poeta. His woman. But after apartment hunting, her brown curly hair was frizzy from the salt air, her rotund belly felt grotesque. She felt like an indigenous woman in a Diego Rivera painting. She'd paint some maize in her arms, and she'd be set. Had she really internalized a Western standard of beauty so deeply that now she was even disrespecting the indigenous women she'd come from?— her bisabuela and her bisabuela's mother, who'd crossed the Sonoran to birth her on this side. And still, she felt so full of herself, so ironically self-absorbed, indulging in self-loathing. There were bigger problems in the world than feeling judged by people who might not have been judging her. She should have been holding her head high, proud of her body, thick as masa, proud of her heritage. Still, she was convinced that these Newport residents looked at her like their cleaning lady—right through her. Not as La Profesora, as Gabe's family called her.

Her feet hurt from walking all day, her back ached. Gabe was in a bad mood. "I don't know how we'll afford it out here," he said. "With you not working."

"I can work."

"But for how long? You'll have to take maternity leave. Who's gonna have to pay for that? Me. I'll have to. And I still have to send money back to Katrina and Lana."

He slammed his truck door closed as she slid into the passenger seat.

On the dashboard was a pile of job applications and apartment pamphlets. He grabbed them and threw them to the back seat.

"We could look for somewhere less expensive, closer to LA County," she said. "We don't have to start out at the beach."

"This whole thing was a stupid idea."

"Why does it have to be here, Gabe? Why can't we settle for something else, for now?"

"Because. That's why."

He had a picture of what his life would be like. Was Bianca part of that picture?

"We don't have to make any decisions today. Let's see how things go with getting a job, and we'll keep searching. There must be someplace we can afford."

He started the ignition.

His frustration was palpable, an object on the center console between them. She reached over, set her hand on his leg. "You want to pick up fish and chips and go back to the hotel, watch a movie?"

"I told Frank's daughter, Adriana, we would meet her for dinner."

She pulled her hand back. "Frank's daughter?"

"My nino, Frank. You've met him and his ex-wife, Belen."

"Your *cousin*, Adriana?"

"She's not my cousin. We're not related."

"Your padrinos aren't your aunt and uncle?"

"No."

Bianca's padrinos were *her* aunt and uncle. She'd assumed the same for his. That's why she'd never asked any questions about Adriana. She wasn't his cousin? That bothered Bianca.

"Hey, Gabe. I'm tired. Maybe it's Braxton Hicks; I'm all achy."

"I promised her already. I can't ditch her. I can drop you off at the motel."

"No. I'll go with you."

A few months ago, he'd left her in the empty house alone with the stomach flu while he'd gone to a bar with Adriana, who was in town visiting.

She wasn't his cousin?

Then what the hell were they doing together at that bar? And what might they do at dinner if Bianca weren't there? Her anger was dampened only by her foolishness that her life had turned into a telenovela, a sappy daytime reality show. Would the pregnant girlfriend end up alone?

"Fine."

Eating at Joe's crab shack with Adriana wasn't the romantic dinner at the beach Bianca had imagined. She was frustrated he hadn't shared his plans. How long ago had he made them? She was more surprised by Adriana. Frank and Belen's daughter, Bianca had thought would look like them—perhaps chubby with dark hair. Not so. Adriana was molded straight from the teen drama *The O.C.* Rachel Bilson could've played Adriana's character in a movie—after getting some shining blond highlights for that perfect sun-kissed look. Petite and thin, Adriana's hips jutted out against her skinny jeans, and her collarbones made her look like a strangely seductive clothes hanger in her plunging halter top. Bianca would bet Adriana didn't need to wear a bra.

Gabe ordered the Crab Daddy feast, a big bucket of crab, corn on the cob, and red potatoes. He and Adriana each had two Corona Lights apiece. Bianca ordered a Diet Coke but felt guilty because of the caffeine. All through dinner, Adriana and Gabe joked and laughed. Adriana hugged Gabe a few too many times. How often did their hands brush as they reached for the bucket? Something made Bianca sick. The baby didn't like crab. Or didn't like Adriana.

Adriana barely spoke a word to Bianca all night and focused all her pretty blond attention on Gabe. Bianca rolled her eyes at Adriana's lame jokes. She didn't seem smart. If anything was going on between her and Gabe, Bianca would find out. She wouldn't be the other woman again. Not for Gabe. That role was behind her. She thought of a line from H. D.'s poem "Eurydice"—

hell must break before I am lost;

before I am lost,
hell must open like a red rose
for the dead to pass.

Sylvia Plath would rather have stuck her head in an oven than be the other woman.

But Bianca could become a chiasmus, her whole splintered self—a crossing. Hell would have to open like a red rose before Gabe dragged her back to feeling ashamed. Before she went back to that, the dead would have to pass.

Or she'd drag them all down with her.

TWENTY-EIGHT
ONE BIRTHDAY,
A FEW DROPS OF BLOOD

WITH JUBILEE

Today was Jubilee's birthday.

Bee had said so.

Easter the week before had been a bust. Joshua, too scared and guilty to celebrate, put a rift between him and Bee. They dyed eggs and hunted with Jayden in the grass outside the apartments by the communal barbecues, collecting coins and candies, but Joshua's heart wasn't in it. The social worker was coming soon, and Joshua still hadn't figured out a plan. How to keep his wife from a breakdown, how to keep their lives together, how to keep everyone safe.

Today, Wednesday, April 21, he slumped over at the kitchen table, chin in hands, watching Bee and Jayden bake a cake. Beside them in the high chair, Jubilee stared ahead.

Joshua sighed, reaching into his pocket. He'd needed his inhaler more often lately. He hadn't been sleeping much either. Every night, he watched Bee snoring away, deep and dreaming (he could tell by the fluttering of her eyelids) as she curled on her left side clutching the body pillow between him and the bed, her swelling belly sinking into the cushion. Her body formed a question mark. But he didn't know the answer. How could he break her heart? Would she ever forgive him?

He and Jayden had bought a birthday present for Jubilee. A book they'd found on display in the children's section of Barnes & Noble, beside a stuffed rabbit. Jayden had said, "Bee likes rabbits, like Velveteen." It was called *The Runaway Bunny*. In the book, when the little bunny announces he'll run away, his mama says she'll run after him. He counters he'll become *a fish in a trout stream and swim away* from her, but that mama was smart. She says if he becomes a fish in a trout stream, she'll become a fisherman and fish for him. Not outdone, he says he'll become a ship and sail away. But that mama says she'll become a wind cloud and blow him in the direction she wants. And so it goes. Whatever he becomes, she becomes the thing that can catch him or guide him back until the bunny gives up and decides to stay with his mama. *Eat a carrot*, she says.

Joshua figured the book would be good for Bee. She was a mother to something that couldn't ever leave. She was baking Jubilee a cake she could not eat. Joshua tried not to be bitter. It was hard. He remembered Bee quoting something from one of her essays on Chicana poets earlier in the semester. *Feeding is the beginning and end of what a mother knows to do for her offspring.* Bee told him Ana Castillo said that. He didn't know who Ana Castillo was, but he liked the quote. He would've changed it to *parent*. Fathers didn't know what to do either.

Jayden hopped on the chair propped against the kitchen counter as Bee demonstrated how to frost the cake, not too thick but enough so you didn't catch crumbs in the frosting or it'd be lumpy. Jayden said he liked lumps. She said he *was* a lump, and they both laughed. Joshua felt removed. She handed Jayden a plastic spatula so he could try, but he got more chocolate frosting on his hands and face than on the cake. "Can we eat it now?"

"No, mijo. At a birthday party, we have to sing then blow out the candles first." She pushed a candle in the shape of a number one into the top of the cake. "Come on, let's go sit with your dada and open Jubilee's presents."

"Then cake?"

"Yes, then cake." She laughed, scooping Jubilee from the high chair and onto her lap. Jayden stood on a chair at the table and scooted Jubilee's presents toward her. Matty had sent one home with Bee that day when she'd picked up Jubilee from his house. He still watched her whenever Bee was in class or tutoring at the Writing Center. Joshua had wanted to talk to Matty again, figure out how to end the ritual. But he'd chickened out.

"Open ours first," Jayden called, squirming atop the chair, handing her the present.

As she unwrapped it, she said, "Josh, I keep forgetting to ask you. Matty needs you to confirm Comic-Con. He's getting your ticket for free."

"Okay, I'll call him." They'd been planning a trip to San Diego, but Joshua wasn't looking forward to that anymore. The social worker visit had taken over all his thoughts. It was bullshit. He got up for a soda from the fridge so Bee wouldn't see how upset he was.

From behind the kitchen island, he watched Bee unwrap the present. She tilted her head back and smiled. "Oh, I love this book. Wherever bunny goes, his mother will find him because she is his mother bunny. I remember this from a play I read in my modern drama class. Thank you, guys. This is lovely."

"We picked it because you like rabbits," Jayden said.

Bee laughed. "I do?"

"Yes, Velvet ones."

"Oh, I do. This is perfect. Thank you."

Jayden clapped his hands. Bee looked over at Joshua, so he winked at her, forcing his mouth into a smile. He was trying so damn hard to be with her.

"There's still another present. Open Uncle Matty's. It's *cake* time."

Bee laughed. "What's up with you and cake, mijo?" From the gift bag and tissue, she pulled out a yellow ruffled dress with matching booties and bonnet. It was tiny. He must have bought it in the preemie section.

The number candle on the cake was *One*. Bee had picked it out. It was Jubilee's first birthday. She was a year old. Didn't Bee ever wonder why her baby didn't grow? She'd explained away the crying, imagined diapers needed changing, exchanged the plastic bottle for a real one. But how could she justify her baby staying a baby forever? In her mind. What about Jubilee's third birthday? Her tenth? What would happen in a few short months when their own baby was born? Would she compare her with Jubilee? Would she ever understand the difference?

They needed counseling. Joshua had screwed up. The charade had to end. "That dress looks small. Jubilee is a one-year-old now. Shouldn't she wear a bigger size?"

She looked at Joshua like he'd startled her, squinting, a question on her face, not quite a glare. She looked at the tag on the dress. *You can't backtrack now.* "Is it the right size?" He prodded, trying to keep his voice casual. His heart was racing. He didn't need a freak-out from her today. Not in front of Jayden. He was still scared of the bathtub incident.

"It's NB, size newborn." Her voice was flat.

"That's strange, isn't it? She's not a newborn anymore." *You jerk. She's gonna see through you.*

"Can we eat cake now, *please*? I can't wait. I'm going crazy. I'm starving. *I need cake*." Jayden was pulling on his face with both palms, stretching the skin on his cheeks like a little zombie boy and widening his eyes so the veiny part of the whites showed. "*Cake!*"

"Hang on, little guy. I need to talk to Bee about this. It's important."

"It's a dumb dress. Jubilee has lots of dresses," Jayden said, pouting.

"Bee? What do you think? Why's she still wearing newborn clothes?"

She frowned. "Do you think she's sick? Is that what you're saying? Something's wrong?"

"I don't know. She doesn't look sick. But it doesn't seem normal, does it? For a baby not to grow? By the time Jayden was a year old, he was wearing size twenty-four months. He's a big guy, so we can't compare them. But it's strange, right?"

She nodded. She looked at Jayden, who'd stuck his finger in the cake and licked the frosting. She looked at Jubilee. "I'll keep an eye on her."

"For what, Bee? Think about it. What are you gonna watch her do? She's not growing. She's not changing." *She's not real. Come on, Bee. See it. Please.*

"Stop it, Josh. Just stop. It's her birthday. Not now, not now, not now . . ." She was rocking back and forth.

Fuck. A meltdown. "Hey, Bee. Shhh, I'm sorry. Let's just eat cake." He swallowed back the lump in his throat. *Eat your carrot*, said the mother bunny.

Jayden squealed. "Yay!"

Joshua lit the candle. He and Jayden sang *Happy birthday to you*, but

Bee was silent. After the song finished, the candle kept burning. *Who's gonna blow it out? Who's gonna make a wish?*

Jayden blew a raspberry, and the light flickered out.

Denial wouldn't work. They were falling apart. What happened to a deceit deferred? Did it explode? The social worker was coming the next morning, and he had no idea how to ask his wife to keep her delusion to herself.

"*Josh!* I need help . . ."

He climbed out of bed, groggy, pushing the blankets off his body. He'd dreamt Bee needed something. He couldn't reach her. "Josh!" He wasn't dreaming. Bee *was* calling him.

It was déjà vu. Bee, screaming.

He switched on the bedroom lights and looked around the room. She wasn't there.

He slogged out to the living room where Bee was standing in front of the entertainment center staring into the fishbowl. She was crying.

"What's wrong?"

"The fish."

He came closer, rubbed sleep from his eyes. The goldfish floated upside-down in the water. "Ah, I'm sorry." He reached out to hug her, but she pushed his arms away.

"I can't even keep a fucking fish alive."

"Shhh . . . You're upset, I know, but don't wake Jayden. It'll scare him."

"I know, I'm sorry."

"I'll be right back."

Jayden was asleep. Joshua shut the kid's bedroom door.

Bee lay in a heap on the floor.

"Hey . . . I'm here," he said, kneeling down and stroking her hair.

"Even fucking fish drown. Water should be illegal. All water."

"I know. Damn stuff is dangerous." What was it with her and drowning? It was a goldfish. They don't live long. Why was she so upset? "Can you try to relax? What were you doing awake? Was something wrong?"

"I got up to pee and was spotting so I came out to watch TV. I found the fish. Dead."

Oh shit. She was spotting. *Shit.* Was *that* real? Or like when she thought Jayden was drowning in the bathtub? Joshua would have to check without upsetting her more. If she was bleeding, he'd call the doctor. If not, goddamn. What if not? Was she slipping away from him?

When her crying subsided, he asked, "Is Jubilee asleep?"

"I checked on her before I came out. She's fine. She's always fine, isn't she?" Her tone was bitter. Joshua wasn't used to this Bee. Part of him wanted to call Dr. Norris.

"Was it a lot of blood? And what color?" *What are you doing? You're not a doctor.*

"A few drops and dark tinged, stringy."

"That's not bad." He reassured himself as much as her. "Want to go to the ER in case?"

He'd pushed her at Jubilee's birthday party. She wasn't ready to let go. With the social worker and the pregnancy, it was too much. But Bee was a goddamn mess, huddled on the ground in the middle of the night. If a goldfish dying could upset her, what would happen if Joshua smashed her bubble? All he needed to say was *if you mention Jubilee to the social worker, if you hold her or rock her or sing to her, we could lose our son.* They had to pretend. Long enough to buy time. They could go to counseling. They could get real help, the kind he couldn't give her. *What if she wasn't really bleeding?*

"I don't think I need to go to the ER," she said, pulling herself onto the couch, clutching her belly. "But will you help me check? I'm scared." That made two of them. Joshua breathed as deeply as he could. It wasn't the time to hyperventilate. He helped her to the master bathroom, where she pulled down her flannel pajama pants, grabbed a wad of toilet paper, wiped and showed him.

"Hardly anything," he said, relieved. There was blood. Not enough to be concerned about. Could've been from her exam last week, or from sex the other day. "We'll call the doctor in the morning. I'll make you tea, rub your feet." He walked behind her, holding her close, his body pressed against hers, hands around her waist, footsteps in unison, back toward the bed. "I'll be back with your tea. Honey?"

She smiled in that strange half smile of hers, the corners of her mouth turned down. "Thank you," she said.

"No problem."

"Not for the honey," she said. "Thank you for loving me."

"That's no problem, either." He winked, but as he closed the bedroom door, he thought *She's not the problem, I am.* He'd gone into his profession to help others. Keep them from going through what he'd gone through. Yet there he was on the cusp of disaster. At Patti's doorway listening to her son say there was no room in their house, in their lives, for him. He should've spoken up then. He should've told Patti that he was her boy and she knew it. Not to listen to her son. *But you were a chicken then and you're a chicken now.*

On his way to the kitchen, he stopped in the living room. He took the fishbowl to the hallway bathroom, flushed the fish down the toilet.

He opened the door to Jayden's bedroom. The constellation nightlight glowed amber, and the Big Bear, as Jayden called him, shone on the ceiling. They'd mapped those stars, learning each cluster's name and story. Joshua couldn't let him go. He had to be tough. Patti had given in too easily. He couldn't let that happen.

He walked to the kitchen, determined. He filled the teakettle, ready. He steeped the tea, strong. He whispered aloud to the cabinet doors, practicing, *We have to pretend. I love Jubilee as much as you do. I would never ask you to hide her if it weren't necessary. But it is. The social worker won't understand. She'll deny us. We'll lose Jayden. Bee, we'll lose him.*

She could handle it. She wasn't glass. It wasn't much blood. Normal spotting. She was fine. She wouldn't miscarry. She was ready. If not, it didn't matter. She had to be ready. He poured honey into the tea, the way she liked it, and put the mug on a plate with cookies. She'd forgive him.

He opened their bedroom door. Bee snored loud pregnancy snores, her legs wrapped around a body pillow.

He sighed then gulped her mug of tea, scorching his throat. *Shit.* He dropped the mug to the floor and sank into the rocking chair beside the bed. He stared at Bee, curled on her side, their baby swimming inside her, gullible little fish. *I don't know what you'll be coming out to, kid.*

After the social worker checked on them, they'd pack for Comic-Con in San Diego. They'd dig holes in the sand on the beach. He was overreacting. Everything would be fine. The social worker was coming, and they were going to the beach. Then why was he picturing them on the island of dolls, drowning? He glanced at Jubilee's bassinet in the corner of the room. Even fish drown. Even good parents lose children.

TWENTY-NINE
MARRY ME

BEFORE JUBILEE

On the way home from Newport Beach, in the passenger seat of Gabe's pine-green truck, Bianca imagined what her life might look like, slow-cooked each night in the menudo caldron where vast brown desert shouldered acres of farms in dusty brown lots and field upon field of alfalfa. This place muttered of empty beer cans strewn on yellowing patches of grass, cars parked on lawns, twenty-four-hour doughnut shops that never emptied, and migrant field workers laboring in ungodly heat while the foremen and white farmers sat in their air-conditioned trucks. Her heart burst in this desert with prickly cactus flowers, blooming in the cracks of sun-scorched pavement—hot enough to burn skin, to sear the soft patches of dirt-blackened feet—where grandmothers set out pitchers of tea to brew on their front porches. Where Gabe might leave her. Where she hated herself for not leaving him.

They drove away from the ocean through the rolling hills. Beaumont. The casinos. Off the Arizona freeway, onto the two-lane Highway 86. Out into the arid brown. Down into California's basin—its toilet tank, as Gabe called it.

Past the Salton Sea, the date-farm signs lured: "Stop and drink date shakes here." She'd never stopped for a date shake because dates reminded her of the tall palms in the empty lots behind her house with the No Trespassing signs she ignored, where she picked dates that had fallen to the hard-packed earth and chucked them at passing cars or down into the ravine toward the river. She'd never actually eaten a date, although she'd sucked on figs whole summers through. Dates reminded her of cockroaches, the swollen creatures that scuttled then flew. She could never bring herself to put one in her mouth.

But the signs boasted, "Cold, refreshing, sweet." So she asked Gabe to stop, and he bought her one. Frothy and amber-colored.

She made a face as she took a sip. "Ugh. This is gross. I knew I'd hate dates."

"Then why'd you want a *date* shake? The name kind of implies the dates."

"I don't know. It sounded good."

"Well, don't waste that. Here, give it to me. I'll drink it." They started driving again.

She handed it over, still thirsty. "Date shakes on the side of the road conjure up my feelings for you," she said. "All those drives back and forth through this desert. Away from you. Back to you. Star-crossed, date-crossed."

"What are you talking about?"

"I don't know."

He smelled like Cool Water aftershave and that sickly-sweet fruit. She rubbed her hand against his neck, his short spiky hair prickling her hands.

"Hey, cut that out. I'm trying to drive."

"We've done a lot more than that while you were driving."

"I know. It's just, I don't feel like that right now."

"You know, I've been waiting for you since I was fourteen. Waiting for our life to begin."

"What's it been up till now? Aren't we living?"

"Not the way I imagined."

"That's a lot of pressure on a person, isn't it? To live up to someone's dream?" He sighed, glanced at her quickly, then returned his gaze to the road. "I mean, why me, anyway?"

She'd developed this idea of what they were, and it didn't matter that reality didn't match up. She'd fooled herself with this beautiful idea. That the truth wasn't pretty no longer held relevance.

Except it did.

"You acted like you were on a date with her. What the hell was that?"

"What are you talking about now? I can't even understand you today."

"Adriana."

"Come on, Bee. I've known her all my life."

"She's pretty though, isn't she?"

"I guess."

"What's that mean?"

"It doesn't mean anything. Jesus. What's your problem, Bee? Pregnancy hormones really suck."

"This isn't hormones. This is me being tired of the same old thing."

"I'm tired too."

"We're having a family together. I'm tired of feeling like second string when I should be your first. Your only. I'm tired of not being able to face my family."

"How is it my fault you refuse to see your family?"

"You never take responsibility for anything."

"What do you think I'm doing now?"

"I'm a responsibility. Real nice." She said it like rocks in her mouth, jagged against her tongue.

"I didn't mean it like that."

"Yes, you did."

He sighed again. "Fine. Maybe I did."

"I can raise this baby alone. I'm strong enough. I don't need your help."

"I know that."

She still wanted the colors, the Folklorico dress of her girlhood, spinning and spinning. She wanted his voice and the butterflies he called up in her—even now. Even when she hated him, she loved him. She felt knotted to him, and although she *could* have cut the cord, stripped herself of memory until she was rid of him, slice by slice, she wasn't sure she was ready. Their baby danced inside her. She could feel her wiggling around. Bubbles popping in her belly. Hiccoughs. Laughter. He'd glued pieces of himself inside of her. She felt them there, sticking.

She blurted out, "Marry me." She almost put her hand over her mouth. The words had slipped out. She hadn't realized they were coming.

Two red balloons in the air. An SOS.

Marry. Me.

He pulled the car over to the shoulder, throwing up clouds of dirt beneath the tires, then turned to face her.

"Bee. I love you. I do. And I know what an asshole I can be. I'm trying to do the right thing. I keep trying not to screw up." He looked behind her, out the window. She braced herself and waited—sage brush, tumbleweed, dry arroyo beds—for his answer. "I know marrying you is the right thing. But I'm just not ready. I'm not."

She breathed out sharply, said nothing. Bubbles popping. Inside her.

"I'm sorry," he said again, reaching for her hand, but she pulled away.

THIRTY
THE HOME INSPECTION

WITH JUBILEE

Bee was humming from the bedroom. A bad sign. But the apartment was clean. Joshua had checked the water heater and stocked the fridge and pantry with fruits, vegetables, healthy snacks. On the top shelf of the hall closet, he'd secured first-aid and emergency kits. Jayden wore corduroy pants and a vest, his curls shined and glossed, his teeth brushed. Bee was humming, but she seemed stable enough otherwise.

They were ready.

Footsteps up the stairway meant nothing good was coming. "Come here, big guy." Joshua pulled Jayden into his arms and squeezed him tight.

Jayden laughed, dimples forming at his cheeks. "Fly me like an airplane!"

"To the moon." He buried his face into Jayden's chest and landed him safely. He was crying. *Shit.* The social worker couldn't see him crying. He wiped his eyes on Jayden's shirt then set him down. *Please don't let Jayden say anything suspicious.* How had he let it go so far? Bee in the bedroom, humming to herself, afraid she might still be spotting. He and Jayden waiting for a social worker. Fucking Olivia. Why had she called the social worker? He'd promised to take care of her boy, promised not to let anyone take him away.

Though he knew it was coming, the knock on the door startled him.

Jayden stood straight with his hands clasped behind his back as if trying to appear taller and more dignified. He looked official, like he was awaiting orders. A little solider in a brown checkered vest.

Joshua opened the door and said hello, plastering a grin across his face he hoped appeared natural and sincere (or, at least, wasn't trembling).

"I'm Cristina Long, your social worker. We've spoken on the phone." She offered Joshua her hand. In her other hand, she carried a black brief-case. She had mousy brown hair and an uneven complexion, scarred from acne, and wore a gray suit, threadbare and too large for her frame. She was a small woman and had a kind face. But what could Joshua tell from her face? She could've been pretending, like he was. *Don't trust her. Don't let your guard down. Look out for traps. One step ahead.*

"Please come in. We've been expecting you." Joshua's voice came out strangely ominous, like the creepy butler at the Disneyland Haunted Mansion before locking the parlor, turning out the lights, and flaunting the dead man hanging from the rafter above the ceiling. A siren warned *Intruder.* Alarm bells, residual from childhood. *You don't know what to expect.*

Cristina thanked him and came inside.

Before Joshua realized what was happening, Bee had shuffled into the living room in a sundress and house shoes. She extended one hand to the social worker, keeping her other hand atop her belly. He breathed out relief that she hadn't brought Jubilee with her. "Hi, Cristina. Nice to meet you." Bee flashed one of her gorgeous smiles, her golden eyes sparkling. If he hadn't known better, he would've thought Bee was truly at ease. "I'm Bianca, Joshua's wife. Jayden's mama." Flawless. She was doing great. He'd been worried for nothing.

"Oh my, look at you." Cristina laughed. "When are you due?"

"August second."

Cristina smiled. "That's not far away. Is this your first?"

He hated her already. First what? Pregnancy? Real, living, nondoll baby? She was setting them up for failure. The disappointments and anger he wanted to hurl at Patti, Olivia, and Ms. McCall, maybe even that he should've felt toward Bee, all of it tumbled out at Cristina, the disrespect-ful social worker in her shabby gray suit.

He spoke before Bee could. "We're all excited about the new baby. Aren't we Jayden?"

Cristina turned and noticed, for the first time, Jayden, standing stoically, puffing his chest and clasping his hands behind his back. "Hi there, Jayden," she said, reaching out to shake his hand. "How are you?"

Crisis averted.

Jayden ignored her outstretched hand. Good for him. It was their animal spirit, that owl stalking its prey from a branch up high, waiting to swoop.

Cristina smiled again, but it looked forced. She pulled her hand back when it was clear Jayden wouldn't shake it, then she squatted to his eye-level and tried again. "I'm Cristina, and I'm here to have a little chat with you and your mom and dad. Is that okay?"

Jayden shrugged. "Sure. Do you like to read?"

"I do like to read. What's your favorite book?"

"*Velveteen Rabbit.* Bee, I mean, my *mama* gave it to me." He said *mama* as if trying to prove something. "It's both our favorite. We read it all the time."

"That's a good one. I've read it to my kids."

"You have kids?"

"Yep, two of them. A boy and a girl."

"Cool. Want me to show you my room?"

Joshua tried not to roll his eyes. Classic social worker move, gaining the kids' trust. Jayden had given in too easily. Joshua had never warmed up to a social worker so fast. He used to run and hide behind Patti's couch whenever one would come over. He'd stashed a cache of comics underneath the base of the couch where he would hide, lying on his stomach reading until Patti or Olivia pulled him out by his ankles.

"Sure, I'd love to see your room," Cristina said. She stood to face them. "I'll chat with him a few minutes first, alone, if you don't mind. Then we can have a conversation before I begin the home inspection."

"That's fine," Joshua said. But at the word *inspection*, his gut twisted and he felt out of breath. He resisted the urge to pull out his inhaler in front of Cristina. Oscar's and Olivia's words whirled through his mind, sputtering *wacko. Batshit crazy.* They wouldn't let a crazy take care of Jayden, she'd said. He felt dizzy. *Maybe you're the crazy one, Joshy.*

"What will she ask him?" Bee whispered as they disappeared into Jayden's room. She scooted closer to Joshua and reached for his arms, which he extended, wrapping around her. In his anxiety, he'd forgotten she should've been resting, just in case that spotting was anything to be concerned about.

"I don't know."

They waited in silence, transfixed on the crack in Jayden's doorway. They heard laughter. Pieces of conversation. Joshua couldn't stop imagining the social worker dragging Jayden away.

From Cristina, "How long . . ."

From Jayden, "Dada . . . a baby. Bee . . . came from the beach."

From Cristina, "Excited . . . baby sister?"

From Jayden, "Best big brother."

Joshua heard nothing about Jubilee. He sighed. Maybe God was listening.

A few minutes later, Cristina followed Jayden out of his room, both of them smiling.

"He's a wonderful kid," Cristina said. "You two must be proud."

"I told Cristina how we're going to San Diego this weekend."

"A family trip," Joshua said. *See, we're a normal family who goes on beach vacations.*

"Can I get you anything to drink or eat, Cristina?" Bee asked, leading her to the dining table.

"No, I'm fine. Thank you. You know, he's a great little boy," Cristina reiterated. "He had nothing but positive remarks for both of you."

Joshua almost joked that he was relieved Jayden didn't mention anything about them locking him in the closet. But why risk it? Only Bee thought his lame jokes were funny. Instead, he said, "We couldn't imagine our lives without him."

"So, I have your home study profile all set, but now I need to ask you some perhaps uncomfortable questions. It's routine, really. But I have to ask." He couldn't look at her face. He stared at his hands pressed to his knees, imagining them blue and furry as Beast's.

"Have either of you ever experienced sexual or physical abuse, either as a child or adult?"

They both answered in unison, "No." Though Joshua was fairly certain that wasn't true, especially for Bianca.

"Do either of you have any history of mental illness, anywhere in your family?"

He shook his head no, scratching nervously at his pants leg, trying to stop the shaking that had taken over his body.

Bee said, "Well, my dad dealt with depression for many years. Other than that, no."

"Okay, good to note. Thank you. Let's see, just a few more questions . . . Do either of you or any close family members smoke, take recreational drugs, or consume alcohol?"

"No, neither of us do any of those things. Neither does anyone in our close family," Joshua said. His temples throbbed, his tongue felt too big for his mouth. "As you read in the paperwork, I'm not in contact with any of my family members since I was raised in foster care, so I wouldn't really know what my family does or doesn't do. But Bee's family is mine and Jayden's family now, and they're all upstanding citizens." It was overkill. He sounded like he was reading off some *Happy Family* brochure.

"Good. So we can check that off. Do you own any firearms or other weapons, and, if so, are they stored in the home?"

"No," Bee said. "We don't believe in them."

We're just a hippie, peace-loving family here, ma'am. We're all poets and tree-huggers, but we don't blaze up.

"Okay, this all sounds great. My final question has to do with siblings in the home, so it'll apply to your expected little one." She flashed what was supposed to be a reassuring smile, but Joshua didn't buy it. His fingers tingled. He'd been digging his nails into his legs.

She continued, her voice professional and placid. But Joshua's ears buzzed with Olivia's taunting voice. "The question asks how you feel about the prospective child in relation to other children already in the home, but we can tweak it. Explain how you feel about the new baby in relation to Jayden. For this question, I'd like you to answer individually."

Joshua spoke first, trying to keep his lips from quivering. "Well, for me, Jayden is my son already, and he's been my son since birth. I'm biologically his uncle, I raised him, and, until Bee, we're all each other had. So no matter what, he'll always be my boy. I can't wait for this new baby. I'm excited to raise one with Bee from the beginning. But they're both my kids."

Cristina jotted notes. *She better not be twisting your words, like social workers and judges are prone to do.*

"Yes, I agree," Bee said, her tone matching Cristina's. Wasn't she as anxious as him? How did she hide it so well? "I've only known Jayden for a year, yet I've considered him family from day one. He's the funniest, sweetest, most compassionate little boy I've ever met. He stole my heart from our first date, trying to make a good ''preshun' on me. I fell in love with Josh, of course, and married him, but I also fell in love with Jayden, and married him as well. He's my son, and I'm his Bee. Nothing can change that."

Yes, something can change that. He wiped the sweat from his forehead and pulled at the collar of his button-down shirt. *Cristina could change that.*

But Cristina was smiling as she said, "That's lovely to hear, I have to tell you." His heart was racing. They'd done it. They were in the clear. "Well folks, I have a full report, so all I need to do is conduct the home inspection." He checked his Superman watch. How long did these things last? Time worked differently for grownups than kids. He couldn't remember it ever taking so long when he was at Patti's. He willed Cristina to hurry.

She listed off the items she needed to inspect. Safety plugs in all the outlets. Bookshelves bolted to the wall. Knives, matches, medicine, household-cleaning agents all secured and locked away where children could not reach.

She'd already seen Jayden's bedroom, and that looked great.

"Will he share a room with his sister?" she asked.

"Not at first," Joshua said. "She'll sleep in our room, then a crib in Jayden's room."

"Sounds good. If you don't mind then, I'll need to go ahead and see your room."

"Sure." He opened the door and held his breath. Jubilee was in their room.

"Oh, how sweet," Cristina exclaimed. "You already have it all set for her. What a lovely bassinet."

He nodded. *Keep your mouth shut, Bee. Play along.*

Bee moved across the room and picked up Jubilee. It happened so fast Joshua didn't have time to stop her. What could he have done anyway?

This was it. It was over.

Bee held Jubilee close, patting her back.

Cristina smiled. "I love it."

Joshua sucked in his breath sharply. What? Loved what?

"You two are practicing for when the baby gets here. What a smart idea. I've often encouraged couples to practice for new babies using dolls."

Bee opened her mouth to speak.

What happens to a dream deferred? Maybe it just sags, like a heavy load. Or does it explode?

He couldn't find out.

"Yes, we're practicing. For the baby. With this doll."

He said it, but he couldn't look at Bee.

"That's wonderful. Really wonderful." Cristina jotted a few more notes, smiling.

Bee sank into the rocking chair.

"Bianca?" Cristina asked.

Bee didn't respond. She looked like she'd been punched in the stomach and had the wind knocked out of her, the way she told him had happened once when she'd been playing Superman on the swings and had flown off and landed on her belly on the dirt. She'd tried crying out to her dad but nothing would come out. It was the first time she remembered not being able to talk when she had something to say.

Now Joshua had done that to her. Knocked her into the dirt.

"You know, this happens," he answered Cristina, keeping his voice steady. "She gets exhausted from the pregnancy. But she's a trooper. She'll be fine." He couldn't look at Bee. His stomach coiled, the back of his neck stinging with what felt like scorpions.

"Oh, I remember that, believe me. By seven months, all I wanted to do was sleep. Well, you two, we're pretty much done. And I believe I can safely say that everything appears in tip-top shape. You should hear back from our office soon, but I don't think you have anything to be concerned about. I'm not sure what that call was about, honestly. Seems everything here is in great order. I'm wishing you three all the best with the new little one."

Joshua thanked her, his heart still pounding.

Cristina turned to Bee, who was still clutching Jubilee and staring out the window. "I hope you feel better, Bianca. I wish you a safe, healthy delivery." Bee turned her head, as if she'd just noticed there were still other people in the bedroom. The corners of her mouth were sagging. Gone was the brilliant flash she'd shown before. The amber glow in her eyes had faded. Joshua hated himself. He wanted to hold Bee.

Cristina walked through the doorway, clipboard in hand, assuring them again that they'd hear from her soon but that everything looked great. "We appreciate all your help, Cristina." He no longer hated her. She'd been there to do her job. To protect a kid. To ensure a good family stayed together. She wasn't the enemy. No, he didn't hate her.

Joshua now hated himself.

As he shut the bedroom door behind him to walk Cristina out, Bee said, quietly, under her breath, so softly Joshua was sure Cristina couldn't have heard, "She's not a doll."

He sighed, so goddamn exhausted. At the front door, he shook Cristina's hand again and kept up his mask long enough for final platitudes. They'd passed the test. Now, what did that mean for his wife's mental health?

He reopened the bedroom door, half afraid of what he'd find. She'd remained by the window, clutching Jubilee, an empty glaze over both of their faces.

"I'm so sorry, Bee." He knelt on the floor at her feet, reached out to touch her. She didn't move. She didn't even seem to notice he was there. She just stared and stared. His beautiful, porcelain wife, and her beautiful, porcelain daughter.

"I didn't mean to hurt you. The social worker wouldn't have understood. She would've put a label on you. Don't you know that? She would have taken our son away. I had to say it, Bee. I don't believe it. Jubilee is our daughter. That's what's real. Please know that I never would have said that if it was not absolutely necessary."

She didn't flinch. But he looked up and saw tears streaming down the stone of her face, smearing her black eyeliner and creating sad, dark lines down her cheeks. She grasped Jubilee tighter to her chest and began rocking.

Joshua felt horrible, but he'd done what he had to do. He'd protected them all. Bianca had to see that.

What had Rosana said at Thanksgiving? Just give her time.

THIRTY-ONE
DITCHWATER BEE

BEFORE JUBILEE

From Bianca's mattress on the floor, she stared at Gabe slouching in Lily's old patio chair across the bedroom. He was playing on his phone, and she could tell he was only pretending to listen to her day, her doctor's appointment, updates on the baby. He didn't give her anything more than grunts, and her cheeks burned with a dull red flash. She petted Kanga, curled at her side on the floor beside the mattress, with one hand, bit her fingernails on the other hand until the skin around the edges peeled ragged. They were living in a truce. Some silent in-between, purgatorial holding pen. She felt stuck.

His cell phone rang; Kanga looked up at the noise, the tags on her collar jangling. Bianca could tell from the way Gabe looked at the screen and the way he answered the call that it was Adriana, the skinny beach-girl who was "like his cousin." He cut Bianca off midsentence as she was describing the classified ad for a yard sale she'd responded to at the newspaper. The ad had said, "INFANT GIRL ITEMS: NEVER USED. COMPLETE NURSERY SET: CAR SEAT, CLOTHES, SWING, TOYS, DOLLS & MORE." She thought of the six-word novel often attributed to Ernest Hemingway: "FOR SALE: BABY SHOES, NEVER WORN." The saddest flash fiction ever written. Perhaps this yard sale was less sad: It was a boy instead; the doctors had been wrong. Whatever the reason for the sale,

Bianca had gone and bought everything since the items were brand new and she couldn't have found them so cheap anywhere else. She'd piled the stash in her trunk and back seat, and set up the bassinet in the living room, hoping Gabe would notice when he came over. But he hadn't noticed. He wasn't listening.

On the phone, she overheard Adriana say she was at a furniture store in Newport Beach, buying a couch. Moving out of her mom's place and on her own. Bianca couldn't hear most of what she said, but Gabe was laughing. He never laughed with Bianca anymore. His care for her seemed robotic at best. He set her prenatal vitamin on the bathroom sink. He got up in the middle of the night to get her water. One afternoon she was cramping and spotting in week thirteen, and he drove her to the urgent care. She was fine, the doctor said, but take it easy. No stress. No lifting anything heavy. At week twenty, Gabe had stopped asking her to give him blowjobs when he saw it made her gag.

But he didn't laugh.

He got off the phone, still smiling.

Bianca tried again. "The doctor says she's growing. Everything looks normal and healthy."

"Hmm."

"Want to see a picture?"

"Sure." His voice was noncommittal, and he drew the word out as if it took effort.

Most nights, he camped out with her in the empty house-for-sale. He hated Kanga's dog hair all over everything and how messy Bianca was, so he was always complaining, but he still slept with her. They watched movies and he took her out to dinner and ate the food she cooked for him in her little makeshift kitchen with the hand-me-down supplies. But he'd stopped asking questions about the pregnancy or the baby and never wanted to come to any doctor's appointments. She argued with him about it, angry that he used to go with Katrina to hers. "What do you want from me, Bianca?" he'd ask. "I'm here, aren't I?" *Was he?* She didn't know.

She pulled sonogram photos from her purse. "She's a girl."

"Cool. Do you have a name yet?"

"No, but I'm thinking about biblical names. Maybe something to connect with my mom again, you know. Do you have any suggestions?"

"Nope." He checked his cell phone.

"Are you expecting another call?"

"No, Bianca. I'm not." He said her name like they were strangers, acquaintances at most. "Am I not allowed to look at my phone now?"

Her cheeks burned again. She wanted to snap at him but felt too heavy for a fight. Her stomach swelled and her skin stretched against the baby, kicking all day.

The phone rang. Bianca knew damn well it was Adriana. She stood quickly, startling Kanga, and grabbed the phone from Gabe before he could stop her. "Hello," she started in a melodramatic tone. "This is *Bianca*, Gabe's *pregnant* girlfriend. Who the fuck is this?" She should've grabbed the phone a long time ago, back when Gabe had cheated on her with Katrina.

Adriana stayed quiet on the line.

Gabe lunged toward Bianca, yelling. "Give me back my phone. Come on, this isn't funny." Kanga was barking, like it was a game. Cell phone keep away. Catch the cheating puto in the middle.

Bianca clutched the phone in one hand, her belly with the other, and shuffled toward the living room, Kanga at her heels; she perched on the coffee table beside the artificial Christmas tree and fake presents she'd never taken down although it was nearly May.

She kept Adriana on the phone. In an affected, high-pitched, singsong, she pretended to mask her disdain. "Adriana, poor dear. I hear you've been having some *boyfriend* troubles. As in, causing trouble with other women's boyfriends."

Gabe followed her, snatching for his phone as Bianca scooted away, almost falling off the table but managing to break her fall with her free hand. She still held the phone.

"Excuse me, Adriana. My Gabe is trying to get frisky with me." She was ridiculous but couldn't help it. She was trembling.

She scuttled off the floor and waddled back to the bathroom, locking herself in. *Hide-and-seek. Come find me. God, please, come find me.* Kanga scratched at the door, whining.

"Look, Adriana," Bianca said, the fake sugar gone from her voice. "I know what you're up to. Gabe and I have been together for years and we've gone through a lot. I don't know if he told you, but I've lost a baby before and I don't want to lose this one. All the stress of wondering whether or not my boyfriend is cheating on me, with you, it's too hard to take. Please do us both a favor and have some respect for yourself. Go find a boyfriend who's available. Someone without a pregnant girlfriend and another kid already here."

Adriana remained silent, but she stayed on the phone. Her passive-aggressiveness inflamed Bianca even more. She wanted to reach through the receiver and grab her skinny neck. *Say something, you cunt.*

Outside the bathroom, Gabe pounded his body against the door. "Open up, Bee! You're being so rude. Leave her alone. She hasn't done anything." Bianca hated that he was defending his tramp. She didn't care if Adriana was his godfather's daughter.

"Do we have an understanding?" Bianca asked. Adriana didn't say a word, but Bianca could hear her breathing. "What? I'm not worth answering? That's how low you think of me?"

Still no response.

"You coward," she said. "You fucking cunt. Answer me." The bathroom door burst open in a blast of splintering wood, and Gabe seized the phone from her shaking hand.

"Adriana?" he called into the receiver. "I'm sorry about that. She gets crazy sometimes. Look, I'll talk to you later."

He hung up and glared at Bianca. She plopped onto the toilet seat, tears stinging her eyes. Her crotch and pelvis ached. She was having a contraction.

"Do you love her?"

"Why are you so fucking crazy? Can't I have a friend? I've known Adriana since we were babies. Why do you always think I'm messing around on you?"

"Because you are."

"Because you're insane, that's why. I don't even think you should be having this baby. You'll smother it like you smother me, like you smother everything. God, Bianca. Why do you have to push so hard? Why do you have to make everything into some tragedy?"

"I wanted us to be a family. That's all I've ever wanted."

"I know, Bee. I know. But you push me. Why'd we have to have this baby *now*? We aren't ready and you know it."

"What are you saying?"

He sighed, deeply. Ran his hands through his spiky, black hair. He looked at Bianca like he was afraid of her. Afraid to speak. Finally, he said, "I've been thinking of moving up to Orange County."

"What?"

"There's a job up there, Adriana told me about. With my padrino."

"Were you planning to invite me?"

He sighed again, locked his hands behind his head. "I mean, where would you live? Even with my padrino's help, I don't think I'd make enough to support us both yet, with you on maternity. Would you be able to find a job up there to pay rent?" He wasn't asking.

"So what, Gabe? Say what you're trying to say."

"I think you should go home for a while and stay with your family. I'm not saying I'm leaving you, but I think it's best till we get on our feet. I can't let us stay in this valley."

"You want me to go home to my mama, seven months pregnant, un-married, without a boyfriend in sight, when I haven't told her yet I'm pregnant because I've been waiting, waiting, *waiting* like a fool for you to marry me like you promised years ago? Because I've been a fucking delusional tonta thinking you'll wake up and remember that you love me? That this baby girl inside of me is half you and the other half the me-you-couldn't-get-enough-of, once upon a fucking time?"

"Stop cussing, Bee. You'll teach our baby to cuss."

She wanted to spit at him. She'd never wanted to spit at someone. She wanted to punch him in the face.

He hung his head, fumbled with that damn cell phone. "I'm sorry, Bee. I do love you. But I can't handle this now. It's too much."

"The world is too much, Gabe. Grow up."

"Look, I don't know what you want me to do. I said I'm sorry." He hunched on the bathtub's edge.

"I need more than sorry." She breathed slowly, trying to calm the waves of pain spreading through her crotch and down her legs. She pictured a bone-dry animal pelvis in the desert, crawling with snakes. "I need you to be the man I thought you were."

He sat there on the linoleum, forehead pressed into his palms.

"And what about Lana?"

"I'll come back as often as I can. She'll still go to my mom's every weekend."

"Mm-hmm. And where will you live?" Bianca felt cold. "Up there in Orange County? While I'm at my abuela's with my mama taking care of *our* baby? Where will you live that we can't stay with you?"

He shook his head and sighed, looked up at her face, his eyes glistening, forehead wrinkling.

"With her?" she asked, though she already sensed the answer.

He sighed. "She has an extra room."

"How convenient," she said, her voice rising, her whole face flaming. "Though I don't see why you'd need an extra room. I'm sure you'll be fine fucking her in her own bedroom."

"I knew you couldn't understand."

"Oh, I understand, Gabe. I understand that you're a lying, cheating, disgusting bastard who has to move on once your job is done. Woman pregnant and alone? Check. Time to exit." She felt the vomit rising. "You make me sick."

She shoved him into the bathtub and fumed past him into the living room where she sat cross-legged on the floor, staring at the Christmas decorations. Kanga sat beside her and pressed her wet doggy nose into Bianca's lap. On the brown shag carpet, propped against the wall, glared three strange faces from the paintings that Lily had given her, three distorted surrealist coffee shop figures she'd bought at a yard sale. Their bulging faces, bulbous necks and eyes, their disproportionate hands and worms-for-fingers mocked Bianca. She turned her attention to the empty bassinet beside the bookshelf.

She heard running water. Was Gabe taking a shower? That didn't make sense.

"Gabe?"

Her stomach hurt. Water running, *Bloody Mary, Bloody Mary, Bloody Mary.*

"Gabe? Can we go to the hospital? I don't feel well. I think something's wrong or the baby's upset or I don't know but I don't feel normal."

He didn't answer. The sound of a bath. And beer bottles opening.

A clicking sound.

She looked again at the bassinet and screamed. There was blood. Kanga was barking.

"Gabe!"

He came into the living room. He wasn't wet from the shower. He was dry. He was dry. Why was he dry? Was she hallucinating? Her heart pounded in her ears.

"Gabe?"

He rolled his eyes. "I'm standing right here. What do you need?"

"There's something wrong."

"What?" His eyes were swollen, blacker than usual so it looked like his pupils never bled into iris, like he'd emerged from a tunnel and hadn't adjusted to the light.

"With the crib, over there. Look." She pointed toward the yard sale stuff.

He followed her gaze. "It's just a bunch of baby stuff, Bee. Will you cut it out?"

She looked again. She was going crazy. No blood. It was white and spotless. No blood.

Her head hurt.

"Gabe, take me to the hospital."

"Bee, I just want to go home. You're fine. Go lie down. Sleep it off, okay? I'll come back later and check on you." He marched out through the hallway toward the front door, flung it open, and headed toward his puke-green truck parked in the driveway.

"Wait, Gabe. Don't go yet," she called after him. There was the bathwater again. She *was* going crazy. She clutched her belly and followed him outside, ordering Kanga to stay. The dog sat in the doorway, whining but obedient. The cold air bit Bianca's cheeks and sliced across the tears on her face. Her bare feet stung against the walkway pavement, dead leaves clinging to the pads as she waddled out after him.

"Go inside, Bianca," he called. "It's cold. I'm going home."

"Please wait," she said. "I'm sorry I called your nino's daughter a cunt . . . Stay and talk to me." *I have promises to keep, And miles to go before I sleep, And miles to go before I sleep.*

"There's nothing to talk about. This isn't working. I'm tired. Go inside." He climbed into his truck, turned the ignition, switched the headlights on.

"Wait," she screamed. "Please wait. Don't leave me here. I'm scared." She said this last part as a whisper. *My candle burns at both ends; It will not last the night—*

The headlights reflected on the windows, lighting up the driveway. Her feet burned. Her stomach ached. Dad stood in the doorway. *Daddy?* Why the hell was her dead father standing in her doorway? She walked as fast as she could toward Gabe's truck, clutching her belly. Everything hurt.

"Wait, Gabe. I'm scared. Something's wrong."

The truck switched into gear. He was ignoring her. Why wouldn't he help her? Without thinking, Bianca clambered onto the hood.

"What the fuck?" he yelled, pumping the brake. "What are you doing?"

"Don't go."

She was flying. She was La Llorona.

"Get the fuck off my truck, Bianca!" he hollered, flinging open his door and reaching out to pry her off the hood.

She crawled up higher toward the window, holding onto the windshield wipers like a dying insect. "Please don't leave me alone in this house," she cried, tears pouring down her cheeks. "There's something in there. Something wrong. I feel it."

"Enough, Bianca." He pulled her feet. "You're hysterical."

She pictured the wandering womb. Her womb floating into the night sky. She felt dizzy. He was hurting her.

"Stop," she said. "Or take me with you. Let's go talk somewhere. Figure this out."

"You're not making me want to stay with you." He was yelling. "You're making me want to call the cops. The neighbors are gonna come out. Stop making a scene."

"I don't care. Don't leave me here. This house is haunted, Gabe."

"Then go home to your mama, Bee. Jesus fucking Christ. You're crazier than Katrina."

"You're so mean, Gabe. You're so mean."

"Whatever, Bee. Get off my truck so I can go home."

"No," she said, razors in her throat. She was cramping and wanted to catch her falling belly, for that's what it felt like, dropping and dropping, but she wouldn't let go of the truck. No matter what.

"I don't want to hurt you."

She clasped her fingers tighter to the wipers, curled her feet under her.

"You're denting my truck."

She didn't move.

"You'll hurt the baby."

"Then take me to the hospital," she said.

He looked like he would cry. "Get off," he pleaded. "Take yourself to the hospital. I want to go home. I'm tired of this shit."

She stared into the dark glass, avoiding her reflection. Was she crazy? God help her. Dad help her. Someone please fucking help her. She said nothing, but stared forward, unmoving.

"Fine. You win. Get in the truck."

She slid down, wobbled to the passenger door, which he'd pushed open from inside, and climbed up. Before she could buckle her seatbelt, he was already backing out of the driveway and speeding down her street. He didn't turn right at the alley, toward his house; he turned left, toward the swine barns, and, beyond that, out of town. He was taking her out into the country.

"You want to talk, puta? Talk." He unzipped his pants, still driving, speeding into the fields, turning at the crossroads, toward the hay bales, between the cornstalks and canals. She had to clutch the door handle to keep from swinging wildly in her seat, gripped the floor with her bare feet. Her stomach hurt so bad. But she didn't want to tell him she might vomit. She just stared forward, as the dirt road sprawled ahead.

"Come here," he said, unbuckling her seatbelt, slowing the truck a bit, grasping her arm and pulling her toward him.

She shrank back, groaned, "No, Gabe. Not that. Come on. Let's just talk."

"Talk to my dick, Bee." His voice was deadpan. Cold.

She squished herself back against the passenger door, putting as much space between them as she could. "Let's go back to your house," she said. "Please."

"You wanted to be with me. So be with me."

He grabbed her hand again, pulled her forward, hard, so hard her shoulder popped, and she yelped in pain.

"You're hurting me, Gabe!"

"Then come on, hurry. I want you."

Tears streaming down her face, she tugged away, but he grabbed her head, clamped his fists through her hair, pushed her toward his crotch. The saltwater smell burned her nostrils, and she resisted the urge to gag. He clutched her hair tighter, pulling her scalp.

She opened her mouth, shut it.

"Suck my dick, Bianca." There was her name again. In a stranger's cold tongue.

She was floating. Water rushing in her ears.

She wouldn't be a fish with no fins again.

He slammed her head forward, into the dashboard, grasping her by the hair, then whipped her sharply back toward his lap.

"I said *now*, bitch."

Something wet trickled down her face. Warm and wet. Matted her hair to her forehead.

Her temples ached. They rang.

She needed help. She needed help. God, she needed help.

She grabbed the steering wheel, jerked it as hard as she could, swerving the whole goddamn truck off the road and Gabe with it.

A dam opens to flood the fields, a dam opens to irrigate the living, and growing. All those sprouting things that need water. A farmer opens a dam and the canal water flows. And when a truck swerves into a ditch whose dam has just opened, the water gushes. See how fast the water goes. See how fast the water rises to Bianca's toes. Her knees. Her belly.

Upon impact, Bianca had scrambled back up to her seat. She'd reached the door handle. But it had stayed closed.

Upon impact, the passenger side airbag flowered open.

It punched Bianca in the gut.

She cupped her hands to her ears. Water rushing. Nothing. Nothing. Gabe pulled the handles, clicked the windows. The water was rising. It reached the middle of the door in seconds flat. Bianca would have been counting them, had she not been humming.

"Bianca! Open the glove compartment!"

She heard him now, and pulled it open.

He reached inside, below the rock that was crushing her chest and stomach, and pulled out a little silver hammer with a spike at the end. He handed it to her.

"Break the window!"

She turned, and pounded. Again. The glass shattered, and the water rushed in.

"Go! Crawl out! Go!"

He shoved her, and she crawled through the window, the jagged glass scratching her arms and legs as she burrowed through. She kicked the door hard to push past the suction that the truck and the ditchwater had created around her. A tunnel. A black hole.

The water tasted like iodine in her mouth. The water tasted like blood.

Dark, cold, rushing water that pulled her away from the truck. She fought it. She kicked her legs and stretched out her arms, a girlchild again in swim team, winning first place; a girlchild again, in the ditches that Dippy Duck said avoid. *Stay safe! Swim in a pool!* Gabe had pushed out of the passenger window and was swimming behind her. She turned, briefly, toward the truck, a bird with its head dipped into the water to catch a fish. Her father's mechanical dipping bird, perpetual motion machine, its beak into the water for a quick sip. Bianca cupped the ditchwater with her hands, scooped it back, pumped hard, free-stroking toward the concrete wall on the other side, but the water kept rushing her downstream. The water was cold as needles, jabbing her, prickling her skin.

She couldn't breathe; everything hurt. She almost wanted to stop fighting and let the water take her. She almost wanted to laugh. She wondered if Gabe's pants were still unzipped, and as she grappled for a piece of concrete to stick her hand to, she imagined him swimming with his dick exposed and wished the ditch had sharks.

She shoved her body toward the concrete, and grasped a metal rung jutting out, a tooth in the mouth of a monster, and held on for her life as the water gushed past her. Gabe made it too. He grabbed on beside her. And together, they climbed up the side of the wall, out of the water. She slipped several times, knocking against the cement, the metal rungs. She was scratched and bleeding all over. "Come on, Bee. Climb." She thought of the Cattle Call basin, where they had run as high schoolers. *Up the hill, punk. You can make it.* White flies summerlong swarming her face as she breathed, open-mouthed and ragged, puffing hard up the hill.

At the top, she crawled on hands and knees, wrangling her way up the embankment. Only when she was out of the ditch did she begin to feel the extent of her pain. She wasn't *in pain*. She *was pain*. Nothing didn't hurt. Which meant, maybe she should've just died instead.

"What the fuck! What the fuck, Bee?"

Gabe had made it out, too, which meant he was beginning to feel the extent of his rage.

She couldn't have prepared herself for a fight if she'd wanted to.

But he didn't fight.

Something stopped him.

The blood stopped him.

She had landed in a heap on the embankment. A leaf curled on the unyielding ditch bank. Something wet dripping from her.

He stood above her, his face swollen, his eyes wide.

"Oh my God, Bianca." Running water throbbed in her ears. "Oh my God."

THIRTY-TWO
SWALLOWING ASHES

WITH JUBILEE

When Bianca was a girl, she fed crows. She scattered seed across the back-yard and they swooped like slick black raincoats instead of rain from the dry desert sky. She learned that together they're called a *murder*, but they were kind to Bianca. They brought her gifts. Broken light bulbs, brown beer-bottle glass, pearl-colored plastic beads, a rusted screw, a dead mouse. Anything that could fit in a crow's beaked mouth.

Bianca felt like the crows, bringing her own mangled presents to someone who probably wouldn't understand what they meant or why she had to give them.

She saw Mama through Abuela's bay window. After the social worker visit, she'd gone to see her mom and told her everything that had happened. "I'm not insane, Mama."

"No, mijita. You're not insane."

Rosana held her daughter and rocked her like a little girl the way she should have when Dad died but she'd been frozen or stoic or needed to be unshocked as much as Bianca did, back then, in the Valley. Mama was covered in Bianca's tears and mocos but she didn't let her go or try saying a prayer over her or tell her how disappointed she was or advise her to eat pan dulce or a plate of tacos con carne then tell her she was getting fat. She was fat as could be with her pregnant belly and she had nowhere else to be but in Mama's skinny arms.

Mama helped her into her bed and took her blood pressure with the cuff she kept in her nursing bag. Bianca's pulse was high but that was normal from all the crying, she said. Bianca told her she needed to see Dad.

Mama looked at her like she was backsliding, as if she'd have to explain to her daughter that her father had died then call Dr. Norris and the Mel Gibson, *Braveheart*-sounding priest fast because, boy, Bianca had really gone off the deep end this time.

Before Mama said anything though, Bianca said, "I mean his ashes, Mama." They hadn't buried him and she needed a place to grieve him.

When Bianca was in the Valley, she'd gone to the cemetery beside the swine barns and the garbage dump at the northwestern edge of town, although she knew she wouldn't find him there. In high school, Gabe had taken her between hay bales a few hundred feet farther into the country, and she'd sucked his dick to the brays of barn animals in the distance, feeling dirty and shameful, but, in the way of a teenage girl in love with a boy who needed that love to push back against the disappointment of his own life; it was exciting enough that she could pretend she was there of her own volition. That she was anything other than used. But the year before, when their relationship had turned horror house instead of fun, and she couldn't find her father in the cemetery, she'd stood outside his white Chevy Cavalier parked on the ditch bank beside the canal and cursed La Llorona for dragging her into that terrible myth. *I don't want to be La Llorona. I can't hold this pain anymore. Take it, Witch. Take it!*

No one had heard her. Or no one answered if they had. And she still hadn't said goodbye to Dad.

Mama brought Bianca his urn, which she kept on a shelf in her closet.

"Mija," she said, as if reading Bianca's mind as she held the smooth obsidian jar that held her father. "He's not in there."

The ashes were there, but Bianca knew that Mama meant his spirit wasn't. That Bianca wouldn't find what she was looking for in a jar of ruins.

Still, she asked her mama, "Then why do you keep it?"

"You know, I once thought about swallowing his ashes? When he first died? One of your tonto uncles had brought beer to the funeral, probably Oscar. And there it was in my 'fridgerator, and I thought I should put Martin's ashes in the 'fridgerator too, to stay fresh. Beside the sandwiches."

Bianca pictured Mama putting Dad in the fridge, and she was laughing so hard she was hiccoughing her tears. "You could've poured some into the beer," she suggested. "Or in the sandwich, between the lettuce and tomatoes."

Mama sat beside Bianca on the flowered bedspread, and she was laughing too. She tried to stop laughing long enough to sound ashamed and said, "I did drink a beer, Bee. Can you believe it? Me?"

Bianca howled a laugh at the guilt in her mother's voice. Her tiny mother, once a sprawling force with a brown faux-leather chancla for chasing Bianca through the house, threatening to spank her, had grown big on the inside when Dad died.

"What did it taste like?" Bianca asked.

"The beer?"

Bianca nodded, and Mama made a sour face, showing the fine lines on her forehead and beneath her hazelnut eyes.

"Like vinegar. Con caca!"

They laughed until their sides hurt and panted deep breaths like they were in labor trying to calm themselves down.

Mama hadn't answered Bianca's question about why she kept Dad in an urn instead of spreading his ashes, but maybe she'd meant keeping him in a jar was a better alternative than swallowing him up so he couldn't hurt her anymore.

"Mama," she said when they'd mostly stopped laughing; she stared at the urn. "What do I do?"

Mama hugged Bianca to her much-smaller body.

"My girl. You have to forgive Joshua. Or, better yet, forgive yourself."

Bianca still hadn't said much to Joshua since she got back from her mama's. It had been three long days since he'd called Jubilee a doll, and he'd apologized in a few different ways, but Bianca didn't seem to forgive him even though she said she did. But her mood was taciturn, unpredictable. He didn't blame her, but he didn't know how to make things right with her. She packed for San Diego, she said, because they'd promised Jayden. But she said very little else. On the morning of the trip, Joshua tried to help her lug her suitcase out to the car but she batted his arm away. "You shouldn't be lifting things, Bee. You were spotting the other night. You need to be careful."

"I'm fine. The doctor said I'm fine. No spotting. I'm not some breakable thing, Josh."

"I know that. You're one of the strongest women I know."

She rolled her eyes, brushed past him, and moved toward the car, clutching her bags.

Despite her icy mood, her palpable anger, Joshua breathed in the scent of her as she stood beside him, jostling her suitcase into the trunk; he breathed in her jasmine and lavender, the calming scent of the massage oil that he had nightly lathered across her belly, inside her thighs, before he'd crushed her spirit and betrayed her trust. He sighed. All he'd really done was protect them. She had to see that.

She shoved her suitcase hard against the others, but it wouldn't fit.

"I've got this, Bee. Let me do it."

She rolled her eyes again but stepped aside.

He resisted joking that she needed to be careful or her eyes would stay stuck like that. Instead, he said, "I know you *can* do anything you want, okay? I don't think you're incapable. I'm just trying to help you. Make things easier for you." Joshua heaved himself atop their bags, slamming his body down like a wrestler. *Take that.*

"Hey. What's happening? Earthquake!" Jayden yelled from the back seat.

Bee laughed. "No, mijo, it's fine. Your dad's fighting with the trunk."

At least she was acting normal with Jayden. That was a good sign.

Jayden sat strapped into his booster seat, his fire and rescue trucks in hand, boxed chocolate milk in his cup holder. Beside him, Jubilee lay buckled in her infant car seat.

"We're *moving* to the beach?" Jayden asked, squirming.

"Tontito. We're going for a vacation. Our San Diego Sea World, Comic-Con Beach Extravaganza."

"Can I feed a shark at Sea World?" Jayden asked.

"Only if you want that shark to . . . *bite your arm off*!" Bee pretended to bite, to chomp at his arm.

Jayden screamed, pulling his arm back. "No shark!"

Bee laughed again, tickling him, and said. "Better stick to feeding dolphins then. They don't like little-boy arms, anyway."

Joshua slammed the trunk and with it, the sound of Bee's laughter.

Half an hour later, a quarter of the way into the drive, Joshua checked his rearview mirror because Jayden had stopped pointing out landmarks and interesting cars and palm trees.

"He's out," Joshua whispered.

Jayden snored in response; Bee said nothing.

He glanced over at her. She pressed her forehead to the window, watching the hills rolling into the surf. Desert and ocean collided as they passed Camp Pendleton then the San Onofre power plant. She cradled her belly, which swelled against her cherry-red sundress.

Joshua sighed, frustrated. He'd been holding back the whole time he'd known her. He'd lost control of the situation. He couldn't be husband and father and therapist. It was time to admit failure. He couldn't be therapist. But he could be husband. "Bee . . . we've got to work this out."

"Work what out?"

"Whatever's wrong between us. The home visit. What I said. I fucked up."

She stared out the window, and at first, Joshua wasn't sure she was listening. Then she asked, quietly, "Do you think I'm mad, Josh?"

"Like angry?"

"No. Like crazy."

Don't step on that landmine. He said, emphatically, "Of course not."

She spoke slowly, deliberately, "That's what people think when I'm holding Jubilee and talking to her and she's my baby, right? People think *that woman is crazy.*"

"I've never thought that, Bee."

She faced forward. Her eyes clear and fiery. She stayed quiet so long that Joshua sighed, defeated, sure their conversation would go nowhere, same as all their Jubilee talks had. But she kept talking. "You once said my love is tough, like I'm an artichoke you have to pluck before it blooms. You have to cut off my prickly tips, steam and soften me, work your ass off for what little pulpy meat you can scrape off the leaves with your teeth. Is that what you think of me, Josh? That in my center, there are thin, purplish leaves like tender new skin covering the bulb of a heart, and it's lovely and you want it. But if you don't remove every single, goddamn needle, every thistle, you'll choke to death? Those tiny spines will stab your throat. Am I choking you? Am I fucking up your family? Because I feel like I am. I feel like you regret marrying me. I feel like I'm coming apart." She paused a moment, and he cleared his throat to answer, but she continued, her voice raspy but fervent. "People have asked me, don't I know she's not real? But she is real. Because what is real, Josh? Is the sky really blue? No. We know it's not. We know that if we pass the atmosphere, it's going to turn black. It's nothing. It's empty. It's full, but empty. It's a whole lot of nothing out there. When we look at the sky, it's blue and beautiful and makes us feel something. Is that feeling, that emotion, that awe, that wonder . . . is that *fake*? Past the blue there's really nothing, is it fake? We gaze at the stars, admiring them for hours, studying and creating pictures and telling stories about them. They inspire us. We build machines to see them clearer. Those stars we see? Most are dead already. They're gone. But we still see them. We're still in awe of them. We want to believe that there are stars up there. Not dying. Not dead. *Real.* Living, burning, luminous stars that shine for *us*. Because *we* can see their light, their residual burning through time. For me, that's Jubilee. She is my baby, Josh. Mine."

The muscles in his jaw twitched. He'd met her and loved her the way she was, every part and parcel of her, those quirks, blemishes, flaws, he wouldn't strip away, wouldn't wish away. Her delusion, her belief, her unshakeable knowledge that something was real despite everyone who said different, had all shaped her into a woman Joshua wanted to be with. She could love and love and love. Wasn't that what drew him to her? Wasn't that what made him feel so safe with her? So special? Wasn't that why he wanted her for Jayden's mama? Not to cover up Jubilee. Not to make her disappear.

Bee was crying softly, and a part of him felt like shit. He'd sided with the Oscars and Olivias and social workers of the world. He sighed, and all he could manage in response was, "She wouldn't have understood."

They checked into the motel, and Joshua insisted on carrying their bags up the stairs. That night they had dinner at a Mexican restaurant in Old Town, on the patio with heat lamps that Jayden kept wanting to touch. Jayden refused to order off the kids' menu, insisting he wanted steak fajitas, so Joshua made him a deal. Joshua would order a bean and cheese burrito from the kids' menu because it was free with an adult meal, but once the plates came, they could trade. This made Bee smile, though she'd been pensive and quiet most of the evening. She ordered a bowl of pozole and corn tortillas. Jubilee stayed in her car seat, covered with a plain blanket. Joshua made note of these details, the austereness, the deliberateness with which she seemed to be keeping her distance from everyone, including Jubilee, but said nothing. Any other time he might've asked a penny for her thoughts.

Now he just wanted peace. He was grateful for this truce. And let it be.

Jayden ate most of his steak, rice, and beans, but gave the red and green bell peppers, onions, guacamole, and sour cream to Joshua. Overall, a fair trade. Joshua watched his little family eat, basking in gratitude that the debacle with the social worker was over and they could get on with their lives. He even tried being thankful for Olivia, or at least tried not directing any more anger toward her. Maybe in a couple of months he'd call and check on her. He couldn't think about her cancer, couldn't think that far forward. He was here, now, in San Diego with his family. As far as he could tell, he had absolutely everything he needed.

In the middle of the night, Bianca awoke, sweating and in pain. The hotel mattress hurt her back and swollen hips, exacerbating her sour mood. Joshua and Jayden shared the full-sized bed beside her; she'd asked for a bed all to herself, and Joshua had relented, though his eyes flashed with the hurt she'd been aware of for several days. She hadn't slept alone since she'd moved in with Joshua, since New York. She lay on her side, stuffing each flimsy motel pillow between her legs, under her bulging belly, beside her aching hip supporting her weight. She could not get comfortable. Both guys snored lightly beside her. She glanced at the clock: two a.m. She'd promised to take Jayden to the beach while Joshua went to Comic-Con with her brother and Handro, in exactly eight hours. She needed sleep.

She hadn't taken Jubilee out of her car seat.

Everything ached. The pozole hadn't settled right in her stomach. The baby inside her prickled. A cactus.

She punched a pillow then threw them all to the floor. Rocked herself to a sitting position, lumbered, heavy and swollen, off the bed, stumbled toward the bathroom.

Not again, not again.

She unbuckled Jubilee, whose car seat was propped on a wood and vinyl desk chair beside the dresser holding the television. Held her as she lurched toward the bathroom, tucked under one arm, not nestled, not cradled. Tucked. Between bicep and chest.

In the dark bathroom, she set Jubilee on the closed toilet seat, upright. Then she flicked on the light switch, and the grainy, motel bulbs guttered a moment, lightning bugs, a camera's shutter, before the fluorescent gleaming yellowed her face in the mirror. She wouldn't look at Jubilee. Instead, she steadied herself, gripping the scrub-white sink, wondering how many strangers had spit into its dribble of water, rinsed their mouths and washed their germs down the drain. How many of their mouths were filled with paste or love or cum. How many with regret.

You're safe, Bee.

She nodded at herself. She watched the head shake up and down, watched the muscles in the neck, watched the little bowls of collarbones shadow as she moved.

Here, now. You're safe.

She recited some Emily in her mind, breathing into an imaginary box the way Dr. Norris had shown her. Breathe in, hold, breathe out, hold: "Far safer, of a midnight meeting / External ghost, / Than an interior confronting / That whiter host. // Far safer through an Abbey gallop, / The stones achase, / Than, moonless, one's own self encounter / In lonesome place." Seven times. Breathe in, hold. Breathe out, hold.

She turned on the faucet and waited for any buzzing. Only water.

She splashed her face.

That man in the next room is your husband, that little boy is your little boy. They're your family, Mama. They're yours.

She nodded again, tears mingling with the water. She plucked the scratchy white motel towel from the rack and wiped her face pink.

I'm safe too.

Her face in the mirror crumbled, her chest constricted. She wrapped her arms around herself and held. She held as tight as she could.

Once upon a time, a house grew wild and empty in the desert.

She nodded.

She turned toward Jubilee on the toilet seat, staring blankly ahead. She was so beautiful. She was perfect.

Bianca sank to the bathroom floor, imagining how many stories had played out in this room, how many strangers had stepped naked into the shower, had made love or sobbed or been sick in this room, as she curled her body into a seashell and closed her eyes, shutting out the innocent girlchild propped on the toilet seat.

Her daughter. Herself. And she cried herself to sleep.

Dreams are tunnels. They usher us between landscapes, memories, time. They wormhole us between worlds. Dreams connect us to the many selves we are in other places. The choices we almost made, could have made, but for whatever reason, did not make. Parallels split and some other iteration of the selves we nearly were go strutting about their business, unaware that we were once joined together, once twinned, mirrored at the center. Unaware that one flick of the tongue, flick of the wrist, one detail different, one movement unmade, and it could have been us through the blackness of space, through the membrane-thin wall separating us, and landing on the other side, atoms floating, atoms loving, atoms breaking apart and reshaping in the endless dance of the expansion into whatever comes after nothingness. Dreams are glimpses through all this invisible matter.

On the motel bathroom floor, Bianca dreamt the social worker had heard her. The door hadn't closed. And the social worker heard her say, *not a doll.*

In the many-worlds hypothesis. Bianca was deemed unfit. Jayden was taken away.

And Joshua stopped breathing.

There are worlds beyond this one. Of that, Bianca was sure.

In one, a daughter came back. And the angels rejoiced.

In another, a feisty little boy with corkscrew curls, a wild thing, a lover of cake and owls, a healthy, growing boy who needed his family, whose family needed him, could still get taken away. Could still get pulled by a current stronger than Bianca.

If Bianca couldn't make the choice *in this world* that she knew, deep down, she needed to make.

THIRTY-THREE
HOMECOMING

JUBILEE

It was too late.

Gabe lifted Bianca from the ditch bank and carried her through a field to the nearest crossroad in order to give the paramedics more concrete directions than *help my pregnant girlfriend bleeding to death in my arms somewhere out in the alfalfa fields where I took her to suck my dick because like a fucking goddamn angry asshole I take it out on the women I love.*

He hadn't meant for any of this. Everything he touched turned to shit. It was this valley. He should've gotten them out of this godforsaken shithole.

He took off his ditch-soaked shirt, balled it up and pressed it between Bianca's legs, holding her wet, limp body close to his. Her skin was clammy. He focused on her breathing to be certain she was still alive. His eyes stung and his body shook. He forced himself not to cry. "It's gonna be okay, Bee," he whispered into her ear, "The ambulance is coming."

He didn't say, *Don't you die on me.* He'd already scared her enough for the both of them.

And he'd never forgive himself.

The doctor couldn't find a heartbeat.

Gabe dropped his head to Bianca's hand on the hospital bed and sobbed. "I'm so sorry," he repeated, "So fucking sorry, Bee. My Bee. I never meant for this." His face tugged at her IV line, pinching her skin, sending quick barbs of pain up her arm.

Bianca lay still, focusing on the stinger at her vein where Gabe was crying, his tears like insect venom. She focused all her attention on that pinprick needling into the back of her hand and not the blood soaking a pad beneath her hospital gown. Not the bright-red cactus flowers sprouting from her sheets. She was a surrealist painting. Dreaming. Not carrying a dead baby. Not the empty place. Dreaming.

Gabe lifted his head and tried grasping her hand, but she pulled away.

Her throat ragged, she said, "Get out."

"I want to help." His eyes plum-dark and wet, his face crumpled as a child's brown lunch sack at the end of recess. Tossed in a bin or left on the empty blacktop. If she looked at him too long, gleaming with his own slick repentance, she might be tempted to forgive.

"Get out," she repeated, looking to the doctor for help. Dr. Caldera, her name badge read. A woman with Mama's complexion and long, shiny black hair. A thick pair of square, tortoise-shell glasses rested on her mushroom of a nose. She wasn't Bianca's regular ob-gyn but the hospital's on-call one. Bianca stared at her paisley blouse ruffling beneath the white coat. The kaleidoscope of patterns on her blouse swirled under the fluorescent hospital lighting.

"Bee. Let me stay with you." His voice a plea.

She said nothing. The colors churning across the doctor's chest needed all of Bianca's attention. They were prisms, catching light. They were so beautiful.

Dr. Caldera put her arm on Gabe's shoulder. "I think it's best you leave."

Gabe nodded and pulled away from Bianca. Then he stood up and his shape grew hazy in her peripheral as he walked out of the room.

"Can I call someone else?" Dr. Caldera asked, breaking the spell.

Bianca forced herself to look up from the paisley maze and at the doctor's face. Her thoughts muddied. She was still under ditchwater. She shook her head.

"Someone should be with you for this."

Bianca blinked, wondering if time had stretched, turned viscous. Or if she was moving in slow motion. She blinked again.

Dr. Caldera explained how they would move her to another room soon where she would induce labor. She said since Bianca was past thirty weeks she had to push vaginally. She would give her Pitocin, and she'd start feeling contractions. "Sometime within the next eighteen hours, you'll feel the urge to push."

The nurse squeezed her hand, and Bianca became aware of her presence at the sensation of skin against skin. She hadn't realized anyone else was in the room. The nurse's voice sounded like honey, thick, through a comb, sticky. "Your body will help you, hun. You'll feel what to do. And we'll tell you when it's time. You want us to call someone?" Bianca shut her eyes. "Brave girl," the nurse said. "I'll go get you some ice chips."

She should've called Lily. She should've had a hand to hold.

But she couldn't face anyone with what she'd done. For a second, she almost wanted Gabe's rumpled face to return so she could focus her shame outside herself. Without him, she had to admit the truth. She'd turned the steering wheel. She'd driven them into the ditch.

She was a murderer, as Katrina had called her. A baby killer. La Llorona risen from the night waters. Stealing babies. Drowning babies.

She shouldn't have bought the bassinet and other baby furniture from the yard sale. They were cursed. She shouldn't have bought them second-hand. She'd have to go home to them, empty. Stark and cold and pink.

The nurse brought her ice chips. She ignored them.

"Let me check your IV drip, hun. Gotta make sure we're hydrating you properly."

She watched her blood fill the small tube, then turn clear with fluid. She stared at the nurse's pale-blue scrubs while she finished taking vitals, robin's-egg blue. She would've wanted to know the nurse's name, but her name tag was backward, and all Bianca could see was an empty, white placard. She would've asked. But the fog rolled in. She closed her eyes.

Opened them again. Closed.

It went on like this.

They must've wheeled her to another room, for now she opened her eyes to a room that reminded her of a motel, a seaside inn she'd stayed at once. Or was she dreaming?

At some point, outside her window, night clouds skimmed the moon in puffed gray shapes like the ones on her ceiling above the mattress on the floor in the empty house. Stains in the sky. A parade of babies down the drainpipes.

Coatlicue, mother of all, where are you now?

Sandra Cisneros, cabrona of my heart, where are you now?

A fragment of a poem came to her. Sandra must've known what Bee would do, for she had written,

It Occurs to Me I Am the Creative/Destructive Goddess Coatlicue

> I deserve stones.
> Better leave me the hell alone.

> I am besieged.
> I cannot feed you.
> You may not souvenir my bones.

Coatlicue bore death. Bianca bore death.

She closed her eyes, drifting in and out of sleep, waiting for the urge to push.

The urge came at 10:12 p.m.—a Tuesday night, twenty-four hours after she'd come to the ER for sliding a pine-green truck into the water—on April 21.

"Please don't make me push her out." She clenched the nurse's hand, the nurse whose name she did not know. "Please let me keep her."

"I'm sorry, hun." The nurse held her. "You've got to push. You've got to dig deep. Reach inside yourself. You can do it. I know it's hard. Put your head down honey, your chin to your chest, like this." She pressed her head to her chest. "Now push hard like you've got to go to the bathroom. I know it hurts. I know it's hard. But you've got to push."

Why had she jumped on the truck? Why hadn't she gone back inside the house? Why had she let Gabe drive her to the country?

Pink lines across an empty screen. Pink lines.

A raspberry pressed to her belly.

She'd had pictures. A long stream of pictures, a fold-out wallet of pictures. "It's a girl!" the sonogram tech had typed onto the screen, in the three folds between the legs.

Dr. Caldera held her hands as Bianca imagined Our Lady herself might have. Had she been there.

"Push, Bianca. Push."

An ocean. A sinkhole. A feast of mothered bones.

Somewhere, back home, Mama was baking pancakes on a Saturday morning, after chores. Somewhere Matty was singing. *This is how you hold your head high. This is how you love the world even when it doesn't love you back.* Somewhere Dad was swinging his little girl through the air on a swing set he'd built. *Higher, Daddy. Higher. I want to touch the leaves. I want to fly.*

"A few more, you're almost done."

This is how you say goodbye.

"She's out, honey." The nurse wiped Bianca's face with a white towel. "You can lay back. They have some cleaning to do down there."

The labor room was silent except for the rattling of instruments, the swishing of suction. The dripping into a bucket.

"You want to hold her?"

Bianca nodded.

Wrapped in a hospital blanket, her girl, the size of a doll. Bianca's tears fell on the bluish skin.

"We'll give you some time with her."

Bianca squeezed the tiny creature to her chest. Traced the outline of her nose and lips. Imagined pressing her to her breasts to nurse her. Made the sign of the cross over the heart.

"Do you have a name for her?" the nurse asked, reentering the labor room, breaking the silence. A brittle sound. A name.

Bianca shook her head.

"We have to take her now."

"Can't I keep her?"

The nameless nurse's face softened, her brown eyes crinkled at the edges. "Oh, honey. I'm sorry, no. The hospital policy is we have to take her."

Bianca's chest constricted, her throat tightened. "What will you do with her?"

"I'll give her to the doctors, love. Who can I call for you?"

"My friend Lily." She told the nurse the number, which Bianca had memorized in elementary school.

"I'll call her for you. You rest," she said, reaching for the baby.

Bianca held her tight. She held her until the nurse took her. Out of her arms. Out of the room. Out of the world.

The nurse with no name came back a few minutes later and told her Lily would be there soon. Bianca stared out the window, pretended not to hear. The clouds had scattered. The moon was full. And in its fullness, it was blank.

Gabe stood in the doorway.

"The baby's gone."

He sighed, ran his hands through his spiky hair. He still looked like shit. Like he hadn't slept or showered since the accident. She couldn't look at him before, but now she stared at his face, the face she'd known since she was fourteen. She'd memorized every scar, knew all the stories to go with them. She could add the newest cut to his forehead: truck into ditch. Baby lost.

When his neck muscles twitched he was clenching his jaw, either in anger or trying not to cry. His jaw clenched.

She'd adored that face since he was a boy and she was a girl. She'd believed everything he'd ever said about getting married and settling down, raising a family, opening a restaurant, growing old together. She'd failed to limpia his heart. She wasn't his curandera—her mouth not sage, her tongue no candle. She searched his black eyes. What she'd mistaken for guilt, for angst, for tragedy-ridden love, for some turning point in a romance novel, she saw for what it was: regret. Gabe regretted their life together. And he was right to.

They were over. *La Bee* was gone. She'd lost the last of Gabe's babies.

"I never meant for any of this, Bee. If I could take it all back . . ."

"Me too."

He stepped closer to her bed.

"Is there anything I can do?"

"No. Lily's on her way."

"Do you want a funeral for her?"

"No. Then it's real. This way, I imagine she's still here. She's going home with me."

Gabe choked back a sob, reached for Bianca's hand.

"You should go."

"I love you, Bee. I always will."

"Too little, too late," she whispered to his back as he walked through the recovery room door, the butterflies and music and color fading around him.

Lily came after her shift, with a requisite sweet tea from the donut shop. "I come bearing gifts, m'lady," she said, stooping down to Bianca on the hospital bed and kissing her BFF's cheek. "Drink this elixir and be healed."

"I wish it were so simple," Bee said, but reached for the Styrofoam cup anyway. She swigged several gulps, allowing the sugar to wash over her like holy water. "I hope there's a jelly donut in there."

Lily reached into her tote and fished out a white paper bag. "Do you doubt me?"

Bee grabbed it greedily, snatched one of the two donuts, and took a bite. She almost smiled as the jelly hit her tongue.

"Hey, donut monster. You know, one of those is supposed to be for me."

Bee shrugged, handed her friend the one she'd already bitten into, and pulled out the other for herself.

"You're lucky I tolerate you," Lily said, smiling wryly, then started on the donut, chewed end first.

They sat in sticky silence a few minutes.

"Oh, hey. I found Kanga wandering around the neighborhood and took her back to your house. The front door was wide open, chica. Your dog's safe though. I fed her, gave her water, locked up the house for you."

"Oh, fuck. I can't believe I forgot my pobre boxer. I told her to *stay* and then never came back for her. Thank God you found her, Lil."

She almost couldn't stomach the last of her donut, but hunger took over, and she licked the jelly from her fingers, then swished it all down with the last of the iced tea.

When they'd finished, Lily motioned for Bee to scoot over, and lay down beside her in the bed, resting her head on Bee's shoulder. "We'll get through this," Lily said. Bee nodded, afraid to say anything for fear she'd bring the donut and sweet tea hurling back up. She grabbed Lily's hand and held it tight.

"They got you hooked up like a chupacabra," Lily said, nodding toward the IV pole, where the nurse had left the empty bags of blood they'd pumped into Bee. "That's a sweet setup. Keep you from gnawing on people's necks?"

The deflated bags held remnants of blood and plasma, a yellowish slime, an organ whose life-force had been drained away. The tubes were like veins bubbling with the last splotches of red ink, the inside of a pen that no longer writes. The label flashed a large *A* and beneath that *positive*. "I've earned an A plus at bloodletting, Lil. Aren't you proud of me?"

"Always," Lily replied, matching Bee's snark with rare earnestness. Her voice grew raspy, and she held Bee's hand tighter. "I'm sorry I wasn't here earlier."

"You've got so much already, with your mom and Little Gran being sick, and Sam monopolizing all your time . . ."

Lily pinched Bee's arm, and they both laughed.

"There's nothing you could have done, Lil. It was over already."

Lily sighed, grasped Bee's hand again, entwining their fingers. They'd lay in bed together like this for sleepovers every other night most summers since they were eleven. They'd recited, acting out the motions on each other's head and back, *Crack an egg on your head, let the yolk drip down. Stab a knife in your back, let the blood run down. Spiders crawling up your arms, spiders crawling down your arms (tickle lightly up and down). Cool breeze (blow on the neck), tight squeeze (give a bear hug). Now you've got the chills.* That's still how it felt.

"At least you're rid of Gabe."

Bee wrenched her hand free of Lily's, turned to look at her friend. It was as if she'd stabbed Bee for real. "Rid of his baby, you mean?" She couldn't control the vitriol in her voice. "That's some sick silver lining."

"I didn't mean it like that, Bee. It's just, now you're free of him."

"Just . . . stop talking."

Bee turned toward the empty bags of blood on the IV pole. A Rorschach test. *What do you see?* A failed mother. Someone else's blood. Bee's soaked the ditch bank. Bee's was gone. She would never be free again.

Lily sighed.

She tried making other small talk but Bee shut her eyes, pretended to fall asleep. She stayed silent so long, Lily got up, whispered, "I didn't mean it like that, Bee."

When Bee didn't answer, Lily said, "I'll come pick you up when they discharge you, and stay with you as long as you need."

Bee wanted to answer *Don't bother*, but her throat was coated in jelly.

Every person in this house has died. *Even you. Especially you.* She was misremembering a line from Rigoberto González. A poem from *Black Blossoms* about Lizzie Borden. Why did it feel so apt now?

> This is not your bird and this is not your house
>
> You're not the daughter
> You're not the spouse
>
> You're not at home.
> This is not your burning house.

Kanga snored beside Bianca where she lay on the couch in the living room. She'd slept there because she couldn't stand to sleep on the mattress on the floor in her parents' room. She couldn't stand to go into that bedroom, look out that front window where the truck's presence remained, though the truck itself was gone.

She hadn't wanted to come back to the empty house, but after Lily, there was no one else. She couldn't face Esme. What would she say? What would Gabe tell her? A lie no doubt. A comforting lie.

Lily would check on Bianca, she knew. Even after her friend's tactlessness. Even after kicking Bianca while she was down. To Lily, it was just putting her foot in her mouth. It was a joke. To Bianca, it was unforgivable. But what could she do? Life resumed. As the truck kept driving. As the dog kept snoring. Bianca stroked Kanga's brown fur. She pulled a blanket over her body, imagining she were a corpse in a morgue herself. Would anyone identify her? Edna St. Vincent Millay knew her pain. "Curse thee, Life, I will live with thee no more! / Thou hast mocked me, starved me, beat my body sore!"

It hurt to go to the bathroom so she was trying not to drink anything, despite the doctor's instructions to drink fluids. She was past feeling thirsty.

She did feel cold, though it was in the eighties outside.

Spring in the desert was like summer everywhere else. Daytimes were hot, nights were cold. Monsoons would come, drowning the grasshoppers, winged and mothlike, swarming into town from the drought-ridden desert edges. Mothers would warn their children not to squash them with their chanclas or, worse, their bare feet—not to catch and bottle them with leaves to eat and a napkin covering the lid because a life contained in the hands of a greed-curious child as large as a giant or a monster in comparison, large enough to murder entire nations of grasshoppers, was no life at all. Still, when the chocolate mountain ranges in the distance covered themselves with thick fawn-colored clouds and lightening crackled the sky, even the grasshoppers must have understood their time was nearing its end.

Bianca stood gingerly, pain springing through her thighs and crotch, and hobbled like an old woman toward the bathroom where she'd felt Dad's ghost the other night. *What makes us do it? What makes us hurt ourselves and those we love?*

In the mirror like a girlhood sleepover game of Bloody Mary, she sprinkled sink water on the glass and called, "Dad."

The yellow bathroom walls reminded her of "The Yellow Wallpaper"; she imagined herself trying to climb *in* rather than *out*. "Dad!"

She picked up a hairbrush and hurled it at the mirror, shattering a chunk in the corner.

"I've fucked up, Dad. I've fucked up big time. I need help, Dad. I need help." She sank to the toilet seat, wrapping her arms around herself and sobbing, rocking. Her Dad had joined leagues with God. He was silent. He would not help her. She was past redemption.

All her babies were ghosts.

From the medicine cabinet beneath the sink she took the iron that Lily had let her borrow when she'd told Lily that her boss at the newspaper was upset that Bianca kept coming into work with wrinkled clothes; she walked toward the sliding back doors in the living room, past the fake Christmas tree and the empty wrapped presents with their garish ribbons. She left the sliding glass open and pushed a lawn chair toward a patio rafter. Kanga woke and followed her outside, wagging her boxer's stump of a tail. She ran toward a ball in the grass and brought it back to Bianca for fetch. Bianca ignored her.

Two houses away, splashing in a swimming pool, children's laughter. It was spring break. Easter was coming. Jesus was getting ready to rise from the dead. The maple in the backyard gathered its leaves and nodded in the breeze. Bianca climbed that tree as a girlchild.

The sun would be setting soon.

Kanga watched Bianca balance on the chair, biting her lip to keep from screaming out in pain, wrapping the cord around a beam and tying a knot, the metal part of the iron hanging limp. She'd never tied a noose but figured any knot would work. She slipped her head into the large loop and began to pull it tight.

Her heart was beating fast.

"I'm coming home," she whispered.

Kanga barked.

"Hush, girl."

But the dog kept barking and barking like Bianca was an intruder and she was ready to attack. Bianca imagined herself kicking the chair away. Imagined falling.

Kanga kept barking.

Tears spilled down Bianca's face.

Kanga barked and barked.

Bianca peeled herself free from the cord. She was freezing but sweating. She felt dizzy.

She stepped down from the chair and caressed Kanga, who was licking her hands and shaking her whole brown body. "Let's go inside."

On the bookshelf, a doll she'd found at the yard sale sat beside the bassinet, her shiny brown curls peeking from beneath a pink hood, eyes wide open, smiling. The most lifelike doll she'd ever seen. She hadn't noticed before. The bluish haze beneath her cream-colored skin, like veins fluttering.

It's time to go home. Her back ached. Her gut and thighs and insides were sore. She was soaking a pad and would for a couple of weeks, the nurse whose name she'd never learned had warned. The nurse promised she'd heal just fine.

She'd split open. She'd come undone. She had a story stitched to her ribs. The pen was in her hands. Its ink was red. She'd forge a bridge back.

"Time to go home," she said again, picking up the beautiful, pink-cheeked doll.

Bianca recognized her. Something about the eyes. Gray. Like a storm over Cattle Call arena.

"Hey, little girl," she whispered. "I know you." She cradled the doll in her arms, squeezing tightly. The doll was a bridge back. A bridge across the ditchwater. And with Coatlicue and La Llorona and Sandra Cisneros at her side, she said, "Jubilee, honey. Let's go home."

THIRTY-FOUR
SWIM BACK

WITH JUBILEE

The weather never cooperated. Sun was predicted, but when Joshua awoke, only half-light glinted through the motel curtains. Bianca, not in bed, must've been in the bathroom already. Jayden slept like the dead, funny little zombie boy. He could sleep through an earthquake, and, as a matter of fact, had done so a few times. Joshua set the coffee-pot with decaf, and pulled back the heavy drape, revealing a morning sky so thick with swamps of gray, he doubted whether the sun would push away the marina cloud cover before the afternoon. Maybe they should postpone. Spend the morning together, rather than leaving Bianca alone with Jayden and Jubilee. He hadn't ever loved the idea, but she'd insisted.

"Bee?" he called after a few minutes, and headed toward the bathroom. The door was closed and the light on, but he couldn't hear her jostling about in her typical morning routine. "You okay in there? You sick?"

Still nothing. His pulse fluttered, and he hated that every time she didn't answer, he feared the worst. He told himself to calm down and tried the doorknob. Unlocked. He opened it, slowly. "Bee?"

He wasn't sure what he was seeing. Bee lay curled on the bathroom floor, Jubilee on the toilet, staring at her. Like she'd killed her. He suppressed the urge to yell out and knelt down beside his wife, touched her cheek.

She was warm. He noted the steady motion of her shoulders and back. He grasped her shoulder and shook, softly. "Bee," he said again, "wake up."

She opened her eyes and groaned, turned fitfully from her side onto her back, stretched out, catlike, mewling out the discomfort of her position.

"Why on earth did you sleep in the bathroom? Nausea?"

She sighed, rubbed the sleep out of her eyes. "Something like that. Where's Jubilee?"

He nodded toward the toilet.

"Did you put her there?" he asked, and then realized the ridiculousness of his question. Of course she had. Jubilee hadn't very well put herself in that creepy position.

"Yeah, sorry. It was a rough night." She lurched forward, straining to lift herself up to sitting, but her belly pinned her back. "I'm too fat to sit," she muttered, chuckling.

He helped her up and said, "You're gorgeous. Even when you've been sick all night and sleeping on the floor. No one lights a candle to you, Bee."

She smiled, her face brightening. Maybe she was forgiving him. He inched forward.

"I wish you would've woken me up though, I could've helped you. Held your hair back."

Using the bathtub ledge as stabilizer, she wobbled up to standing, picked up Jubilee, less childlike than usual, he noted. Held her awkwardly, facing outward. Like a toy. Or was he imagining things? Was he wishful thinking?

"Here, can you take her?" she asked, handing Jubilee over. "I need a shower."

"Of course. And your decaf is brewing, my dear."

"Such a gentleman, Joshy."

"Anything for my wife."

This time, she smiled, her whole face glowing, and he couldn't help himself, he leaned forward and kissed her. She sank against him, allowing herself to be kissed, and he knew they were going to be okay. They were going to get through this.

At ten a.m., he dropped them off with a picnic basket and blanket at Mission Beach near the roller coaster. He wanted to go with them, set them up on the sand like he always did, but she shooed him away, saying she could take care of herself and the kids. "You don't have to do everything for us. I am capable, Josh."

She tucked Jubilee under her arm and weaved her fingers through Jayden's. She looked like she was hiding a beach ball under her dress. Joshua felt guilty leaving. Matty and Handro were waiting for him at Comic-Con, and he'd wanted to go since he was a kid, but the timing felt wrong. "I could stay."

"We'll be fine. Go have fun. Give my brother and Handro a kiss from me."

"Or you could come with me. Give it to them yourself."

"It's sold out, Josh. We don't have tickets. Besides, we'll have more fun at the beach. Comics are your thing."

"Really. It's no problem. I'd rather stay with you and the kids." He wanted her to notice how he'd referred to Jubilee as a kid. He was joining her. He wasn't letting her go.

Her eyebrows furrowed, her forehead wrinkled. He could see he'd made her mad, again. "Don't you trust me anymore, Josh? Or did you ever?"

He sighed. If he didn't trust her, then how could he expect anyone else to? "Fine, I'll go. But I have my cell phone so call if you need anything. I'll come right back. The convention center's only a few minutes away."

She nodded and held Jayden's hand in one hand and all their stuff and Jubilee in the other, then padded away in her sandals, kicking up dirt behind her.

"Bye, Dada," Jayden called, turning back and waving with his free hand. "Don't worry. I'll take good care of Bee and Jubilee and the new baby."

Comic-con crawled with heroes. But Joshua wasn't in the mood for comics. Weeks earlier, Bee had encouraged him to dress up as Superman. She'd said Joshua was their superman, but he hadn't wanted to. Now, seeing everyone else dressed up, he felt out of place. Always a sore thumb. He should've let her buy the damn costume.

The convention center was so crowded, he plodded elbow to costumed elbow through the boothed aisles where attendees huddled, blocking rows, excited for the chance to find other fans of their ilk. When he was a kid, he was Beast because both Beast and him were oversized, took up too much space, had big hands and feet. Joshua had been teased for his gorilla nose, his long ape arms and gait. Kids were awful. But Beast and him fought social rejection. They used their keen wit to create a better world for both mutant and man. Every time he'd hung a poster on campus declaring "Black Lives Matter," "Some Bruises Are on the Inside: Stop Bullying," "Marriage Is about Love, Not Gender," or "Take Back the Night: End Domestic Violence," he was Beast, turning blue, growing fur, fighting for change. No one ever knew that about him, why he related with Beast, besides Bee.

He'd told her one night, in bed. She'd said, "You're a beautiful Beast."

He'd laughed. "You're mixing stories. I don't mean the Disney movie."

She'd shrugged. "Either way. You're beautiful," kissing his arms, his hands, his nose.

He wandered the gauntlet of booths and displays, costumed and trench-coated folks fighting each other for an inch of space as they rushed to their heroes, hoping to get close enough to their favorite author or publisher for an autographed picture that would one day validate their lifelong passion. They could, old man or old woman with a grandchild on their lap, say, "I met him," pulling out an autographed photo of the Hulk, "Or, at least, the person who wrote him."

Joshua found Matty and Handro's booth on the printed plan, and trudged through the crowd to get to them. They sat behind a black-tarped sign displaying Matty's comic book, *Crimson Knight*, emblemed with a red hawk on a shield. "Hey, guys," he called out, waving.

"Hey there, Josh."

"Hiya, Joshy!"

They were smiling and stood to hug Joshua as he scooted into Matty's booth.

"You having fun?" Matty asked.

"It's sort of overwhelming."

"It can be crazy. Handro hates it here." Matty poked Handro, who rolled his eyes dramatically. "But he comes with me every year anyway." Matty pulled Handro close and kissed him. Joshua had never seen Matty so openly show his affection for Handro. Comic-Con had made him giddy. "How're Bee and Jayden?"

Joshua cleared his throat. "I'm worried about Bee."

As if an alarm had sounded, Matty's eyebrows rose and he pulled away from Handro. "Why? What's up?" Matty's voice and demeanor changed so abruptly that Joshua felt compelled to fess up, like a shamed child confessing to a parent what he'd done wrong. He told him about the social worker and Olivia, about Ms. McCall and the adoption. About the dead fish. He admitted how worried he was and how weird she'd been acting.

Matty crossed his arms over his chest and lifted a hand to his chin as Joshua spoke, frowning. He didn't say anything, and Joshua let everything spill out.

When he finished unloading what he'd kept bottled since he married Bee, Matty took a deep breath that moved his shoulders, no, his whole body. Then he just wilted. He leaned his arms against his booth of comics, so his body shrank from over six feet tall to a crouched small thing, in grief.

"Matty?" Handro said, putting his arm on his back.

He kept his head down so long, people at other booths were beginning to stare. Matty's hands on the table showed his raw cuticles, the blood-dark scabs where he'd chewed at his skin. Joshua didn't know what to say. He stood there for an uncomfortable length of time, trying to keep from looking at the passersby gawking at the crying comic book writer behind the red hawk sign. Finally Matty took a deep breath and wiped his face with his hands. "Did she tell you how Dad killed himself?"

Joshua sucked in his breath sharply. "He what?" She'd never said a word.

"She never told you?" He seemed as surprised as Joshua. "Shit. I figured. She's been so angry about it. I thought she would have said something . . . We don't understand it. Not completely. He'd gotten sober. My mom won't talk about it. But she found him with an empty twelve-pack. In the bathtub. He'd drowned himself. We know it must've been suicide. But Mom insisted he just fell asleep. That it was an accident."

Joshua's stomach lurched. What an awful way to die. Something hummed in his eardrum. Something Bee had said, after they'd married. She was watching the yellow jackets in the jelly water on the neighbor's balcony and said drowning would be the worst way to die.

And the bathtub. She'd thought Jayden was drowning.

Matty broke his thoughts. "Sometimes I think my mom is the delusional one. When Bee and I were growing up, Mom told us it was an accident the first time too. When Dad laced his Prozac with beer."

Her dad had committed suicide? Why hadn't Bee told him? Why would she keep something that huge from him?

"Jubilee keeps her from having to deal with that." Matty sighed, his expression pensive. "Since she came home, *I've* tried to keep her from having to deal with that." He folded his arms across his chest.

The humming in Joshua's ear grew louder. He pictured those yellow jackets again. Bee curled up beside the toilet, screaming that Jayden was drowning. But she wouldn't hurt Jayden. Joshua told the guys how on the car ride over, she'd talked as lucid as he'd ever heard her talk about Jubilee. Like she understood. Like she knew Jubilee was a doll.

Matty nodded. "I know what you mean." He unfolded his arms and leaned forward. "She was a mess. Mom wanted Bee to stay at the hospital or go back to Abuela's with her, at first, but Bee didn't want to be with Mom. Honestly, I don't think Bee wanted to be with me either, but she thought of me as the lesser evil. Mom was there when Dad died. She didn't save him. When Bee came home from the hospital, she kept saying, 'She almost drowned.' Handro and I figured out she meant Jubilee because she'd hold her up and tell us, 'My baby.' It was scary. Then one morning, she kind of snapped out of it. She came to the breakfast table and said, 'We need to get Jubilee a high chair.' And that was that."

Handro was nodding, his eyebrows knitted.

Joshua's head hurt. Jubilee had almost drowned. He felt a prickling on the back of his neck. Something was wrong. He felt the same tingling when Bee had told him she was pregnant, and when Olivia had taken Jayden to the motel, the night she left him and got arrested. Joshua shouldn't have left Bee with Jayden. A humming in his ears, pulling him. Something wasn't right. He shouldn't have come to Comic-Con and left them alone at the beach.

"I need to go," he said, and he rushed back through the crowd, stumbling through the parking lot, then speeding the few miles back to the beach from the convention center, past Sea World, exiting at Mission Beach, cursing the full lot. Even on a stormy, cloudy day, the beach was crowded. He finally found a space, threw quarters into the meter, jogged toward the sand, past the roller coaster, the tattoo parlors, the concession stand, the surfers and children rinsing themselves in the outdoor showers.

He scanned the packed afternoon shoreline for Bee's red dress, for Jayden's curly dark hair. The waves crashed against the surf. The image of Bee huddled beside the bathtub screaming at him that his kid was drowning. The image of Bee or Jayden drowned on that damn horror island. This morning, Bee on the bathroom floor, Jubilee above her. Why had he left them alone?

At the edge of the sand, where children splashed water in buckets and ran from the waves before their feet or knees or hips submerged, Joshua spotted Jayden, his little brown body glistening with salt crystals. Joshua breathed relief. He was safe. God, he'd been worried for nothing. He wanted to laugh at his stupid self for mistrusting Bee. He smiled broadly and waved at Jayden, who turned around just then, as if he sensed his father nearby. But the prickling at Joshua's neck returned. Something still wasn't right.

Jayden was frowning. "Dada!" He motioned for Joshua to hurry.

"Where's Bee?" he yelled back, clomping through the sand, his boots sinking in.

"Out there!" Jayden screamed, pointing toward the ocean.

Joshua ran, panting, his muscles burning. He caught up to Jayden on the wet sand. Jayden wasn't just frowning, but crying. "Where's Bee?"

Jayden pulled Joshua's arm and pointed to where Bee was swimming several hundred feet into the water, at the end of the massive algae-covered posts supporting the pier. He could barely make her out among the surfers, but knew her tangled, dark hair, her bright-red bathing suit. A bloodstain against the gray sky and water.

"Why's she out there?" His heart raced. He felt sick. He pulled off his boots.

"Jubilee."

"What happened?" Joshua yanked his wallet, cell phone, keys, loose change, and inhaler from his jeans pockets and dropped them inside his boots on the wet sand.

"The wave pulled her away from me," Jayden cried. "I'm sorry."

"It's okay. I'll get them." He hugged Jayden. "Sit down. Don't move. I'll be back."

Joshua made sure the boy sat on the sand before he ran to the water and dove in. He hadn't been swimming in the ocean since the one unsuccessful time his freshman year in college when he'd tried learning to surf. He fought each wave crashing against his face and body, free-stroking with all the power he could muster. *Swim, Joshy. Don't you dare fucking let her drown.*

His lungs already burned. Why hadn't a lifeguard seen her? A surfer? Why had no one else helped her? Maybe no one else realized the danger. Maybe they just saw a woman taking a swim.

He fought the waves. *You're not a strong swimmer. The current's too strong.* He felt a familiar burning in his chest and knew he would need his inhaler soon if he couldn't keep calm. Even if he could keep calm, his asthma was flaring. *Breathe. One, two, three. Breathe.* He could see Bianca bobbing near the end of the pier, where an undercurrent could pull her under. Or out to sea. *Swim, goddamn you.*

"Bee! I'm coming! Hang on!" He gulped in saltwater and coughed. His eyes stung.

When he reached her, he called her name again. "Are you okay? I'm here." She stopped paddling, and turned, treading water. He grabbed hold of her, the water raising them both up, dropping them down, and tried to hold her from behind, the way he'd seen lifeguards on television save drowning victims, but she pulled away from him.

"Jubilee's over there," Bee called, pointing to the doll, who in the water looked like a real drowning infant, whose curls and bright pink dress Joshua could make out floating beside a concrete post at the end of the pier. "I can't get to her. The waves keep pulling me back."

His legs were already cramping, his stomach ached, and his chest compressed. *You get your wife back to the shore, Joshy . . .*

"Bee, let me get you out. I'll come back for Jubilee. Let me get you back to shore. Please."

"No! Josh . . ."

He could've asked someone to help. But what lifeguard in their right mind would've helped Joshua save a doll from the ocean? And by the time he'd returned to the water, Jubilee could've been carried out too far to reach. *Bee would be too far to reach.*

"Goddamnit, Bee. Fine. Swim back then. Now! I'll get her. You swim back!"

She shook her head. "I can't leave her."

"You aren't leaving her. I'll get her. Please, swim back to the shore."

She turned back, and he propelled forward, straining his body toward the pier, pushing against the waves. He dove through the tumult and spray, pushed and pushed. He had to save her. He couldn't let her drown. "Jubilee," he found himself calling. Like he'd gone crazy. Swallowing saltwater and coughing, he thought of Bee's dad and, for one gruesome second, imagined himself drowning too. He couldn't let that happen to Jayden. He couldn't let that happen to any of them. Breathing as deeply as he could manage with his burning lungs, he thrust his way beneath the water and pumped his legs hard, sweeping back the water with his big hands. He was Beast. He was a superhero. He could save his wife.

The cramping in his legs spread upward, and he couldn't breathe.

Jubilee floated farther and farther out.

He shoved forward, but the waves were too strong. He was swallowing water. He coughed as wave after wave crashed over him.

He fought for air. He couldn't breathe. *Come on, Joshy. Come on.* Salt in his eyes. Salt in his lungs. The water was too heavy. It was like a chain around his legs, the cramping. He couldn't free himself.

Someone was calling his name. *Joshy! Come on.*

"Josh!"

It was Bee. She hadn't swum back to shore. Goddamnit.

She was lifting him the way he was supposed to be lifting her.

"I've got you."

"No, go back, Bee. I'll get Jubilee."

She shook her head, her eyes bright red, her face scrunched in concentration, but she was focused, serious, dead set. "No, Josh. You won't."

She grabbed his hand, pulled him away from the pier. And with strong, deliberate strokes, set them both flowing with the waves, using the water to carry them.

"I can get her for you, Bee. I can." He couldn't lose her. He couldn't lose his wife.

She said nothing but held his arm tight, gripped him so tight, and kept rowing them atop the waves. She was crying, but she was a strong swimmer, he could see that. Much stronger than he was. And she was leading them back toward the shore.

Where the water shallowed, he planted his feet into the sand, stood firm, tried to balance her upward. But his lungs ached. His breath was coming in shallow wheezes. He meant to support her, but his vision was narrowing, everything—the shore, the crowds, Jayden—becoming fuzzy.

"Breathe, love. Breathe, I'm here. I've got you," she said, supporting his weight.

Together, they lurched onto the shore, and Jayden ran toward them, clutching Joshua's inhaler, a familiar sight, Jayden coming to the rescue with his inhaler. Bianca grabbed it, "Thank you, mijo. It's okay, it's okay." She steadied it at Joshua's mouth and guided his shaking hands as he pressed down, sucked in the cold, compressed air, waiting for the familiar expansion in his chest. Coughed. Again. Again.

"Breathe, Joshy. Breathe," Bianca said, as Joshua kneeled onto the sand, trying to pull the air into his lungs.

The lifeguards circled now, like birds at a picnic. The lights from their truck flashing.

Joshua closed his eyes.

The lifeguards covered his mouth with an oxygen mask, and although he wanted to resist the fuss over him, wanted to pull it off and tell them to leave him alone, the air was a welcome relief, and he breathed, deeply, finally. Over the next several minutes, the lifeguards continued taking his vitals, asking questions, monitoring them. He explained his condition, assuring them that his albuterol had kicked in; he'd be shipshape again in no time. Though that felt only half true. He told them to check on Bianca. She was six months pregnant and shouldn't have been straining to swim in the ocean like that.

"We've already checked her, sir. She's in great condition."

Joshua looked over toward Bianca. She sat nearby, on the sand, her feet crossed in front of her, a towel wrapped around her shoulders, Jayden next to her, digging with a shovel and dumping the sand into a bucket, then overturning it onto the ground, building a castle.

The lifeguards, satisfied Joshua was breathing and could take it from here, rode away in their bright-yellow trucks and ATVs.

He scooched closer to his wife. Was she watching for Jubilee? He followed her gaze to the ocean, gray and tumultuous and expansive. What could he say? He didn't have the words.

He reached out for her hand, and she clasped her fingers through his.

They stayed that way for a while, hands locked together, him tracing shapes with his fingers into her wrist. Her, solemn but brighter-eyed than he'd seen her in a long time, staring at the water. Neither saying anything. Jayden scooping sand. A tableau of a family. No, not just a picture. The real thing. They stayed that way until they were all hungry and cold and tired, and then they walked, together, toward the car where, before Jayden was buckled in, he turned back toward the ocean and said, "Goodbye, Jubilee." And the waves behind them must've washed away the indentations they'd made as they sat there, watching Jubilee float away.

Jubilee, who was a bridge. Who'd carried Bianca safely to the other side.

THIRTY-FIVE
DAUGHTER, I RISE

AFTER JUBILEE

The downtown Fullerton lights gleamed bright on the back patio of the Mexican restaurant where the reading was held. Her familia was there to cheer her on, Joshua and Jayden, her mama, Matty and Handro, Abuela and Abuelo even. And Lily. Of course Lily, who'd brought Sam. They wouldn't have missed it. Tonight was her first public reading of her first published poem in a literary journal, and her family was so proud. Elena, her poetry mentor at Cal State Fullerton, had come to hear her read, and they all sat together at a large table under a heat lamp that cool, November evening, eating chips and salsa, listening to the other poets.

Bianca held her one-year-old daughter, Alba, strapped to her chest in a Moby wrap, and Alba sucked on her fists as her mama dog-eared the page of the journal that held her poem. She took a deep, steadying breath as her name was called from the microphone, and she stood, straightened her blouse beneath the wrap, and walked, tall and proud, up to the stage.

"Thank you for having me here tonight," she said. "I'm so excited and nervous to read you my first published poem." Everyone applauded, and she could hear her family whistling and cheering. "I've brought my daughter, Alba, onstage with me because this poem is dedicated to her, and I want my girl to know from an early age what it means to speak her truths, aloud, and never, ever be afraid to follow her heart and her dreams, like I'm following mine."

More cheering, more applause.

"For Alba, whose name means *the dawn* . . .

"Not all women need a daughter to make them strong. But for some of us a daughter is the strength that's been inside us all along, just waiting to rise."

Some nights Bee could still hear Esme's voice. *It's been a long time, mija. Come in, let me fix you a plate.*

Someday, Bee would take her family back to the Valley.

Rio Vista would beckon, and Bee would introduce the people she loved—Joshy, Jayden, and Alba—to the place that had raised her. To the place that had made her a mother.

Where the sweet tea still brews in the sun on Nana's porch. Where her girlhood house crouches above the canyon's edge, skirting the New River. Where her dreams, from the fissures of her fifteen-year-old heart, remain as real as any she knew.

THIRTY-SIX
LETTER TO JUBILEE

Once upon a time, a house grew wild and empty in the desert. The cacti scrubbed its floors with dirt. The death birds scavenged. They picked clean the bones. The jeweled beetles scuttled. In and out. All night and day. And once each year, the bats came.

Girlchild, that house was a wreck. That house bore a girlchild.
And she held me tight. Baby girl. You held me so tight.

Hush now.
The wreck that was your mama rests at last.
(Forgive me.)

Forgive me for letting you go.

ACKNOWLEDGMENTS

Thank you, Mama. You never gave up on *Jubilee*, like you've never given up on me. I love you forever. Thank you for taking care of my family while I wrote this heart for us.

I am immensely grateful to my family, Andrew, Lina, Jer; my dad, Philip Boese, and my mama, Dr. Suzanne Casas Boese, thank you for helping me raise my babies so I could write these stories; my big brother, Paul Gonzales, and his husband, Mark Lopez; and my little brother, David Boese, and his wife, Karissa, I couldn't have done any of this without you—Grandma Marge, fierce advocate, Grandma Linda and the whole Casas family—you all who have taken care of me and kept me safe. Lisa, my better than best. Sally, for loving me in the Valley. Nikki, high school bestie I'll always adore. Renee in heaven. My dear poetry hermanas, Alicia Elkort, Stephanie Bryant Anderson, Leslie Contreras Schwartz, Avra Elliott, Sherine Gilmour, Stacey Balkun, and Jennifer Krohn—y'all bruja loves cast protective light over me, draft after draft. So much gratitude to Eliza Dreier, who saw in Bee's story exactly what my heart needed to keep believing, dear kindred soul. Bordistas Lauren Fleming and Jesenia Lua. Lynn Hightower, my wonderful teacher and best novel mentor. Sisters who read *Jubilee* throughout this decade-long journey, including Jessamyn Smith, LaToya Jordan, Stefani Freele, Molly Sutton Kiefer, Mandy Rose, Nandini Dhar, and Shaindel Beers, thank you.

And for Reyna Grande, for reading the first draft and seeing what I couldn't see then, gracias, hermana.

For the works and teachings of Rigoberto González and Sandra Cisneros.

For my first and greatest mentor, Irena Praitis—thank you for teaching me to speak my truths.

In loving memory of Mr. Croghan, the finest English and humanities teacher a poeta could ask for. I still have the postcard. I hope you knew what your belief in me meant to my spirit.

I thank my lucky stars for my agent, Laura Blake Peterson, and her guidance and support for my writing. And Vikki Warner, for seeing me and the empowering stories for women that we could share. You lights. I'm so grateful.

For my whole Blackstone Publishing fam. Y'all are such fierce advocates. Lauren Maturo, you wonder. Thank you.

My dear editor, Peggy Hageman. You ask all the best questions. I adore you.

So many other lights in my life—please know your kindness has buoyed my heart.

Thank you, Dr. Raina J. León, editor of the *Acentos Review*, where Bee's voice debuted when "Pyre for Waiting: She May Have Been a Witch" appeared in 2012; this journal gives Latinx folks such a generous platform and welcomes us with open arms. I am forever grateful. Thank you, dear Lorinda Toledo, fiction editor at *Witness Magazine*, where "La Bee Goes Bar Crashing" first appeared in 2017, for your faith in Bee's story and your astute edits. To my dear sister-in-writing, Frances Badgett, fiction editor at *Contrary Magazine*, where "Cattle Call Leaves, A Ghost Story" first appeared in 2013, for your first *yes* to Bee, and your faithful friendship since that time. And for my dearest Stephanie Bryant Anderson, then fiction editor at *Up the Staircase Quarterly*, where "Labyrinths in Smoke" first appeared in 2012, for opening your heart to Bee and me, beginning the sisterhood I've always needed.

Y'all who said yes and gave me the courage to keep banging down doors and climbing up fire escapes, thank you.

This book is for the girls and women in the borderlands. I see you. You fierce queens. Keep singing your truths. Keep believing, no matter what. Never let anyone take that beautiful light away from you. Keep rising. Keep crossing bridges. I love you.

CREDITS

Toni Morison. *Sula*. NY: Knopf/Vintage, 1992.

Maroon Five. "Come Away to the Water."

Simon and Garfunkel: "Bridge over Troubled Water."

Emily Dickinson: "A wounded deer."

Emily Dickinson. "If I can stop one heart from breaking."

Emily Dickinson. "Hope is the thing with feathers."

"Harlem" and "Dream" from *The Collected Poems of Langston Hughes* by Langston Hughes, edited by Arnold Rampersad with David Roessel, Associate Editor, copyright © 1994 by the Estate of Langston Hughes. Used with permission of Alfred A. Knopf, an imprint of the Knopf Doubleday Publishing Group, a division of Penguin Random House LLC. All rights reserved.

MGM/Judy Garland. "Somewhere over the Rainbow."

Selena. "Bidi Bidi Bom Bom."

Shakespeare. "Sonnet 116."

Laura Esquivel. *Como agua para chocolate.*

Sandra Cisneros. "Loose Woman." *Loose Woman.* NY: Knopf, 1994.
    Reprinted with permission from the author.

Sandra Cisneros. "You My Saltwater Pearl." *Loose Woman.* NY: Knopf,
    1994. Reprinted with permission from the author.

Margery Williams. *The Velveteen Rabbit.*

Gloria Anzaldúa. *La Conciencia de la Mestiza: Towards a New Consciousness.*

Elvis Crespo. "Suavamente."

Stephen King. "Why We Crave Horror Movies."

Sandra Cisneros. "Full Moon and You're Not Here." *Loose Woman.* NY:
    Knopf, 1994. Reprinted with permission from the author.

Jerry Herman. *Hello, Dolly!*

Bob Merrill and Jule Styne. *Funny Girl.*

Jennifer Givhan. "I Believed All Poets Were Dead" from *Protection
    Spell.* Copyright © 2017 by the University of Arkansas Press. Re-
    produced with the permission of the University of Arkansas Press,
    www.UAPress.com

Excerpt from the poem "Black Blossoms" from *Black Blossoms* © 2011 by Rigoberto González. Reprinted with permission of Four Way Books. All rights reserved.

AsapSCIENCE. "The UPDATED Periodic Table Song."

Shakira. "My Hips Don't Lie."

Edgar Allen Poe. "The Raven."

John Donne. "Song: Sweetest Love I Do Not Go."

The Clash. "Should I Stay or Should I Go."

Bob Marley. "No Woman No Cry."

Emily Dickinson. "After Great Pain, A Formal Feeling Comes."

Robert Louis Stevenson. "The Swing."

Lynyrd Skynyrd. "Free Bird."

H. D. "Eurydice."

Margaret Wise Brown. *The Runaway Bunny*.

Ana Castillo. *So Far from God*, W.W. Norton, 1993. 48-49.

Robert Frost. "Stopping by Woods on a Snowy Evening."

Edna St. Vincent Millay. "First Fig."

Emily Dickinson. "One Need Not be a Chamber to be Haunted."